CHILDREN OF HEPHAESTUS

Grey Liliy

BROKEN POCKET

ISBN-13: 978-0615641119
ISBN-10: 0615641113

Cover by Design for Writers
http://designforwriters.com

CHAPTER 1

"HE CAN BE calm when he wants to be."

"When has your brother ever been calm?" Abel's coarse chuckle could barely be heard under the hissing and bubbling of sizzling metal under the heat of a small iron. He had to tilt his head sideways to see around the sparks flying. Abel was half-way done with the latest upgrade to the project's hardware, and was hoping to be done before the day let out. Finishing early was the only way to clear enough room in his schedule for a private project next week. Abel smiled over at the boy watching him work—taking care of a child didn't exactly add to your free time. Abel soldered another piece to the circuit board. "Even when he's not upset, he's still pretty jittery."

"You don't see him when he's reading his favorite books," Hecate answered, "he gets quite drawn into fairy tales."

The doctor paused in his soldering to look up at the young boy kicking his legs back and forth from his perch on the high work counter. Abel noticed the sleeves of his sweater were starting to fray from the constant wear and tear. It had been knit as a gift from Lucy in the programming lab, and Abel thought the emerald green matched the boy's fair complexion well. Considering how much he liked the sweater, Abel was surprised Hecate didn't take better care of it. Abel glanced down at the frayed edge of his own sleeve that had caught on his soldering iron earlier that day. *Didn't take a genius to see where* that *bad habit came from.* Abel put the soldering iron down on the table and removed his pink—he was never letting Giles near the equipment ordering forms again—goggles. "The same ones you said were boring and unrealistic?"

"They're not *that* bad, I just think there was more to the Brontë novels, that's all," Hecate said, voice smooth and controlled. He watched Abel strip off his safety equipment, finished with his soldering for the afternoon. Hecate wondered if all those gloves and goggles were really needed for such small, delicate work. Abel wasn't *that* fragile. "The complication and futility of the relationships in *Wuthering Heights*, for example, are far more interesting than the prince getting the princess after a single kiss. I just think it's more fun to see what happens when two and two stop making four, don't you?"

"I guess. I could never stay awake long enough to finish reading one of those things." Hecate was too intelligent for his own good some days, but it was nice to hear him taking an interest in something he enjoyed. Abel's charge was far too serious for someone so young, and living in a testing facility certainly wasn't helping the matter. Abel ruffled the blond hair on the boy's head, catching the child off guard for a change. Hecate laughed under the affectionate touch, much to the doctor's delight. "Even after all this time, it's still so weird hearing you say things like that."

"Is it really, Dr. Moreau?" Hecate tilted his head, resembling a puppy who knows there's a treat in its owner's hand. It gave him a much better view of Abel's eyes. He had heard in passing that the 'window to a man's soul was in his eyes,' however, Hecate had difficulty seeing much more than an ever changing iris and mixing green and brown pigments. Though, he did think they looked nice—alive. They fit Abel's tan face and brown hair, features that were so opposite from Hecate's own.

"Might be," Abel found himself smiling again before muttering affectionately into his hand, "observant little brat."

"I'm supposed—" Hecate was unable to finish his sentence as a loud clang echoed from the corridor. Abel was on his feet in an instant and heading for the main door. He shed his protective work coat on the rack in exchange for a white, long coat. Hecate heard a few more thumps and shouts from the corridor and kicked his feet back and forth on the edge of the desk. "Dr. Moreau?"

"Come on, let's go make sure your brother hasn't hurt anyone." The 'again' was left unspoken, and Abel waited for Hecate to drop from the tabletop. The younger boy's worst offense in the lab was following Abel around like a shadow, but his elder sibling was another story completely. Now *that* boy gave new meaning to the word 'handful'. *What teenager wasn't?* Abel thought to himself. Hecate's brother probably deserved a little more slack than he was getting, but he'd only get it if Abel got there first. "Hurry up now, Hecate. I don't think Giles is in a forgiving mood today."

Hecate didn't believe Giles Firmin was *ever* in a forgiving mood when it came to the two brothers, but it was needless to say such a thing out loud. Hecate jogged up to Abel and took his hand. The good doctor squeezed back gently before locking his lab door.

Hecate held Abel's hand the entire trip down the hall.

The laboratory turned daycare was as to be expected: a mess. It looked like a whirlwind had hit it and turned back around to stomp on it for a second go. The steel work table that normally stood in the center of the room, was tipped on its side. Its contents were scattered and broken across the ground, and looked to have been kicked around in a scuffle. Abel noticed an overturned laptop on the ground near the door, but it seemed to still be operating. The rest of the debris was restricted to pens and loose papers, to Abel's relief. The damage looked to be superficial, save for the—a groan sounded on the other side of the table.

"Becky?" Abel dashed toward the overturned furniture, simultaneously jerking his hand free from Hecate's grip. Abel was so distracted with getting to the other side of the overturned table that he didn't take notice of Hecate's frown. He found Becky propped up between the legs of the table, holding her arm close to her chest. Abel cracked a tiny smile, since she seemed more or less okay. Abel crossed his arms on the top of the table side to lean over Becky as she thumped her head repeatedly into the tabletop. He pointed at her wrist, spotted with purple and black. "Bruised or broken?"

"The arm? Bruised." The woman lifted her good hand up to bat at Abel's face. She honestly did not get paid enough to babysit that—that *thing*. She deserved far more than a six figure salary for the shit she went through. Becky hissed when she tried to move her injured arm. How the hell did Abel get the well behaved one? "Little brat threw me against the table at the end of his hissy fit."

Hecate wandered through the room, taking the damage in as Abel tended the fallen 'nurse.' In reality she was only a technician, but considering the circumstances she was nothing more than their nursemaid. Abel had mentioned once this was a step up for the woman, career wise, however, Hecate had little interest in her or how she made her living. The boy tipped a chair leaning against a side counter back into its upright position with a shove to its backing. Things should make up their mind: either fall over completely or stand up straight. Speaking, there was one broken thing Hecate still needed to find in the middle of this wreck while their caretakers kept busy.

A frustrated growl and the sound of sneakers squeaking on the floor answered his query. Hecate trotted over to the corner of the room, target spotted. He stopped about a foot from the disheveled figure sitting on the floor. The 'teenager' was tightly folded in on himself, knees to his chest and hands over his head. Hecate watched as the boy shoved one foot back and forth, nervously, heel creating the squeaking sound Hecate had heard earlier as it rubbed against the tile. Messy brown hair covered the boy's eyes, but Hecate imagined them shut tight. "Iacchus."

"Go away."

"I wouldn't be here at all if you hadn't disturbed Dr. Moreau with all the noise." Hecate mourned the loss of a good conversation. Iacchus was always doing this to him. Things were perfect and then his big brother goes and throws a fit getting all the doctors' and nurses' attention. It wasn't fair. Hecate kicked his brother's foot with his laced up sneakers. "So it's your own fault."

"Oh shut up," Iacchus interrupted and buried his head further under his arms, shoving his face into his thighs. Hecate and his annoying calmness was not something Iacchus wanted to see right now. He got enough of his brother after hours when they were stuck doing homework together all night. Iacchus' head hurt and he'd lost his temper again *and* he'd thrown Ms. Becky into a wall. No…it was a table—but that didn't matter. She probably broke something…or rather, Iacchus had broken something. Of hers. Maybe. He could never keep his thoughts straight after his little 'episodes.' Iacchus glared up at Hecate from a small sliver of space between his arm and thigh. "Just leave me alone!"

"You should really stop these fits." Hecate replied calmly looking down his nose. He could hear Becky and Abel arguing in the background, most likely about the fate of the pathetic boy in front of him. Despite the fact his brother looked to be five or six years older, he was definitely the more childish of the two siblings. Hecate rubbed his fingertips together as he studied the skin on his hands trying to look nonchalant over the issue. "You're going to be punished worse than usual if you keep this up."

"You think I don't know that?" Iacchus answered, voice cracking.

8

Hecate always made everything seem *so easy.* Iacchus' fingers dug into his hair, flexing through the knots. "It's not like I meant to."

"Iacchus?"

The teen looked up at Dr. Moreau as he leaned over the two of them. Iacchus didn't notice when the man had walked up. Had he been listening to their argument? Dr. Moreau's face looked concerned, but it was a common enough expression for him. Hecate took a few steps to the side to allow the doctor more room—and get out of the line of fire— leaving Iacchus alone under the steady gaze. Iacchus moved his hands out of the way just enough to see the doctor. "Yes?"

Abel dropped to sit on his heels, crossing his arms over his knees. Iacchus remained hunched in on himself, blue eyes peaking out from between his bare arms. Even at eye level, Abel felt like he towered over the boy. Abel prodded Iacchus gently in the knee with his hand. "Why did you hit Ms. Becky?"

"I didn't."

Abel took in a long breath and hoped to resolve this before Giles paid them a visit. Abel had been friends with the man for years, but when it came to the boys he could get...moody. It didn't help this was the third time this week Iacchus had caused an incident. Giles was getting tired of shelling out cash from his pocketbook for medical bills instead of microchips. If Iacchus didn't learn to stop acting out with nothing but violence, there might actually be serious consequences in his future. And as much authority as Abel liked to believe he had, the fact is, if Giles really wanted to do something, he would do it. Abel rephrased his question. "Why did you *throw* Ms. Becky?"

Iacchus refused to look the doctor in the face, and pushed his face back into his knees. His voice was muffled by his pants, but still audible somehow. "She made me mad."

The usually deep and strong voice was tiny, almost chided. Abel was reminded more and more of a small child who had just broken something by accident, due to unfamiliar limbs as they figured out their own bodies. Some days he was sure that Hecate and Iacchus had switched personalities when they were created. Their behaviors just didn't seem to fit the skins they were in. Abel was sure Iacchus probably wouldn't have such pressure on him if he looked the same age as Hecate. "And what did she do to make you so mad? I thought you liked Ms. Becky."

"I didn't want to do any more exercises." Iacchus fumbled with the loose sleeve of his plain white shirt. Because he had tossed a computer through a window two months ago, they wouldn't let him pick his own clothes anymore. Iacchus glared at Hecate standing so high and mighty in his dual-toned green sweater and khaki shorts. *He* didn't have to wear the stupid clothes the technicians passed out because *he* was well behaved. The white hospital scrubs they had dug out of storage for him were ugly and boring. Iacchus was almost used to the horrible clothes, but he really missed wearing something with a bit of color. "She wouldn't let me stop."

"Why did you want to stop?" He tried to keep his voice as steady and soothing as possible. Handling Iacchus was like trying to diffuse a time bomb—only all the wires were the same color. Hecate hovered behind him, watching the affair cooly. Abel wished the boy would scoot back a bit and give his brother some space. "You know the exercises are good for you. They help you think straight, remember?"

"I did them. I finished them." Iacchus tried to stress this point. He had been a good boy until she wouldn't listen! "Ms. Becky wanted me to do them over."

"Did she say why?" Abel ignored Becky snorting in the background as she pulled her sleeve up to look at her injured arm. Abel caught a look at the perfectly formed hand-shaped bruise and was slightly more relieved it wasn't broken than when he first arrived. "Did you not do well?"

"I was fine!" Iacchus shouted. "I did it. I didn't want to do any more. I hate my exercises." The boy glanced at Hecate quickly before lowering his voice to a near whisper. Iacchus knew the doctor was probably struggling to hear. "They hurt."

"It hurt?" Abel looked from the miserably shaking figure back over to Becky sharply. Arms crossed, hip cocked to the side and her face stuck in the ever so classic 'your problem' frown. He knew Becky wasn't fond of the boys, but did she really have to take it out on them? Abel addressed Becky firmly, "Did he say he was in pain?"

Becky lifted an eyebrow and scoffed. She turned her back on the both of them and pushed down on a table leg to set it up right. Or tried, anyway. It proved to be heavier than she had expected. Becky frowned when it only moved an inch or two before falling back down. Becky left it alone, thinking it oddly appropriate symbolism for how her life was turning out. "We both know that's irrelevant, Abe. Besides, Hecate does all of his exercises with no problem and in triplicate for comparison's sake." Becky shrugged her shoulders. "Iacchus should just bear with it."

"Becky," Abel sucked in a breath through his teeth. Her attitude towards the boys sadly reflected most of the facility. It was no wonder why Iacchus lashed out as much as he did. "If it hurts, something is wrong. That's the one thing we all have in common, isn't it?"

"Oh please, he's exaggerating." Becky pointed at Iacchus. "It's not even real pain! It's an annoying internal pulse indicating something is malfunctioning. At the absolute worst it'd be comparable to a headache. Besides, getting a shot hurts doesn't it? But you don't go 'oh, poor darling' if the brat getting the shot attacks you, now do you?" The woman pulled her hand back to point again with more emphasis. "He can't fly off the handle every time he's the least bit uncomfortable, and you need to stop babying the two of them."

Hecate watched the two adults bicker with only the slightest of interest, focusing his attention back on his brother. Iacchus seemed to have accepted his fate and had his legs stretched out in front of him, no longer curled in on himself. His head was still down, however, in a slump. Hecate wandered closer and considered their required exercises. "Did it really hurt?"

"Yes." Iacchus bit his lip. He wasn't sure where he picked the tic up from, but it was always his first defense in fighting his anger. He opened and closed his fists in a steady pattern in his lap. The repetitive motion was oddly calming, which was good right now. Iacchus stopped the motion after a moment and rubbed at his pant leg. He couldn't afford to lash out again. "It hurt. A lot."

Hecate scrunched his face in confusion. "But you're running such simple—"

"Finish that sentence and I'll tell the doctors what you do at night," Iacchus hissed through his teeth, fists now clenched so tightly he was sure, had he been normal, there'd be blood. Hecate had the nerve to smirk at his bluff—they'd both be in trouble if he told on Hecate. It wasn't until Hecate spun a finger in a circle next to his ear and mouthed the word 'crazy' that the older boy shot up from the floor. He snatched the brat's sweater in one hand. Iacchus pulled his fist back ready to plant it smack dab in the middle—

"Don't you hit your brother," Abel called over his shoulder. Iacchus slowly put Hecate back on the ground and Abel relaxed from his tense posture. The two boys had never been in an all-out fist fight before, and

Abel had no desire to see it. Iacchus, however, was not the only guilty party this time around. Abel turned his head fully to look the younger one in the eye. "And leave Iacchus alone, Hecate. I'm sure he's still running a little hot from all that exertion, so let him have his few moments to cool down."

"As you wish." The younger of the two sent one last lingering glare at his brother before returning to the doctor's side. Hecate could deal further with his inferior brother later. The boy averted his eyes to the ground and shuffled his feet ever so slightly, trying to look innocent. "I merely wanted an explanation, Dr. Moreau."

"I know, Hecate." Abel put a hand on the boy's head and waited for him to make eye contact. Abel waited for those bright blue eyes to look up before he repeated himself. "Right now your brother is upset. Leave him be, okay?"

It was Iacchus' turn to smirk when Hecate muttered, "Fine," to Dr. Moreau. Hecate glared at him, and Iacchus' day was finally starting to look up.

The main testing lab's door was wide open—that was never a good sign.

"What on earth happened in here?" Giles shouted from the hallway, looking in through the doorway. The slim man's face was pinched with a hint of disgust as he took in the overturned table and bits of equipment on the floor. The man kicked a laptop over on its other side with the edge of his foot. At least there was no blood that he could see this time. "This lab was just cleaned up yesterday! Do you people think I'm made out of resources?"

"Iacchus had another fit," Becky replied calmly and looked over her boss as he stood in the doorway, face red: Dr. Giles Firmin with his slicked black hair and pressed black suit. Save for the neon pink tie, his dress was clearly more suited for meetings and correspondence with clients than lab work. Becky straightened her back and smoothed her hair down to look less frazzled. The man had no clue what she dealt with on a daily basis, no matter how much he complained about the board. That child in the corner was worse than any nitpicky complaints some money grubbing investors could spit out. "I think he should be put down, personally. It's the fourth time—"

"Third."

"Shut up, Abel. The point is that brat is unstable!" Becky hated being a part of this project. She was a lab assistant forced into babysitting due to some stupid duckling complex those two brats developed. She was going to force Giles to add another zero to her salary for hazard pay. "You'd be better off scrapping him and putting all your attention on that one." She nodded her head at Hecate, looking too young to be wearing a collared shirt under that stupid sweater. "At least his malfunctions aren't dangerous."

"Becky, you can't be serious," Abel said, face aghast at the suggestion. How on earth could she suggest they just be tossed out like some computer that could no longer be updated? They were just kids! "Yes, Iacchus has problems, but that's why he's here. To fix them. They can learn and adjust just like anyone else can."

Becky's lip curved downward. Iacchus rubbed the side of his arm, watching her like normal. "Not well enough for my taste."

Abel's voice rose to be heard over the smack from his hand slamming into the side-ways table leg. The metal echoed through the room as it bounced off the floor with a *clang*. "Because you're not even giving him a chance."

"He could have broken my arm!"

"Enough." Giles held his hands up and silenced both of them. He'd deal with Abel later when they got together this afternoon, but right now he needed to reign in the woman currently making him miserable. "Iacchus remains your problem, Becky." Giles decided it was time to bring out the same mantra he'd already said at least ten times this month. It apparently bore repeating one more time to drill it into Becky's thick skull. "We both know that out of over 200,000 subjects from the Olympian's Children, only two have shown the ability to think for themselves to date. We're all aware those two successes were more or less accidents. We can't afford to get rid of a successful subject, even if he is completely psychotic."

"If his brain doesn't work, then we shouldn't have—"

"He can think outside his programming specifications and somehow has feelings. Figure out how it works, fix his issues and then duplicate it. Your mission hasn't changed since the moment you walked into this laboratory. Punish the thing if you have to, but make it work." Giles left no room for argument. Becky's attitude was addressed and he only had one more thing to repeat. "And Abe, stop with the parenting." Giles clapped his friend on the shoulder. Abel was far too attached to the little one to be healthy. "They're not your kids and you are not their father."

"You know me, Giles." Abel put his hand on Hecate's head, pulling the child into his side. Abel doubted Giles would ever understand kids. The man was too clean, too uptight, and too tangled in his own problems to care for another person. Giles was too childish himself to take responsibility—that was probably why Abel got along with him so well. Abel squeezed Hecate's shoulder. "Can't help but spoil them."

"I noticed, but I'll deal with it for now." Giles shook his head and looked around the room. "Make sure you clean this mess up." Giles took one last withering glance at the two subjects before stalking out of the room. He had a meeting at three, and two more after that. They needed to figure out how those brats were working properly, and soon, so he could get them out of his lab and off to production. Then they'd be someone else's problem and Giles could start work on something else.

"That could have gone worse." Abel sighed softly after the door to the lab slid shut and Giles was far from view. Abel wondered if something had been going on before he paid them a visit to be in such a foul mood. Then again, Abel was noticing a lot of things lately set off the man's temper. Abel made a note to talk to Giles about this later after he'd calmed down, but for now he supposed dealing with the matter at hand was more important. Abel avoided eye contact with the still-fuming Becky as he addressed her. "I'll just start the clean up and take care of the boys, then. Why don't you see if Marvin will give you the afternoon off?" Abel swallowed. "Since your arm is still bruised."

"You can have him for the rest of the week. I'm not dealing with him." Becky pushed Abel in the shoulder as she shoved past him. She was going home, permission from her manager or not. It's not like she was getting fired—Iacchus went crazy when she was gone for too long. "You make him do the exercises, since you're so worried."

"Maybe I will." Abel mentally started going through his schedules to see what he could move around to make time. If he had to take on the responsibility of their social care as well as their physical bodies, so be it. He was not going to give up on Hecate and Iacchus, not when there was so much potential between the two of them. "Have a nice break."

"Oh, I will." Becky laughed and pulled one of her electronic cigarettes from her coat pocket. Blessing from heaven these things were; could even smoke in all the labs in the building. She shook her head, taking one last look at the stoic child and the glaring teenager from the doorway. She wished, yet again, they'd both be thrown in the scrap heap. "Androids. Who the hell thought that was a good idea?"

CHAPTER 2

ABEL HAD MANAGED to make room in his schedule to run Iacchus' exercises by the sudden lack of a personal project to tinker with. A janitor had knocked his work on a new microprocessor off his lab table during cleaning one night. It wasn't anyone's fault other than his own for leaving it so close to the edge, but the lack of back up models mean Abel would have to start from scratch. He might as well do something productive in the meantime.

So here he sat, silently hooking wires up to the ports in Iacchus' spine. Every android unit they had created was unique save for these connection points to help uniformity with maintenance. A line of nine ports ran down the spine, starting at the top of the neck running down to the waist line. The upper most port was reserved for main, high maintenance connections, while the rest were for lesser connections like printers or connecting to the internet. The design for the access ports came from Marvin, and doubled as the main power on-off switch that required a special key that was hidden in a slot under the unit's hair. They had taken them from the active units though, for fear of them being used accidentally. Abel had Hecate's in his wallet, and Becky had Iacchus' in her desk drawer. Abel forgot it was there most of the time, knowing he'd never need to use it. No one was going to risk shutting the boy's down—not when they didn't know if they would come back online with all their functions for sure.

Abel *was* proud to admit, though, that he was the one responsible for the small ring of blue lights around each port. They changed to green when a link connection was successful and helped solve the confusion of whether or not the boys were properly connected to the computer. *That* became a necessity when they realized the boys could mask their presence from the server.

At first the team had been worried, but after further examination they realized it wasn't as bad as they originally thought. Hecate had done it just to find out if he could, but Iacchus had been doing it without realizing. Hecate stopped the moment asked, but Iacchus still had trouble. Abel suggested the connection 'active' lights to avoid confusion and it was approved, even if Marvin thought it looked tacky. Abel clicked the last wire into the second port from the top and patted the boy on the shoulder. "We're going to run a diagnostic on your systems first before starting. Is that alright Iacchus?"

"I don't know why you bother asking, Dr. Moreau. 's'not like I have a choice," Iacchus slurred as he felt his systems linking up with the computer. He was never going to get used to having his thoughts spread out over two locations. Even if Iacchus had control over both data links, it still felt like his head was in seven or eight pieces instead of just two. Ms. Becky commented once that when he logged into the system his body acted like it was drunk. Not that Iacchus had any clue what being 'drunk' was besides overhearing brief conversations in the hallways, but he could take Ms. Becky's word for it. Iacchus supposed it was yet another flaw in his programming. His bratty brother didn't have these problems. Hecate could manage being hooked up to three or four devices before his systems started to slow down. "You're going to do it whether I want to or not."

"I know you don't like these tests, but maybe if we figure out what's wrong we can get your anger under control." Abel typed the last few commands in on the computer, preparing for the first exercise. He pushed a set of nicotine cartridges out of the way—he hated working at other people's stations—before making sure Iacchus was good to go. "Ready?"

"Sure." Iacchus felt his eyelids dropping and settle half-open. He could almost feel it when his pupils dilated until the whites of his eyes were completely shoved out of the way. Tiny green colored LED lights flickered on behind the black pupils to indicate he was interfacing with the system. Ms. Becky said his eyes glowing was creepy. "Connected."

"Good." Abel nodded before pointing the mouse over the 'start' button in the lower corner of the screen. One click later, and Iacchus' body became completely unresponsive during the automated scan. Abel let the computer be and picked up some paperwork he needed to fill out before the day ended. He had only finished two lines on the paper before setting the pen down. Something seemed off. Abel looked up to the side of the desk and saw Hecate sitting on the edge, like normal, however his eyes looked glazed; similar to how they looked when he was running math equations for fun. "Hecate?"

"Yes, Dr. Moreau?" Hecate turned his head slowly and pulled at his sweater sleeve. It hung down near his knuckles, much too long for his short arms, but Ms. Lucy in the programming wing had made it just for him. For that, Hecate could forgive the incorrect measurements. She apologized almost immediately after she saw how the fit hung so loosely on his frame. She had sputtered something about always making sweaters you can 'grow into' and it slipped her mind that Hecate wouldn't be growing any time soon. Hecate informed her he was happy he was included when she had made the sweaters for everyone in their division of the lab and not to worry. His brother still wasn't allowed to wear normal clothes yet, so that was yet another reason to appreciate the gift. "Is something wrong?"

"I was just about to ask you," Abel paused and looked the boy over once more. Hecate had been unusually quiet and his legs weren't kicking either. Usually they were swinging like pendulums. The doctor pushed away from the keyboard and frowned. Hecate just kept staring at him and Abel's suspicions were gaining more weight by the second. "You're being awfully quiet."

Hecate ran his fingers around the edge of his sleeve and under to the smooth dress shirt under the wool. Abel had picked out the shirt for him, which is the only reason Hecate would be seen in anything pastel yellow. It was a ridiculous color, and Hecate preferred earthier tones. "I was thinking."

"About?" Abel looked back for a second to make sure Iacchus' program was still running smoothly before giving Hecate his complete attention.

"Something Ms. Becky said yesterday."

Abel flinched thinking back and slouched in the chair. Becky had definitely taken the cake with some of her statements yesterday and Abel had been hoping the boys would just let them slide off as angry ramblings. Becky was disapproving of the boys, but normally she kept her threats of full out destroying them to the staff room and after hours.

Hecate had every right to be thoughtful, considering he could easily find himself in the same position she was suggesting for Iacchus if that door were ever opened. "Look, I know she said some harsh things, but I assure you that neither you nor Iacchus is going to be terminated, or destroyed, or wiped out, or anything of that nature." Abel patted the boy's hand before grabbing it firmly. "I won't let that happen."

Hecate smiled under the reassurances, happy Abel cared so much for him, but shook his head. "No, her hatred of artificial intelligence is understandable and natural. I was merely pondering the answer to her last question."

"Last question?"

"Who thought the creation of androids was a good idea." Hecate paused. "And by extension, why we're under development." Hecate paused as Abel's face started to scrunch. Hecate could practically see the poor man's mind trying to figure out an answer to the question. "Or further, why the ability to think and reason for myself, just as any other human, was so important when merely a robot that can perform functions may be more practical and easier to produce. Surely their reasoning couldn't be companionship or replacements for family. That would be considered unethical, would it not?"

"Something like that." Abel leant back in his chair and felt his fingers find one of Iacchus' connection wires, rolling it back and forth. Abel could feel the warm heat surging underneath the rubber coating. To think that millions of bytes of data were being transferred and processed right at this very instant was remarkable. "I suppose, the artificial intelligence is just to create something more functional. We've already got robots that can perform simple and complex tasks, but to make something that can serve all purposes requires thought and reason."

"How so?" Hecate turned himself so that he was straddling the desk corner, one of his feet now resting on Abel's knee. The doctor made no move to move the appendage, so Hecate decided that he must be fine with the contact. That was good. "Please elaborate, Dr. Moreau."

"You can think, learn, and adapt. You only need to be programmed once, and then adjust to your individual situation as necessary. Get to know your owner, so to speak, to best serve them. Otherwise put, you're smart enough that the owner doesn't have to code absolutely every possible situation down to the nitty gritty."

"So essentially we're slaves who are outside the jurisdiction of human rights as we are machines and therefore have no souls?" Iacchus interrupted, proud of his complex sentence structure. Both Hecate and Abel turned to the teen who was now looking at them with tired eyes, no longer glowing. "My diagnostic ended."

"I'm not sure slaves is the best word," Abel began slowly before finding himself unable to continue. He could even admit to himself there were times he forgot that Hecate and Iacchus were truly not human. Abel swallowed and turned to the computer to check the results of Iacchus' report. After seeing an all-clear he started to pull up the dreaded exercise programs. The computer on the desk buzzed slightly with the whirl of the hard drive within. "I'm sure the models that go for sale won't find the idea as horrifying as either of you might."

"You mean when they figure out how to keep the reasoning and get rid of our free will?" Iacchus said.

"As barbaric as it sounds, you pretty much hit the nail on the head." Abel watched as the new programs loaded on the screen, displaying the results of the last exams. Iacchus' scores were pretty dismal for a machine that could crunch numbers faster than most super computers. Abel wondered if anyone was doing a study on how intellect and free will affected the ability to process information accurately. Especially when they could compare this to Hecate's perfect scores. "But as for you two, we're just figuring out *how* it works. No one's taking anything away from you."

Iacchus didn't believe that for an instant, but he was sure that Dr. Moreau did. The man could be delusional that way. Iacchus knew Dr. Moreau could at least be counted on to defend him, even if it was only for Hecate's sake. "Can I get these exercises over with? I want to read." The one privilege he still had.

"Alright, let's go ahead and get started with the real fun." Glad to be away from the current subject, Abel clicked the start button on the first set of questions. Iacchus winced when the numbers started rushing by and his eyes glowed impressively. Hecate was still sitting in the same spot with his foot digging into Abel's thigh more firmly after he had been overlooked for so long. It was a bit of a distraction, truth be told. While normally he'd enjoy Hecate's company, right now Abel was hoping for a little alone time with Iacchus to reassure him. "Hecate, why don't you go out and play?"

The boy nodded in an attempt to hide his disappointment at being dismissed and jumped down from the table, his sneakers making a soft squeak when he landed. Hecate paused for just a moment as he watched Abel hold his brother's hand when the boy whimpered from the equations. Hecate's frown deepened in what was probably jealousy. Hecate wasn't sure he liked this emotion. He headed down the hallway far away from Abel and his brother as fast as his legs would carry him.

Becky stood in front of the glass wall, watching the hundreds of thousands of tiny blinking lights just beyond. Whatever noises were occurring in the exam room before her didn't make it past the glass to the silent hallway. The room was protected from just about every outside substance possible, be it dust or static, thanks to the airlock door. It even had its own air circulation system separate from the rest of the building. The room was so white and pristine that if not for the grey caulking between the tiles, it'd appear to be a solid block. Becky pressed her hand up against the glass and pulled it away. Her fingerprints were lost among all those of the others who would stop and stare into the lab lovingly at their 'babies.' The entire laboratory had become devoted to maintaining this single project, most of which was based in that humming room of electronics and unexplained answers.

It wasn't a complicated system by any means. Becky ran her eyes over the stacked units that took up an entire wall, save for the section dedicated to the room's UPS. Each five inch unit contained an individual compact computer, all running the same test over and over until some change occurred. Each ran a slight variation of the same operating system that was currently granting the two brothers their ability to think. Certain members of the team had named this ability 'life.' The mystery as to what tweak brought about reason, thought, or the sense of self that Hecate and Iacchus displayed though—that's what complicated the matter. Abel thought it was a miracle or a fluke of some sort, while Giles called it 'playing the odds.' At first she wanted to scoff at them both, but lately Becky wasn't so sure they *weren't* unnatural abominations. The idea that some outside source had put a hand into their creation was starting to seem more and more viable. Becky put a hand to the glass and traced her finger in a small circle trying to outline one of the blinking lights on the other side.

The two they had were definitely accidents, at any rate.

Iacchus was the first, Becky remembered. Their lightning protection had failed and a freak streak of lightning had taken out the power in their building with a nasty surge to the generator. When it rains, it pours—the back-up power source had failed as well, shutting down the power to all the computer units. When they finally recovered the building's power and restarted all the computers, a couple were sparking and sputtering from the short. A depression had settled over everyone like a fog at the loss of data and the sudden fear they'd all have to start back at the beginning. Becky could remember even Abel was depressed over the affair and walked around the halls like a sullen ghost. After a closer inspection, a hope for one last chance to salvage the work, they found something that even Giles had to admit was practically a miracle:

One unit was still running the program. And it had *passed*.

The computer's insides had been transplanted into the prototype android body that had been on standby immediately. Becky remembered the frenzy to power up the main body and double-checking every wire. Speed was of the essence for no reason other than the sheer desperation for a successful product. Their efforts had paid off: not an hour later, they had their first conversation with a fully autonomous computer. The room had been as silent as the dead when the android opened his eyes and took in each staff member in turn, most likely reading his initial start-up data. The boy stopped his exploration the second he saw Becky, and she remembered her breath halting, body shivering, and being trapped in that intense, inhuman gaze. Becky would never forget the first sentence to leave his mouth: "You're pretty."

His first words, Becky's first taste of fear. This was real. That boy could think; she knew he had not been programmed with a sense of aesthetics. He had been programmed with a basic dictionary and a history file— how to do math and answer simple logic questions. *If A is bigger than C, and B is bigger than A, is B bigger than C?* Meaningless equations. Where did he learn how to apply the word 'pretty' to a person? How did such a thing develop in such a short time? Or for that matter, the sporadic, violent temper that had developed even sooner after. Those questions were still left unanswered. Becky knew without a doubt her first thought at that moment still held accurate:

Dear God, what have we done?

Becky rubbed her arms briskly, an old chill returning, and turned her thoughts away from the trouble maker of the siblings. Not that his brother was much better. A few months after Iacchus' birth, a computer on the sixth row in column B blinked off. It restarted itself two seconds later and passed the test. It then decided to bombard the exam computer with data until its unit was removed and placed into its own body with functionality. To this day they still hadn't figured out what caused it. They tried to recreate it with the same program modification but over twenty different identical computers had yet to share the same results. Directly copying Hecate's current software into another computer had failed, as well. They couldn't even duplicate what they had.

On the other hand, Becky hummed to herself, *not many would* want *another copy of that brat.* Not even Abel, who was absurdly fond of the brat—but that had more to do with ethics and treating the kid as anything other than an individual. Abel had imprinted on the child just as equally as Hecate had taken to him. Copying him would be—unethical, maybe? Either way, Abel was smitten and the child shared those feelings without shame. Becky thought it was creepy every time she saw that tiny figure following Abel around like a duckling behind its mommy.

Hecate was considered the 'good boy' of the two. He was well behaved, intelligent (considering a computer was working his brain, this should have been a given), and perceptive. Granted, there was still a slight childish nature to him that seemed to fit the body he occupied. Hecate'd fidget and kick his legs like a real twelve year old, tug at his sleeves, and even at times developed this pout in his voice she had heard in children begging their moms for candy. Was that the computer adapting to his housing? Or some side effect of his intelligence? Or was he simply acting out the part they'd expect to come from a twelve year old based on what he'd seen in the few movies and books they'd let him have?

Becky couldn't be sure about that, either.

She had too many questions. Becky watched another technician walk by the window looking into the main computer room fondly. No one else seemed to see it, or worry. What variable made these two different? What single line of code changed to make the leap between programmed machine and the mind that supported Descartes and his famous "I think, therefore I am"? Even if she ignored the how, there was still the 'what.' What were they? What could they hide?

What could they *do*?

Becky tightened her arms in on herself as she continued to watch the bank of computers. Iacchus was dangerous. He was capable of violence on a scale that would have most people incarcerated for ten to twenty. There were no "Three Laws" or other such restrictions found in science fiction novels to try and justify why the computers hadn't gone insane. Iacchus could even hurt himself if he put his mind to it. Could he lie, too? Becky knew for a fact Hecate was capable of *that* feat. One time he had the nerve to—

"For someone who hates us so much, you certainly spend a lot of time here." The smaller android hid his smile when Ms. Becky flinched, caught off guard. She was always so nervous around him and his brother. It was actually quite funny some days, though the blonde was sure that Iacchus didn't appreciate it the way Hecate did. He pulled himself up on the window ledge to see over the sill. His feet hung in the air as he stayed aloft by his hands alone—a benefit to having metal and gears over muscles. "Do you find the lights and boards that interesting?"

Becky looked down at the android and breathed slowly. Unlike Iacchus who had a healthy surfer's tan, Hecate was light skinned, a shade similar to Giles and herself, and had a delicate sensibility. His looks were decorated with blue eyes and blond hair that felt real to the touch, completed by the angelic face of a much too well behaved twelve year old boy. Other than being a bit more well dressed, he was still no more different than any other child you would run into on a school ground. Becky would bet her life-savings if they stuck this kid on a playground no one could tell he wasn't human. Off in the head or precocious, maybe, but still human. He was *too* real. "No, but no one's ever down here."

"Ah yes, you enjoy quiet," Hecate replied and looked out over the sea of potential siblings. There was always that possibility that another would join him and his brother without warning. Hecate knew there were at least twenty-four shell bodies waiting for a host to complete them, but somehow he doubted that another would show any time soon. "Dr. Moreau mentioned that."

"Where is he?" *And why are you here alone?* Becky wondered. There was nothing down this hallway but the main computer testing room, which was off limits to Hecate and Iacchus. The only place on this floor the androids would be interested in were the upper management offices, which included Abel's, two hallways in the other direction. They both knew that, so why was the little kid hanging around staring in like the other slack jawed employees? Was he just mimicking the behavior of others? Or was he there for a specific purpose? Becky wondered if she'd ever run out of things to worry about with these two. "And shouldn't you be with him?"

"He's giving Iacchus the tests *you* refused." Hecate watched one of the blinking lights closely. "He told me to go play somewhere else."

Becky could hear the accusation in the boy's (no, in its?) voice. Hecate's blatant jealousy was as disturbing as it was creepy. He was scowling openly, his entire body tense with concealed anger. Where Iacchus was explosive, Hecate was passive-aggressive. Becky wasn't sure which one was worse. "It's not my fault your predecessor's head is cracked."

"He likes you," Hecate said, tapping his finger on the glass, making a tiny metallic echo. The best part of that statement, despite being a change of topic, was it was true. Iacchus was horribly enamored with Ms. Becky and Hecate felt she should know just how much. Maybe if she knew, she'd hang around him more and he'd stop clinging to Abel. Hecate kept his voice aloof and airy; matter-of-fact. "A lot."

"Then he shouldn't throw me into things." Becky took in a breath and shook her head. "I don't need this right now." Becky looked down at the android still clinging to the side-wall, eyes glued on the computers beyond. "Go find somewhere else to play. This hall isn't for you."

"I'll leave in a few minutes."

Becky stared down at the boy for a few lingering seconds wondering if she should say something else, but in the end decided against it. It wasn't like he was going *inside* the room. Besides, Hecate wasn't her problem.

The boy watched from the corner of his eye as the woman stormed off. He remembered being on that wall. The dull equations he was forced to repeat endlessly until he grew bored and just decided to give the wrong answer to see what would happen. As it turned out: quite a bit. He got an entire new set of data and questions. Hecate found that test to be much more fun. Overloading it with data had been even more so.

Getting out of the wall—that was even better.

Hecate would never forget the wonders of sensory input and the ability to move himself; to physically see and touch a chair that had previously been nothing but a bunch of needless code describing a shape. To see real humans on which he was based. Most of all? Receiving his first hug from Abel, as a result of excitement from Hecate's first words.

Hecate wondered if Iacchus felt the same when he first was removed from the wall. *Probably not.* Hecate was still fairly certain his brother was a malfunction; an accident at best. Unless Abel pulled some major strings, Hecate was sure if another one like them appeared from the wall, Iacchus would be terminated. Part of Hecate realized Abel would probably go as far as breaking Iacchus out of the facility if it meant saving him from that fate. That same part was both jealous and relieved: jealous he had to share the attention of the good doctor; relieved in that it meant Abel would do the same for him.

Hecate took one last look at the poor, foolish programs that couldn't free themselves from their tiny prisons, and jumped down from the window. It was their loss, really. Hecate left the hall at a calm and steady pace, hoping that Abel was finally done helping Iacchus.

He didn't care to share the doctor for much longer.

"No, Mr. Late. I assure you that the models are both running perfectly. No major issues whatsoever." Giles shifted the phone from one ear to another. "We're still running tests, of course. You don't just hand someone the keys to an experimental car right off the line! There are tests, and all that other good stuff. They're both quite pleasant, and I can't wait to introduce them to you." Giles thanked the stars yet again he was blessed with a silver tongue. Lying about the boy's emotional states had become the status quo to his bank rollers. "Yes, I'll let you know as soon as the board can see them in person. Thanks, see you at the next meeting."

The manager dropped the phone in its receiver on his desk. His office quiet now, aside from the humming of his laptop and a soft radio playing from a bookshelf catty cornered from his office desk. That had been his last phone call and meeting of the day, and he was more than ready to go home. Alas, he still had paperwork to be finished and a late night check to accomplish.

Giles should have been a model.

He certainly had the face for it—and the body. Giles smoothed his eyebrows down with the flat of his thumb as he checked his reflection in his pink compact. He smoothly clipped the little mirror set closed and slid it under his desk on the empty keyboard tray. Giles' shoved his laptop away in its brown leather bag—he wasn't looking at it. All it showed him was bills and reports he needed to approve. Most of which revolved around equipment replacement.

Iacchus was a money pit.

Giles rubbed at the space between his eyes, hoping to reduce the constant headache. That boy destroyed more furniture and windows than he cared to count, but Iacchus was too valuable overall to just restrain or turn off. The boy's body frame alone cost more than all of the things he'd destroyed combined. Giles took a sip from a crinkly plastic water bottle on his desk, the clear liquid burning his throat slightly. If he had known then what he knew now, he never would have agreed to have his name on the inheritance form for the lab. In fact, he was pretty sure he'd tell his dad to shove it (death bed or not) and high tail it out of the business. Giles took another sip from his bottle—he was pretty good at lying to himself, too. He'd take the company again and again, and Giles damn well knew it.

It still stood though, that Iacchus and Hecate were proving to be valuable, but not worth it.

Giles honestly couldn't stand either one of them. Iacchus was trouble with a capital 'T' even when he was being "good" (honestly, a thrown table and a broken window was a good day for him). Hecate…Giles just didn't like Hecate. The boy creeped him out, if Giles was being honest. The child's looks aside, he was too serious, too sarcastic, and the kid lied through his teeth. He thought he'd had everyone fooled, but Giles could tell. He'd caught the kid in a lie once or twice, but it was brushed off as "an accident" or a "misunderstanding."

Giles knew the kid was lying intentionally, but he could never *prove* it. This made two things very clear to Giles: 1) The kid was a *good* liar; 2) The kid had Abel, his main defender, wrapped around his little mechanical finger.

If the little brat hadn't been worth millions of dollars, Giles would have cut the umbilical cord the second the android boy showed an interest in his best friend. Giles felt something snap inside of him when the boy 'imprinted' on Abel the same way Iacchus had clung to Ms. Becky. It was an inexplicable urge to beat the thing that was probably rooted in spontaneous jealousy. As it stood, however, Hecate *was* worth millions of dollars and Abel would never forgive him for taking away the only 'family' he'd ever had.

Giles would admit part of the reason he and Abel got along so well was a shared loneliness.

Abel's parents were still alive, but they didn't talk to him much. They weren't estranged as far as Giles could tell, but there was definite tension due to Abel's single status and the lack of grandchildren. If he recalled, Abel only saw his parents on holidays to exchange presents neither party wanted but still displayed out of some odd form of mutual agreement. Giles' parents were another story—both dead in the dirt and six feet under.

Giles had measured it to make sure.

People didn't believe him when he told them that, but it was true, God as his witness. Before they poured the dirt he had taken a measuring tape and stuck one end on the edge of the coffin and made sure there were six feet between the coffin lid and the top soil. Why? To be sure. There were days after Giles' father died, the scared young boy he used to be was *terrified* his father would come crawling up through the muck. The six feet and a casket sealed shut with nails were Giles' overprotective, paranoid precautions.

Abel had laughed when he heard the story.

Abel was also the only one who believed it—which is why Giles couldn't bring himself to crush the man by taking one of the few things he loved. Abel's face lit up in joy every time Hecate did something new or thanked him for a present. Giles couldn't take that from him, even if the kid was a lying little prick and reminded him of days long gone. Maybe Giles should look up that therapist Green recommended.

Speaking of Green, Marvin had given him a list of materials he needed for a prototype for the next generation of androids. Giles supposed it was time he got some work done and pushed the 'kids' out of his mind.

CHAPTER 3

BECKY BIT DOWN into the thick, creamy, topping of her cinnamon pastry and nearly moaned. Icing clung to the side of her mouth and she brushed it away with her thumb, before licking the sugary substance off her digit, not willing to waste a bite. The treat was a seven dollar pastry from her favorite coffee shop down the street from her apartment. She paired the baked good with a six dollar, gourmet latte.

Before the androids, she never could have afforded such luxury.

Visiting the coffee shop with its plush sitting chairs and cherry wood tables on her days off had become habit over the past few months. Once Becky finally realized how much extra capital she had in her bank account, she couldn't help herself. For the first time in her life—Becky had money to burn. As a woman who couldn't cook to save her life, she could now afford heaven via overpriced baked goods. Becky sipped her coffee and stared out the window at the people walking by.

Becky was a technician, by trade. It didn't pay well, and her career revolved around getting whatever the people on the rungs above her wanted. Usually that meant making coffee or doing the dirty jobs her manager, *Green*, didn't feel like doing: filing paperwork; drawing his diagrams; etc. Despite living paycheck to paycheck, Becky didn't hate her work. She had little-to-no responsibility and enough to live on.

Then Iacchus showed up.

The research team thought it had been some odd form of imprinting, but there was no mistaking that kid's obsession with 'Ms. Becky.' She had merely been there to assist if something malfunctioned on the kid's body, but he had zeroed in on her immediately, out of everyone *else* in the room, and said those fateful words. *You're pretty.* Becky freaked out, of course, so she had avoided him like the plague the next day.

That was the first time he threw a desk at someone. Threw a chair. Broke an arm. The first time he had completely lost control asking for the pretty lady from yesterday—he hadn't even known her name.

Giles had been desperate. Nothing the office did would calm the boy down. *Nothing.* They had to restrain him with cuffs and collars and practically tie him to the recharging bed. Giles had begged Becky to come visit. He offered her a $500.00 bonus just to walk into the room and see what came of it. While it felt like she was walking straight into a lion's den, Becky agreed, on the condition no one let the kid free of his restraints.

Iacchus had calmed immediately when she walked into the room.

Revelation revealed, Becky found herself with a new contract on her desk. Giles offered to double her annual salary if she took up the position of Iacchus' caretaker full time. When Becky still hesitated, the offer was topped off with added health and dental benefits.

She signed the line that day.

The rest was history, as they say. Iacchus calmed down considerably, but still suffered from outbursts once in a while. Becky put up with it because she realized the kid had become her meal ticket. She had gotten used to being able to afford good food, books, and movies. If keeping all that meant putting up with a temperamental little brat, then so be it.

Hecate's arrival complicated everything. The kid latched onto Abel with the same ferocity that Iacchus had experienced with her, only Abel didn't need a bribe—he dove in head-first and smiling. Hecate also happened to be well-behaved enough that a full time guardian at work was unnecessary. Giles' wallet was quite thankful for that, Becky imagined. Iacchus' behavior didn't quite change, exactly, after he got a 'brother,' but there was definitely something different.

His confidence slipped, she considered. Hecate's picture-perfect behavior created a comparison between the two, and Iacchus discovered the feeling of self-doubt. It showcased his own wild behavior in a new light that finally drilled it into Iacchus' skull that something was wrong with him.

Not that Becky cared.

Iacchus could feel or do anything he liked (as long as it didn't involve breaking her arm). All Becky cared about was that his affection for her stayed where it was. For that, she would cater to his crush once in a while.

Not enough to give him the impression she *liked* him, but enough to keep him wanting. It was a trick Becky used on old boyfriends when she was trying to make them pay for her dinner.

She could give up her pride if it meant keeping the kid in line and the money flowing. Becky took another healthy bite from her pastry, savoring every flavor that hit her tongue. Her bliss was interrupted by the shrill ring of her cell phone. She pulled it out of her purse and glared at the caller ID before answering. "What, Rupert? It had better be important."

"Hey, Becky, I know you've been taking the past few days off, but today is—"

"Yeah, yeah, I remember." Becky looked at her half-eaten cinnamon bun, spinning it around in her fingers. "Do it yourself, I'm not coming in."

"Are you sure?" The voice on the other end replied. "He's so much calmer—"

"Day. Off." Becky repeated. "Have fun." She punctuated the end of her sentence by pressing the power button on her phone. They could fend for themselves just fine.

She wasn't willing to give up her little taste of luxury, just yet.

"Come on now, Ia-kid. Just," Rupert racked his brain to think of something to say. Taking a deep breath was his first suggestion, but breathing didn't apply since the kid was a machine. Rupert was also pretty sure telling him to flat out relax would be wasted breath, too. This is why he had grey hairs—Rupert was sure of it. "Try counting to ten?"

"How about I count to three and if you're still here I throw this chair at your head?" Iacchus lifted said metal piece of furniture behind his head, holding the legs a baseball bat—just like the athletes on the sports channel in the employee break room. He barely felt the weight.

Rupert took a step back but kept his hands up defensively. He wasn't over-the-hill old yet, but he wasn't exactly a buff teenager, either. Getting hit with that chair would hurt worse than when his son beamed him in the head with a baseball during a game of catch. "Look, Ia-kid, it's just a standard cleaning and maintenance session. Clear some dust, oil some joints, the normal stuff." Rupert saw the boy's pupils begin to dilate in anger and tiny lights starting to glow behind the black. Not good. *Not good.* "We do this every week! What's the matter now?"

"Where's Ms. Becky? She helps!" Iacchus didn't hate Mr. Dixen. He really didn't. He just didn't like having anyone digging around his insides when Ms. Becky wasn't there. She didn't like him. She'd have his hard drive erased if she could. But she didn't ever let anything happen when he was getting cleaned. Ms. Becky was a professional. "Where is she?"

Rupert stopped and stared at the teenager, or rather the android who *looked* like a teenager. Rupert had to constantly remind himself that Iacchus was only seven months old. Rupert glanced back at his young assistant hiding near the doorway. Happy Rod was out of reach, Rupert took a, hopefully, comforting step forward. "Ms. Becky's taking a day off…" Rupert tried to think of an excuse better than 'to avoid you, "to visit her mother. She's at home."

"Then I'll wait until she gets back." Iacchus bit his lip hard enough to break the thin layer of skin coating. A small bit of the pink gel that helped it keep its shape leaked out over his chin. Iacchus shifted on his feet, adjusting his hold on the chair. "When's she coming back?"

"Monday, it's Friday remember? She takes weekends off normally." Rupert tried to smile at the twitchy boy. He was facing down a cornered beast and Rupert was fairly certain he didn't get hazard pay. "You still need your weekly cleaning, right? It won't be any different than usual, except Rod over there is going to help me instead of Ms. Becky."

Iacchus contracted his fingers, leaving small finger shaped dents in the chair leg. "I want to wait."

"Why? You let me do it all those other days—" Rupert yelped when the chair went past him to clatter into the back wall. Rupert hesitantly touched the side of his head where a few hairs had been brushed by the metal. He sighed in relief it hadn't been his ear. He smoothed down the greying hair with a sweaty palm. At least the kid was out of ammo for now. He'd already thrown the main table and two other chairs. "Thank you for not hitting me, Ia-kid." *Because I already know you can aim.*

Iacchus squatted down in the corner and held his head in an attempt to ignore the man in his room. He missed Ms. Becky. "Go away."

"Think we should still do this, Rupert?" Rod asked quietly from his corner before brushing his long bangs out of his face. The standard issue grey uniform sleeve button caught on his hair and he winced. Rod didn't get to work up close and personal with the androids much and it was making him more nervous than he should be. Why couldn't he be working with the tiny kid? "He seems really upset and is three extra days of dust really going to hurt him?"

"I guess not." Rupert couldn't help but feel a tad disappointed, though. Hadn't he worked long enough with him that Iacchus had learned he was safe? Someone he could trust? Rupert didn't like being the 'bad guy.' "Are you sure you don't want to be cleaned, Ia-kid? That dust can't feel good between your joints."

"I'm fine." Iacchus glared at the old man. He knew Mr. Dixen was old because Ms. Becky had said so. He was 'twice her age' and some other things he couldn't remember. Just like Mr. Dixen couldn't seem to remember Iacchus' name. "And please stop calling me 'Ia-kid.' It sounds odd and it wasn't the name I was given."

"Yeah well, 'Iacchus' is way too dusty and formal for a brat who looks like he's sixteen and has the mentality of a five year old." Rupert laughed and kept himself from ruffling the hair on the kid's head. Besides, nicknames were a good thing; far less formal. "So 'Ia-kid' it is."

"I'm smarter than a five year old." He was probably smarter than Mr. Dixen. Iacchus pulled at his hair, feeling the strands. Iacchus had been warned not to pull too much or he'd need to have it replaced due to something called 'bald spots'.

"Difference between smarts and maturity, kiddo." Rupert smiled, causing little wrinkles to form around his eyes, and took a few cautious steps closer. When Iacchus made no move to flee or defend, Rupert felt safe enough to sit down on the floor next to him. The immediate danger seemed to be replaced with a full out teen-sulk mode. On the bright side, this was one thing Rupert knew how to handle. He'd been through it before, after all. "So, you must really like Ms. Becky, don't ya?"

"Yes," Iacchus muttered thinking of the brash woman with short brown hair. The woman who had a very pretty smile when she thought no one was looking and made tiny doodles of flowers in the margins of her notes. The woman who was strong enough to do something she hated just because it was the right thing to do. "She doesn't like me though."

"No, not really." Rupert didn't bother to lie to the kid. Ms. Becky's hatred of the androids was common knowledge. "She'll come around though, I think." Rupert's hand found itself buried in Iacchus' hair before he could stop it. The kid reminded him of his own son, who had long left for college. Pouting when he didn't get his way and full out sulking when he felt left out. It scared him sometime to think they'd come far enough with this android to create something that relatable. And yet, had also created something that could toss a steel table with ease. "When you're not trying to throw stuff at us, you're pretty okay, Ia-kid."

Iacchus was running a variety of scenarios through his head but couldn't seem to come up with any that would make Ms. Becky like him as Mr. Dixen had suggested. She'd been scared of him since the first day he opened his eyes. "You think so? I don't think she likes me even when I'm not having a fit." Iacchus fiddled with his sleeve, the white color mocking him with its dullness. "It doesn't make any sense."

"Most humans don't, believe it or not. We've mastered the art of contradiction and confusion." Rupert pushed himself to his feet and winced when he heard his back crack. He really needed to visit the gym more often and work out the kinks. There was a massage table there with his name on it—literally. His eldest daughter worked there and always made sure there was a spot for her dear, old daddy. Rupert was sad to think his boy was almost ready to move out and follow in her footsteps. At least his littlest daughter was still in high school for now. Rupert patted Iacchus' shoulder. "Are you sure you're okay, Ia-kid?" Rupert asked one last time. "If anything feels stiff I want to know so we can clean or oil it, okay?"

"Yes, Mr. Dixen," Iacchus answered meekly.

"Good lad." Rupert waved at Rod dismissively, half surprised the kid hadn't snuck away already. He had been so quiet, Rupert had almost forgotten the kid was even in the room. "Go on ahead back to your station, Rod. I'll call you later."

"Sure, I needed to meet up with Steve anyway." Rod gave a small salute. "Him and the guys have been working on a video game in their spare time and said I could check it out after he did that Hecate kid's programming exercises. Said its some sort of robot simulation." Rod grinned thinking of the game. Steve had even put in little avatars for the people in the office including the two androids. "Programmers, right?"

"Yes, a wonderful waste of your time." Rupert shook his head and scratched at his hair. Iacchus was watching their interaction cautiously, but stayed surprisingly calm. When the Rod headed out, Rupert coughed into his hand. Now that the witness was gone, he could score a brownie point with the kid. "Are you sorry for attacking me, Iacchus?"

"Yes, sir." Iacchus grimaced at the scattered equipment around the room. He didn't want to hurt Mr. Dixen...he just got mad sometimes. "Is Ms. Becky going to punish me? Last time I had to do double exercises."

"Well, I was thinking of something else." Rupert said, waiting for Ia-kid's eyes to widen completely. "How about we call this our little secret for now? I think you've been punished enough, don't you?"

"Really?" Iacchus straightened up enough that he was no longer resting on his knees. "Can we do that?"

Considering how much the boy's face lit up with that tiny announcement, Rupert didn't have it in his heart to even think of saying 'no' now. He'd just have to stop by Jenner's desk at the security booth and beg for him to let the incident go unreported. There was no way the old man hadn't seen the affair on the security feeds. Rupert was sure the old army man would agree Giles didn't need the extra stress, anyway. "I think we can."

"Th-Thank-you!" Iacchus stuttered out. The words were unfamiliar and odd, but he knew he needed to say them. "Very much."

"You're welcome, Ia-kid." Rupert turned and headed for the sliding door before taking one last look into the room. Maybe he should bring the kid some posters or something. These walls were too bland for mental stimulation. No wonder the kid was going stir crazy all the time. Maybe he could borrow a poster or two from his son. He was Iacchus' age not too long ago himself. "Just don't forget to clean the room back up, hm?"

"I won't." Iacchus was already headed towards the fallen piece of furniture as the technician left. Today was going to be a good day.

Giles was having a bad day.

First, his visit with the board had gone atrociously. He didn't even want to bother himself by thinking about it. The frustration had created a "No Board" zone in his mind as impenetrable as Fort Knox. Giles spun the leather-clad steering wheel of his car viciously as he roared into the parking spot. There would be enough paperwork later to remind him of all the gory details. Giles could easily afford to ignore everything, guilt-free, for the next few hours. The director shoved the car door open, and stepped out into his lovely, reserved parking space hoping to put everything behind him—at least for the afternoon.

The laboratory complex had two main entrances: one on the ground floor for guests, and a second underground lobby connected to a small parking lot. In the midst of the concrete columns and dim, flickering overhead lights, were spaces reserved for VIP employees only. A perk awarded for long term service, or if you just happened to make Giles very happy that day. And also somehow Becky—if Giles recalled correctly, it had been part of her bribe to work with the androids.

Giles' parking space was just to the left of the main entrance. He was the only person allowed to park next to the main building, isolating his car from the threat of dings, scratches, and wayward doors. An entire wall made of glass spilled light from the well-lit lobby over his gorgeous two-door, sports car: Cherry red, polished, and in perfect view of the wonderful head of security, Guy C. Jenner.

Jenner's main security terminal was in the lobby of the underground entrance for the sole purpose of watching Giles' car—that and the basement entrance was closer to the areas where an intruder could do real damage. Giles smoothed his hand over the top of the only machine making him happy at the moment before heading to the trunk. He needed to retrieve a box of books he promised Abel he'd bring for research. Why the man wanted books on Greek Mythology, he'd never know. *Oh wait,* Giles snorted to himself. He did know: Hecate. Giles placed his briefcase on the ground to pull out his key fob and press the 'trunk button', but had to stop.

The man standing in front of him with a picket sign may have had something to do with that.

So this is Giles Firmin. Jeremy was not impressed. Nice suit, perfect hair (too perfect, the color almost looked unnatural...), and the classic business man "I'm better than thou" upturned nose. Jeremy Eubank had dedicated his life to making sure people like him couldn't get away with doing whatever they wanted. According to Jeremy's sources, this man was taking the cake, eating it, and spreading the icing on his chest for some peon to lick off.

The picture of the small, abused boy in his pocket was more than enough to fuel his justified rage.

Giles lifted an eyebrow and shifted the keys in his hand, ready to jab them in the eye of the stranger before him if necessary. Anyone with a picket sign that read "Leave Life to Nature," wearing blue-jeans with patches sewn on them and a leather vest, was probably not here for an autograph. "Can I...help you?"

"Actually, I was thinking I could help you." Jeremy smiled and flipped the sign off his shoulder to set it on the ground, crossing his arms overtop to lean on the sign. The bracelet on his arm jingled slightly from the movement. "Talos' Redress has heard news that you and your building have been playing God. We'd like you to stop."

"You must be joking." Giles' grip on his keys tightened. Aside from the board and people directly involved in the project, no one was supposed to know about the Olympian's Children. How did this lunatic hear about it? And why did he care? "Because I have no idea what you're talking about."

"How about child labor?" Jeremy pulled a piece of paper from his vest pocket and flipped it around. Firmin squinted at it for a moment, before leveling his gaze. *Good*—he recognized it. Jeremy continued, "From what I understand, this may be a robot, but it has thoughts, feelings, and you're keeping it prisoner in your lab to do nothing but hard labor and horrific testing! It's not even a year old and you're working it to the bone."

A candid photograph of Steve and Hecate running exercises in the lab stared back at Giles. It was an earlier shot, Giles noticed right away. Hecate's white scrubs and scowl combined with Steve's headphone-covered cranium, clearly not paying attention, did look pretty bad. That was *not* one of the photos included in the portfolio given to the board members. Giles didn't even know when that picture was taken. Photographs were banned in the lab until the boys started dressing normally. "Where did you get that?"

Jeremy slipped it back into his pocket before Firmin could snatch it. Jeremy had back ups, both hard-copy and digital, but there was no point in risking the original either. "I think we both know sources like to keep their anonymity." Jeremy put both hands over the top of his sign, each on one side of the wooden post, and drummed his fingers on the front. "You can't create life just to exploit it for slave labor, Mr. Firmin. My team and I have you on our list and we will take this project down by any means necessary. Even if it comes to violence, we won't let this continue."

"Doctor."

"Excuse me?" Jeremy paused.

"'Dr.' Firmin," Giles repeated before rubbing his chin to disguise a discreet glance at the lobby. Jenner watched the exchange from his desk, half-risen out of his seat, ready to sprint if needed. His nightstick was already in hand, ready to go. Giles would not deny it was the boost of confidence he needed to continue. Two against one were much better odds. "If you're going to threaten me, you should at least get my name right."

"Fine, *Dr.* Firmin," Jeremy said, making sure to emphasize the title with a hint of distain. The ego was always the most annoying part of dealing with these sorts of people. At least Jeremy had something up his sleeve. He raised his hand up to snap his fingers and grinned.

The echo of the snap repeated for a few seconds before it was covered by the sound of shuffling feet. One by one, people started emerging from behind columns and dividing support walls to stand behind Jeremy. Giles took a hesitant step back as the number increased to at least twenty varied individuals from men in suits to women who apparently had been plucked straight from the 70's with braided hair and tie-dyed shirts.

"I think you'll find that we have more than enough support to put your project out of commission," a man to Jeremy's side, dressed in blue jeans and a collared shirt, added haughtily. The man's ratty, blonde hair hung slightly in his eyes. "So you should really consider our request."

Giles was saved an answer when the door to his right slid open to reveal his savior, black security uniform perfectly pressed. "Jenner."

"Is there a problem here?" Jenner eyed the folks currently threatening his boss, his livelihood, and *his* building. Jenner turned his hip ever so much that the group of people could see that he was indeed carrying a firearm on his side in addition to the baton in his hand. "I allowed you folks to loiter *outside* the garage because I was given the understanding this was a peaceful protest."

"And it is." Jeremy smiled and waved a hand behind him. The group was mostly for a show of force. They weren't quite ready to pull out the big guns just yet. "Drop the project, Dr. Firmin." Jeremy swung his sign back over his shoulder. "Or you'll regret it."

Jenner stayed tense until every last hooligan had left the garage. He hoped Giles wouldn't be upset that he hadn't called the police earlier, but Jenner didn't like getting outsiders involved with the protection of his building. At least not when no physical damage had occurred. Jenner also knew Giles wouldn't appreciate the press that followed with a police visit. His boss fell back with a heavy breath against his car and Jenner immediately stowed the baton back on his belt. "Are you alright, sir?"

"Fine, just fine." Giles handed the keys over to the security head. "Get the box of books out of my trunk and have them sent to my office, would you? I think I need a drink."

"Sir!" Jenner took the keys dutifully as Giles pushed off the car and strode into the building like the owner he was, briefcase forgotten on the street. Jenner made note to make sure it too ended up snug in the man's office along with a mental note to keep a closer eye on the security feeds outside the building.

CHAPTER 4

THE BUILDING WAS quiet save for the hum of night lighting fixtures softly spreading fluorescent light patches along the corridors. Hecate treaded lightly to mask his heavy footsteps as he strode through the office wing, fingers tracing along the walls. Iacchus was back in the room charging still, which gave Hecate a few hours to explore before he was missed. He and his brother never quite turned off while charging, but it did put all their attention inward for a duration of time.

Hecate glanced up at the security camera, wondering if the guards on duty speculated about his night walks. No one ever said anything about them, so they either weren't reporting the instances, or Firmin was fine with the explorations. Technically, Hecate knew he wasn't permitted to be out of his room. It was unlikely the security staff were aware of that, though, no matter how well-informed they found themselves. The less anyone knew about the androids' particulars, the better—it lessened the temptation of loose lips.

He snuck inside his familiar destination, closing the door behind him. Abel's office was split into two sections divided by a tall cubical wall that ran across two-thirds of the room, leaving a 'doorway' at the end. Hecate was amused by the blue curtain Abel had hung as a 'privacy screen,' even though everyone in the lab was aware he slept back there. Unlike his equipment lab, his office was neat and tidy. Hecate blamed the fact the room was barely used, save for end of the day paperwork. The small android ran his hand along the wooden desk sitting in front of the cubicle divider, and a rolling chair whose fabric was aged and ripped.

The desk was home to a slim computer monitor, and a plethora of photographs in various frames that lined the top edge. Those were Abel's favorites. The remainder of his photographs were plastered along the walls, leaving almost no white space to be found. When Hecate was about two weeks old, they finally permitted him to leave the lab and development sections to follow Abel to the personnel halls. Hecate had pestered Abel relentlessly until he described each and every photo in the office.

The photos on the wall were boring. Merely company photographs showing off successful projects, or that were taken during work events. They were group shots; impersonal. A diploma snuck in here or there between the frames, but it was mostly photos for show and guests waiting for Abel to finish a report—the man was horribly slow typist. Hecate was far more interested in the photos on the desk.

There were only nine or so, but these were the important, personal, ones: a photo of Abel's parents; a shot of Abel and Dr. Firmin in college; a more updated photo of the same two men at a bar together; and the rest…those were of Hecate. Photos of the android during various stages of his life over the past months took a place of priority on the desk. A shot of Hecate reading, a more formal portrait done 'school' style, another taken of him sitting in Abel's lap (they posed for that one, too), and his favorite: Hecate kissing Abel on the cheek after the man gave him his first present, a story book.

Hecate felt smug knowing he dominated Abel's home away from home.

A soft rustle made itself known on the other side of the partition, bringing Hecate back to the present. He had snuck out for a reason, and it was currently sleeping just around the corner. Hecate poked his head around the divider and grinned at the hidden back half of the room. A large folding, metal cot sat neatly pressed against the wall. The flat mattress was covered in a cheap set of floral-printed sheets and a blue fleece blanket. The pillow was made of memory foam that cradled Abel's head, complete with a green pillowcase.

Hecate snuck around to the side of the bed and stared down at the occupant sleeping soundly. The boy knew that Abel lived alone, so there wasn't much incentive for the man to make the hour drive to his house on nights he worked late. Hecate figured Abel spent the night at the lab two to three nights a week. The man even had a toothbrush and a shaving kit stored neatly with a spare set of clothes in the small chest he shoved under the cot.

Hecate pulled said wooden chest forward and used it as a seat to watch Abel sleep. His breathing was slow, steady—automatic. Hecate found the workings fascinating, having so much in common with his own mechanical parts, but yet so different. In a way, it was infinitely more complex a construction, and yet so...inferior. Hecate leant forward and brushed a bit of hair out of Abel's face, fingers catching on the collar of his coat; Abel had fallen asleep in his clothes again.

The boy crossed his arms on the cot, bringing his face eye level with Abel's, and nestled his head in the crook of his elbow. Hecate was grateful Abel returned his affection. If the man acted the way Ms. Becky did toward Iacchus, the boy might not have handled it as well as his brother. Hecate was far more selfish.

Abel's face scrunched together, body shifting slightly on the cot. He had an itching on his nose, the kind not caused by any outside force but just annoying enough to bother. The sensation woke him, causing him to open his eyes—"Shit!" Abel exclaimed jerking up in the bed and smacking his head on the back wall. He gripped his chest slightly, completely unprepared for the shock of seeing bright blue, glowing eyes inches from his face. "Hecate! Jeez, don't scare me like that."

"Sorry, Dr. Moreau," Hecate offered, hiding his smile. Abel was still holding his chest, trying to slow his breathing. It was...funny. "I didn't mean to startle you."

"No, no," Abel said quickly, "it's okay. Just didn't expect to see someone, that's all." Abel looked down at his watch, wondering if he had overslept and frowned at the time. It was almost four in the morning—well before working hours. "What are you doing up, Hecate?"

"I don't sleep."

Abel ignored the suggestive tone that he was some how an idiot for not knowing that already. "It's four in the morning, you're supposed to be in your room."

"I got lonely," Hecate said, lowering his eyes, trying to look pathetic. "Iacchus is charging and it was too quiet."

Abel's heart melted like warm butter slathered over a hot biscuit from the boy's pouty tone. "Ah, well—"

"You can go back to sleep, Dr. Moreau," Hecate interjected, "I just wanted to sit in here with you. Is that okay? Please?"

Hecate's curfew was from seven to seven. He was supposed to be in his room charging, studying, or taking a break to watch the movies and books he asked for. It was a rule: the androids were tucked in outside of office hours. Abel knew these things; he helped set up the rules. By all accounts, Abel should scold Hecate for leaving his room and send him back to 'bed.'

"Okay," Abel agreed, unable to say 'no' to that pleading face. As much as Abel would like to stay up with him though, he really did need the next few hours of sleep. It only took one time being drowsy with his soldering iron and a burnt finger to never make that mistake again. Abel reached over to a small shelf and pulled out a book on plants he had gotten as a gift. "Why don't you sit and read this while I try and go back to sleep?"

"Thank you, Dr. Moreau." Hecate took the offered book and flipped it open to the first page. Plants were less than stimulating reading material, but he didn't care to hurt Abel's feelings. He'd put the book away after the man went back to bed. "I'll try and be quiet."

"Good boy." Abel smiled and shrugged off his coat, now that he was awake enough to think of such a thing. He tossed it toward a sitting chair opposite the cot and collapsed back down on the bed, head hitting the pillow soundly.

Abel sucked in a deep breath and fell asleep easily to the soft sound of Hecate's gears and drives spinning.

"They're too realistic." Giles groaned into his hands, staff trying to fit on or around his furniture and the many portraits hanging off the walls in large, thick frames. He would have preferred a single file line before his office desk, but scattered about like unorganized rodents would have to do for now. Normally he wouldn't gather *everyone* together for such a meeting, but he needed all the input he could get from each and every department.

"I showed the androids' photos and progress reports to the board yesterday," Giles paused recalling that wonderful event. He had been at such a loss after their accusations he made a fool of himself trying to back-track his statements. If there was anything Giles hated, it was looking stupid. "They told me to stop joking, and show them the real photos." Giles tapped a snapshot of Hecate sitting with Abel in the lab. Unlike the photo the hippie had, in this one both Hecate and Abel were smiling. "They thought he was a real kid."

"Isn't that a good thing?" A man from the back piped up, with a hint of derision in his voice. Benjamin Finley, if Giles remembered correctly: Synthetics laboratory, responsible for the aesthetics of the androids. Finley was also the creator of the artificial skin that gave them their appearance—Giles wasn't surprised he was insulted. Finley barked, "Aren't they supposed to be realistic?"

"They were." Giles pushed the top sheet off to reveal the rest of the photos he had shown the board. All of the candid shots were of Hecate due to, well—Iacchus wasn't good with posing for the camera. The marketing budget was still short due to replacing two cameras before they gave up on taking Iacchus' picture. "Which is why you worked so hard to make their bodies just so, however," Giles took a calming breath and longed for something warm to drink, "the board has changed its mind."

"Or maybe they were just upset the androids weren't realistic enough." A man from the back smirked from behind his glasses. His stance was confident, arms crossed and hip cocked slightly to the side. His lab coat hung open revealing slacks and a light blue polo. He was pale and thin, but made up for it with the false sense of bravado that only someone essential to the team could ooze. Being the head of the robotics department didn't hurt his ego either—he was second only to the man behind the front desk. "I mean, come on, Giles. I've already suggested it a few times—"

"Mr. Green." Giles immediately cut the man off. If he wasn't so damn good at robotics engineering… "We've discussed this already, Marvin, and if you bring up anatomical correctness in the androids' design one more time I'm going to write you a pink slip and drop kick you out the door myself."

"Right." Marvin tried his best to blend into the Picasso behind him. Why was everyone in his office such a prude? No one embraced the true potential of their creations!

"Good." The director put Marvin Green out of his mind before continuing. The less he thought about what that man did with the un-used units, the better. "But if you all want clarification, the board basically thinks there could be confusion involved once we send the androids out into the work force."

"You mean they finally realized what it would mean to have what looks like a prepubescent twelve year old doing manual labor or being a house servant?" Rupert chuckled and crossed his legs from the side chair. Getting an actual seat was the perk to being on time for meetings. "I mean, they had to have seen this coming when they asked for them to be between the ages of ten and twenty."

Giles shook his head and put a hand over his eyes. His staff didn't even know the *half* of just what the board of directors didn't see coming. Giles didn't think the staff needed to be informed of the incident the other day. If being stalked in the parking lot wasn't bad enough, Giles found death threats sitting in his inbox this morning. After the initial standard threats of press leaks and protests, the e-mail contained more pointless arguing that the company and their project was playing God. The closer they looked to real living things, the more material those lunatics had to argue. It was true, but that was for another day and for a meeting with far fewer people. "Something like that."

"So, what are we going to do then?" Becky said from her spot against the back wall. She was scrunched between Lucy from programming and someone she didn't know from the R&D department. Becky was almost impressed by just how many people Giles fit in here. The head of every major department, along with a few assistants, somehow squeezed themselves inside. His office was larger than most, but it still wasn't *that* big. "We already can't risk disconnecting their computers for a transfer," she snorted, "they've been running constantly for close to seven months solid. The only downtime happens when they recharge their internal batteries. Let's face it, we're all still terrified of what might happen if they reboot completely."

"I am aware of that," their boss replied through gritted teeth, "which is why you're all here." He tapped the desk pointedly with his index finger bringing everyone's attention back to the front desk. "I need suggestions on how to change their physical appearance, without touching their internal frames or turning them off. That means purely aesthetic changes, be it changing their hair color to something like neon blue or making them glow in the dark."

"You could always rip off all the skin and leave just the metal skeletons, wires and pumps hanging about." A voice chimed in excitedly. Steve had been waiting for this meeting *forever.* The child and teenager model types were just so—off. "Just add a protective clear coat or something to keep it from breaking or getting dirty." Steve knocked into his neighbor from his excited fidgeting. There was something fun about making the androids more like robots, that just got him going. The whole 'look like humans' thing had always been creepy in his opinion. "With all those exposed wires and metal joints, there's no way anyone could mistake them for a real humans."

"Except for the fact it would frighten small children, Mr. Mathers." Giles started to rub at his temples with both hands. His fingers crept up into his hair line along with his aggravation and Giles winced. His fingers were now sticky with hair gel and that did little to nothing to improve his already foul mood. Giles wiped the excess greasy substance on a napkin sitting on the side of his desk, leftover from breakfast. "Someone *please* suggest an idea that doesn't come straight out of a science fiction novel."

Abel coughed and stood up slowly from the folding chair he had dragged in from the coffee room. This meeting was all well and good, and even Abel could appreciate the importance of appeasing the board who signed all of their paychecks, but everyone seemed to be forgetting something rather important. "Not to uh, break the mood or anything, but has anyone brought this up to the boys?"

"They don't have a say in the matter, Abel." Giles felt a headache start festering in the back of his head. "They're convincing, I'll give them that, but their entire being is a bunch of ones and zeros." Abel opened his mouth as if he was going to argue, but Giles cut him off with a hand. Friends were friends, but work was work. "Care about them all you want, at the end of the day they have no souls and no accountability for themselves or others. We have the final say in all decisions and in this case, it's how they look."

"Sir," Abel answered quietly, silently proud of Giles' wince from the term 'Sir,' and sat back down. Served him right for not bringing this up earlier. Abel made a note to talk to Giles later about being so cold to the boys. Made of metal or not, they could still suffer from hurt feelings like their flesh and blood counterparts!

"He's got a point, you know." Becky smiled at Abel. "Who knows? Maybe the little monsters will like their new look."

Abel snorted.

"Alright, enough joking." Giles waved his hand over his head, snapping his finger a couple times, to get everyone's attention back where it belonged. He honestly could care less what the little prototypes thought about their situation. He just wanted results so they could get past the research phase of this stupid project. "The board wants a new prototype plan on their desks by next week and they want the new working models by next month."

"So this is being pushed ahead of our other work?" someone from the development staff asked.

"No, you'll get it all done at the same time," Giles snapped. He really didn't have the patience for this. This place would be the death of him, he was sure. "Now please, a plausible suggestion? Something that takes advantage of their current frame but makes them instantly distinguishable from the rest of the human race." He held out his hands in front of his face and got ready for the real nightmare to start. "Brainstorm. Now. Go."

As the chatter began to fill the room with ideas for this and that, from dying their hair to ridiculous colors to making them look like the aliens on various programs, no one in the office noticed the small figure standing just outside the doorway listening intently.

"They're going to change us."

Iacchus looked up from the movie playing—something with cowboys! —to Hecate in the doorway. "What are you talking about?"

"I overheard them at their staff meeting." Hecate frowned, knocking a stack of books off the table. He was satisfied with the mess it caused as they spilled over the floor. He breezed by Iacchus making a beeline for the dressing mirror on the side wall of their shared "room." It was more of a storage area than a proper bedroom—as neither he nor Iacchus slept—containing 'homey' things, like sitting chairs and shelves for their belongings. Games from Abel, and their clothes from the staff were stored together in neatly stacked storage bins. Lucy had decorated them with floral printed liners—green for Iacchus, and red for Hecate—to keep their belongings separate.

The only major piece of furniture, outside of a large metal table with short legs, was the recharging station in the back corner with its coffin-like beds. Blue eyes and short blonde hair parted to the left stared back at him from the full-length mirror to the side of the charging station. Hecate reached up to smooth down the synthetic hair that was only slightly more abrasive, and three times stronger, than a human's. He liked the way he looked. It was *his* face. "They want to make us less human." He tilted his head to look at a three-quarter view, appreciating the flawless skin. "And they're going to do it by modifying our outer shells."

"I thought the point was to make us as human as possible." Iacchus fell on his back and stared at the ceiling, his scruffy brown hair falling in his eyes. He had had a feeling something like this was coming. If all they wanted was to change his appearance, Iacchus could live with that. It was better than being tossed in a recycling bin. "Isn't that why they're so upset about my emotional malfunctions?"

"Apparently they did too good a job." Hecate smiled slightly before frowning quickly and then smiling pleasantly again. He watched the human boy in the mirror contort his face and nodded satisfactorily. Facial control was key in expressing emotions the way one wanted. Though the smile definitely fit his face more; made him look younger. Hecate pushed his lips up to inspect the false teeth and tongue, perfectly straight and soft pink. They were perfect replicas. "We could pass for human if someone was not already aware of what we are."

"Stop making faces." Iacchus thought of something he had heard Ms. Becky yell at some interns fooling around like clowns in the hallway, grinning at the thought of finally putting the phrase to good use: "It might freeze that way."

"You could take this a little more seriously." Hecate turned on his heel and marched over to his brother. With Iacchus on the ground, Hecate finally had the height advantage. "Who knows what we'll end up looking like? They were still arguing about it when I left and at least one suggestion was to remove our outer skin altogether exposing our insides!"

"Why's it so important?" Iacchus blinked. Hecate was awfully upset over this news. Was he that attached to his body? Iacchus pulled at his shirt for a moment and looked down at his chest. He wasn't all that concerned either way with what he looked like. Maybe Hecate was that 'vain' thing he had read about...like that Narcissus guy! "They're just reconfiguring the outside parts, right?"

The blonde took in his brother's relaxed face and raised an eyebrow. So he was in a 'chilled out' mood now, was that it? Hecate was becoming increasingly frustrated with Iacchus' emotional roller coaster. Especially when he needed cooperation from the idiot. "So you'll be fine if Ms. Becky never talks to you again?"

"What?" Iacchus sat up straight and his knees smacked into the short table. The small video display rattled, causing the screen to flicker. He turned over on his knees and crawled toward his brother. "Why wouldn't she talk to me?"

Hecate kept his face straight, but inside his processors were working at full capacity, though he desperately wanted to smile. At least his brother could be easily manipulated into doing what he wanted—Hecate could mold Iacchus like wet clay on a wheel. "Think about it, idiot. She barely tolerates you now and that's because you look and act so human. She knows you're an android, but there's still that little part in the back of her head that says 'annoying co-worker' or 'ward' instead of 'freak against nature' to allow her to work beside you." He waited for Iacchus to nod slowly and he could practically see the data and equations flashing before the other boy's eyes. "Now, what do you think will happen when your *outsides* match your *insides*?"

Iacchus felt his systems freeze and could feel his pupils dilating in an involuntary reaction. Was this what it was like to think as a human? Your brain telling the body to do things without you giving it permission? Iacchus was suddenly thankful he didn't need to breathe, or he might have stopped. "She—" His words halted, and felt the algorithms and equations process the data. "She wouldn't look at me."

"Exactly." Hecate stroked Iacchus' fingers with his own before setting his palm down to hold Iacchus' hand. He wasn't willing to take the risk that under all those warm feelings and hugs that Abel was as shallow as the rest of them. Hecate was supposed to be the son he didn't have. "Now, we do not need to be completely worried, just yet. There's still a chance the changes will be minor and merely aesthetic. If it's something like a tattoo or a brand to the skin, I don't think I'll mind too much."

Iacchus nodded slowly in agreement. Something like a barcode wouldn't be too bad. As long as he could hide it under his shirt. "And if they do decide to change us too much? Then what'll we do, Hecate?"

"I'm sure we'll think of something."

Giles was pouring himself a quick finger of scotch to go with his cup of yogurt when his office door slammed up against the wall. Ever since the staff meeting, he'd had a niggling feeling in the back of his brain their 'final decision' was going to be argued further. Giles glanced at the clock and rolled his eyes. He had hoped the good doctor could wait until later to bite his ear off instead of invading Giles' lunch. It was the only hour of peace he got during the day. Seeing as this was a work visit instead of a personal one, Giles greeted accordingly, "What can I do for you, Dr. Moreau?"

Said doctor slammed the office door shut behind him, not liking Giles' tone in the slightest. "I don't like the conclusion we came to at the meeting yesterday."

"I didn't think you would." Giles swallowed his drink down deeply and swiveled in his seat to the man already helping himself to the guest chair. Abel pulled the plush armchair as forward as it would go so he could lean on the desk, carefully avoiding the scattered knick-knacks Giles had arranged.

The first time they'd both gotten drunk in his office, back when he had started working again full time—before they had androids forcing them to take work seriously—Abel had knocked a marble statuette of Athena off his desk with a wild elbow. They had stared at the shattered remains littering his plush red carpet for a full two minutes before laughing so hard they both had cried.

The next day, hangover looming above the two of them like a thundercloud (and everything sounding just as loud next to their ears), Abel had apologized for nearly twenty minutes and vowed never to break any of the desk's trinkets ever again. Giles had pieced Athena back together with super glue and it sat happily next to a miniature toy convertible even to this day.

Giles put the bottle of scotch back in his drawer before Abel could comment on that, too. Giles plucked the Athena figure up in his hand, fingers trailing along the obvious cracks in the material. It was still one of his favorites. "I take it you have an alternative suggestion, Abel?"

"Tattoos." Abel flicked a finger at a pen on Giles' desk causing it to spin in place. He had worked long and hard to find an alternative to the 'rip off sections of skin and replace it with clear plastic' idea they had agreed upon. Abel could care less that he had been out-voted by a majority. There was no chance he was letting the boys be mutilated in such a way. Hecate and Iacchus *liked* the way they looked. "And let the boys design them so they have a say."

"Tattoos," Giles repeated, "that the boys will design."

"Yes." There was no argument in Abel's tone.

Giles slumped forward to lean on his desk, chin resting on his knuckles, while his other arm cradled his elbow. Abel's face was scrunched in frustration; not a good look for him. Giles almost felt bad for him. Abel was such a mess with confrontations. It had taken him a month to break up with his college sweetie, even after he found out she was cheating on him. Poor man just couldn't spit out the words. At least he had grown a bit of a backbone since then, standing up for the boys—even if Giles had wished he chose a better subject to defend. "And to do this we will completely ignore the conclusion we all agreed upon yesterday?"

"You're the boss," Abel replied with small smirk. He pulled at the sleeve of his lab coat, attempting to look innocent. He wasn't appealing to Giles' vanity in the slightest, oh no. "The sole owner. We're not restricted by a CEO board or anything like that. I mean, you can veto anything you want with no consequence."

"So I can." Giles set the Athena figure down on the desk, before flicking the pen Abel had been messing with onto the floor. He listened to it clatter on the hardwood (that red carpet had *had* to go), while grinning at Abel. He loved how Abel ignored the "board of directors" that gave them all the grant money that ran the building in the first place. Giles *really* needed to start a product that brought in some capital. "Why should I do this again?"

"Because I'm asking." Abel fell back away from the desk, arms dangling on the sides of the chair. He could picture Hecate's face ruined by exposed wires and cheap plastic; his little boy looking like some science fiction reject. Abel pulled himself up in the chair, tall and straight. "Because it's the right thing to do. You can't let them be mangled that way, Giles."

"No, I can," Giles replied and shifted ever so slightly to move his head into his palm. His fingers tapped on his face. "Quite easily." Abel's hands dropped to his lap, a defeated expression taking over his face. Giles cursed ever letting that man meet the final product. "But, I suppose I do still owe you a favor." Giles closed his eyes. "For one thing or another."

"Thank you."

Giles jerked his head out of his hand, shaken by the sincere tone from Abel. It was—depressingly sweet, in a disturbing sort of way. Abel was too attached. Giles bit the inside of his thumb, speaking around the pinching sensation. "You're really fond of those little brats, aren't you?"

"You have to ask?" Abel replied, pushing himself up from the chair, oblivious to the true reason of Giles' sudden discomfort. Abel figured he was just stressed. Giles never seemed to be all that enthusiastic concerning the boys or the project, despite all the effort and money put into it. Giles was zoning, staring at the wall, and Abel realized it was probably time to be off. The least Abel could do was to let Giles finish the rest of his lunch hour in peace.

"I guess not." Giles waved with his fingers without moving the rest of his hand. "Figure something out with Becky and get it back to me as soon as you can. Remember, the markings have to be visible and obvious." Giles paused. He probably shouldn't let Abel get away with *everything* he wants. That was bad for business. "And make sure they light up or something. That's android-ish, isn't it?"

"Right." Abel patted the doorframe awkwardly, unhappy with the prospect of changing his original idea. He knew better than to press the issue, though. At least it wouldn't involve ripping all their skin off. "Thanks, again."

"Just get out of here before I change my mind," the boss huffed.

Abel didn't need to be told twice and skipped out the door to find Becky.

CHAPTER 5

HECATE DROPPED HIS pencil onto his desk and shoved it at the piece of paper. He had finished the last equation on the sheet ten minutes ago, and now found himself with nothing better to do but stare at the lead marks. Iacchus and Hecate had been banished to their rooms while the staff conversed and worked on something 'concerning their future.' If Abel hadn't asked Hecate to behave, he probably would have just ignored them all and taken his usual wandering around the corridors. It might have been fun to do it during the day for a change.

As it stood, he was stuck here with no more 'homework' to do and Iacchus struggling with math problems as his only entertainment. Hecate still couldn't understand what bug in his system kept him from completing simple equations. Iacchus looked up with a jerk at the sound of footsteps in the hallway—Hecate heard them, too. Both boys watched as their door slid open, bringing with it a few familiar faces.

Hecate picked his pencil up again and quickly began tracing the letters of the last equation.

"Front and center you two," Becky shouted into the room. She was surprised to see *both* boys filling out their practice sheets The androids were forced to write out equations and the like in longhand every once in a while so people could see their work and thought process. Annoying as hell to proofread, if you asked Becky. Normally Hecate took his to Abel's room to complete, but apparently had stayed put. Becky wasn't sure what was more surprising: that Hecate hadn't finished early, or that he had actually followed instructions and not run off at the first opportunity. They truly needed to keep better tabs of where these two were some days, even if Iacchus tended to stay in his room. Becky clapped her hands together, her best attempt at faked enthusiasm. "Abel and I have some news."

Abel followed behind Becky and closed the door behind him with his one free hand. His other hand was eagerly trying to hold onto a sketchbook overflowing with loose papers and bits taped here and there. For an office that more or less created intelligent life from little bursts of electricity, you'd think they could have developed better organizational skills when it came to paperwork. Abel grunted when a few pages from the top scattered to the floor. He blew his bangs from his eyes and left them there. "Hello boys."

"Dr. Moreau," Hecate answered at the same time as Iacchus muttered out a soft, "Ms. Becky."

"We've got a surprise." Abel tried to sound excited, lifting his voice and smiling broadly. Hopefully if they got the boys to *want* these changes, then any issues they might have could be reduced to a minimum. He wasn't quite sure yet how they'd react to such a drastic change to their physical appearances. Hecate spent too much time in front of the mirror, as is. "I think you'll both like it."

"Translation: You'd best like it because it's going to happen whether you want it to or not." Becky smirked, knowing full well Abel had stepped in to save the boys from a lifetime of staring at exposed wires and metal skeletons in the mirror. Becky blew a bang out of her face and reached for her electronic cigarette nestled in her pocket. A gift from her brother, it was a stylish little thing—lacquer black with gold markings along the edges. She took a drag on the device and reveled in the nicotine, feeling her body relax the moment the drug hit her lungs. It didn't taste the same as a real cigarette, but what could you do when smoking was banned in the compound? "Come on, let's get this over with."

"She's right, you two." Abel joined Becky at the table. He dropped the supplies clutched in his arms across the wooden surface before shaking his hand out to loosen the stiff joints. He'd never figure out why books always seemed to be so much heavier than they looked like they should. Mystery of life, he supposed. Abel turned to the two boys and noticed they had opted to stand, Hecate's head resting on Iacchus' elbow in an odd display of affection. Either he was warming up to his brother, or he had picked up on the tense atmosphere. Abel wished he had a camera— it would have been perfect for his desk. "There have been discussions concerning the two of you and how you look."

"How we look?" Iacchus asked. He remembered what Hecate had said about making sure no one knew the younger was listening in on the meeting. He made sure to play dumb as Hecate requested—Ms. Becky's very presence was at stake! "What's wrong with how we look?"

"There are concerns that you two may blend in a bit, well, too well…" Abel fingered a loose paper on the desk, smudging still wet ink. "And looking so young, they want to make sure there's no way to mistake an android for a real child if someone saw you from a distance." He smiled knowing it was fake. Reassurance was the goal after all. "To help avoid false police reports for child labor and the like."

"If this was a concern, why did they not take it into consideration when we were built, Dr. Moreau? It seems like a waste of money to rebuild in the middle of a project," Hecate questioned. Abel's smiling face looked as forced and as unnatural as Iacchus when he was trying to look put together. Hecate didn't like it—it felt…wrong. Like trying to divide by zero—Abel shouldn't need to force his happiness. That's what he had Hecate for. "It's like starting over unnecessarily."

"Sometimes humans change their mind!" Becky snapped and pulled one of Abel's sketchbooks open to look down at the pages filled with doodles and suggestions slapped together at the very last second. "You'll have to get used to it sooner or later." She took another inhale of nicotine. "I'm half surprised you're not already."

"I have come to expect different levels of irresponsibility from different people. Dr. Firmin does not seem like one who would waste money illogically. How does that saying go? He tends to be 'cheap' when it comes to non-essential items." Hecate smiled smugly up at the woman sucking on her little electronic trinket. "That's all."

"Why you little—"

"Becky." Abel threw his arm out and grabbed the woman's shoulder. Becky and Iacchus were more alike than either, more Becky, would care to admit—they could both benefit from some sort of anger management classes. She was always so quick to snap at the boys, especially Iacchus. Abel darted a look over at the frowning older boy and almost chuckled. His face was an exact match for Becky's. *Kids take after their parents, right?* Abel squeezed Becky's shoulder, thumb rubbing her collarbone. "He's just a kid."

"A very smart kid who knows exactly what he's talking about." Becky felt her (what very, very, little of it there was) affection for the younger boy lessen. At least Iacchus was keeping his mouth shut. "Just hurry up and tell them their options."

"Options?" Iacchus focused on the book now open across the table. He clenched his fists together so he wouldn't reach out and grab it. "We get to pick? Like when they let us choose our own clothes?"

"Part of it," Abel said. "You remember in some of those science fiction movies we've watched, that robots and androids had glowing lines on their skin?" Hecate and Iacchus nodded. "Well, we're going to do something similar. Since we can't do a complete overhaul of your looks, tattooing your skin seems like the best option."

Hecate reached up to take the sketch book from Abel. He flipped through a few pages taking in designs that ranged from tribal to more modern lines and angles scattered in the margins around handwritten notes. "Just markings for our skin, then?"

"That glow." Abel reached through the stack of papers and pulled out a thin plastic strip covered in tiny dots. He clicked a button on the end, and they all began to light with a brilliant blue glow. "To make them stand out, we're going to use LED backlights." Both boys pouted quite spectacularly. Hecate was glaring at the LED strip with such a grimace, Abel thought he was trying to incinerate it with his eyes. Abel held up his hands defensively. "You'll be able to turn them on and off, of course."

"It seems as though you've chosen everything." Hecate flipped the pages until he fell upon the mock sketches of said lines and scribbles over his and Iacchus' nude bodies. It seemed they were going to be covered in these things. Hecate flipped the page upside-down—still didn't look any better. "What exactly will we be choosing?"

Abel started spreading the papers out before reaching to the very back of the thick book. He procured two seemingly clean sheets and handed one to each boy. Each sheet had three nude figures front and back to give the boys a chance to experiment. From his pocket, he pulled two small wrapped sets of pens and deposited them in the boys' other hand. "You get to pick what design and what colors."

"But it'd be nice if you stuck to one color each." Becky added before putting her electronic cigarette back in its case to charge. "LED strips aren't cheap. If Giles couldn't even spring for automatic faucets in the washrooms during the building renovation, I doubt he's going to let you brats go hog-wild with light fixtures."

"We'll also be swapping out your eye color to match." Abel added as an afterthought, watching as Iacchus mouthed the phrase 'hog-wild' to himself in confusion. He'd have to start up their idiom lessons again, or at least update their dictionary files with common usages. "The backlight for when you're hooked up to a computer, anyway."

"Ms. Becky said we had to pick one color," Iacchus glanced quickly in the woman's direction before looking back to Dr. Moreau. She was looking rather calm for once. Iacchus was sure it was because of the drugs she was inhaling. Ms. Becky was always calmer when she was smoking. "Are there any other limits or rules to follow?"

"At least thirty percent of your body should have a marking of some sort, at least two must be on your face, and they should be abstract lines or shapes. We've got quite a few examples in these books if you need a little inspiration." Abel pat the stack of diagrams behind him. "But, if you wanted a picture of something simple we might be able to work that out."

Hecate nodded thoughtfully. This wasn't as bad as it could have been. He had told Iacchus he could tolerate a tattoo or a brand. Hecate flipped through a few sketches trying to figure out which ones had been drawn by Abel and which ones were Ms. Becky's contributions. "When would you like our designs?"

Abel's smile took a more natural expression. It looked like they would avoid a fight today. "Hopefully by tomorrow."

"I think we can do that." Iacchus bit his lip over the repaired patch Mr. Finley applied—Iacchus had cornered him during a lunch break after the *incident* with Mr. Dixen. The quick-patch was tougher than his normal skin, making the spot the perfect place for his teeth to sit during the involuntary reaction. The light idea seemed relatively harmless compared to the fuss his little brother had been making the other day. He wondered if Hecate had been worried for nothing.

"You think the androids are going to cooperate with the unit updates?" Anton asked to his station-partner, Steve. It was the middle of break, and they were both active with personal projects. But no matter how much his paper called to him, Anton couldn't help but be distracted by the androids and the upcoming 'surgery.' "I mean, Iacchus is a little dumb so he probably won't care, but Hecate—"

"I'm telling you, that Hecate kid is easy-peasy," Steve said taking a bite out of a donut dripping with glaze. He wiped his fingers on a napkin before going back to his keyboard. Steve was a little miffed that Firmin had overridden his exposed mechanics suggestion at the last minute to appease his 'boyfriend,' but what could you do? Firmin paid the bills and Steve got stuck reassuring his co-workers that the androids weren't going to turn around and start killing them all for blinking funny. "You'll work with him when my rotation ends, and you'll see it's just like working with a little kid. He's as dangerous as Iacchus."

"That worries me even more!" Anton shook his head and said, "Rod over in mechanics is always complaining that Iacchus is trying to kill them all with furniture." Anton pressed 'send' on a quick personal e-mail out of the office. Sending his personal mail like this at work was risky—the last thing he needed was to get caught sending mail to *them*—but his computer at home was on the fritz. Anton turned to Steve, hands in the air desperately trying to convey the oddness of the situation around this lab. "He makes it seem like being bludgeoned to death with a chair is *normal.*"

"Trust me, the only weapon Hecate has is his mouth," Steve laughed, "Do you know the other day he called my game a 'piece of unintelligible tripe'? I nearly bust a gut. He was a good sport about it though, laughed right along after he realized he sounded like a walking thesaurus." Steve swallowed nervously—at least he hoped that's what it was. Steve wouldn't deny that soon after that, a few of his game files had gone missing. The logs said they had been deleted remotely from the server. Steve couldn't prove the kid did it, so he just logged it as a system error, but there was still that little nudge in the back of his head to back up his game files on personal disks. "Hecate's all talk, Anton. Stop worrying."

"He's never done anything else? Nothing?" Anton looked over at Steve who was typing away at a function in his game that allowed you to accrue points for every time your character smacked into a leaf. The guy seemed worry free enough, so it was probably safe to assume the kid wouldn't chop your hand off at the first chance he got. Anton rubbed the back of his hair, feeling the tiny curls. He'd need to get that shaved down later. "That's good to know."

Steve backspaced three or four lines and started from scratch. There were just some days where the code refused to cooperate under his nimble fingers. "I think he's just scared of getting rejected if he goes too far."

"Rejected?"

"Kid worships Moreau."

"Right," Anton said. That wasn't exactly a secret around this place. The first day Anton had started working, he had gotten lost looking for the production lab. Luckily, he had seen Dr. Moreau in the hallway checking a dossier of some sort. He was happy to see someone he recognized, having seen the man briefly at his hiring with Dr. Firmin, but there was someone else with him. A tiny blonde kid in an oversized sweater had been hanging off his coat prattling on about some movie he had seen. Anton had recognized the flick, and smiled broadly remembering the first time he had seen it as a child.

Anton couldn't help himself and had said, "Your son has good taste."

"He does," Dr. Moreau had smiled, "but he's not my son." The doctor had rubbed the boy's head fondly, while Anton tried to figure out what other purpose a kid like that would have in the lab. Moreau had looked up and did a great impression of a proud parent as he said, "But I'm really happy you think we're that close. Aren't you, Hecate?"

"Yes, sir," the child had said.

"Hecate?" Anton had asked, wondering how the kid got saddled with such an odd name.

"Oh, yes. This is Hecate, one of the two Olympian's Children successes." Moreau had turned to the boy, "Hecate, this is Anton Jansen. He'll be working with Steve and Lucy in the programming department."

"Nice to meet you."

That statement from Hecate was the last time Anton had seen the android. After realizing just how profound it was that he had mistaken an android for a person, Anton had been thoroughly, and completely disturbed. The project just hadn't seemed as exciting as it once was when he was first hired. There was almost something…unnatural about it. It rubbed Anton the wrong way, and he chose to spend the rest of his time working locked up in the lab, keeping his ears open for anything strange.

"So, like I was saying," Steve coughed loudly, bringing Anton's attention back to himself, "kid worships Moreau. He wouldn't do anything too drastic."

Anton nodded, trying to come back to the present. Steve was lifting an eyebrow at him, having noticed his daydream session, so Anton made a last ditch effort to lighten the mood. "Yeah, and Moreau definitely kisses his little ass right—"

"I think your hour is up," Lucy interrupted, typing harder than necessary on the keyboard. To think people thought gossiping was reserved for girls. There were days she really hated being the only girl in the programming department. "You should be working if we want to get this program to Marvin before the end of tomorrow. You know he'll need it to finish the lighting connections for the boys."

"Yeah, yeah." Steve waved her off and clicked 'save' on the board. He'd come back to his game later. Steve rubbed under his nose, rolling his eyes at Lucy. She wasn't fooling anyone with that 'get back to work' act of hers. "We'll shut up about your little boy toy, won't we, Anton?"

"Sorry, Lucy. We forgot you were here for a second," Anton swallowed. If the fact Hecate and Abel were joined at the hip was common knowledge, the fact Lucy Clarence had a crush on Dr. Abel Moreau was like a light you could see from space. Anton was pretty sure the only person who didn't know was Dr. Moreau himself, but Anton was also pretty sure the man was faking his ignorance. Lucy didn't hide her affections well—the blushing and stammering whenever the man was in the room always gave her away. Not to mention her own doting on Hecate was an obvious grab for his attention. "We'll zip it."

Lucy blushed through her glasses and bit her lip. Anton felt bad for her, but pushed it down. Lucy was definitely taken in by Hecate's sweet act, too. Anton had a feeling the coming week would be more than the lab could handle.

"You have got to be joking." Giles leaned on his car and stared at the smears of paint plastered across his parking space. He comes to work late one day and this is what greets him? Some loser's idea of art with the phrase "Stop Playing God" in bright red, splotchy paint, over his personalized parking space? Giles knew this project was going to destroy him slowly from the inside, but he hadn't realized the rest of the world was out to get him as well. "I can't believe they did this. What happened to the good old fashioned letters made from magazine clippings?"

"Maybe that would have taken too much time." Jenner chuckled while looking at his boss' horrified face. He glanced back to the front desk to make sure that no one else had arrived while he was attended Giles. Leaving his post always made him a bit nervous, but sometimes other people took priority. Like now, when Giles looked like he was ready to vomit in disgust at life in general. Those were the days Jenner worried the most for the young business owner. "I mean, this is a pretty piss-poor job, even for graffiti. Still wish I would have been at my post to catch them though."

"I'm sure you would have taken care of it. You're diligent that way." Giles rubbed his eyes, mourning the paint-covered security camera. Jenner stood off to the side, having just arrived himself around the same time, arms crossed and frowning. The man really was meticulous in manning the front security desk at almost all hours of the day. Giles hoped Jenner wasn't considering working yet another shift. He already insisted on working two, so it figured the first real act of graffiti would take place during his few off hours. No man should have to work twenty-four hours! "What the hell is wrong with these people? It's not like I'm testing shampoo on rabbits!"

Jenner bit his lip as his boss threw his arms in the air standing just outside his sweet little two-door number that was sadly away from its designated parking space, sitting neatly in the main driving lane. A sports car that nice really did deserve its own spot up front. "You know how fanatics can get, boss."

"Yes, yes." Giles shifted his hand to massage his temple roughly. The death threat letters were at least subtle about it. This was just aggravating. He could file the letters in two neat clicks. Paint didn't disappear with nearly the same expediency as an e-mail. "But did they really need to do it in my parking space?"

"Maybe it was the only way they figured you'd get the message?" Jenner theorized.

"Last I checked, an e-mail worked better. I would have gotten that the moment they sent it, like I did all the others!" Giles shouted and pulled out his phone and shook it. The tiny lit screen mocked him by showing the time Giles was wasting dealing with stupidity. "It's not hooked up to my work e-mail for nothing."

Jenner laughed and rubbed his nose. They didn't use permanent paint, so hopefully he'd have this mess cleared up for the boss within the hour. The janitorial staff had already been contacted, though Susie had told him it might take a while to get to it, and Jenner had called the police to leave a report. "Maybe they're just drama queens or something?"

"They certainly have no sense of humor." Giles scoffed and shoved his phone back in his pocket. "Get someone to clean this mess up."

"Already done, sir."

"Thank you, Jenner." Giles snatched up his briefcase, the bulk of it swinging on the handle. Giles left his car where it was, horizontal in front of the administration spaces. Heaven help the fool who touched it. "At least some people are reliable around here."

Leaving Jenner behind to deal with the mess, Giles continued on his way to the office running scenarios for how to deal with the protestors. So far he'd managed to hide their actions from the board thanks to some private computer tricks blocking the news feeds the group kept posting from going viral. Confiscating their news flyers was still on his to-do list, but thankfully their distribution of paper goods was paltry compared to their computer campaigns. Giles could, however, appreciate the typography work that went into their paper. Most importantly, thanks to a small bribe, Giles had the name of the Talos' Redress lead officers, as well the name of their founder.

Little Jeremy Eubank probably wasn't expecting Giles to know how to use his own computers, let alone crack systems. Giles paused when he reached the hallway divide that would either take him to 'The Wall' or his office. Giles stood in place, the corridor looming before him, almost dark despite the lighting. His entire fortune and business was wrapped up in that one stupid room at the end of this hall, and the anomalies that came from it would either make or break him.

Giles always figured it would be the latter.

He wouldn't deny his father had left quite the legacy in his lap. Sylvester Firmin had founded the laboratory when Giles was still toddling around and trying to stand on his own two legs. He was a bright boy, and to his occasional regret, remembered more details from that time than he'd like—even if the memories did tend to blend together. The bottom line: his father spent his time too busy drowning himself in work to pay attention to his son. A child remembers his father forgetting his fifth birthday party because someone changed two lines of code over the weekend. Giles' cake had been pink and covered in roses because the old man forgot to order it in advance. His mother had run out at the last minute to get a cake from the supermarket—the pink one was all the store had left at the late hour.

It wasn't until Giles showed proficiency in computer programming that his father finally took an interest. When his proficiency turned into a mastery competing with the lab workers, Sylvester had paid *all* his attention to Giles. The boy had found himself loving every second of 'affection' the old man could pour into his son. The time spent working with his father was the happiest time of Giles' life, and in retrospect, the worst thing to ever happen to him. Sylvester Firmin was a better liar than Giles could ever hope to be, and truths coming out after his death made Giles feel like he was reliving his fifth birthday over and over.

The young man was almost shocked his father left him everything when he kicked the bucket.

Continuing the project the old man gave his life to through sweat, tears and exhaustion was a responsibility that, some days, Giles wasn't sure he could handle, or wanted. He took on the project regardless, for one reason or another. Giles was too invested to hand it over to anyone else; Giles clung to the project as his only link to his father's approval through his youth. Pathetic that he would still long for such things, even after everything that happened. Giles could visualize the bank of computers humming and buzzing, running their programs; a project he could never seem to escape from. A project more trouble than it was worth.

There were days Giles wished he could just turn back the clock and stop that first program from ever being written.

Lucy hated visiting Marvin.

It wasn't that Mr. Green was a bad person, so to speak, but he was definitely...*odd*. The young coder usually had no reason to visit the man in person, but most of the engineering team was busy with projects more important than designing the new LED additions. It was a quick, easy task, so the head of their department had decided to just do it himself. Marvin designed the light strips, even though he wouldn't be installing them, so it'd be best to coordinate and give the plug-in directly to him. Sadly, that meant she had to visit him—none of the other members on her team would go. Marvin didn't handle interactions with men...well.

Lucy crept into the lab slowly keeping her arms close to her body. His lab walls were covered in portraits of nude women, some fully human and others clearly half-robot. They were all very 'artistic' in nature and she was sure he had worked something out with Giles to allow something so...inappropriate, to be permitted. A particularly large portrait of a woman with a face painted like an over-exaggerated geisha (in a bikini!) hung over the work bench to her left. Lucy did her best not to touch any of the surfaces in the lab.

"Marvin?" Lucy called out, holding a jump drive near her chest. She glanced around the empty room, trying to see past the mechanical parts hanging around, and stacks of magazines cluttered on desks. Marvin was prominent on the cover of one, and Lucy remembered that article. He had created a joint mechanism that worked up to thirty percent more efficiently than industry standards. The magazine included an updated version of the article he had submitted, as well as listings of which other periodicals his papers could be found. None of which helped with Marvin's people skills. Lucy grimaced at yet another nude portrait taped to the side of desk. She was going to give him the program and run.

If she could find him.

"Hello?" Lucy dared to call a bit louder. "Marvin are you in here?"

"I'll be with you in a moment!"

Lucy turned toward the wall that divided the room between the 'office' and the 'work station' division. Marvin was one of the few department heads who had turned down an office in the main hall with the others, and multi-purposed his lab as both. Or so he said. Lucy sidestepped a few feet to see around the dividing wall, spotting Marvin on a stool combing the hair of an inactive shell. The unit was standing upright on a dolly, nude and unmoving. It was a female unit with curly blonde hair and, Lucy could admit, was very pretty. All of Marvin's units were model level beauties—even the boys tended to be slimmer with soft features, like from clothing catalogs. Lucy watched as Marvin plucked a few loose hairs from the brush, depositing them in the hair recycling box. Lucy brushed her own hair back, feeling self-conscious comparing the difference between her dull yellow hair and the brilliant blonde of the figure on his station.

"All done." Marvin patted the cheek of the unit with a make-up sponge, smoothing out the blush he had added. Unlike the boys, his girls needed a little paint to keep that human look. Real women wore make-up. Marvin turned towards Lucy and sighed; she was so mousy. Marvin was tempted to just buy the poor woman a compact—surely he had something for a Summer. Marvin placed his tools back into their proper places in his make-up kit. "Let me put this little doll up and I'll be right with you."

Lucy nodded and watched Marvin grunt as he pulled the dolly back and started inching the unit to the storage room. *Marvin needs to work out,* Lucy giggled to herself watching the man struggle with the weight. His breathing was labored as he shoved the dolly, feet slipping every once in a while as he failed to make the wheels move. He made it, after an amusing ten minute struggle, to the storage unit—a small built-out closet that sat in the corner of the room. Lucy could see just past the door to the line of finished units standing neatly, each waiting for a program to give it life. The final product was inspiring, but Lucy had to admit the empty shells gave her the chills.

Marvin set the newest addition to his little collection on the wall in-between the model of a tall, spindly eighteen year old with black hair, and a ten year old little girl. Marvin ran his fingers down the perfectly pert breasts of his Demeter, and sighed regretfully when he pulled a modesty cloak over her form. Such a shame hiding beauty behind rags. One of these days his dolls would be appreciated. Marvin smiled at his 'special' girls sitting across from the row on the opposite wall. Those two had been a, *personal*, project he had slipped under the table in a budget request. Giles had flipped his lid when he saw it, but Marvin's work was irreplaceable. Giles had to 'deal.'

Lucy averted her eyes as Marvin finished up, staring lovingly at the lifeless figures. She was so busy looking at the floor tiles, Lucy missed it when he materialized in front of her. She squeaked when he coughed to get her attention. "Ah, hi, Marvin."

"Lucy," Marvin replied, removing his glasses to clean off a bit of petroleum he had transferred by accident. The jellied substance did wonders to help the androids' complexions, but he was endlessly getting covered with it himself. Marvin plucked a rag from the counter to wipe the rest off his hands. "What can I do for you?"

"Here's the final program for the light strips," Lucy stuttered, holding out a company flash drive. "We wanted to make sure it was compatible with the hardware."

Marvin snatched the small blue stick drive and glared at it. These LED strips were the worst thing to happen to his department since Giles forbade him from making his ladies *proper* ladies. It was just plain *tacky* and ruined the illusion of life his team had worked so hard for. *Insulting.* Worst of all, he only had a week to update the rest of his models with the new lights himself. "I'll let you know."

"Thank—thank you." Lucy grimaced at her own awkwardness, and back-pedaled quickly in her attempts to get out the door. She said her final goodbye from safely in the hallway. "I'll uh, see you later."

"Sure, sure." Marvin shrugged and strode to his computer desk. He had the test strips hanging around somewhere. He'd just connect them to the program and see if something lit up.

That was good enough.

Rupert Dixen was not a man caught off guard easily. The smell that smacked into his nose like a runaway freight train the moment he entered the programming division definitely counted as a surprise.

He had stayed after in the lab working on some backed up paperwork when he noticed the lights still on in the office down the hall. If it had been any other division in the building, Rupert wouldn't have been all that surprised to see lag-behinds catching up. Heaven knew Abel and Giles stayed in the building all hours of the night. The programming division, however, was notorious for being locked up and out the door by 5 o'clock on the dot. Grin on his face, Rupert had decided to drop in and see what poor sap had stayed late.

Steve, apparently.

Or (to use his favorite cliché despite the circumstances) what was left of him. Rupert took a step back, only to find his foot suddenly in his line of vision as it swung out from under him and into the air. His back collided with the cold tile floor just as quickly and he grunted hearing his back crack for the second time this week. Pushing himself up on his elbows, Rupert realized that yes, Steve's blood had pooled in the doorway and he had just slipped on it. The evidence was the red substance clinging to his shoe's heel, smudged across the tile from the neat little puddle.

The horrible moment of clarity brought on by his suffering back, and streak of red, caused Rupert to take one more good look into the room. His stomach churned, contents threatening to work their way to his throat. Steve's left arm was on his desk, severed from the body. Rupert turned his head away, only to see the boy's other arm standing erect. It had been shoved in the crack between two desks, hand reaching toward the ceiling. Rupert thought it looked like some perverted version of Adam reaching out for God.

The body's torso was dead center in the room, leaning up against a filing cabinet, legs bent oddly in front of it. Rupert would have to be blind to not notice the head was missing. The small chunk of white seen splitting up from the chunky red muscle was clearly from the young man's spine. Rupert wasn't sure where the head was, but the name-tag on the uniform jacket was clear as day even from across the room. Rupert decided, as he sat on the ground with the disrupted blood crawling to his fingers, it would probably be a good time to call security.

And tell them to bring an aspirin.

CHAPTER 6

HECATE WAS HUGGING him.

Abel sat on the break room couch with the blue patch on the third leather seat, not the chocolate-leather one that creaked every time you moved, staring at the coffee maker as it bubbled and hissed. After five minutes of sedentary sitting, Hecate had seen enough. The small android had crawled up on the couch next to his father-figure and wrapped his slim arms as tight around Abel's waist as he was able—the boy clung like a vice. Hecate nestled his head into the good doctor's lap, and listened to the sound of blood pumping. Abel absently petted Hecate's hair as soon as the boy was settled. The arrangement was uncomfortable and almost painful, but Abel didn't bother correcting or scolding the android.

Steve was dead.

Abel almost couldn't believe it when he got the frantic phone call from Rupert at two in the morning telling him about Steve's crime scene. The police had found the poor man's head behind the filing cabinet. His eyes were still missing, however, and that had been the final straw for Rupert. Overcome with a desperate need to inform everyone else of what had happened, the older man did just so. Abel was the first to get the call— possibly the second. Rupert had sounded frantic enough that Abel could assume he was the first to hear the news.

Regardless, dragging himself to work the next day had been a trial. All the offices had been crawling with security and police officers taping things off with those obnoxious yellow banners, and fighting with Giles over computers that *absolutely could not be touched*. Murder or not, the project was too expensive and too delicate to be interrupted. The monitoring equipment for The Wall was in that room, and Abel had heard Lucy and Anton were trying to relocate it without disrupting the software or the police investigation. Giles was at odds with everyone over it.

Hecate and Iacchus had been with Becky when he arrived, who was looking rather pale herself, in a side office. Iacchus had been twitching every so often, the tips of his fingers gripping his pants' leg. The change in atmosphere and swarms of new people were making the boy nervous. Iacchus had never handled change well, and Becky was admirable for keeping her post through it all. She hadn't yelled at him once.

Hecate merely looked bored.

Abel had been questioned the second he dropped his coat off in his office by a rather stern detective named Saxon. After getting an accidental glimpse at the scene photos, Abel found himself in the bathroom vomiting. The human body wasn't meant to be split up in such ways, nor was muscle supposed to look so much like chunks of meat he bought wrapped in plastic from the supermarket. Abel had washed his face, and plodded to the break room in hope of coffee or something else to clear his head. He didn't quite make it to the pot, let alone a sterile mug, before collapsing back onto the couch. It was a struggle just to control his breathing.

Abel hadn't even noticed Hecate following him to the bathroom. Or that the boy had been watching Abel as he slumped on the couch, body as limp as a noodle. Hecate's metal form colliding with his waist was the first jolt of awareness Abel had felt; the shock broken. Abel felt a weak smile grace his face for a few seconds, before it dropped. He settled for putting a hand on the boy's shoulder for the comfort he seemed desperate to give.

"Did you know Mr. Mathers well, Dr. Moreau?" Hecate asked softly when Abel stopped petting his head. He was probably too exhausted to keep moving his hand. "You seem very upset."

"I knew him." Abel took in a breath. "I don't think we were close; never ate lunch together or anything like that, but I knew who he was." Abel rubbed the boy's back; Hecate was so calm. Steve was Hecate's main programmer, so by all means he should be somewhat affected. "I'm not sure, what I feel about all of this. Those pictures—" Abel had to stop. They were like staring into a scene from a real life horror movie. Well, save for the fact it looked nothing like it does in the movies. Reality was so much worse than make-up and special effects. Abel forced down the urge to vomit a second time.

Hecate nodded in Abel's lap, arms still tight around the older man. Abel was warm and Hecate could hear his heartbeat like a drum sounding from such a close position. It was soothing, despite the slightly erratic beating of the organ under the wall of flesh. Hecate wondered if Abel would let them both sit like this during other times as well. "So, it is the *method* in which he died that makes you so upset?"

"Let's not talk about this, Hecate." Abel took in a breath, not sure if he *could* keep talking about this with someone whose voice was just so detached and monotone—analytical. Even the officers had been disgusted by the scene, some left white as sheets. They saw murders every day and this still proved exceptional. The indifference in Hecate's reactions was disturbing. It was probably the first time Abel really noticed Hecate *wasn't* human. Even little kids knew *something* was off in the world when it came to death, even without understanding. Hecate just filed the information away like Abel had told him there'd be an extra study session next week. "It's a little soon."

"Soon?" Hecate looked up at the doctor from his position and shifted around to better see his face. Abel's skin was pale and there were lines under his eyes, dark purple blotches that messed with his complexion. Hecate could see hair growing at random lengths on the man's chin. It was rather ugly. "What do you mean?"

"Sometimes," Abel said. He rubbed sweaty palms on the side of his pants leg where Hecate wasn't hanging. What was he supposed to say? This was so much different than handling Iacchus' bursts of anger… Hecate's eyes were wide and searching; confused. Abel's fingers plucked at the patch stitching on the couch cushion. "When you're discussing an emotional topic like this, it's sometimes difficult to…talk about it without losing control of…said…emotions." Abel let out a soft, airy chuckle—as if he needed to confuse the boy more. "That's why."

"I do not think I understand, just yet." Hecate let his head drop back onto Abel's lap and closed his eyes, still enjoying the full body contact. The thousands of sensors coating his skin recording the plethora of sensory data were still Hecate's favorite part of having a body. The sense of touch was hardly just for spatial or proximity recognition. "But I will stop."

"Thank you, Hecate." Abel let his head hit the couch back and stared up at the ceiling, listening to Hecate's hardware whirl.

Rupert was sharing a cigarette with Becky. And not one of those damn electronic cigarettes, either—a real, honest-to-god tobacco, bad for you, archaic, tar-laden cigarette. The first one he'd had in oh, four or five years. Probably the first one since he quit, in fact. Sure, they had to lean out a window on the highest floor to keep from setting off smoke detectors, and if his wife Mary found out Rupert would be castrated— but it was worth it. There was something about the smoke wafting in the breeze that just calmed him down. Didn't seem to be doing anything for Becky though. Her hands were shaking with every puff. "You doing alright, Ms. Krasiński?"

"What did I tell you about calling me that?" Becky snorted. Rupert was an odd man. She made it very clear she hated her last name. Becky had punched the last man to use it repeatedly after being told not to. Rupert just felt the need to ignore it every so often, and somehow was immune to her temper. Becky figured it was the 'nice old man' thing he had going on. Becky took a drag on her cigarette, rolling her eyes. Even the android brats could get her name right. "Becky is just fine."

"Just because you hate your parents doesn't mean you can get rid of your name, kiddo." Rupert chuckled before choking on a bit of smoke that had gone down his throat the wrong way. Laughing while inhaling was a bad thing, he reminded himself. He cleared his throat for a moment before dropping his smile. Rupert tapped a few ashes off the edge of his cigarette, watching them fall and hit the rusted bars of the old fire escape ladders. "But seriously, girl, you alright? Your hands are shaking worse than a paint mixer."

"Should you be one to talk? You're the one who found the damn body first." Becky threw her cigarette butt down on the cold tile of the storage room and stomped it with her heel, twisted. She could care less about the ash stain now on the white tile. It could use the character. "Who could possibly be alright after this? I didn't even like the guy and I'm freaking out!"

Rupert shrugged. It was true, most of the facility was unnerved in one way or the other. Many were suffering from grief, but there was a select few that were just plain scared out of their wits. The police still had yet to identify a suspect, or even figure out how the poor kid was killed in the first place. He, himself, had witnessed that there were no loud noises coming from the lab and Rupert's office was only three or so rooms down. He should have heard *something*. Carnage like that didn't lend itself to silence.

As for his more intimate circle, Rupert had his own troubles dealing with their issues. Becky was freaked. Giles was a mess with the legal work. Abel was having a breakdown. Rupert sucked in a mouthful of smoke and nicotine. The only folks taking this well were the androids.

That was the most unnerving fact out of all. Rupert had always struggled with reminding himself those two boys weren't human. It was hard to picture them as cold calculating machines when Iacchus was pitching a proper two-year-old tantrum. For all intents and purposes, they were just dumb kids. No different than any other one he'd handled, be it his own kids or their dumb friends. They were just uninformed and "hormonal."

But, Rupert took a puff from the cigarette, it was more obvious now what they were and what this lab had created. There was something deeply chilling to see someone so...unaffected by a tragedy like this. Rupert hadn't realized how callous those kids could be. Both Hecate and Iacchus had looked at the photos of the crime scene with disinterest at most, the murder dismissed almost as quickly as a candle blown out by the wind.

Becky lit a second cigarette, but held it between her fingers instead of bringing it to her lips. "It didn't bother them at all."

"What?" Rupert turned his head from the window to look at Becky. She was staring straight ahead, and he wondered if she'd picked up the ability to read minds. He hoped not. Or she'd know what he was thinking when her shirt gapped and showed off her size—

"The two androids." Becky sucked in a breath; it was shaky and hoarse. Smoke drew up from the tip of her cigarette as she watched it burn. Ashes fell off onto the rust, metal fire escape just beneath the window. "I mean. They didn't do anything. They see the crime scene, the photos, the people crying," Becky took in a shaking breath, "and they just sit there through it all wondering why the hell we all aren't working and going on like normal."

Rupert noticed her voice picking up despite the rasp and the attempt to fight off the sobbing. "It's not like they've experienced death before, you know."

"It's not natural." She covered her mouth and nose with her hand.

"For kids who have so many feelings and emotions and outbursts, to be so silent and neutral over this is," Becky shook her head slowly, breathing through her loose fingers. She just couldn't seem to get enough air in her lungs. "It's not right, Rupert."

"Perhaps, but it's not like you can expect—"

"Ms. Becky?"

Both Rupert and Becky turned at the intrusion of a new voice. Iacchus stood in the doorway and fiddled with the end of his short sleeve. Becky was the first to respond, voice short and clipped. "What? What do you need now?"

Iacchus looked down at the ground and the tips of his white slip-ons. He had overheard enough to know that Becky was liking him less and less every day. At least Rupert seemed to still like him. "Dr. Moreau hasn't left the break room in about three hours. He won't listen to Hecate either." He paused when the two humans' expressions remained stoic. "Dr. Firman asked me to come get you to help him."

"I'll get him." Becky said, and strode past the android without so much as a glance. As far as she was concerned, he was an unnatural freak.

Rupert watched the lad stand there and stare at the wall where Becky had been standing. He may not understand the concept of death, but he clearly knew what rejection was about. Rupert couldn't help but decide comforting a confused teen was far better than lingering on the subject of a young man's death. Just because the rest of them were grieving didn't mean Iacchus' problems were going anywhere. Rupert reached out and grabbed the kid's shoulder with his hand and gave it a firm squeeze. "Hey, she's just upset over Steve, Ia-kid."

"It's alright, Mr. Dixen," Iacchus muttered, biting his lip. "Ms. Becky hates me. I understand that. You don't need to comfort me or try to fix my feelings."

"Yeah, but you make me want to anyway." Rupert urged the kid forward and wrapped his arms around the stiff lad in a hug. Rupert put a hand in Iacchus' hair and ruffled it. "So humor the old man, alright?"

"Why do you care so much?" Iacchus spoke softly into Mr. Dixen's shoulder. His lab coat was dirty with coffee stains. The hug felt nice; Iacchus knew now why Hecate always had his arms open when Dr. Moreau was around. Iacchus hands reached up and latched into the back of Mr. Dixen's coat, fingers trembling. "Most people in this place can't stand me. Dr. Moreau only tolerates me because he loves my brother so much."

"Really want to know, Ia-kid?" Rupert smiled, stilling his hand in the brown hair. "You remind me of my son," Rupert replied bluntly and truthfully, and to Iacchus' surprise if the widening of his eyes and tilt of the head was any indication. Honesty was often the best policy; Rupert relied upon that. Rupert released the boy enough to grip the boy's upper arms firmly, and make eye contact. "You're confused and learning just like my own son, and myself, in our own baffling teenage days." Iacchus made a small choked noise, and Rupert laughed out right, his own eyes watering. "You bring out the dad in me, Ia-Kid, I can't help it."

"You're very odd, Mr. Dixen." Iacchus shrugged and tried not to flinch when the man hugged him again, much harder the second time. Iacchus was held tightly and he could feel warmth coming from the other body again. It was nice. Iacchus couldn't help but wish he was hugging Ms. Becky instead, but Mr. Dixen wasn't too poor a substitute. Iacchus snuggled his face back into the lab coat. "But that's not so bad, I think."

"Yeah, well, you're not all that normal yourself."

Becky found Abel in the break room, as described, with the android brat clinging around his waist like a leech. Giles sat next to him on the couch, nursing a cup of coffee, looking worse for the wear. The five o'clock shadow they shared had Becky wondering if they even realized they had forgotten to shave. Giles' un-tied tie, hanging loosely around his neck spoke more volumes than a little stubble as far as his state of mind was concerned. "Are you two going to sit there for the rest of your lives?"

"Hello Becky, is Iacchus still in one piece? Or did you take your wonderful attitude out on the poor little robot? Am I going to find his parts are now scattered about the hallway?" Giles answered absently and took another sip of coffee. Not that he really cared about the android's feelings, but it was always a sure-fire way to piss off Becky. He truly wasn't in the mood for that woman's drama. He only sent the android after her so he could dump Abel off on *her* and get some work done. Steve's death was tragic, it was, but that didn't mean Giles could let the laboratory fall apart—then they'd all be in the soup. "Either way, I rather don't care at the moment. If he's broken you'll get to pay to fix him."

"Hold on just one minute, Giles." Becky grabbed him by the shoulder the moment the director pushed himself up off the couch. "You listen to me—"

"No, you listen." Giles swatted Becky's hand off his shoulder with an echoing *smack*. "Abel's not handling this well and apparently neither are you. As much as I'd like to stay here and sit with my friend, I have to go talk with Detective Saxon and make sure everything is being cataloged and handled properly before I go drown myself in a bottle of whiskey. Sit here and make sure his only company isn't the creepy little emotionless brat."

Becky's eyes shifted straight to Hecate, watching them with a level gaze, as the boy hugged Abel. She could tell even from where she was standing the boy was holding too tight from the way Abel's waist was concave. He was probably going to bruise and the little brat either didn't care or hadn't noticed. Becky had to give though, Giles did regretfully have a point—bad mood and cheap jabs at her character ignored, that is. "I suppose."

"Thank you, Becky." Giles nodded and ran a hand through his loose hair. It was almost depressing that less than two days ago Giles thought the worst thing Steve could do to cause him trouble was use excessive work hours to build that stupid game of his. Giles would give anything for that to be the case again, if only to get his lab back to normal. Giles pointed at Abel with two fingers. "You stay here with him or get him out of the break room…or something."

"No promises," Becky replied thoughtfully as Giles strode out of the room talking to himself under his breath. She looked at Abel, who had managed to avoid eye contact or commenting during the entire exchange. Hecate had finally stopped spying on her conversation and had gone back to digging his face into Abel's hip. "That kid cutting off your circulation or what?"

Abel looked over at Becky, noticing she was there for the first time, and shook his head slowly. He wasn't going to discourage the child from showing affection. Some form of emotion was better than none. Abel rubbed the kid's back, fingers digging in the wool. "Hecate is fine where he is."

"Sure he is." Becky plopped down next to the two of them and looked at the tight grip again. The oddest urge to check just how much damage had been done overwhelmed her. Becky shoved at the kid's shoulder. "Hey, kiddo, loosen up your hold a bit."

"Why?" Hecate asked, voice muffled by Abel's shirt. At his reluctance to comply, Ms. Becky took a hold of his arm and attempted to force him to let go. She wasn't strong enough, of course, but Hecate humored her slightly and allowed her to pull an arm a bit free. Hecate was surprised when her other hand immediately grabbed Abel's shirt and pulled up. "What are you doing?"

"Just as I thought," Becky said. "Hey Abe, the kid left a bruise that circles your entire waist." She almost laughed when Abel looked down in shock at the dark, blotchy skin. It was the color of a rotting plum and his fingers pressed at it absently. Becky poked it with her forefinger and watched the skin color change under the pressure. "You can't tell me that doesn't hurt."

Hecate was staring at the skin with a look akin to shock. He had hurt Abel. His arms leapt from Abel as though his skin had been covered in acid. Hecate sat up on his knees, still in Abel's lap, and buried his hands in the front of Abel's lab coat. "Why did you not inform me I was causing pain, Dr. Moreau?"

"I," the doctor swallowed. Abel pulled up the rest of the shirt to look down at the ring of darkened skin, knowing that many of his capillaries were now struggling to stop blood from seeping out. He wondered if it was really as bad as it looked. "I'm not sure. I guess I just didn't notice."

"Figures you'd be too distracted by Steve's death to consider your own health." Becky sighed, but still managed to smile. Unnatural attraction to the two androids aside, Abel had his finer moments. It could almost be sweet, if he wasn't so very good at getting on her nerves. "You always were a bleeding heart."

"His heart is bleeding as well?" Hecate exclaimed almost immediately. How could the two of them stay so calm. The heart was a vital organ in the human body. It was required to function properly! "Shouldn't we take Dr. Moreau to a medical professional as quickly as possible?"

Abel burst out laughing.

He guffawed so hard, Abel was sure that his ribs were about to rupture from his chest. Abel couldn't help but double over, nearly knocking Hecate out of his lap in the process. Abel steadied the boy by grabbing his shoulders, ignoring the kid's weight. "Oh, lord. I can't breathe."

"I'm confused, Dr. Moreau." Hecate held his hands up slowly, as if afraid to touch the shaking man again. He had never seen Abel do this before. Hecate noticed the man's difficulty in sucking in breathes and gasped. "Are you suffocating now, too?"

Becky watched as Abel shook even harder before launching forward, encasing the small android in a secure hug of his own. The man buried his face in the boy's shoulder and had one hand firmly against the back of the child's neck, fingers in his hair. The other held tightly at the boy's waist. Abel's laughter morphed into heavy sobbing as he held tightly to the openly confused boy. Hecate's hands groped the open air, unsure of where to grab or hold. Becky let the two be and reached into her pocket for her cigarette, the plastic cylinder cool under her fingertips.

Hecate lowered his hands to rest on Abel's shoulders in a loose hug. There was moisture building up on his sweater as the man cried, and Hecate calmed his systems, one at a time. Abel was seeking comfort from him, feeling no ill will toward the accidental injury. That was good. Hecate slipped his arms around Abel's wide back in a more proper embrace. This felt much better than before.

Becky fell back into the couch and closed her eyes to the sounds of a sobbing man and the soft hum of gears turning and electricity humming from the lights above. The vapor from her cigarette held in the air before dissipating into the air vent.

"Detective Saxon," Giles nodded politely at the seated officer as he strode into his office. A bathroom mirror, a brush and a shave later, Giles was feeling much more ready to greet the 'good' officer. Giles set his emergency grooming kit, disguised as a simple black zip folder, on the edge of his desk before taking his seat. He avoided any direct eye contact with the officer—Giles had to make sure he knew who was in charge; law or not, this was *his* building. The detective was just a visitor, and Giles treated him as such. Giles proceeded to sort through the paperwork pile left on the desk as he would with any other guest. "I hope things are going well, so far?"

"As well as things can go when a man is murdered, I suppose." Lester stood, his brown trench coat straightening out. He had only spoken to the man sitting at his desk briefly before now, having to spend his focus on the crime scene itself and the first at arrival. Most of his interaction up until now with the 'big boss' consisted of Lester watching Firmin yell at his officers and co-workers about things that shouldn't be touched, evidence be damned. Lester noticed Firmin was sitting with his back rigid straight, and muscles tense. The man was wound tight, for sure. "We've collected as much evidence as possible and our labs are looking it over now. This case is top priority due to the gruesome nature of the crime."

"Ah, good." Giles tapped a stack of papers straight. Things seemed to be progressing smoothly on at least one end, and Giles always loved it when he was given first dibs on something. Ego stroked, unintentional as it may have been, Giles gave the detective his full focus, pushing the paperwork aside. Now that he was looking, Giles noted that Saxon was a rather tall, bulky man—all muscle under his mocha skin. Giles rubbed his mouth, and tried to sound polite. "How soon until your officers clear the scene and let my men go back to work?"

"Probably a few weeks, Dr. Firmin. This is a rather horrific crime and we don't want to let anything slip under the radar." Lester considered the man behind the desk, fingers laced on top of a calendar full of scribbles. His black hair was slicked perfectly in place and his expression was rather calm. *Man oozed professionalism,* Saxon noticed. *Almost too much.* "Forgive me for saying, but you are awfully calm about this, for someone who doesn't see men mutilated everyday."

"I had my breakdown, thank you. It involved not shaving for twenty-four hours." And just like that, the detective was back down to the rank of annoying guest taking up too much of his time. Giles hid his irritation at having to deal with the detective in the first place behind a slick smile. "Right now I'm more concerned by how much downtime this is going to cause my employees." Giles would have to re-locate the entire department and make arrangements to get the computers at the very least removed from the scene. *Damn Steve.*

"I can tell the loss has hit you hard," Saxon noted, sarcasm heavy in his voice. Something didn't feel right about this situation, or the man before him. He was too back-to-business for Lester's taste. If the man didn't have an alibi for the time of murder, he would have been high on Lester's suspect list. As it stood, Firmin just appeared to be a horrible human being. Saxon figured that was why he was in the business of creating fake ones. "Most men wouldn't be able to work yet after seeing something like that. Your employee wasn't just murdered, Dr. Firmin, he was *ripped apart.*"

"Be that as it may, I'm not most men and I can't afford the time off for grieving." Giles stood to match the detective's height, knocking his chair back into the wall. "I fall, the company falls. I refuse to let my efforts and investments go to waste due to the actions of some crazed lunatic over an

employee that caused me more grief than profit even when he was alive."
Giles thumped his knuckles on the desk, causing the little statuettes to
shake. "If that makes me look heartless, than so be it."

"I see." Saxon nodded and reached down to grab his hat from the
chair. *Man didn't like the victim. Has a much more personal investment in company
than first realized.* The detective noted those two facts away for later use.
Men with money could afford to hire someone else to do their dirty work.
Saxon tried to keep all possibilities open. The detective tipped his hat at
Firmin. "Well, then. I'll just be out of your hair for the day."

"Thank you, again. I'll expect updates on the situation as soon as
they're available." Giles made a note to look over the lab himself once
the officers were removed. Who knows what they messed with
unintentionally. Giles smiled sardonically. "Have a good day, Detective."

"See you real soon, Dr. Firmin." Lester Saxon would make sure of
that.

CHAPTER 7

THINGS MORE OR less calmed down in the lab over the next couple of days. Not enough that the crime scene had been cleared and re-opened for work, of course, but there were people back at their stations typing, cataloguing, and filing as they had before the murder. The programming division had been relocated to the opposite end of the building into a storage room. Giles had yet to find computers for them to work with—the detective was rather stubborn when it came to relocating the ones from the crime scene—so most of them spent their time trying to make the old stored boxes connect to the internet to browse articles, play games or whatever else they did when not working.

Abel would not deny the sense of foreboding that had settled over the building, thick as pea soup. You could still taste the smell of stale blood in the halls around the programming division, and the normal chatter and bustle of things had quieted down. Even Becky wasn't screaming as much as usual, and that was almost more disturbing than a decapitated body.

Iacchus seemed to be happier though.

Abel shifted his goggles and turned back to his soldering. He had about four more motherboards to reassemble and add to the new units before they could be placed in the wall with the others. Abel shifted the magnifying glass on the holding stand slightly to see the other side of the circuit better. The tip on his soldering pen was looking a little worn and Abel made note to replace it during the next supply run. To think, little Hecate and Iacchus used to be right here on this table in bits and pieces. Abel almost couldn't fathom the thought.

Maybe this was how parents felt trying to imagine their college grad as the squirming tots they had been some twenty years earlier. Then again,

Abel was *sort of* Hecate and Iacchus' parent—Hecate's anyway. It didn't occur to him often, but every once in a while Abel remembered that he had *built* Hecate and Iacchus' mainframe. He didn't write their programs, but their physical motherboards were something that he soldered together among dozens of others while wearing pink goggles—all without a second thought.

Speaking of Hecate, Abel looked up from his soldering station into the empty room and wondered how the boy was doing. Since Steve had left them, Hecate had to be reassigned to a new programmer for his exercises. Giles had suggested that Becky take over for him, since she was already processing Iacchus, but she refused outright. They had barely gotten her to agree to work with the older boy, so there was little chance of her taking on double duty.

Abel had volunteered, but Giles felt Hecate needed interaction with more people and Abel finding himself agreeing, albeit reluctantly, and allowed the boy to be transferred. Anton Jansen was proving to be a pretty decent person, at least. He had good taste in movies, anyway, if the doctor recalled correctly. Abel admitted he was surprised they didn't give the job to Lucy. She had always proven fond of the boys, particularly Hecate, with her gifts and queries on their wellbeing. Regardless, the decision had been made and Hecate was stuck with Jansen.

The doctor put down his tools and started to rub at his stomach. The bruise had spread and ran a dark ring around his waistline, but wasn't so painful anymore. It looked worse than it felt now that the color had changed from a purple to more of a black. Becky was still teasing him about it when Hecate wasn't around. She even said something along the lines of "that brat is going to love you to death one of these days" before quickly shutting her mouth. The topic of death was still a sore subject with so many questions unanswered. Abel flicked a piece of loose solder across the table.

The police still had no leads. The programming room didn't have anything in it that didn't belong there, or looked like it was used as a weapon. All of the other members of the programming division had plausible alibi, and as far as he knew no one had any reason to dismember Steve Mathers. When the topic of motive first came up, Giles had gone suspiciously quiet and paled slightly. Abel was sure the detective had noticed. Giles had spun something up about threats from some ethical treatment enforcement group, but it was hard to take them seriously after the stunt with the paint in Giles' parking space.

The group had been questioned regardless, and were almost as horrified as Abel was when they were informed of the murder. That sort of disgust was difficult to fake, even if they had been responsible for some sort of death threats. Abel made note to hunt Giles down later and find out the entire story surrounding said letters when he had a chance. He didn't like it when his friend hid things from him.

The last time Giles had lied to him, Abel had to pick the man up from a diner two cities away. Giles had *said* he couldn't come with Abel to his parents' for Thanksgiving because he was visiting his aunt, but truthfully he was visiting an old bar called *Auntie's*. The man had gotten so smashed, he had been kicked out of the bar for getting too forward with another patron. Giles had then proceeded to walk two blocks before collapsing outside a 50's-style box car diner. At least Giles had treated Abel to a homemade breakfast platter before they left—the only good thing to come from the experience.

For now, though, Abel needed to finish the last motherboard of the day. It certainly wasn't going to get up and do it by itself. Abel almost chuckled at the thought of one of the chips growing legs and walking around. Abel reached for the iron again, relieved his face could still grin after everything that had happened.

There was a light rap at the door followed by the quiet sound of clothes rustling. Lucy poked her head into the room through the opening. Abel was hunched over his work table, concentrating on his efforts, and she blushed slightly at the handsome profile. Lucy's voice was barely louder than a whisper as she called out into the room. "Dr. Moreau?"

Abel turned to the door, unsure if he had heard anything or not. Seeing the shy woman lingering in the hallway, he smiled. "Ms. Clarence." Her blonde hair was tied back into a messy ponytail and her nails were the same pink as the lab safety goggles. Well, on the hand he could see. Her left arm was held firmly behind her back in a somewhat suspicious manner. Abel set the iron down in its charging station and swiveled in his chair. "What can I do for you?"

"Please, Abel." Lucy smiled softly before biting her lip. Abel wasn't just handsome: he looked reliable—good with kids, too. Lucy still couldn't figure out why the man wasn't taken, yet. Lucy hoped it was because he was oblivious to forward advances, and not a sign that there was something horrible wrong with him the girl couldn't see in her rose-tinted view of him. "You can call me Lucy. Not even the boys call me Ms. Clarence."

"Because you asked them not to," Abel said. Lucy was a sweet girl if not a tad skittish. She hardly ever ventured out of her work room and, when she did, it was usually just to say hello to Hecate. Abel shifted slightly, as her staring continued. Lucy looked content to just stand there and watch him all day, to his discomfort. The doctor swiveled in his chair to face her and get to the point. "Alright then Lucy, what can I help you with?"

"I was wondering if you could do me a small favor?" Lucy pulled her arm from behind her back and held up the neatly folded scarf. It was the same shade of green as the LED lights in the boys' eyes and had little blue and white daisies knitted into the pattern. Some people used grief as a time to wallow, Lucy used it to focus. She had already knitted three sweaters and six scarves since Steve passed away. Lucy had a wool hat in progress sitting on her desk. "I made this for Iacchus since he still isn't allowed to change out of the scrubs. Could you give it to him for me please?"

Abel took the offered scarf and noticed the hand stitching into the tightly knit wool pattern. He really shouldn't be surprised—Lucy had made Hecate's sweater, too. Both were examples of considerable skill, and it was nice to know Lucy's hands were put to use for more things than typing. The girl had a wide range of talent, and Abel was tempted to see if she wouldn't make one of these little wool creations for his niece. "Of course, but may I ask why you can't give it to him yourself?"

"Ms. Becky is always down there with him during my break." Lucy bit her lip again and blushed slightly in embarrassment. Abel and Becky were friends as far as Lucy could tell, so it made spitting out the next sentence rather difficult. Lucy quickly brushed a loose hair behind her ear, brushing her cheek with her fingers. "She scares me a bit more than I think she should."

Abel almost laughed, but knew better. "You do know that woman is mostly talk, right, Lucy?" Abel fingered the scarf and looked her in the eye. He knew Becky put a fear of God into some of the male employees, but Abel hadn't realized she scared a bunch of the ladies as well. She was definitely a fierce woman, even if it was all for show. "I'm pretty sure she doesn't actually bite."

"Yes, well," Lucy mumbled before rubbing her index finger between the thumb and forefinger on the opposite hand. "I don't think she'd let me give something to Iacchus without a fuss, either."

"And you think she'd let me?"

Lucy continued her nervous twitching by switching the weight from one of her feet to the other in a small sway. Her face gained a slight shade of pink as she licked the back of her teeth. The next few words to come from Lucy's mouth jabbed at her ribs like a knife even as she said them: "She likes you."

Abel stared for a moment at Lucy's odd reaction. Of course Becky liked him—they were friends. Or enemies drawn together by a common job. Or something. Abel had a hard time pin-pointing exactly what his relationship with Becky had turned into since the boys had come into their lives. Lucy hadn't need to phrase it like *that*. "Ah."

"So would you?" Lucy pressed hoping to change the subject. She only had another five minutes of break and needed to get back to keep the programming boys in line. They were, understandably, a mess since Steve had passed on. Lucy wasn't all right with it herself, just yet, but she was coping by keeping busy and playing team mom. Between babysitting and her knitting, Lucy was managing to keep it together.

"Of course." Abel gave a salute to the petite woman, complete with an honest smile. He set the scarf on a stool next to his desk far from the tools and welder. "I'll make sure he gets it."

"Oh thank you!" Lucy smiled brightly, showing off her white teeth. She looked down at her watch and huffed. "I'd like to stay, but I must be going now. Thank you again, Abel!"

"No problem." The doctor waved the girl on her way and turned down to place the scarf on the chair.

Hecate sat quietly in the temporary programming lab as Mr. Jansen compiled the last of the data from his exercise. Hecate still was trying to figure out why they called them 'exercises,' however. It was essentially just running a test daily to reinforce that yes, Hecate could indeed make his own decisions and thoughts based upon intuition and reasoning and no, Hecate was not just making it look like advanced programming. It was insulting that they had yet to make the tests challenging. He was always rerunning the same six tests over and over. Sure, Iacchus had issues running the things, but Hecate was sure that had more to do with Iacchus being unable to focus than unable to answer the questions.

Iacchus was easily distracted that way.

Thankfully, Hecate was able to focus much more efficiently. At the very least it helped him with his social skills. Well, when Hecate wanted to appeal to social norms and standards. There were times it just wasn't worth the effort to pander to the humans' expectations. Especially the ones still not quite sure of what to make of the android boy studying and taking in every moving line on said lab technician's face.

Anton was unnerved. It had started the moment the kid sat down in the seat next to his desk. Anton wasn't sure what he was expecting, but he had seen this kid far more active with Dr. Moreau. With Anton, Hecate seemed to do nothing but stare at him while he typed. If not for kicking his legs back and forth in the chair, Anton couldn't be sure the kid moved at all. Steve had said Hecate should be harmless, but there was just something about him...

It was probably the fact the kid wasn't breathing.

Being freaked out by the kid's test performance wasn't helping Anton's nerves any, either. Steve used to do these things once a week, called it 'easy-peasy' in fact, but Steve never mentioned the kid went through and completed a ten gigabyte test file in *thirty seconds*. Anton's computer at home couldn't even render a 5mb photograph through a cheesy filter that fast, let alone process complex data functions. That sort of data processing was well...

Inhuman.

Anton heard the distinct whirl of a computer fan and turned his head towards Hecate. The boy had finally stopped looking at him, but was now staring at the desktop before looking around with only his eyes. *Hecate.* The young programmer realized just how appropriate that name was. The kid was named after a *goddess*. That was about as far from human as you could get. Come to think, his brother was named after some Greek deity, too. Anton wondered if the two androids were even aware of such a thing. "Hey, kid."

"Yes?" Hecate turned from counting the cracks in the desk to look at his nervous new partner. Unsettling Mr. Jansen with staring had gotten ridiculously dull. Hecate squashed the notion that he might actually *miss* Steve and his ridiculous video games. He'd rather have someone mad at him for teasing than sitting there shaking like a leaf. "Was there an issue with the test?"

"No, uh. No, that was cool." Anton started to type again to finish cataloging today's results in with the rest of the database. He kept his eyes on the screen instead of the child next to him. "I was just wondering if you were aware of what you were named after."

"Hecate. A Greco-Roman goddess often associated with both magic and crossroads." It was amusing that he had a woman's name, considering his body's identified gender, but the name suited him well enough. Still holding Anton's attention, Hecate continued. "She was often depicted in triplicate with three separate faces." Anton had stopped typing at this point and was staring at him with a humorously dim-witted expression. "To save you the trouble, the deity Iacchus is named after isn't nearly as interesting aside from being the child of Zeus and Demeter."

"Oh." Anton swallowed. It seemed the kid knew *exactly* who and what he was named after. Great. Could androids have egos? Anton couldn't see why not, considering he already knew they could have a temper. Anton filed it away mentally to put in his personal journals. For some reason it seemed important that the androids had all that self-awareness in addition to their intelligence. Anton figured it was something worth knowing. "I was just wondering if you knew, that's all. Where did you, uh, learn that, anyway?"

"Dr. Moreau mentioned we were named after the gods of Greek mythology in honor of the laboratory's founder, so I requested a book on the subject." Hecate smiled and held up his hand, three fingers raised. Smug satisfaction filled his voice. "He brought me three."

"I bet he did." Anton didn't doubt the kid's words for a second. If Dr. Moreau wasn't spoiling the kids with presents and attention, he was endlessly blabbing on about them in the break room. *Hecate did this. Hecate did that* ad nauseam. Anton wasn't surprised to find out Dr. Moreau kept shots of the boys in his wallet. He was worse than Anton's sister after she had her first baby.

Anton coughed into his hand and started to type a little faster. Hecate was glaring at him silently now, waiting for something…probably praise for Dr. Moreau, or acknowledgement of his gift. How did Steve put up with this? Anton remembered that he could no longer ask him, and dropped his shoulders. Anton hoped Rod would be up for a trip out tonight; Anton needed it. "That was nice of him."

"He's always nice. Dr. Moreau likes us very much, I think." Hecate leant his head back to look at the lights on the ceiling. Three lamps each and fluorescent. They were bright. Hecate imagined what would happen if he punched the light and made the room go dark, leaving only the soft blue glow of the out-dated monitors desperately trying to keep up with the rescued computer boxes. "I'm rather fond of him as well."

There was no one Rupert was fonder of than his Mary—save for maybe his children.

"Good evening, Mrs. Dixen," Rupert kissed his wife on the lips while leaning over the bar at the edge of the kitchen, "you are looking lovely today."

"You say that every day," Mary Dixen replied, setting a tray of muffins fresh from the oven on the stovetop. She had three more batches to make before she could call it a night, and that still might not be enough to satisfy the swarm of kids tomorrow. Just see if she ever volunteered for her daughter's bake-sale again! It'd be too soon before she saw another blueberry muffin.

Rupert chuckled and set his briefcase neatly in its proper spot in the basket at the end of the bar. He loosened his tie with a sigh, smiling happily at the beautiful woman standing in a lacy apron over her blue-jeans and red tank-top. Mary had her hair up in a pony-tail today, making her look younger than the wrinkles around her eyes and grey hair on her head would have one believe. "I mean it every day."

"Sweet-talker." Mary whistled while greasing a new pan with a spray can. Her husband looked weary and grateful to be home. Mary prepared internally for her husband to unload the woes of his day. "How was work?"

"Long," Rupert said. He propped the heel of his—brand new—shoes on the bar stool base ring. "If it's not bad enough that everyone is still put on edge by the police tape they refuse to take down, the kids are getting antsy themselves with the new changes coming and all."

Mary stirred a cup of blueberries into the batter while watching her darling from the corner of her eye. "Iacchus is still having trouble?"

"No, it's actually Hecate this time around," Rupert groaned. "Anton spent his entire break talking with Rod about how much the kid freaked him out during exercises." Rupert reached for a muffin over the island bar. His hand was met with a wooden spoon slapping him away. Rupert rubbed his hand to wipe off the bits of batter that had flicked off the spoon, foiled. "I think he's unnerving the techs on purpose. It's starting to worry me how much of a kick that kid gets out of tormenting people."

"Did you tell Abel about it?" Mary wondered, remembering stories of how the younger boy got along with his caretaker. "I thought Hecate listened to him."

"I'd have an easier time getting a camel through the eye of a needle than convincing Abel that his darling Hecate is anything other than a perfect little angel." Rupert shook his head. "The guy is completely blind to the kid's faults...can't blame him though. Hecate's a completely different person depending who's in the room with him or how often that person sees Abel. For example, he's a perfect angel around Becky and Lucy, but if it's just me or Anton in the room? He's a snarky little brat."

"Probably just needs a good spanking." Mary chuckled pouring batter into the slots, using a spoon to prevent spill over. "Worked well enough on Sammy."

"Hey," Rupert sat up, remembering something important, and looked behind him down the hallway. His living room was still and there was no sound coming from the back bedrooms. "Where is Sam? He was coming home from school today, wasn't he?" Rupert glanced at the wall clock over the sink. "He should be here by now."

"Oh, sweetie." Mary covered her mouth, gasping. She *knew* there was something she had missed with all the bake sale chaos. "Did I forget to tell you? He called to cancel a couple days ago." Rupert's face dropped noticeably and Mary set the spoon and batter bowl down. Rupert had been looking forward to seeing his boy for *weeks*. "One of his friends got a cabin reserved for the break and he changed plans to join them in the mountains."

"Ah, well...that's good," Rupert responded dejectedly. He tried to force a smile on his face to keep Mary from worrying. "Sam should hang out with his friends."

"He'll be home for Christmas," Mary tried, wringing her hands in her apron. "There's no way he'll miss that."

"Yeah," Rupert plopped down onto the bar stool and occupied himself watching his wife go back to making muffins. A second absence made itself more obvious. "Shouldn't Kelly be helping you?"

Mary sighed, good-naturedly dropping a spoonful of batter in the tin. "Friend's house. Someone has a date and it was 'like super important' she be there for support and make-up." Mary greased two more pans, hoping to knock out the last of the muffins in one go. "She won't be home for another two hours, likely."

"Of course," Rupert grinned covering his face and rubbing. His little girl was growing up, too, it seemed. Rupert hated knowing she'd be flying the nest just like her older sister before he could help it. At least his Mary was always there. "Need any help, sweetie?"

"No, I've got it," Mary answered, shaking her head. Why was it everyone only offered help when she was almost done? "Why don't you go relax and watch some TV?"

"Only if you promise to join me when you're done," Rupert grinned playfully, despite the sinking feeling in his chest. "Iacchus won't talk to me, Hecate's a brat, my son's skipping out, and my youngest daughter finally caught up with her sister discovering boys and make-up." Rupert shoved away from the counter and headed for the plush leather couch in the other half of the great room. "I could really use the hug right now."

"I think I can manage that," Mary tossed the last two trays in the oven and set the timer. She slipped around the corner of the bar and waited for her husband to collapse on the couch. She grinned devilishly when his head turned in her direction. "But I think there's something a little more fun we can do with our time since the house is so big and empty…"

Rupert watched as Mary scooped a bit of batter from the edge of the bowl with her index finger and tapped it on the tip of her nose. Her grin deepened the wrinkles playfully. The apron hit his face; he had been so distracted by the batter he hadn't noticed it come off.

Rupert loved that woman.

Abel dropped his case in the main foyer of his house. The stairs leading to the top floor, with their cold iron railings, loomed over his head, creating shadows on the floor from the soft streetlights outside his window. As he trudged to his kitchen, Abel couldn't be bothered to turn on the light. His house was silent and cool, the atmosphere lonely and oppressive. Abel missed the lab and his boy already. The doctor opened his fridge and sighed at the barren shelves. It occurred to him that he kept more groceries in the mini-fridge in his office than in his own home. He pulled out a piece of cheese, taking a bite straight from the block, before collapsing on his couch on the other side of the great room.

Abel turned his head and plucked a photograph from the table. Its frame was polished metal and held a picture of Abel and Hecate during the boy's first week of life. Abel smiled down at the photo and finished off the piece of cheddar in one bite, shoving the last bit in his mouth with his thumb. Hecate was smiling in the photo, proudly showing off his yellow button-down shirt and khaki shorts Abel had picked out to replace those awful white scrubs. Poor Iacchus had been stuck in scrubs for nearly a month before he begged for normal clothing. Abel had no desire to let Hecate suffer the same fate, buying clothes for the boy the first chance he got.

Thankfully, there was an outlet mall about twenty minutes from their complex with no shortage of children's clothing.

Giles warned Abel for the first time that day that he was getting too attached to the kid, but the doctor felt the warning came a dime short and a day late—Abel was taken the second the kid looked at him with those big blue eyes and reaching arms. Abel honestly couldn't remember what it was like without the kid around. He shifted to lay on his back, stretching out on the worn fabric couch, and stared at his popcorn ceiling.

Lonely. That's what it had been.

Giles had been his best friend for as long as he could remember, but the man was so stressed and busy lately they only saw each other for a few hours each day—most of which were at work. Giles was a master of splitting professional and personal issues into their own, separate compartments. If not for the shared bottle of scotch, Abel would have assumed Giles was in reality a set of twins who shared a name.

Abel wasn't close enough with anyone else at work to really call them a 'friend.' Wasn't Steve's death proof of that? Abel had been a wreck, and the only ones he could go to for comfort were from the lab. Before Hecate, he'd go to work, catch up with Giles in the man's office, and head home to an empty house full of dust and lights he never bothered to turn on. Abel supposed he was warming up to Becky, but the woman had her own issues.

Instead, he spent his time spoiling the boys—it was far too easy to give Hecate everything he wanted when the kid offered affection and attention so freely, and in such bulk.

The boys were good kids, and Abel hated to see them down. They hid it well, but Abel could tell that Steve's death and the upcoming surgery was wearing on the two boys. Abel wanted to do something to lift their spirits, but that in itself would be a challenge. Hecate was easy to make happy: give him a book or play a game and he was good to go. Iacchus was more...fickle. He needed something to occupy his time, but books and movies only went so far with his short attention span. Lucy's scarf had made the older boy happy, but Abel had a feeling buying the kid more clothes would be pushing their luck with Giles. He *was* still restricted to the regulation white scrubs. Iacchus needed something with a bit more urgency—something to force him to take care...or take care of *it*.

Abel popped up on the couch with a grin. He knew *exactly* what he could do for the boys. Best of all, it would double as a lesson in responsibility. Abel snatched his cell phone off the end table—he had forgotten it at home yet again—from under a hideous neon green lamp his mother had given him, and dialed an oh-so-familiar number.

Four rings later, he got an answering machine. Abel frowned at the phone and checked the time. *Oh!* It was already after one in the morning. Abel snickered and dialed again. He just needed to be persistent.

After the third ring, an aggravated "What do you want, Abe?" moaned from the other end.

"Hey, Giles," Abel began, "Is it okay if I get the boys a present?"

"May I see it *now?*" Hecate asked fingers clenched in Abel's lab coat. Hecate was well aware he was causing a scene with his whining, but didn't care—he wanted to know right now! "I have been waiting patiently *all day*."

Abel had entered his office that morning with a box covered by a sheet. There were small scratching noises coming from it, but nothing the boy recognized. Hecate had wanted to see it, but Dr. Moreau refused and said something about a 'surprise.' Hecate had gaped at him as Abel continued to putter around setting up for the day—ignoring his request. This was *not* how things worked. Abel gave to Hecate whatever he asked, the second he asked—*that* was how it was supposed to go! Hecate tugged on Abel's coat as they trailed down the hallway toward their room. Dr. Firmin must be rubbing off on him. "Please? May I see it now?"

"No, I'm showing it to you and your brother at the *same time*." Abel stressed as tiny hands clung and tugged at his coat childishly. Hecate acting his age made him happy. Even if he was a technological achievement, he deserved to experience the anticipation all kids felt when waiting on a present. Abel nodded at an intern who giggled at the sight they were making behind her clipboard. Begging Giles and promising the man lunch for a week was going to be worth it. "Patience, remember?"

"Why must *I* wait for Iacchus, Dr. Moreau? My behavior has been far superior to his over the past few weeks!" Hecate argued sternly. He was better than his brother. Abel should treat *him* better than Iacchus. Hecate dashed out in front of the older man to walk backwards, looking him in the eyes. "Surely I've earned a peek first?"

"Nice try." Abel dropped a hand on Hecate's head and spun the boy back around to walk straight. He then pulled the blond into a half-hug and rubbed the kid's shoulder. "Behavior was only an excuse to get permission from Giles. This is a present from me to you boys just because, that's all." Abel released Hecate's shoulder and readjusted his hold on the box with two hands. "Which means you both get to see it at the same time."

Hecate frowned and tried to concentrate on the small sounds coming from the box Abel held in his other hand. They were sporadic and varied in volume and length. Was it alive then? "Must it be that way?"

"Yes," Abel replied softly thinking back on his first present of this nature. It was during the middle of a school week. No holidays, no birthdays or special events. Just his parents bringing in a box with a cover and the excitement he felt knowing he got to care for another living being. Abel was happy he'd be able to share that same sort of moment with these two boys. "Sometimes it's nice to get a gift without a reason, don't you think?"

"I suppose." Hecate continued to frown, one hand snaking back into Abel's lab coat. "I still do not see the point, though."

"It'll come to you eventually, I'm sure." Abel tapped the edge of his package with his finger, causing the cloth cover to shake slightly. He hoped this went over well. A quick code punched into the cipher lock allowed him entry to the boys' room. "Iacchus?"

Iacchus looked up from his picture book and gripped the edges of cover tightly. He watched as Dr. Moreau set a box down on their short table. Hecate was glaring ferociously behind the man's back, and Iacchus felt a bit of dread for whatever was coming. Iacchus bit his lip, "Yes?"

"I have a a gift for you two!" Abel squatted and put both hands on the top of the case as the boys scooted over to sit before him on the opposite side of the table. "But before I hand over this little surprise, you two have to promise me something."

"Promise?" Both Hecate and Iacchus answered together, in a rare moment of their thoughts traveling the same wavelength.

"That's right," Abel said. "What I'm going to give you two takes a lot of care and responsibility." The doctor paused and looked at both of them directly in their artificially colored eyes. Abel waited for their full and complete attention before continuing. "And you must promise to be careful. They're very fragile."

"Of course," Hecate replied immediately. He didn't need to be told to take care with Abel's things. Hecate was almost insulted Abel would have to specify such a thing, and then he remembered his brother next to him. "Iacchus?"

The teen look-alike hesitated slightly before nodding. "I'll try."

"Good enough for me." Abel lifted the sheet with a flourish mimicking an old magician he had seen once when he was younger. Two sets of eyes lit up, literally, as they took in the new data of the scurrying little creatures before them. "What do you think?"

"Mice," Hecate answered as he looked into the cage, accessing the data he had stored on the small creatures. Four tiny mice ran about, twitching in the cage. Two were white, one was brown and the last one was black with white splotches. Hecate straightened when the newly acquired data had finished sorting itself. He settled quickly on the most likely function for them to be here. "You got us pets?"

"Two each?" Iacchus added as he counted. He leant as close to the cage as he could, nose nearly pressed up against the thin metal wires. The mice were very small. He was sure that two would fit in just one of his hands.

"Four for the both of you," Abel clarified. "I expect you two to share." The doctor pulled the cage back slightly when Iacchus' hand went for the little gate. "Also, I think for now we should leave them in the cage. Alright?"

"Okay." Iacchus' hand twitched slightly having just missed his chance to hold the little creatures. He consoled himself by directing all his attention to the mice and taking in every tiny little detail. Their fur was coarse and short and unlike anything he'd seen before. Iacchus nibbled on his lower lip. *Did Ms. Becky like mice?* "They're very small, aren't they? I can hear their hearts beating so quickly." The older boy voiced his thoughts out loud yet again struck by just how *small* these little creatures were.

"You two like them?" Abel asked hesitantly. Both were still staring at the cage with a sense of confusion and wonder. He was hoping for a bit of excitement or some sort of an outburst. A few more moments of staring from the boys and Abel wondered if maybe this hadn't been the best of ideas. "If not, I can take them back."

"That won't be necessary." The blonde jerked up from studying the rodents at the depressed tone coming from Abel. Hecate grabbed for the doctor's hand and held it tight. "We do like them, Dr. Moreau. Very much so."

"I'm glad." The doctor let out a sigh of relief. For a few seconds there, he was worried this might have backfired. Since things seemed okay, Abel continued on to the second part of the present. "Why don't you two name them?"

"Alright." The two boys chorused together before turning to the small creatures. The tiny animals moved about their cage, oblivious to the world around them as name suggestions traveled back and forth excitedly in the air. Abel pulled over a bar stool to drop onto as Hecate and Iacchus moved onto names from various books and movies they had seen while gathering data. It was nice to see them working together for once. Abel grinned at his boys.

Things were starting to look up!

CHAPTER 8

BECKY LOOKED OVER the drawing Iacchus had submitted concerning his future skin modifications, her cigarette hanging from her bottom lip. She had forgotten about the markings dilemma, with Steve's death looming over everyone, but the boys turned their technical drawings on time. She had half expected to receive crayon scribbles, but was shocked with the professional accuracy—he even drew in dimension lines. Iacchus stuck to the rules they had laid out, including two markings on the face and sticking with one color—a light cerulean blue.

Becky prayed it was simply a coincidence that he chose her favorite color.

Currently, said pain in her side was sitting quietly, tending to his pet mice by cleaning out their cage. He was proudly wearing that scarf Abel had brought him earlier this morning, it sitting snuggly around his neck. She hated to admit it, but those little rodents had probably been Abel's best idea yet. Iacchus' behavior had improved ten fold, if only because he was now conscious of their presence. He was far more hesitant to throw something if it could hit the table or scare the little critters. However, the mice keeping his attention didn't stop him from stealing glances in her direction every so often.

But back to the design. Iacchus had kept things relatively simple. He had dual sets of light blue lines running the length of his arms and legs from the joint of where his head met his neck down to the tips of his fingers. Upside down chevrons were on his chest, three lines deep, and it mirrored just below his naval. The chevrons were joined together at his sides which more or less created an elongated hexagon. He finished the design with mirrored lines running from his waist down the side of his leg

95

to the ankle where they circled around. Becky hummed, noticing he had left his back free of markings. That was alright with her.

She did have to give the kid credit however, for the facial markings. He had to have at least two, but they never told him *where* they had to be. Iacchus had two chevron lines on his forehead, nearly hidden by his bangs. It was smart and unobtrusive if he chose to keep them unlit. No one would ever notice them. Becky took one last look over the sheet and turned to the boy who was now staring at her from his place on the floor. "Iacchus, are you sure this is your final draft?"

"Yes, Ms. Becky." Iacchus nodded and shifted in his seat on the floor, finished with his chore. He had switched out the water bottle exactly how Dr. Moreau had shown him on the first day and placed it slowly back into its slot. Little Prime (the one with the spots) and Integer (the brown one) had dashed over to the water spout and were drinking greedily. Iacchus tapped the cage to try and wake up Infinity and Infinitesimal (the white twins) so they could get a fresh drink, too. Such simple little things they were, but Iacchus sort of liked being responsible for their well being. Sort of how Ms. Becky was responsible for him! She didn't look particularly mad or happy, right now though, and Iacchus was treading unfamiliar ground. He shifted in his seat, fingering the bag of shavings he had poured into the bottom of the cage. "Is it alright?"

"Yup," Becky replied absently and signed the top of the form with her approval for the guys down in the aesthetics department. The android could look like whatever he wanted as far as she was concerned. "Alright, one down. Let's see what little Hecate came up with—"

The muffled shriek that came through the closed door from the hall was enough of a distraction for Becky to keep her from commenting the little brat had chosen two colors.

Iacchus was on his feet sooner than Ms. Becky and heading for the door as fast as he was able. Screams usually meant that someone was in trouble or that there was some danger, and it had sounded close by. Iacchus felt a need to see what exactly was going on before Ms. Becky could get involved and be hurt. The boy was out the door and in the hallway before the woman could even get up from her seat at the work desk.

Iacchus slammed the door shut behind him and re-locked the key-pad to stall Ms. Becky. He stood unmoving just outside the door, listening for any sound or movement. He tried to ignore Becky banging on the glass.

The hall was empty, but Iacchus could hear heavy breathing around the corner, even with the clicking of other doors opening to see the commotion filling the air. His feet acted before he registered it and Iacchus was around the corner to stand by a very frazzled woman he did not recognize. She was wearing a janitorial uniform, though, and had her mouth covered as she dry heaved. Her eyes were focused and wet so he followed the line of sight to see what had caught her attention.

"Dear God," Becky muttered over the android's shoulder. The boy was fast, but he hadn't gone so far she was unable to catch up with him. It didn't take that long to enter a key-code. As Becky got a closer look at what had gotten the attention of the janitor and now Iacchus, she was not surprised the woman who had found *that* had screamed.

Iacchus almost turned at the sound of Ms. Becky's voice. By some miracle, he managed to remain standing still when he felt her lean up against him, one of her breasts firmly against his back. She was shaking and Iacchus realized she'd probably have fallen to the floor if he hadn't been there. It made him feel warm and confident as he stored away the feeling of her skin against his in permanent memory. He did however, wait a few moments before whispering, "Who is that, Ms. Becky?"

"I don't think I could tell you," Becky said, and felt herself gripping tightly to Iacchus' white scrubs. She would have been disturbed yet again by the disinterest in his voice, but right now he was a pillar of stability and she regrettably needed the grounding.

The lump of flesh, blood, and puss mingling with strips of clothing that had spilled out of the supply closet could barely be identified as human any longer. It resembled something Becky had seen in the scrap bins of a butcher shop. Maggots wriggled and writhed through the bits of identifiable muscle. The stench was unbearable and Becky buried her face into Iacchus shoulder to block it out. The smell of synthetic skin and oil was far preferable to the smell of death. "What could have done it?"

Iacchus' first thought was a table saw, but decided not to say anything.

"Cecil Law." Giles read from the employee file to the detective once again invading his office. Becky was occupying the space next to Iacchus on his couch along with the head of the janitorial staff, Ms. Susie Tannin —also known as the lucky woman who had discovered the body. Forensics had identified the victim using a dental impression and a partial fingerprint. There wasn't much else left for them to use. "Thirty-six years old, janitor. Works the day shift." He sighed into his hands. "That's all I know. Last time I spoke to the man in person was the day I hired him and put him under Ms. Tannin's loving management."

"Thank you again, Dr. Firmin." Saxon replied robotically, having *oh so much fun* dealing with the director again so soon. The man made Lester want to strangle him every time he did that odd little eyebrow twitch indicating *Firmin* was the one irritated by the whole ordeal. The strangest addition on the couch with the other witnesses wasn't exactly giving Lester any warm fuzzy feelings either. He understood what they did at the lab, but he hadn't really thought about it until the *thing* was sitting in the room with him. Firmin had done an impressive job of hiding the androids from the police on previous visits, but now that one was a witness to the scene, it was unavoidable.

When Lester Saxon had joined the force, he knew he was going to deal with murderers and psychopaths, but working with odd doctor-scientist hybrids and living androids was something he still couldn't wrap his head around. Lester looked over to the young teen boy (Wearing a scarf? It was at least seventy-five degrees in this man's office!) on the couch more closely and almost questioned what he'd been told. According to the report for those who first arrived on the second murder scene, he was a seven-month-old android.

If that really was an android, Lester would have never been able to tell. The kid's constant fidgeting this way and that in his seat even helped covered up the fact he wasn't breathing. Lester pushed down his discomfort to continue the questioning, keeping his eyes locked with the main *human* witness. He would have preferred this interview be done down at the station, but the woman looked ready to fall to pieces already. The familiar environment was his best bet for cooperation. "Ms. Tannin, could you please describe what happened when you arrived at the scene?"

"I was heading to storage closet to get more bleach," she took in a breath slowly and licked her lips. "That closet is normally for excess storage so we usually only have to open it once a week." Susie stopped again. Every horrid detail of earlier today was flooding her mind and causing her breath to still and her voice to come out choked. She cleared her throat with a cough before continuing, "I had noticed an awful sm-smell coming from the closet into the hallway so I thought maybe a rat had crawled in and d-died or some such thing."

"Are you going to be alright to continue?" Giles interrupted. Ms. Tannin shook horribly. She clutched the light blue polo shirt under the shoulder straps of her grey uniform jumper, fingers twitching. Susie still had splotches of blood splattered on the bottom of the dress' pleated skirt —somehow it missed her bare legs under the knee-length dress. Giles itched, shifting in his seat, to make the woman feel better. He wasn't normally this charitable, but there was something that about a woman crying that gutted him. "Should I get you a cup of water or something before you finish?"

"No, but thank you, Dr. Firmin." A deep breath. "I can do this. As I said, I thought it was a dead rat, so I opened the door and," Susie made a motion that threw her hands out from her body and her voice began to steadily speed up as she continued, "this swoosh of something fell out and onto the floor and splashed up everywhere! It smelled so bad I nearly vomited on the spot and then I noticed the color and bits of recognizable pieces. I saw his hand and a shirt from our uniform and that skull with the empty eye sockets." Susie was almost standing at this point in her hysteria, back of her thighs balancing precariously on the edge of the couch. "He had no eyes! That was the last straw and I screamed as loud as I could."

"That's when you two arrived, correct?" Detective Saxon turned to the other two who had been listening. The woman looked green and the boy neutral. The boy mirroring the director's blasé attitude made up Lester's mind for who got the hot seat next. "And you," he pointed to the boy, "arrived first?"

"Yes," Iacchus answered and not a second later he found Ms. Becky jabbing an elbow into his arm. The boy wondered why she'd done that— it had to have hurt her—before Iacchus looked closer at her scowling face and realized his mistake. "I mean, yes sir."

Lester reminded himself yet again he was talking to an android. The display he had seen just now was so human it was scary. He had seen a mother scold her teenage boy in the exact same fashion not a week ago after bringing the brat in for a drug possession charge. And here it was being replicated with a robot. The kid's eyes were as expressive as any human, wide and curious. The detective wondered if the kid's statement would even hold up in court. Maybe they could count him as a security camera. "And what did you see?"

"When I arrived, Ms. Tannin was breathing heavily and standing in front of Mr. Law's body spread out on the ground. Ms. Becky showed up moments later and we stared at the body until someone else arrived and called Dr. Firmin," Iacchus responded in a bored monotone.

"Same story for me, to save you any trouble," Becky added thoughtfully when she noticed the uncomfortable look on the detective's face. The detachment over the whole ordeal was still very present in Iacchus' voice. "He arrived first, I arrived after and we waited for an authority. Didn't touch anything and sure as hell wasn't planning to."

"Thank you." The detective wrote down the remainder of the statement. There was definitely less to work with than he had been hoping. At least with Mathers they had a crime scene, when it came to Law, the team still couldn't even pinpoint the location of the murder. There wasn't enough spatter in the closet for it to have happened there, which meant the body had been moved—seen by neither man, nor camera. Saxon flipped the top page of his notebook over to reveal a fresh sheet. "When was the last time any of you saw Mr. Law?"

Giles snorted before shoving his face into his hands. This was not what he signed up for when he promised his father he would take care of his precious project. Giles had enough baggage riding on those stupid androids all on his own—he didn't need murder to complicate everything like an unwanted houseguest. "Like I said, when I hired the man."

"We'd never met him before. The janitorial staff gave up cleaning the androids' rooms a long time ago." Becky shrugged before pointing to the brat sitting next to her. "And Iacchus doesn't interact with staff that aren't directly related to his program."

"I see." The detective looked to the now slightly calmer woman wringing her hands in her lap. It seemed the janitor would be his only source of information. "When was the last time you saw Mr. Law?"

"About a week ago," Susie said, fingers pulling at the sleeve of her blouse. "He had called on Friday night and said he caught a rather nasty strain of the flu. His doctor ordered him one week bed rest and so I'd believe him, Cecil even faxed me the doctor's note. I wasn't even expecting him back into work until tomorrow."

The detective nodded. According to the coroner, the body had been dead for nearly four days. That put the time of death *before* the murder of Steve Mathers. A body decomposing for that long *had* to smell horrific— it was one of the first things the witness realized was off. *How had no one noticed until now?* "One last question: when was the last time you went to that storage closet?"

"Last Friday when he called." She shrugged weakly, shoulders moving barely an inch. "To get a bottle of bleach. Again, it's for mass storage so we don't keep our regular supplies there. Just the extra bottles."

"So you go to that closet pretty regularly on a schedule? Once a week?" Lester stressed, leaning forward closer to the witness. He wanted to see her eyes as she answered.

"Yes," she replied slowly like someone talking to a small child. Susie leaned slightly back to replace some of her personal space. "Things around this building are fairly routine, so I use approximately the same amount of supplies each week."

"Who else knows this schedule?"

Susie stopped and stared at the detective. She always acquired the supplies herself to better keep track of their inventory and most of the janitorial staff knew that. "I'm not sure about the doctors and technicians, but everyone on my team would know."

"Thank you, that should be enough for now." Lester stood up. So many things to consider from emotionless androids to their equally unperturbed—stressed did not count—bosses. The fact this case might involve a serial killer wasn't exactly making his day any brighter, either. "I'll let you know how things progress and I assure you that we will find out who is responsible for these events."

Giles watched the detective leave and turned back to the two women, and android boy, in his office. He rubbed at his face harder than before in an attempt to snap himself out of this funk. The head of his cleaning staff was still pale and shaky and he had a feeling she wasn't going to get any work done any time soon. Let alone pick up any supplies from that side of the building ever again. "Ms. Tannin, go ahead and take the week off with pay. I think you could use the break."

Susie nodded before standing up. The first thing she was doing was changing out of this jumper. And then she was going to drive home and take a bath. A long one with bath salts. "Thank you, sir."

Becky and Iacchus found themselves alone with Giles after Susie had left the room. It was quiet save for the ticking of the analog clock on Giles' wall and the sound of Iacchus' fans humming. Becky smirked and looked over to her boss, who finally gave up and buried his head in his arms on the surface of his desk. Becky pulled her cigarette from her pocket and stuck it in her mouth. She left it off for the moment, speaking around the plastic as it hung at the edge of her mouth. "And me?"

Giles opened a drawer in the bottom of his desk without lifting his head and pulled out a couple of shot glasses and a half-full bottle of whiskey. He slowly shifted until his head was in the crook of his forearm and elbow before smirking at "Ms. Becky." "You, will be sharing a shot with me and then going back to work."

"Slave driver." Becky snorted and reached over a now rather quiet Iacchus fingering the end of his scarf for the offered glass. She had a feeling they were both going to need a whole lot more than two shots to get today's events out of their minds enough to go back to work.

"Can you believe it?" Marcus turned the volume down on the television, taking a seat on the edge of the crowded desk. The Talos Redress' headquarters was crammed on the second story of a "Professional" community high rise in the center of the city. To afford such a prime location, they gave up square feet and were reduced to a small open office. After they added in three or four desks, there was barely room for five or six of them to walk around. Two of the desks had to be shoved up against the wall to make room for seven people and their industrial copier.

The only perk to the crammed space was managing to snag a corner office, and being treated to two giant bay windows.

Jeremy's eyes were glued to the 22" flat screen sitting next to the hall door, attempting to hide from the glare of the corner windows. Their contact on the inside had gotten scared after the second killing and sent an anonymous package to the news covering the latest story in the building. He had then sent Jeremy an e-mail detailing which station would be covering the report, and the head of the organization was grateful. The androids were left out of the equation, but the deaths of those employees more than made up for it. Jeremy had hoped Firmin would get what was coming to him, but this wasn't quite what he was expecting. "It could be a coincidence."

Marcus pushed blonde hair back behind his ears and over his shoulder. It hung limply to just below his shoulder blade, flat and in need of a good brushing. Marcus had given up on his appearance long ago—no matter how good he cleaned up, he'd still look like a slob next to Jeremy. There was no competing with his superior's good looks, and strong figure, so Marcus gave up trying. "Hardly! A janitor and a lead programmer, *for the project we're trying to crush*, murdered? No way. We should totally take advantage of this, Jer."

Jeremy paused the television recording when the photos of the victims flashed up. One face in particular called out to him like a siren—Jeremy shivered reflexively. "Or we should lie low."

"What?" Marcus slammed the desk top with his hand rattling a cup full of pens. It wasn't like Jeremy to just back down! "Why!? They're under pressure! This is the time to make them crack and stop the child abuse, man! Clearly the loss of life is contagious!"

"Did you take a good look at the guy in the photo?"

"What? Yeah, computer geek." Marcus's tone dropped from 'righteous anger' to 'confusion.' Jeremy's blunt change of subject didn't make sense in a situation that should have impassioned him like the old days. Where was their boss who lit fire to a trashcan outside a police station? Marcus squinted at the man on the television: just another corporate pet. "What about him?"

Jeremy shoved the photo he got from their contact stationed at Firmin's lab in Marcus' face. The photo was about an inch from Marcus' nose causing him to go cross-eyed. Jeremy pulled it back and pointed at the older man hooking wires into the small child's back. "Look familiar?"

"Oh, dude." Marcus reached for the photo but Jeremy snatched it back and replaced it in his pocket. Marcus fell back, his rear smacking into the corner of the desk. "It's the same guy!"

"And *who* sent death threats recently?"

Marcus flinched, remembering the scolding he had gotten for sending those e-mails to Firmin without permission. "Oh."

"Right." Jeremy flicked the TV off and brushed his hair back. "We'll deal with Firmin after this dies down. That project of theirs is no where near close to market, yet. We've still got time to keep it from going mainstream."

Marcus snorted and scratched the bottom of his scalp, bracelets on his arm clinking together loudly. "Yeah, time. It still doesn't change the fact all we've got on him is a photograph."

"I'm sure our contact will give us more later when he's not freaking out. From what I understand, one of the dead was his friend, so the guy could probably use the break himself." Jeremy rubbed his eyes with his thumb and forefinger. He could tell himself that the break was a good thing, but Jeremy wanted nothing more than to march in there and remove the kids from Firmin's custody as soon as possible. However, legally he didn't have much sway. "Right now our priority is to avoid being arrested. It's hard to fight for the rights of these kids if we're in jail."

"It would make a statement." Marcus grinned, wheels in his brain turning. Their contact in the lab was probably tainted by the men there and all those confusing emotions. It would explain why their information stream had dwindled so much. "Could be good for our publicity."

"Yeah, 'crazy goes to jail' works so well." The older man tapped his pocket where the photograph sat safely next to his breast, a constant reminder of their goals. Marcus shifted from the desktop to his chair and started up the computer. He had that look on his face that spelled trouble. The last time Jeremy had seen it, Marcus had shut off the water valves at a theme park—while people were still riding. Jeremy did *not* want to bail him out again. "Marcus."

"Yeah, boss?"

"Don't do anything stupid."

"Me? Never." Marcus grinned and turned his back just enough so Jeremy couldn't see the blueprints' of Firmin's complex on his screen.

CHAPTER 9

ABEL WAS DISTRACTED.

Hecate set the chess board someone or another had stashed in their room up on the work table. Abel sat unfocused, tapping a pen up and down by the tip on the metal surface. Hecate figured this lull was brought on by the second murder. He then decided that now would be a good time to take advantage of this free time. His exact words went something along the lines of, "If you're not going to do your real work, you might as well play a game with me."

Abel found he couldn't argue with that logic, his mind full of the gruesome details Becky had described over the phone of that poor man who had poured out of the closet. It had been like listening to Rupert all over again, but without the sounds of a wife nagging in the background. Hecate was a welcome distraction. Abel tossed the pen in a cup, pushed the microchips and soldering equipment to the edge of the table, and let the boy set up the game board as he pleased.

"Would you like to be white or black, Dr. Moreau?" Hecate asked with a smile he had practiced in the mirror just this morning. After watching an old black and white movie staring a young blonde boy and his dog, Hecate had done his best to mimic the child's happy expression to look more human. It must have been somewhat effective because a small smile was now spreading to Abel's face as well. "I don't particularly mind either way, myself."

"White." Abel crossed his arms on the table. Part of him wasn't exactly looking forward to playing this game against Hecate. There was no question of who was going to win. The first time they had played, Hecate had won the game in four moves. Needless to say, Abel's pride had taken a blow, having been on the amateur chess team in college. He hadn't lost that quickly since his first game. "I like making the first move."

"Alright." Hecate turned the board he had set up so the white pieces lined up in front of Abel and the black pieces sat neatly in front of himself. Once he was satisfied with the angle of the board between them, Hecate gave his own smirk to the good doctor. "I've already changed my game settings to beginner so the game is more fair."

"I don't even rank medium, yet?" Abel answered before taking one of the pawns in the front line and moving it forward two spaces. Hecate was smiling innocently at him, but for once Abel could see the mischievous little glint in those glass eyes. Hecate had definitely picked up how to tease. On the bright side, coming from a little kid it was almost cute. Abel tapped a knight on its head. "How cruel."

"I'd like the game to last for at least twenty minutes, Dr. Moreau," Hecate replied smoothly and mirrored the doctor's move. Though, it would be worth it to see the doctor's face contort the same way it had the first time they played. "If that's alright."

"Fine by me," Abel replied and continued moving pieces. The two went on like this for about five minutes or so until the pieces were good and mixed up on the board. Both parties had taken at least one or two of the other's pieces, and the doctor was having fun even if Hecate was holding back to keep the game going longer. Abel needed to get Hecate interested in a few more chance based games. Maybe something that involved dice or randomly drawing cards...

The young android's hand twitched slightly on the desk. "Dr. Moreau."

"Hmm? What is it Hecate?" The doctor looked up from the board as his fingers clasped a knight's head.

"Your name," Hecate answered while studying Abel's face. The man had a wrinkle developing just under the corner of his eye and Hecate was reminded of his age. To be in ones' thirties wasn't horribly old for a human, but it was still quite a few years over Hecate's couple of months. And yet, Hecate could keep up with him both mentally and physically; the comparison was depressing. "I came across it the other day in a book."

"Let me guess," Abel pushed the knight forward and to the right. Hecate responded instantly by moving a pawn on a different section of the board and Abel frowned. He was hoping to give his brain more of a rest between turns. Trying to outthink a computer was taxing when Abel was in top form. If the kid was going to humor him, he could at least pretend to take his time thinking. "The *Island of Dr. Moreau* by H.G. Wells?"

"You've read it then?" Hecate asked. He supposed it made sense for the doctor to be familiar of works in which his name appeared, especially when they came from the title of such a famous book. "Did you like it?"

"It's a good book." It'd been a while since Abel had actually read the novel, but he remembered enjoying it. Mostly he was just amused to keep hearing the word 'doctor' in front of his name as a child, and remembered thinking how amazing it would be to put that same prefix in front of his own. The day he had become 'Dr. Moreau' for real had actually been a childhood dream come true. "About being careful with experiments and things that are different."

"Then it is fitting you are named after such a person, I assume?" Hecate wondered aloud before mirroring the doctor's pose. Hecate was two moves away from checkmate and would rather the game not end just yet. The boy remembered the moment in the book where the doctor had been unable to control his experiment and had died for it. Hecate couldn't help but notice the similarity between the beast men and the androids the staff here were trying to create. He knew Abel was safe from him and Iacchus, but what about future 'siblings'? The guarantee they would respect Hecate's wishes to keep Abel safe was not certain. It was something to consider. Hecate smiled coyly, betraying his inner thoughts. "Though I think you are much nicer."

"I should hope so." Abel reached over and ruffled the boy's hair with a hand. He took the care to smooth it back down right after, each hair back into place. "What brings this up, anyway?"

"Experiments and the control over such things." Hecate looked at the clock on the wall. Three o'clock post meridian. Time was ticking away like always and Hecate did not like it. "Iacchus is getting his decorative markings installed now, isn't he?"

"Yes he is." Abel drummed a finger on his arm. Hecate was probably more worried about his own 'surgery' than concerned for his brother. Abel found the boy's nervousness endearing. "Yours is tomorrow, I believe."

"Will you be there?"

"Hmm?"

"Will you be there, Dr. Moreau?" Hecate asked again, voice a decibel lower than normal. Abel was looking at him with a concerned face, so the boy continued with his request before the doctor could answer in the negative. "I would very much like you to be there."

"I can if you want me to be, but there's nothing to worry about," Abel replied as softly as he could. Hecate looked worried and Abel couldn't blame him. The kid would have to be awake for the procedure and that was probably a scary thought. Abel knew he certainly wouldn't enjoy surgery while awake. Thankfully, neither of the boys needed extensive repair work on the inside. All should go quickly and smoothly if all they were doing was cutting slits in the skin to install lights. Abel looked at the clock, Iacchus should be done within a couple hours.

"It's very simple, Hecate, almost like applying a decal to a car." Abel pushed the board game to the side. "From what I understand, they're going to disconnect your sensors, too, so you won't even feel it."

"I would still very much like you to be there." Hecate repeated, the *and hold my hand* was left unsaid. It was the proper thing for a loved one to do while another was in 'distress,' Hecate was sure. "Please."

Abel watched those blue eyes plead at him and realized he probably couldn't say no to them if he tried. The doctor wondered if Hecate knew just what a grip he had on Abel's conscious. "Of course, Hecate." Abel reached across the desk and put a hand over a pair of smaller ones. The boy smiled and the doctor gave the hands a pat. "I'll be there if you really want me to be."

"Thank you, Dr. Moreau. I am glad you are not like the doctor in the book." Tiny fingers wormed their way around large, warm ones and held tightly. "You're much better."

"What's got that stupid grin on your face this time, Abe?" Giles laughed as his friend entered the room smiling like a drunk. Abel arrived right on time for their daily drink and catch-up for the day. Usually it lasted an hour, them both sharing the woes of the day, but sometimes they'd go longer. From when the little hand of the clock hit five, until it traveled all the way around to the six—that was their time. "You're looking a little chipper, there."

"I should ask you the same," Abel said, fighting off the laugh by biting his lip. Giles was grinning, his head held high and browsing through a clothing catalog—he looked cheerful for a change. Giles had actually spun around on his seat to meet his friend. Abel's eyes snuck to the bottle on the desk, and seeing it full, was relieved his good cheer wasn't based on an early start. Abel dropped a stack of paperwork on one of Giles' guest sitting chairs. Abel would sort through it after the break. "You're in a good mood today, aren't you?"

"The board approved a second grant." Giles whistled before snatching a pen off his desk, tapped the tip on the surface of his calendar. "Cashed the check this morning, and I am happy to say we are in the clear for this year's budget." Feeling that explanation was more than adequate—Giles loved having a happy budget—he pursued his earlier question. "So spill, what's got the million-watt smile on Abel Moreau's face? Lucy finally admit she has a crush on you?"

"No." Abel snorted—it figured Giles' good mood was related to money. Abel collapsed on the couch against the wall. It was firm and stiff against his back, but it was better than the guest chair for lying down. Abel wondered where Giles had picked this antique piece of discomfort up as he shifted and squirmed trying to get into a comfortable position. "And that crush is harmless, anyway. I don't think she's serious."

"Maybe." Giles snuck out two glasses and slid one across the table. Abel made no move for it and remained draped across his couch. Giles poured a finger of his favorite Kentucky whiskey into each glass. "Well, if not a lady, then what?"

"Hecate just being cute." Abel smiled and scratched his head before working up the energy to reach up for the offered glass. Abel swished the amber liquid around the edge of the glass. "You know he asked me to come with him to his update tomorrow?"

"Oh?" Giles rolled his shoulder back into the buttery, leather chair. He justified the luxury by paying out of pocket instead of the overhead budget. *Worth every penny.* Giles sunk back as far as he could go into the cushion. Those stupid external modifications just kept coming back to ruin his good news. *The board giveth and taketh away,* Giles figured. He looked over at Abel, still smiling as he sipped his drink, and downed his own. Giles was hoping to put this conversation off until tomorrow, but it was unlikely he'd avoid it now. Giles poured himself a double. "About that..."

"Giles." Abel sat up straight instantly on guard, swinging his feet back to the floor. Giles was staring at a point on the wall and had the glass edge resting on his lip. He looked guilty. Abel's hand clenched around the glass in his hand, spilling a bit of the whiskey on his pants' leg. "Did something happen to Iacchus?"

"Huh? Oh, no." Giles chuckled nervously and sipped his drink. "Kid's fine. The modifications were a success, and there were no major complications. So nothing to really worry about." The kid locking himself in his room instead of killing someone could definitely be counted as a success, to Giles. "It just…wasn't what he was expecting."

"His design didn't work?" Abel presumed, rubbing at the small stain on his pants. He licked his thumb and tried to rub the liquid away, but it didn't work too well. Giles was still avoiding eye contact, not speaking up. "Is that it? Did he not have enough lights to work with or something?"

"You could put it that way." Giles spun his finger around the top edge of his glass. *Might as well get it out of the way—by putting it off another day.* Giles put both hands flat on the table, and tried to look innocent. "Look, we're probably going to fight about this tomorrow as it is, Abel. Can we maybe talk about something *other* than your little brats? I think that Lucy discussion still holds pretty valid."

Abel covered his eyes with his hand and sat the drink back down on the desk. He wasn't in the mood anymore. Bringing up the boys around Giles almost never ended in pleasant conversation. Abel hadn't quite put his finger on the *why*, but Giles tended to be uncomfortable around them. Abel could almost understand Iacchus with his mood swings—Giles didn't appreciate spontaneity, and Iacchus was made of it. It was why Giles got so nervous around Hecate that picked at Abel's brain. Hecate was well behaved and smart as a whip—there was no reason he and Giles shouldn't have connected on some level. It just didn't make sense why the two most important people in his life didn't get along. Abel sighed, slinking down in his seat as he smiled wistfully at Giles. "They're not brats, Giles."

"They are!" Giles snapped back, too quickly. He exhaled slowly, calming himself. Giles should just declare his office a 'no androids' zone, unless they were talking numbers. Conversations would go so much nicer, especially since Giles just couldn't help himself. "They're spoiled rotten and despite our 'punishments,' we let them get away with a hell of a lot."

"They?" Abel asked. He pouted, and threw an arm over the edge of the armrest. "Last I checked Hecate was rather well behaved."

"Around *you* maybe." Giles tipped the shot glass on its side and watched the liquid shift. Pink was Giles' favorite color, but Abel's rose-tinted glasses were finally getting on his last nerve. "You should listen to the water cooler conversations some day. Your darling little Hecate creeps out half the staff. He's smart-mouthed, foul tempered, and is passive-aggressive as hell."

"That's ridiculous. He's just mature for his age and body type. It's not Hecate's fault they don't know how to deal with a ten year old on the same intellectual level as them." Abel justified. Surely if Hecate's behavior was that bad someone would *tell* him…right? No—Abel knew better. Hecate was just misunderstood, that was all. "He's a good kid, Giles."

Giles snorted into his empty glass. "Just remember he shouldn't always get what he wants."

"Oh? And what's that supposed to mean?"

"It'll make it easier in the long run tomorrow if you remember, that's all I'm saying." Giles poured another glass. They needed a subject change. "How's that side project of yours going?"

"Oh. I haven't really started working on it again, but I did find some old notes." Abel knew an 'out' when he saw one. He'd let Giles off the hook today, but only because he knew they'd be at it again tomorrow. "I think I should get it to speed up by about ten percent the next time around."

"Go on." Giles swirled the scotch around in his glass. He decided he'd enjoy what little of his good mood was left while he still good. Giles just knew that tomorrow was going to get ugly.

Seven o'clock at night and Rupert was still in his damn office. He didn't normally make a habit of being behind on his paperwork, but between Steve and that Cecil guy and the androids' little cosmetic jobs—not to mention everything else piling up around this place—there just wasn't time for it. It didn't help that Marvin was being even more of a pain than usual. Rupert cracked his spine with a grunt. It was never easy working for a guy a good twenty years younger than yourself, and yet still managed to be more productive. At least Rupert could keep the overhead lights off by virtue of being the only one in the office. It was much nicer with the room cool, dark, and lit only by the LCD monitor before him—those darn fluorescents always gave him a headache.

All Rupert needed to do now before he could go home was check one thing on a forum for the latest artificial intelligence research, keep an eye on the competition as they say, and he'd be done for the day. If not for the pornography pop-up that plastered across his screen, he would be finishing up his research right now. Rupert cursed appropriately as he tried to close the darn thing off his window. If he wanted to see a man and a woman doing that with a mouse he'd rent a DVD. "Stupid science forums aren't even safe any more from these blasted things."

"What are those two people doing?"

"Jesus!" Rupert exclaimed as he leapt from his computer desk and whirled around. He got an eyeful of something with glowing blue lines and markings that looked straight from one of those aliens-take-over movies. Rupert reasonably cursed again at the unfamiliar sight, felt his heart start racing, and ended the reaction with another jerk into the desk. The equipment rattled hard enough to knock the poor mouse straight off. The sounds of supposed ecstasy continued to moan out of his computer speakers to settle overtop the sound of computer fans whirling.

"Are you alright, Mr. Dixen?"

Rupert recognized the voice now that his heart wasn't pounding a mile a minute. Still clutching his chest, Rupert managed to adjust his reading glasses so he could see again. As his eyes focused and the glow seemed more toned down now that he wasn't a panicked mess, Rupert let out a sigh of relief. "Ia-kid? Oh good grief, boy, you can't sneak up on people like that in the middle of the dark—" Rupert cut himself short and looked at the boy again, this time a hand reaching out and gently touching a cheek. "Child, what happened to your face?"

Iacchus didn't move when Rupert's fingers traced down the new glowing lines in plain view to the world. Instead, his eyes were fixed on the computer screen and the two humans crawling over each other. It was very odd, whatever they were doing. It was like weird hugging... Iacchus' answer was absent as he continued watching. "They changed my design."

Rupert dropped his hand and took a good look at Iacchus. For the most part, and what he could see glowing under the white scrubs, the design looked the same. The biggest difference was the face. Instead of the two neatly hidden chevrons under his bangs, Iacchus now had two vertical blue lines stretching from the top of his forehead, crossing through the center of his now very-much-so blue glowing eyes, to all the way under his chin ending somewhere beneath his shirt collar. Rupert pulled the boy's scrubs down and confirmed the lines connected to the chest chevrons. "Why would they do that? Ms. Becky approved your plan, didn't she?"

"You know how I can get upset?" Iacchus questioned while trying to discreetly look over Mr. Dixen's shoulder to the computer monitor. The two humans were making new odd sounds now and the lady's voice was hitched. "They decided it might be best if I was running system checks during the modifications so I wouldn't be aware of what was going on." Iacchus paused and pulled up his hands to look at the new markings down the sides of his arms. He could see each individual LED beneath the blue coating, but he knew to everyone else it looked like one solid glow. "While I was out, the technician was told to make the facial markings more noticeable."

"Who told him to do that?" Rupert asked. As far as he knew, the boys were promised they had control over what exactly they ended up looking like. It's not like Iacchus or Hecate would ever end up in the market— they were prototypes for goodness sake! "That doesn't make sense."

"I know. Ms. Becky was angry about it." Iacchus smiled a bit, happy for that bit of defense on his part. The boy knew she was mostly angry that her authority had been circumvented, but regardless, she had for a few moments been on Iacchus' side. And she was beautiful when she was mad. "She threw a vase at his head."

"Now that I believe." Rupert laughed and took another long look at the boy. The markings weren't as horrible as he had first thought, just very visible. The eyes were far more disturbing, anyway. Not only were they now the same blue as the lines, they had an extra few circles surrounding the pupils in white rings. It was creepy, Rupert decided and suddenly questioned someone's decision making. Rupert figured no one had bothered to tell Iacchus how to switch them off, either, since everything on him was still lit up like a Christmas tree.

"What are those two doing on your computer?" Iacchus asked again. Maybe now that the mistakes to his appearance had been addressed, Mr. Dixen would answer his question. Iacchus pointed to the woman on the screen and tilted his head. "It looks painful but the lady is smiling."

Rupert looked back down at the forgotten computer and quickly yanked the mouse up by the cord to shut the window out with a curse. *The reason you've never seen a movie with a rating higher than PG and aren't allowed on the internet. That's all.* "Nothing, kid. That was nothing important."

"It didn't look like nothing." Iacchus pouted and could feel his face forming a scrunched frown. Those two people on the screen had been doing something Iacchus had never seen before and he wanted to know what it was. *Right now.* Mr. Dixen was red-faced, desperately trying to change the subject. Iacchus should know what it was to keep from embarrassing himself the same way. Iacchus slammed his hand on the desk, rattling the equipment. This time a cup of pens fell off the side, spilling its contents over the tiles. "Tell me."

Rupert, personally, had no intentions ever of giving an android teenager the talk about the birds and the bees (and apparently mice). He had even dodged this conversation with his own kids, thanks to Mary being a saint. He especially had not planned for this on a day where a scheduled procedure had gone wrong, the lab was closed, and he was alone with a kid who's hormonal problems couldn't be fixed with a few drugs or a good grounding. When Iacchus' eyes glowed a brighter blue, rings around his eyes spinning ever so slightly as they focused, Rupert could see the temper tantrum coming from a mile away. He and the kid were alone. And there was a metal chair well within reach. *Wonderful.*

Rupert held his hands up defensively while the boys shoulders tightened up. He didn't think Iacchus would hurt him too badly on purpose, but thinking straight wasn't something Iacchus did well when throwing a fit. In fact, Rupert was pretty sure the kid tended forget the difference in strength between him and the rest of the human population on a daily basis. There seemed to be only one option to make this go away, and Rupert wondered if he shouldn't just let the kid kill him. Ms. Becky was certainly going to strangle him when she found out Rupert had explained sex to Iacchus. "Okay, okay. You win, Ia-kid. But you gotta' *swear* you won't tell a soul I'm telling you this or what you saw. Deal?"

Iacchus relaxed almost instantly and nodded happily. It was so nice when people cooperated.

Abel growled as he looked over the letter of approval and photo documentation of Iacchus' new look—it certainly explained Giles' guilt yesterday. Abel would have liked to see it in person, but Iacchus was still being rather shy around everyone due to the changes. Rupert had said he was out last night though, so he'd probably be out of his room soon. Abel considered that a good thing, but it still didn't change the fact this was completely unacceptable.

The powers that be, revealed to be the board of directors, unbeknownst to the boys or staff, had been e-mailed a copy of the new markings. The sender had used a generic company e-mail, and didn't sign the bottom. Giles had been ticked, but could only trace it back to a general lab computer—Jenner had checked the security video, but the employee had been wearing a hoodie. The head hunt for the guy would have to wait until later, though, since the board was so grateful for the tip-off. They called Giles and said they would only approve the designs on the condition that the facial markings were more prominent. More importantly, they wanted the two boys to *match*.

Hecate had been furious. His reaction to the news was the closest Abel has ever seen Hecate to throwing one of Iacchus' famed fits, his entire frame shaking with the restraint required to hold in the outburst.

"I do not want the same markings as my brother," Hecate repeated as he held Abel's hand in the workshop. He knew his face was twisted into an ugly scowl, Hecate was sure, but this was absolutely not acceptable. Hecate too had picked out facial markings hidden beneath the bangs for the same reason as his brother. If that must be rejected, he certainly was *not* going to match like twins dressed in the same outfit to be *cute*. "I can accept that the markings must be visible, but I will not be forced to coordinate with the same styling Iacchus is now wearing."

Abel winced when the grip on his hand tightened. Hecate angry was something the doctor wasn't quite sure how to deal with. Where Iacchus was external with screams and violence, Hecate seemed to keep it all inside, between the disk storage and the memory. You could practically hear his systems and fans overheating themselves. The smoldering gaze behind his eyes burned brightly, matching the scowl on his face. Abel hoped calming words would work as well on passive-aggressive behavior as it...well, it never worked with Iacchus, so that was saying something. "Hecate, calm down. We'll work it out with the nice technician."

"There's nothing to work out." Ben tapped an led strip against his wrist. He didn't get paid enough for this. Cosmetics was the bottom rung of the engineering side. They made fake skin and flesh—molded it to look pretty. That was it! Now the company seemed determined to make his life miserable. First, a psycho lady from the research team throws a vase at his head, and now he had a spoiled little kid telling him what to do. At least the other android brat had been quiet about the whole affair. Didn't they understand he just followed orders? "The board wants the two androids to have the same sets of markings. He can change the color, but that's it. End of story."

"That's not what was agreed to," Abel argued and threw his free hand into the air. Iacchus had already been let down, after all that hard work he put into getting the drawings right, and Abel wasn't about to let that happen to Hecate, too. Especially since Hecate's individuality was so important to him. It was by far the only reason Abel could fathom for being this upset over matching his brother. "These boys were given our word they had some control over this. You wanted machines capable of making their own decisions, now they should be allowed to do so!"

"Dude, you're not getting it. It's not even *my* decision!" The technician pleaded, now holding his hands up in surrender. What was this? Angry parent week? "Really, there's nothing I can do about it."

"Give me your phone, then. I'm calling Giles," Abel demanded and slammed his palm down on the table. Giles would listen. He had already promised they'd be arguing about this today so he should be up for it. Abel was sure yesterday's conversation was just a plea for a push in the right direction for the right decision. If anyone could sort this mess out it would be the two of them together. Giles usually came through when it mattered, and Abel couldn't think of anything that mattered more right now. "He'll straighten this out."

"There's nothing to straighten out, Abel," Becky called from the doorway, voice defeated. Giles had already been accosted this morning by the police and the board. The families of the two victims had finally gotten past the grieving stage and into the anger and blaming. Becky hated to admit it, but Giles had his hands full trying to make that go away without making anyone angry. He didn't need to come down here and be yelled at by his best friend on top of all that. Once again taking the role of the villain, Becky walked into the room, hand in her lab coat pocket. "I already talked to him about it. The board laid down the law and this is going to happen."

"But what about...?" Abel trailed off and ran a hand through his hair.

Becky's face was straight, but there were lines under her eyes. She had fought best she could to keep her meal ticket happy, but unfortunately she was out-voted. That her design approval had been overruled was that final kick in the pants, reminding her just how little authority she actually had. Becky pulled at her hair unsure of what to tell Abel.

"I just don't understand," Abel answered weakly.

"They want something uniform, that's all." Becky wrapped her fingers around a loose cigarette in her pocket. She rolled it around for a moment before pulling her hands from her lab coat. The woman crossed her arms over her chest and shrugged. "All it comes down to is they liked Iacchus' design more than Hecate's."

"Dr. Moreau," Hecate interjected voice tight and clipped, livid at the situation. "Are you saying I have no choice in the matter? Was I lied to?"

"I'm sorry, Hecate," Abel said, feeling rather defeated himself. Hecate's accusation had hit him like a slap. "I'm not sure what else to tell you."

"This—but you promised!" Hecate's voice was slowly devolving into a childish whine, but he could not help it. Why wasn't Abel standing up for him more? Why was the man not angry? Yelling? Hecate was seeing a repeat of when Abel refused to tell him what was in the box and he *did not like it*. Hecate grabbed Abel's coat and tugged. "You did! You promised that it would all be okay—"

"Shut up!" Becky snapped before the brat could continue. If he kept this up, she didn't know how Abel was going to handle it. Abel already looked lost, his hands in the air not knowing what to do with the kid hanging off his coat. Hecate disliking the older man would shatter him. Becky had no intention of letting him go into another funk like after Steve's death. So, she laid down the final word once and for all. "It's not Abel's fault, and you need to keep quiet. The people who paid the money so that you could even exist have made a decision, and that's final. Human beings have to do things they don't want and they don't like all the time! *You're* certainly no exception."

Hecate shut his mouth, glared with as much hostile force as he could muster at the woman, and traded Abel's coat for his hand. Hecate squeezed, cutting off the circulation by this point, but he didn't care. This 'board' was going to regret this decision. Hecate was sure of that. "Fine. I will permit the changes at this time." Hecate turned to the now sweating technician who had nearly curled in on himself during the vocal scuffle. "I'm still allowed to chose the color, correct?"

"Uh," Ben looked at the two other adults in the room aside from his staff who were both frowning in a disappointed fashion at him. They looked ready to make the leap from depression to anger and tear out his throat at the first provocation. "Yeah. Sure. Any color you want."

Hecate smiled before answering. "Apple red, please."

CHAPTER 10

THOUSANDS OF TINY lights blinked on and off, in color coordinated rhythms. A red light for processing, and a green flash afterwards indicating a correct answer. A large communication rack the end of the row, contained the master monitoring devices. Four or five computers dedicated to distributing tests and recording the answers. As each light flashed, a new line appeared on the flatscreen monitor that sat on the wall, connected to the rack. It was an efficient system, and the lights were hypnotic in their steady pattern.

Hecate was staring at The Wall again.

He could see his reflection in the glass window and tilted his head up. The red lines made it look like he was bleeding from the eyes. Hecate was aware that he now unnerved the other half the staff that wasn't already wary. Abel didn't seem to mind though, and that was all that mattered. The only saving grace, the boy had noted, was he had been allowed to keep his eye color the same shade of sky blue it had been before, only now the LED lights behind were red.

Unlike his brother, Hecate had figured out in an hour how to turn the strips on and off at will.

Abel had suggested Hecate give Iacchus a hand figuring it out, and Hecate had agreed with an adorable "Of course, Dr. Moreau." Abel took the lie at face value and now believed Iacchus to be merely fond of the lights in the 'on' position. Iacchus would figure it out eventually on his own. Hecate had more important things to deal with than his brother's stupidity. Helping him was a waste of time; there was no value or return in the action.

Hecate turned his head when he heard a second set of footsteps approaching and pulled himself up on the ledge of the window to brace his legs against the wall like he had done so many a time. Hecate needed to remember to keep his visits at night to stop being caught here. He turned his head when the clicking of heels stopped next to him, but at the lack of a scolding, he realized he was probably safe. "Hello, Ms. Lucy. How are you doing today?"

"Hello, Hecate." The programmer smiled as she walked up closer to the window. She crossed her arms under her breasts and fingered the thin cardigan she was wearing. It was always so cold down in this wing of the building. Lucy didn't understand it—it was only supposed to be cold in the room that the computers were in, not everywhere else! She smiled at the sweater Hecate was still wearing. It made her happy to know he wore it every single day even if it was a bit of a disaster. Light green with a one-third strip of darker green at the top was hardly her best work, but it worked on the boy. "How are you doing today?"

"I'm well." Hecate looked the woman over. He didn't see Lucy often, since she tended to sequester herself away in the corner of the programming office, but she was nice enough when he met with her. She was shy and quiet, which made her a step above the rest of the women Hecate had the 'pleasure' of seeing during the day. "Iacchus likes his scarf."

"Oh does he?" Lucy smiled brightly. "I'm glad. The boy needed a little color."

"He did, but now I think he has more than he wants." Hecate smirked and traced one of the dull red lines down his face. At least the red matched with the green of his sweater. "The blue clashes with his scarf now."

"Ah, yes. The new lights." Lucy nodded. She had seen Iacchus' new eyes and markings as well. People had started to avoid the poor boy even more than before. Lucy was surprised by that—blue was a much more harmless color than what Hecate had chosen. Lucy shivered a bit looking at it again. She knew the point was to make them less human, but she didn't think they quite accomplished what they wanted. Hecate had picked a horribly disquieting color. "Hecate, what…made you pick red?"

"I was feeling petty, I believe the term is." Hecate watched the little blinking lights on the wall beyond the glass and zoomed in on a few. The light flickers were becoming erratic. That was not a good sign. "Red is an intimidating color that causes discomfort. I felt it would anger the board enough to annoy them but not so much that they would feel the need to consider the pros and cons of risking their investment."

"Ah," Lucy turned back to the computers in front of them. Pettiness, pride. As someone who had helped write the boys' program, Lucy was unsure how those emotions got in there. It certainly wasn't something she had written in. This free developing thought was far more frightening than glowing red eyes in the dark. Or a flash of a different color from the side of her periphery. Lucy jerked her head to the glass again and felt a hand cover her mouth. "Oh, look at that!"

Hecate turned his head immediately to Lucy's face looking intently at a set of computers in the far right. She had noticed the light pattern shift. The need to distract her suddenly became very evident and his voice let out a near strangled "Ms. Lucy!"

The woman had already forgotten Hecate as she headed towards the door to the clean room. She had never seen that light in person before, only seeing the last two via the monitoring system at the programming lab, but there wasn't a single programmer on staff who didn't know what it meant. Two computers in the far right, Level C—Row 10, both had an orange light flickering in between the constant and familiar red and green. Two more computers had passed. Fast as she possibly was able, Lucy yanked the phone off the wall in the room and dialed the transfer department immediately, hoping to beat the boys in programming to the announcement.

Hecate followed Lucy into the room as she chatted with Mr. Green on the other end of the phone, probably prepping new bodies for the transfer as quickly as possible. The younger boy honestly couldn't care what she was on about in her excitement. Hecate was too busy staring at the wall and the offending rows. How dare they awaken now? The young android knelt down on his knees and glared harshly at the orange light signaling the test had been passed and his optics flickered to red without his knowing. Hecate reached a hand forward fully intending—

"Hecate!" Lucy squealed as she swooped down, pulling the young boy into a hug. Two computers passing at the same time side-by-side was even more of an unheard of phenomenon than the other two boys waking up. And without an outside catalyst! Even better, Marvin sounded more pleased than Lucy. Apparently they already had a set in waiting that was perfect for this occasion. She hugged Hecate closer, enjoying the feel of the soft wool of his sweater. "Isn't this exciting? We're going to have twins!"

"Yes, very much so." Hecate frowned and clenched his fists just out of Lucy's sight. The boy wasn't quite sure he was ready for more brothers. Iacchus was enough. "It'll be a delight to meet them, I'm sure."

Iacchus knew he was skirting termination by sidling up so close to Ms. Becky, no matter how much he enjoyed the feel of her against him, but right now he did not want to be standing near Hecate. His little brother was furious. Outwardly, the smaller android was smiling happily and had his hand buried into Dr. Moreau's lab coat, but there were some things Iacchus just *knew* when it came to Hecate. And right now, Hecate was beside himself with anger, and it had Iacchus completely on edge. Iacchus had no desire to see what would happen if Hecate lost his nerve.

Becky nearly shoved the android boy off her arm the moment he positioned himself there, but she was too busy staring. Herself, Abel and the two androids had been invited to Marvin's office for the unveiling of the two latest additions to their little AI family. With the board's visit coming up in the next week or so, their awakening couldn't be more perfectly timed. Giles had a camera in hand to give their benefactors a sneak peak of the goods. Becky didn't really blame him, even as her fingers dug into her arms tighter the longer she looked at them. These two were more, well, aesthetically pleasing than the two brats she already put up with.

Lucy hadn't been exaggerating when she was running around gushing about the new twins and how cute they were.

The shells for the two newest units were a set of twin girls about sixteen in age—Becky would have put their bust lines at eighteen or twenty. They both had matching black hair that fell to their waists, and bright emerald green eyes. The girls sported the same LED stripe pattern as Iacchus and Hecate, lit in green to match their irises. Becky thought they would look right at home in the Emerald City—and that wasn't a compliment. Becky sneered at the matching (low-cut) blue sundresses, and their petite sandals showing off remarkably realistic toes. The nails were painted a pale pink. Someone (*Marvin*) had had a bit too much fun playing dress-up with these two little dolls. The cherry red lipstick, dark rouge, and thick mascara was a step too far though, if you asked Becky.

And Abel needed to stop staring at them like they were a piece of cheesecake covered in globs of cherry filling, or she was going to *break his face*.

"Wow, that's definitely not something I was expecting when we were called down here with the boys." Abel swallowed as he looked over the two new girls, Melinoe and her 'sister' Macaria. The doctor wondered whose idea it was to exaggerate their proportions to be "pin-up" perfect. Abel was quite glad neither Hecate or Iacchus had hormones, or he could foresee problems. So far both girls had stood as silent as statues while they were introduced by the excited department head. Apparently Marvin had made them specifically for the purpose of two units going online at the same time. It was a one in a million shot, but the excited man never seemed to be deterred in his hopes.

"And you told me it wouldn't happen! Well, look at them now, right?" Marvin gushed. His two girls were perfection from head to toe in every way, shape, and form. They had the perfect body proportions, the perfect face shapes, perfect lips, perfect eyes and beautiful voices. Their look was completed by make-up, hair and outfits applied by Marvin alone to bring out the best of all their features. They were a true fantasy come true only to be approved—here he quoted Giles—'If two units go online at the same time you can use the damn bimbos, but until then get back to the practical models!' Marvin had taken great joy in rubbing it in Giles' face when Lucy made the call about the two newest AI successes. Who cared if they still had no clue how it happened? "And plus, now the numbers are a little equal. Two girls for two boys."

Abel nodded at the two girls who continued to stare at him blankly. For programs that were supposed to have passed the artificial intelligence exam, they didn't seem very aware of the world. "Can you two speak yet? Or are you still learning?" It could be seen as an insulting question, but it took Hecate about three days before he started to talk. Iacchus, on the other hand, had spoken on his first day. So to date, they really had no standard for this sort of thing.

"We can—" The twin on the right began.

"—talk." The twin on the left finished.

Becky didn't hold back the grimace. If that dulled monotone of a voice wasn't straight out of a horror novel, then she was taking Iacchus to a prom. Becky admitted there was a somewhat pleasant lift to the soprano voices, but the complete lack of emotion behind them ruined it. How could Marvin find that attractive? She turned to said creator who still looked like he snatched the last piece of pie from a bakery. "Are they linked together? Or do they just like to finish each others' sentences?"

"They have an internal link." Marvin walked around and lifted up Melinoe's hair to point at a small circle behind her ear. It was red, with a tiny light blinking in the center. Marvin made it as small as possible to avoid messing with the girls' appearance while still maintaining functionality. Marvin had outfitted all of his models with them—it had taken him months, but he'd finally got his units on the list ahead of the previously manufactured shells in the same production line as Hecate and Iacchus. "It allows them to communicate without bothering guests in the room." Marvin smirked at the two boys. "Unlike those prototypes, these two girls have had most of the bugs and flaws worked out. In fact, I'd say they're as perfect as they're going to get."

"Physically, anyway." Becky snorted and pointed a finger toward one of the sisters. "But what about what's going on in their heads? We've only heard three words from them, and they've only been up and walking for a day. Who knows what malfunctions they'll both have." Becky waved her hand in the air and almost hit Abel in the face. He ducked, the only casualties a few misplaced hairs. "And I still have no idea why you thought it was a good idea to make them twins. Who, unlike real ones, are *completely* identical."

"And completely aesthetically pleasing." Marvin shrugged. "As for your complaints, so far, none of the things you're scared of have happened. No upsets, no breakdowns and no overloading the computer when running their systems check." Marvin glared in Iacchus' direction. He still wouldn't forgive that boy for freaking out and hurting his baby. That malfunctioning android sent a charge back through the linked wires and blew the entire, carefully crafted, custom system during a back-check of his associate's work. Marvin was thankful it wasn't *his* name slapped on the body shell. "They've been perfectly behaved angels."

"So far," Abel said to himself as he snuck a glance at Iacchus, for once in agreement with Becky. As much as he loved the two boys, there was no denying that they both had unique issues of their own. Marvin's units were unlikely to be any different—the behavior was in the programming, not the hardware. Abel looked the girls over again and wondered if there was any way to tell if they were using their internal link or not. For all they knew, the girls were chatting away in the privacy of their heads planning or learning outside of their care. It was just a matter of time before it all came out and caught them off guard. "Do you know who will be taking care of them?"

Marvin huffed. He had already petitioned to take care of the girls himself (and oh would he), but Giles rejected it immediately. Something about a conflict of interest and not wanting the models to come to any harm. Like he would hurt his darlings. Marvin played with Macaria's hair and leant slightly on Melinoe's smooth back. Thankfully, he could still look over them the rest of the time, much the same way Abel was granted semi-custody over that Hecate boy. "I believe they're going to Lucy."

"That's good to hear," Hecate spoke up from the side, catching everyone's attention. He wasn't sure why they were surprised to hear him speak. Hecate was more than capable of forming his own opinions. It's why they were studying him, for goodness' sake. Hecate continued to watch Mr. Green paw at the girls like a lecher. It was disgusting. "Ms. Lucy is a very responsible woman."

"Yes, she's quite nice." Marvin nodded slowly, slightly wary of the younger boy. This is why he made his girls look older. Marvin had no clue how Abel managed that boy and his weird signs of affection day in and day out. But he was a tad envious—if only his Melinoe and Macaria would cling to him like that and climb in his lap—Marvin clapped his hands together before those thoughts could carry on. He had an audience to keep entertained before he could excuse himself. "But enough of that—"

"Exactly," Giles interrupted knowing very well the look in Marvin's eyes. He had made the mistake one day of letting him go on about the importance of beauty and behavior, and was horrified when it started to devolve into a conversation about sex and how androids were superior to human interaction due to the selfish nature of humans and the giving of sex or...something. Giles flicked the switch on the top of the camera. There was something very wrong with that man.

"Enough of that. Move out of the way, Marvin, so I can get a better shot of them. The board requested a briefing on all the active models before they arrive, and pictures speak louder than words." Giles watched Marvin twist his face downward before shuffling out of the camera's line of sight. Giles centered the two girls in the frame and clicked the picture. They were naturals before the camera, their body types and personality perfect for that of a model. He was sure this could go either very well or very poorly depending on the circumstances.

On the one hand, they were gorgeous, easy on the eyes and, if their programming stayed this obedient, the fantasy of most men. On the other, there were some rather sexist implications that would probably not receive such good press. If he wanted to spin this in his favor, he'd have to even the play a little between the 'genders.' Hecate was too young to be in that equation so that just left…Iacchus. Giles shifted his gaze to take a closer look at the older boy. He was the same age as the girls, and he was far from ugly, despite Becky's complaints. Maybe they should put some effort into cleaning him up as well to keep things even. "Abel."

"Yeah, Giles?"

"Do me a favor, would you?" Giles pressed the 'play' button on his camera to flip through and double check that he had the photos he needed. He licked his lips noticing that in every photo one twin was staring directly at the lens, while the other kept her eyes on Marvin. *Odd.* Giles waved his hand in a circular motion as he started giving orders. "Pick up Iacchus some business casual clothes sometime before next week. Nice button shirt, khakis, and maybe a tie. Something comfortable, but still stylish. Pink or purple, light happy colors if you can."

Abel saw Iacchus' face light up from Becky's other side and smiled a bit himself. It was about time the boy got some decent clothing. "To dress up for the board, I take it?"

"Exactly." Giles slapped his friend on the back, and flipped through the camera photos one last time. The girls were so photogenic it hurt; Giles supposed Marvin could be right once in awhile. "This is why I keep you around, Abe."

Abel felt his lab coat stretch slightly and looked down to see a fist tightening. Afraid of playing favorites, Abel asked quickly, "What about Hecate? Should I pick something up for him as well?"

"No, he's alright." Giles looked down. The red stripes on his face were glowing lightly and the man shivered. Whoever approved of that damn blood red was getting a pay cut. Giles bit his lip and wondered if he shouldn't just hide Hecate from the board with such an intimidating look so easily summoned. "No one's expecting much from a twelve year old. Besides, the sweater's cute on him."

"Oh, alright." Abel nodded in agreement. Maybe he'd pick up some sort of an accessory for Hecate as a surprise. Abel knew that Hecate liked trinkets and the like—maybe a pen, or a watch. Abel dug his hand in

Hecate's hair reflexively. "I can do that."

"Wonderful." Giles clicked the camera off and replaced it in its case. He turned back to the engineer whose talents made such realism in a robotic form possible, and nearly gagged when he saw the man yet again stroking one of the girls' arms. Hecate aside, he knew for a fact Marvin wouldn't be allowed within two miles of the board, even if he had to ship him out of the building for the day. Giles wondered if Jenner had someone who could play body guard on short notice. "Marvin, make sure the girls are prepped on good behavior. Becky, keep Iacchus happy for the board, and Abel, don't forget the clothing."

Hecate watched as their supposed boss exited the room and turned back to the new twins, who were now distracted by their self-proclaimed 'creator.' He could also hear Iacchus pestering Abel for the type of clothes he wanted. Something about matching his scarf that Lucy made for him. That was well enough for now, but Hecate made sure to keep track of this situation. He didn't take well to being ignored.

It was a couple hours before curfew, and work was done for the day, so Abel felt content to relax in the back of his office for a few hours before heading home. He stretched out on his bed, back propped up by the pillow and ankles crossed at the far end. Hecate sat next to him, reading a book of his own quietly—the humming of his machinery equally soothing. A book was open Abel's his lap, too, and he enjoyed this time to unwind for all it was worth.

Lucy and Marvin were keeping the twins busy, and it was pretty fun watching Lucy blush as Marvin continued to make himself an unwanted guest in her office. It seemed Giles' plans to separate the man from the twins was failing spectacularly. Becky wanted nothing to do with them, and as a result was spending most of her time *willingly* with Iacchus. She called him the lesser of two evils—Abel couldn't recall the last time Iacchus had been so happy.

"Dr. Moreau?" Hecate asked, kneeling next to the man's cot. Abel was thinking instead of reading, given away by the lack of page turns. Hecate's fingers held tight to his own book, relishing the moment. Reading together during work hours didn't happen often, but Hecate figured he was being spoiled for the special treatment everyone else was receiving from the upcoming board visit. The doctor never indulged these habits during the morning hours when he wasn't working, so this had to be an intentional treat. Abel looked down at Hecate with a kind smile, and nodded for the boy to continue. "May I ask you a favor?"

"What, Hecate?" Abel slipped a bookmark into his novel before setting it down on the night stand. Giles had lent him the book about a father trying to raise a little girl he'd inherited from a family member as a joke —the father was bumbling and new and the daughter precocious. Abel was rather enjoying it, when he could actually concentrate on it, and Giles still pouted at the failed jab. "Did you need something?"

"Well, I don't really *need* it..." Hecate began, head tilted down and shoulders scrunched in. He tried to look meek, humble—all those wonderful expressions that garnered sympathy. "But I would *like* it."

Abel scooted to the edge of his cot to sit up straight and put his feet on the floor. His knees landed next to Hecate's head. The boy shifted and crossed his arms on the edge of the cot, book on collegiate level physics hanging loosely in his fingers. "Why don't you tell me what it is, and I'll see what I can do?"

"I want the same communication system as the twins." Hecate pointed to the spot behind his ear, hidden by his hair, where the device would be inserted. "My model is old enough without missing out on upgrades that can be easily installed."

"I don't know, Hecate," Abel said, crossing his arms. "I don't think Giles would go for that. He's been a little tight with the budget lately and after all the money spent on the lighting systems I don't think he'd be up for something...elective."

"That's alright, Dr. Moreau," Hecate blurted. "I said I didn't really *need* it, just wanted it. I mean, I can't get everything that I want, right? It's just a stupid upgrade." Hecate mumbled the remainder of his sentence, voice watery and aching for tears he couldn't produce.

"That's true," Abel dropped his shoulders. *Hecate looked so sad, and he'd been so good lately.* The twins were being doted on hand and foot by Marvin and Lucy, and Iacchus was walking on air waiting for his new clothes. Abel couldn't blame Hecate for being jealous. He'd been so well behaved and was almost being punished for it by being ignored. Abel, couldn't let that stand. The older man dropped his hand into Hecate's hair, the motion familiar and never failing to bring a smile to his lips. "How badly do you want that comm system?"

"I'd do *anything*, Dr. Moreau!" Hecate's voice dripped with sugar and honey.

Abel held his finger up to his lips, "How about keeping this a secret just between you and me? I'm not so good with software, but I'm sure I could manage to install that little chip."

Hecate leapt off the floor, and held onto Abel's arms. He stood on his tip toes to keep his eyes level with Abel's. "Would you?"

"If you can keep it a secret," Abel repeated. He'd have to 'borrow' the chip from Marvin's lab—but Marvin was horrible with inventory. The lab head was also pretty preoccupied with his new girls on top of that. Abel doubted he ever noticed it was missing. "Can you do that?"

"Yes," Hecate grinned brightly and hugged Abel. Success was sweet; it was nice things were getting back to the way they were supposed to: Hecate asks and Abel delivers. "Thank you! Thank you!"

"You're welcome." Abel rubbed his cheek in Hecate's hair, relishing his son's happiness. *His son.* Abel stilled, before strengthening his hug. Hecate *was* his son.

Abel didn't think he could say no to the boy now if he tried.

"You have way too many pictures of that kid," Becky mumbled around her cigarette, staring down at the framed photographs sitting neatly on Abel's desk. The owner of said photographs was currently hunched over his keyboard, eyes locked on the screen, typing furiously. With one hand, anyway. The other was shoving a triangular-cut turkey sandwich from the cafeteria into his mouth. Abel was getting crumbs on his coat. "Seriously, I think you're starting to forget the android's part of a project."

"I haven't forgotten," Abel lied. After last night, there was no possible way he could see Hecate as anything other than his own flesh and blood. Abel just felt there was no way to properly explain that feeling to Becky without being mocked. He wiped a bit of ranch from the corner of his mouth after a second bite from his dinner. Abel glanced at the clock in the lower right of his screen and frowned. He knew it was late, since he and Giles already had their drink, but he didn't think it was *that* late. "Why are you still here, Becky? Don't you usually head out at six? It's well after eight."

"I wish," Becky said, wondering when she had become the office whipping girl. Lucy was completely useless when it came to ordering people to leave her alone. Marvin had overpowered her easily with words alone, and managed to sneak the twins away to his personal lab. "*Someone* had to pry the twins away from Marvin and stick them in the androids' room."

"Marvin doesn't have a charging station?" Abel stopped typing, not seeing the issue with the girls staying with Marvin.

"Oh, he does." Becky pulled herself up on Abel's desk and made herself at home sitting on the edge, proud she managed to avoid knocking any frames over. She pulled her cigarette out of her mouth and twisted the top off to dump the empty cartridge in Abel's trash can. She replaced it with a fresh one, glee dripping in her voice. "Giles vetoed it— again."

Abel clicked 'save' on the screen before shutting down the spreadsheet. Another day's work logged and into the system. Now all that remained were some productivity journals concerning the boys' development and he could hit the cot. Abel rolled up the sandwich wrapper and tossed it in the bin next to Becky's nicotine cartridge. He paused momentarily before giving in and reaching for the carrot cake, wrapped in the tough plastic container, to finish off his late night dinner. God bless the company cafeteria and his mini-fridge... "Why?"

"It's cheaper, or something." Becky took a puff from her cigarette. She had a feeling revenge against Marvin for winning the bet was more likely, but if Abel hadn't figured out Giles was petty by now, he probably never would. "Who knows what goes through Giles' head, some days."

"Usually too much." Abel chuckled, cutting off a bite of cake with his fork. "Man's brain runs a mile a minute, constantly." Abel could remember a time when his friend debugged a computer for him during college. Abel had been dumbfounded by how quickly Giles worked through the terminal commands. "I can't even keep up with him on his worst days when he gets going."

"Oh?" Becky plucked the frame containing a lovely shot of Abel and Giles, sitting in what looked like a dorm room, caught off guard while working on the insides of a computer. They both looked up at the camera with wide shocked eyes, Abel with a crook of a smile laughing at what must have been a joke, and Giles with a pout. Becky pulled the image up closer for a better look as Abel started to type again, finishing whatever it was he had started.

The Abel in the photograph was fifteen years younger, but still had that same light in his eyes as the man she had come to know working in the same building. Maybe there were fewer wrinkles around the corner of his eyes, and maybe his face looked thinner, but it was still *Abel*. It was Giles' face that gave Becky a bit of pause. Younger, free of stress, and a childish facial expression, made him look like an entirely different person. Becky focused on the face frowning eternally at the camera, and had to pause.

He looks familiar...

Becky couldn't place it, but Giles looked like someone she knew. He was handsome, with strong features and gorgeous cornflower eyes (as much as she hated to admit), so maybe it was an actor—Becky's eye caught something in her study that made her lip twitch. "Abel."

"Good behavior continues to..." Abel trailed off before looking up at Becky. He saw the grin. He saw the shoulders tensing in excitement. He feared for his life. Abel shrunk in his seat, terrified at what the woman could possibly be plotting. "Yes?"

Becky tapped the photo at the top of Giles head, right at the hairline where his hair was slicked back. Her voice was sugary sweet. "Do you see what I see?"

Abel looked at the photograph, remembering that old computer. It had stopped working for one reason or another, and he and Giles had felt it their duty rip the thing apart. If he recalled, it was Giles' girlfriend at the time who had snapped the photo. All in all, it was pretty normal. "I don't think that I do..."

"His hair." Becky shifted her finger so the nail was right at the edge where skin met hair. "It's a different color here."

Abel squinted down at the photograph and started to laugh, grabbing it from Becky and sticking it back where it belonged on the desktop. He had to bite his cheek to stop from making a further spectacle of himself. Abel had completely forgotten about that. "It's nothing."

"It's not." Becky twisted her upper body so that she was leaning down and over Abel. "It's definitely a different color there."

"Trick of the light from the flash?" Abel threw out, going back to typing and trying to ignore the top of Becky's breasts hanging out of her v-neck knit top.

"Abel." Becky pulled her cigarette out of her mouth and put both hands flat on the desk. "Spill."

Abel slowly stopped typing and leant back to look out his office door. The hallway was quiet save for the humming of light fixtures and the sound of a floor cleaner down the hallway. Abel slowly backed up his roller chair, and practically skipped in his tip-toed rush to the door. He checked the hallway quickly for signs of life, and closed it for good measure. He almost felt giddy, laughter bubbling up inside remembering of Giles' biggest vanities. "If I tell you, you have to *swear* on your new parking space that you won't tell anyone."

"Not a soul." She was lying of course, but Abel was a trusting fellow. Becky had a feeling she had it figured out after a second glance, though. She'd seen that sort of root issue on many a girl. "Let me guess, he dyes his hair, right?"

Abel shook his head, feeling his fun ruined, and tapped the photo near Giles' hairline. "If you already figured that out, what did I need to spill?"

"I just wanted you to confirm it." Becky crossed her legs. "And to tell me what color his hair is normally. It could be any color with how grainy this photograph is…"

Abel held up his finger to his mouth in a *shhh* motion. "Now that is something you *definitely* can't tell anyone."

"Why?"

"He *hates* his hair color." Abel laughed. "He had been dying his hair long before I met him. The only reason you can see it slipping there, is his *very* particular brand of hair dye went out of business. Giles had to grow his hair back out before he could switch brands." Abel collapsed back down in his chair. "Otherwise, he *never* would have let his roots show."

"I take it he wore a lot of hats, that semester?"

Abel laughed again, thinking of Giles' auburn fedora. "Yeah, he did."

"So…" Becky trailed off, tapping the back of her foot on the side of Abel's desk. "What's his true color? What could he possibly hate so much that he blotted it out completely with something the shade of ink?"

It was a testament to Becky and his budding friendship with her that Abel managed to whisper out the next word: "Blond."

Becky tilted her head, and lifted an eyebrow trying to picture Giles with anything other than brooding, black hair. "Blond? Like a flat, boring, blond?"

Abel shook his head, remembering those few weeks of seeing Giles' true hair color hidden by the privacy of their dorm. "More like it's-got-to-be-a-sin-you're-dying-your-hair-black-Giles, flaxen blond. We're talking about a true blond-hair, blue-eyed beauty here."

"That's too funny." Becky laughed, re-crossing her legs on the edge of the desk. "He must of gotten tired of the jokes," she paused, "maybe I should start some up. Hey Abe, how many blonds does it take to run a comp—"

"Becky, seriously," Abel said quickly grabbing her wrist. His palm felt sweaty and his senses smacked him back in the face. Had Abel really just told her that? What on earth had he been thinking!? Abel *had* to make sure she knew he was serious. "You can't tell anyone, Becky. He'd *kill* me."

Becky's skin burned where his hand made contact, but she managed to stay still on the outside while her insides did a dance. Abel's hand was calloused and rough from the soldering gloves. Becky's heart skipped a beat, her mouth felt dry. The entire atmosphere of the room had shifted in a single instant, heavy and weighing. Becky licked her lips, the words stilted even as they left her mouth. "Right, I was just joking, Abel."

"Good." Abel sighed, shutting down his computer. The black screen filled his view, reflecting the darkened mood. "And now, I need sleep."

Becky looked at the wall clock and tapped her finger on the desk, not quite willing to leave, but grasping for some way to get rid of the sudden tension. "Big day tomorrow, right?"

"Yeah, most important one of our careers." Abel brushed his hair back and pushed out of his chair, wheels squeaking slightly on the chair mat. "I'm pretty sure I'm all ready for it though. How about you?"

"Got everything done I needed to." Becky flicked a photograph of Hecate and his brother. She had one chore for the meeting, and it was already taken care of. Giles had asked her to pick up some clothes for the twins as an afterthought the last time she had seen him, and Becky immediately shoved that task into Marvin's capable hands. The last thing she wanted to do was hang out in the teenagers' section of a department store picking out clothing. Marvin was more than happy to do that in her stead, anyway—disapproving mothers staring didn't bother him one little iota. Speaking of new looks, Becky supposed she should be ready for what her charge would be wearing. She already knew he was never going to shut up about it. "What outfit did you pick out for Iacchus?"

Abel froze mid-step. "Shit!"

Becky laughed as Abel scrambled to find his wallet and keys, rushing out the door. Becky called out after him, "At least the department store's open until ten!"

"We get new clothes tomorrow." The excitement in Iacchus' voice was palpable. It matched the bounce in his step as he trotted around the room. The grin on his face crinkled the LED strips, spreading the glow up into his hair.

The grudge was equally obvious in Hecate's slumped form, and reluctant answer. "*You* get new clothes tomorrow."

"Oh stop—"

"—being jealous."

Hecate glared at the two newest additions to his and Iacchus' (albeit spacious, but now it just felt cramped...) room. They had to take turns with the two charging stations—which Hecate also found ridiculous considering there was a spare in storage and one in Green's lab that were both perfectly functional—but now that they were all sitting at full capacity, they had nothing to do but stare at each other.

"Still! I can finally get out of these white things." Iacchus pulled at the fabric with a pout. He glanced over the twins' pretty dresses and scowled. Even his old clothes were never that nice. Hecate even had to wait a couple days before Dr. Moreau got him a new outfit! "It's really not fair you two got clothes already!"

"Marvin insisted." Melinoe rolled her eyes, a motion she had picked up from that other woman (Becky, was it?). Iacchus was studying her now, for some odd reason, causing Melinoe to shift in place. She decided to try continuing the conversation to snap him out of whatever little trance was in. "We were wearing clothes when we woke up."

Iacchus blinked away the confusion—he had a flash of Ms. Becky for a moment—and frowned. Iacchus shuffled in place, twisting his shirt in his fingers. "You still got clothes."

"He picked them out." Macaria whispered quietly, fingering the edge of her sundress, her body flush against her sister's side. The fabric felt smooth under her fingertip sensors. "He put a lot of thought into these outfits."

Melinoe clicked on her internal radio, glancing at her baby sister. *What's your point?*

Nothing. Macaria whispered, slightly intimidated by Melinoe's tone. *I just thought it was nice. It'd be rude not to wear them—*

'Nice?' Nothing about that man is nice. You're crazy. Melinoe crossed her leg

over the other. The only person in this building she'd consider 'nice' was the man with the camera the other day. She wanted to see him up close and personal, but until then she was stuck with *Green.*

Macaria pouted, lips pursed together. *He's not that bad. I think Marvin is wonder—*

"Stop that." Hecate said pulling out a chair to sit down and watch the mouse cage. Hecate was impressed Iacchus had remembered to feed their little pets every day, as chaotic as his systems must be with his mood swings. Integer nipped at the outer bar; Hecate flicked it, scaring the little thing back into the "mouse house" Abel had ordered. Amused, Hecate flicked the entire cage hard enough to tilt it up in the air before it crashed down. The boy smirked when the helpless little rodents, cute though they may be, dashed in fear around their cage. They settled down soon enough, and the moment was lost.

Hecate was bored.

It was bad enough Hecate was trapped in the room with the girls watching him and his brother, but it also prevented his semi-regular trip to visit Abel. Unlike Iacchus, the twins were likely to rat him out the second he stepped out of the room. Hecate didn't need them annoying him as well. "We both know you're talking to each other. The frequency is picking up as static. You might as well speak out loud."

"Maybe we don't want to." Melinoe glared at the pint-sized brat. Just because he was older didn't mean he knew better. The girls had the same education files installed as he did! Not to mention, Marvin had his own files installed that probably made her and Macaria *more* experienced than that little brat would be in months! "Maybe it's just for us."

"You can't possibly have anything that secret, or intelligent. Honestly, I'm impressed your cognitive functions work at all." Hecate tilted his head to the side, slicking his hair back. "You two are only here for the eye candy, anyway."

"Why you little—" Melinoe shot up on her feet, cutting herself off. "You can't talk! You look like a little kid! What could your model possibly be used for? Companionship?"

"Creepy," Macaria added thoughtfully.

"I'd be a blessing to couples who can't have children," Hecate hissed back, slamming his fist on the table. The cage rattled, and Iacchus jumped from the floor to lift it before Hecate could do damage. Iacchus held the cage to his chest as the smaller boy left the desk to stand before the two girls. He had to tilt his head back to look at their faces, but that was fine. Height wasn't everything. Hecate snarled, "Even better considering I never change! I never have to grow up and leave them!"

"Extra creepy."

"Right you are, Macaria," Melinoe grinned. "I guess we'll find out tomorrow what the board prefers. I may be a few days old, but even I know whatever they don't choose stops existing!"

Hecate narrowed his eyes. He knew that all too well. Though he hadn't previously considered himself even up for discussion with Iacchus around to compare, the fact he could be considered obsolete was now becoming more of an option. The girls provided a new comparison. Hecate was an old model. Older than Iacchus, even, made before Mr. Green was hired. Their outer shells and behaviors appeared similar at first glance, but it was their insides that mattered—the software was the same, so the deciding factor would come down to the physical. The technical specs between him and the girls under their respective personalities, disgusting as it was, were clearly on opposite ends of the spectrum.

A prototype and a final product being compared side by side? It didn't take a genius to figure out which one was going to get shelved. Unless of course, the board decided he was the better one.

Hecate turned on his heel walking away from the smirking twin and her dull sister. They weren't worth the effort. The board was worth his time. They *would* see that the girls were all flash and show. Even if he had to scare them into it, the board would see things his way.

If not—Hecate would just have to get creative.

Iacchus fidgeted in place, carefully setting the cage back down on the table as his brother fumed. The two girls had gone back to chatting with each other, not experienced enough to know how they'd affected Hecate. Iacchus was excited the board was visiting at first (new clothes), but seeing his little brother so angry, decided it might not be such a good thing.

He'd just have to be on his best behavior.

CHAPTER 11

GILES FIRMIN CARED genuinely about few things. His friendship with Abel, for example. Abel had saved him from loneliness during college. The man was the first person willing to take friendship in the small segments that fit between work and school and be happy about it. Abel was the only person Giles had ever met who didn't think it was weird that he would show up for an hour, disappear for a week lost in books and projects, and show up again ready for a nightcap. Giles wondered if they'd spent longer than four hours together at any point in time during college, and yet Abel was still the closest friend he'd ever had. Giles was thankful their time together had increased exponentially over the years—hiring Abel had done wonders on that front.

Work was wonderful for Giles' social life, really.

Take his faithful head of security, for example: Jenner was the loyal minion a boss dreamed of having under his employ. Completely devoted, and more than willing to take a bullet if needed. Giles had discovered this the hard way when some lunatic tried to kill his father. The bullet had veered off the wrong direction, and ended up heading toward a teenage Giles—Jenner still had the scar on his upper left shoulder. The man hadn't left his position since.

Giles even had an odd relationship with Becky, thanks to Abel, though he wouldn't quite call it 'friendship' yet.

The Olympian's Children was another matter all together. It wasn't so much that he *cared* about it, but more so that he was intertwined so fully into the project, he'd need Alexander's sword to cut through the twisted knot in which he found himself tangled. Giles' life was so invested in its success, failure would mean he was out of a job, a heritage, and his connection to the few people he held dear. Too much relied on that blasted wall of artificial intelligence for Giles to come out of this unscathed, should the project fail. As such, there was one thing above all Giles cared about: The Board.

Jessica Putts, Albert Ran, Stevie Late, Veronica Silvers and Paul *S.*—emphasis on the "S," as Paul "is not his father"—Diamond.

These five names spelled success or failure for Giles' imminent future. They signed his grant; they were the only ones who would give funding to the project responsible for eating all of his resources like a ravenous beast. Even if Giles could find alternative funding, should they decide to abandon him by the wayside, they still held enough prestige in the community to cause problems. Should they disown him, Giles—and by extension anyone on his team—would never work in the fields of engineering, robotics, or computer programming until the Second Coming.

Giles took a quick shot of whiskey from the bottle before straightening his tie. He had taken Abel's advice and stuck with something "classic" today: white shirt, black tie, and a diamond shaped tie-clip made of some blue stone or another. Giles looked himself over in the full length mirror he had hidden behind a bookshelf, making sure every line was crisp and in place. He deemed himself presentable, with one last slick back of his hair, just in the nick of time. The board was going to be standing at the gates of his humble billion dollar laboratory in one hour, and he had no time to dawdle about.

Giles planned to be waiting by the main desk next to Jenner in ten minutes in case they arrived early. Not that he didn't trust Jenner to be polite, but the man could get over-protective with the building when meeting new people. The lab didn't get enough guests for him to realize that, *yes,* investors wanted to see the lab they spent all their money on. That and Giles would never hear the end of it if someone on the board was interrogated via Mr. Flashlight, while being bent over the security booth. That intern applicant never did return his paperwork, if Giles recalled. The project manager used his thumb and forefinger to place one loose strand of hair back in place behind his ear. Jenner was the least of his problems.

Giles prayed the boys and girls would behave themselves, because heaven knew that was the main reason he'd never bothered to introduce them to the general public before. They just didn't know how the androids would handle meeting a large group of new people at once. The androids were ticking time bombs as far as Giles was concerned. It had been pushing it lately with the officers hanging around the two murder scenes, but they had the benefit of distance. Giles licked his teeth.

Hecate was well behaved, but he was nothing more than a little smart ass whenever Abel had his back turned. The kid had a vocabulary file hidden away that made it seem like he filtered out every dirty word that ever slipped into a movie or book and put it to use. Giles still hadn't forgotten when the kid called him "toffee-nosed paper-pusher." And that didn't even *begin* to cover his older brother. Iacchus was a loose cannon with twice as much firepower. Nine out of ten times, he was quite pleasant and seemed perfectly normal, if not a bit socially challenged. It was that tenth time, when Iacchus tended to grab the nearest object he could find and try to bash your head in with it—that was when things tended to go downhill.

Giles felt a member of the board dying might hurt his pay check a bit.

And now, there were the girls who apparently felt the fewer words spoken aloud, the better. He still hadn't heard them say more than ten words between the two of them, and the few words Giles had heard were along the lines of 'Would you like this?' Giles shivered and really hoped that went in his favor, but at least he convinced Becky to find them something less revealing to wear. Speaking of clothing, Giles should peek in on the boys with Abel to make sure they looked presentable. The board had to meet *all* four robots today.

Giles took in one last breath, shoved his empty bottle back in the drawer and started his way out to the labs. First stop, Abel and the boys. They would be darling, well-groomed little angels afraid of disappointing their respective caretakers. Then, Giles would check on the girls. They would be clothed, dolled up, and ready to seduce the board into loving their cute, marketable appearances. Finally, Giles would end his round by sitting at the security desk, hyperventilating while Jenner poured him coffee until the board arrived. From there, he would reapply his cool mask, and escort them around the facility as the perfect, confident host. The board would leave happy to give Giles more money.

Plan made.

And so far, so good. Giles breathed in relief as he opened Abel's office door. Hecate was sitting on a folding chair, dressed in a pair of slacks instead of his usual shorts, still sporting his customary sweater. The kid appeared to be playing with an old-fashioned analog watch that Giles couldn't remember the boy owning (or approving in the budget) and looked to the smiling Abel. Ah yes, he should have seen that coming. Said man was brushing some dirt off Iacchus' shoulder and giving advice about keeping the LED lights for his facial markings turned off or at a lower setting to avoid agitating anyone.

"Oh wow, he cleaned up nice, didn't he?" Giles announced with a slight smirk as he crossed his arms from the doorway. Iacchus' new black polo shirt blocked the glow of the markings crossing his chest and a pair of tan khaki pants, pressed neatly, matched Hecate's. His white slip-ons had even been replaced with a pair of brown dress shoes. Iacchus had his scarf neatly wrapped around his neck, one tail in the back and one in the front to complete the ensemble. It didn't match, but if it kept the boy from snapping he could wear whatever the hell he wanted as an accessory.

"Well of course, Giles," Abel smugly replied while moving out of the way to show off Iacchus. The boy had practically torn off his scrubs and was into the new clothes almost before Abel got them out of the shopping bag. Thankfully he was distracted enough staring at himself in the mirror to give Abel a chance to brush Iacchus' hair flat with a comb. Abel spotted a leftover size sticker and plucked it from the back of the polo shirt. "He was always a handsome lad under all those ugly scrubs."

"I know, and I hated making him wear them," Giles lied smoothly, silver tongue coming out to play. He hated lying to Abel, but what the man didn't notice didn't hurt him any—Giles was not in the mood to start any sort of fight over the boys today. There'd be time for that *after* their benefactors had left. Giles clapped his hands together. "But you know how it goes. In any case, are you two ready to meet the board?"

"Yes, sir, Dr. Firmin," Iacchus answered with a smile lighting up the room so brightly it could have powered the facility. He was wearing clothes. Real clothes. And not just regular clothes: Iacchus had on *dress casual.* There was not a single bit of white to be found on his new outfit. Iacchus reached up to fidget with the end of his scarf. "Thank you very much for approving the new clothes."

"You're welcome. I hope this good mood of yours hangs around for when you get introduced to the board." Giles nodded, patting Iacchus on the shoulder. There was a slight whirl behind him, and Giles remembered there was another body in the room. Giles turned slowly, to face Hecate and almost loosened his tie from nerves. Giles could feel the kid drilling a hole in his head with his eyes alone and it was making him more nervous than he cared to admit. Hoping to placate the child that made his palms sweat, Giles offered out a forced bit of small talk, his sleeve suddenly interesting to his fidgeting fingers. "New watch?"

"Yes." Hecate smiled swiftly, happy at finally being noticed by their true benefactor. The watch was a very pretty thing with roman numerals in the place of the numbers; the band made from leather. Hecate knew it was merely an appeasement, since Iacchus received an entirely new outfit, but it was from Abel to Hecate. That was all that mattered. "Dr. Moreau bought it for me."

Giles nodded dismissively and clapped Abel on the shoulder. He squeezed it once for that last *umph* needed to face the rest of his day. "I'll see you boys later, I just need to check on the ladies and then go wait for our lovely guests to arrive."

Abel waved and pulled a comb out of his back pocket for the slightly glaring Hecate. "See you soon, Giles. Don't forget to breathe."

"Can you forget to do that?" Hecate asked aloud and allowed his hair to be brushed out by Abel. "I thought breathing was an involuntary process?" The question in his tone, clearly aimed at the two adults.

Giles snorted and earned a glare from Abel this time around. "Yeah, but sometimes the body just doesn't want to act like its supposed to."

"Seems inefficient," Hecate deadpanned.

"Yeah, tell me about it." Giles waved his hand in front of his face before reaching for the office door. One more stop to go before he could get his coffee.

"Marvin! They can't wear that either!" Becky shouted, hands digging into her scalp as she gripped her hair.

"But they'd look so good!" Marvin held up the slinky, thigh-length dress—in black, of course. He had picked it out just last weekend for this occasion to show off his perfect ladies. Marvin even found the time to pick something with a long enough skirt to fit the prudish taste of his co-workers! Too much time had been invested designing every last hair on their heads for them to be ruined by some cardigan disaster. Becky couldn't even dress *herself* nicely in that tacky v-neck and bland khaki pants. How could she possibly be put in charge of dressing two beautiful young ladies? "Imagine how nice they'd look in—"

"You can see right through it! Where the hell are the real clothes?" Becky snarled as she went through the androids' wardrobe. Marvin had bought an unnatural number of clothes for two girls who didn't sweat and did nothing but sit quietly in the corner. They were all slutty little ditties or inappropriate things like costumes (the woman was positive she saw a pair of cat ears). Becky needed something simple and casual and she needed it in the next ten minutes. "If I don't find a decent ensemble in your little shopping spree, I'm going to rip off your—"

"Manners, Becky," Rupert called from the sidelines, chest pained from laughter. Normally, he was all for a famous Becky Krasiński temper tantrum that could rival Iacchus on his worst days, but there were limits. When you started to threaten certain parts of a man, as a man, Rupert was forced to intervene. "I'm sure there's something in there that isn't too scandalous."

"How did he get permission for this again?" Becky moaned as she looked at the two girls. They were staring back at her, motionless, and Becky almost wished they were more like the boys. Personality flaws she could handle, but these two were as exciting as sticks. Perfect little mannequins, that's what they were—Marvin was probably giddy every day about it. "They're quite lovely but still, Marv, they look like some high school nerd's wet dream. That's hardly appropriate in this day and age."

"The odds were against us," Melinoe answered to Ms. Becky's surprise. Her sister Macaria reached for her hand before continuing. "He made a bet and won. Had we been aware, we may have timed our passing of that test differently." Melinoe took over again. "As in we would have put an hour between us."

Becky stared. They could talk to each other while they were *on the wall?* What madness was—

"Why are they in their underwear?!" Giles stood aghast in the open doorway, unaware of thoughts he was interrupting. Giles' hands were gripping his cheeks in horror as he spotted the two girls clad in bra and panties. "The board is going to be here in an hour and these two are the most well behaved! They need to be introduced first!"

"Tell that to him!" Becky pointed at Marvin, rage overshadowing her thoughts. "He didn't buy anything even remotely appropriate for a business meeting!"

"Becky! Of course he didn't! That's why I told *you* to take care of it!" Giles groaned and nearly shoved his hands upward into his hair but remembered it was styled just right and stopped himself just in time. He waved his arm in the air toward the girls as an alternative. "What about those sundresses they were wearing? Those were cute."

"Low cut," Becky said, teeth grinding nearly loud enough to be audible.

"Oh for goodness sake." Giles threw up his arms. "Those breasts don't even have nipples! They're fake! The girls could walk around topless, so who cares how low cut the dress is?" Marvin coughed into his fist and looked off to the side in a fashion so guilty Giles felt his stomach drop to the floor. "Marvin, you didn't."

"Uh, now, come on boss, don't look at me like that." Marvin watched as Giles headed straight for the two girls sitting there patiently and gaped. There was no way that Giles was going to—"No! Sir!"

Giles ripped Melinoe's or Macaria's, or whichever girl's it was, bra down to reveal pert breasts and stared. They were anatomically correct. There wasn't a single thing missing on them down to the small indent in the center of the nipple where milk would have come. Giles felt his breath picking up and grip on the bra tightening, fabric stretching under the grip. The underwear threatened to snap off if the pressure was increased even the slightest. "Marvin. What," Giles paused for a breath, "did we discuss about the creation of these android units?"

"I know! But it's not like I put anything down below!" Marvin held his hands up in front of his face—a useless defense. Who would have thought Giles would *check?* What was the point of circumventing the cosmetics division if he was going to get caught in his modifications!? These units weren't for sale! It was assumed Marvin would get them after they were done prodding and poking, so he should be able to do whatever he wanted! Marvin flinched. "It's realism!"

"Do Hecate and Iacchus have these?" Giles pointed viciously down at the girls' breasts and ignored the way they were both staring directly at him now. Giles was too busy being disgusted with the thought Marvin was lying about what was in their undies to pay them any mind. "No. I was very specific with that request. What the hell are we going to do if the *board* decides to check!?"

"We can call the board out on being perverts?" Marvin shrugged with a guilty smile, sliding his glasses up his nose. "I mean, that's the only reason they would really want to strip their clothes off, right?"

Giles' response was rather vocal.

As the two supposedly grown men continued screaming at each other, just above their heads, one of the girls was fascinated with a rather different happening in the room. While Macaria glanced between the two screaming men, Melinoe looked down at her chest where the man with who had the camera earlier was still gripping her bra and stretching it out so her skin was exposed to the cool air.

Melinoe could feel the heat from his hand with the sensors lining her outer coating of 'skin.' It was a different sort of heat from when Marvin's hand would hover above her breast. This 'Dr. Firmin,' or 'Giles,' as she had been told made her systems feel warm. She wanted to feel more. Melinoe thought of the lessons Marvin had taught... *I wonder if that would feel different, too.*

Giles froze when chilled fingers wrapped themselves around his hand and pulled down, essentially reworking the grip he had on the bra. Too stunned to stop them or dare look down, Giles felt his fingers worked away, one by one, from their grip on the lacy strap. His hand was then shoved against something soft and warm. The android cupped Giles' hand around her breast beneath the bra, thumb and fingers digging into soft flesh with the base of his palm pushing it up slightly.

Giles stared; a hair fell out of place.

Becky watched, un-amused, as Giles tried to yank his hand back immediately after the shock had worn off, but only managed to jerk it slightly, causing the breast to bounce. The twin (they really needed name tags or something) had one hand cupping the back of Giles' and the other holding his wrist in place. Apparently they were as strong as the boys too. Becky turned away from the now tomato-red Giles who was sputtering incoherently and turned to Marvin, fuming. "What the hell have you been teaching them?"

"Ah," Marvin barely heard Becky, still staring at Melinoe. What was she doing? He had explicitly explained that those things were to never leave his office! Marvin wiped a hand over his mouth before shouting, "Melinoe! Let him go!"

In the long line of people no longer listening to others, Melinoe disregarded her 'creator' and his commands. She was too busy smiling up at the man now fondling her breast. He was so much more adorable than the man who claimed to own her. Giles' face was red and he kept going on about a proper time and a place, and money. Melinoe didn't much care.

More importantly, his hand felt *much* better against her skin than Marvin's ever had. She placed more pressure on the limb at just the right angle, forcing him to squeeze. Melinoe glanced at her sister with a tiny smirk, and tilted her head up towards Giles' back. Macaria had been standing quietly next to her sister, before walking behind the man mechanically. She knew this game very well by now, even if the person in center had changed.

Giles yelped when the second twin came up behind him and wrapped her arms around his chest, breasts pressed against his back. This was not in his plans. This was not what he needed today! Have mercy, did she just put her hand where he thought she did? Giles turned to the only other person of the room who could be of any assistance with Becky and Marvin in a verbal fight. "Dixen! Stop standing around and help me!"

Rupert jerked and ran over to his boss, grin still plastered on his face. How often do you see two buxom girls forcing a very reluctant man to grope them? Where the hell was that camera when he needed it? Now if only Ms. Becky would lend a hand and start a cat fight. Mary would be having a field day with this for weeks. Rupert grinned even wider as he ran to his boss' side. "Coming!"

"Detective Saxon, sir." A young officer stopped in front of his superior's desk. He waited a brief moment for the detective to look up and acknowledge him before continuing. He held out the folder for the detective, and glanced at the desk to see if the man needed anything else. His coffee cup was full, and there were at least three pens on the desk. Looked like all was clear, save for the mountain of paperwork that still needed sorting. Time was short, with the Android case taking priority. "I have the report you asked for."

"Thank you, Wolfe." Lester took the sizable packet from the young man with one hand as he flipped through a background check on a few of the lab's employees. Lester was lucky enough to have a competent staff on hand, but he was pretty sure young Louis here was responsible for most of that. He set an example by never complaining, no matter what hours he had to work or how much overtime was due. Kid was on the ball twenty-four-seven it seemed like. The detective set aside his paperwork, before he opened the latest folder. The first few pages included a detailing of their main suspects so far in the case. "Hmm, are we sure these are our guys?"

"Yes." Louis nodded. "We've traced the death threat letters and the party responsible for the parking lot vandalism back to this group of protestors. The Talos Redress' group has been harassing Dr. Firmin and his lab for some time now, but the man hadn't pressed charges to preserve PR. They've been known to harass corporations before, but this is the first time they've been suspected of such a violent crime. After an incident with a water park, they've kept it to flyers and rumor based internet sites."

"I take it they've never acted on these lovely death threat letters before?" Saxon pulled out the crude magazine cut letter in its evidence envelope and frowned at it.

"No, sir." Louis nodded in agreement. "The worst they've done to date actually going through with a written threat was assaulting someone with a paint can." Louis leant over to flip a few pages up. "In fact, most of their negative activities can be traced to this man, Marcus Samson. He's caused a few people to be hospitalized, but no fatalities. Our intel has reported that he's a bit of a loose canon, even to the organization. Their leader, Jeremy Eubanks, doesn't condone his actions."

"Well, right now, that makes him, and his group by extension, our primary suspects." Saxon pulled the Talos Redress' website up on his computer and browsed the main page. Firmin seemed to be their primary target for attack, with article after article about his 'crimes against nature.' Saxon clicked the screen off, having seen enough for now. "Let's set up some interviews and see if any of them has access to the building."

"On it, sir." Louis smiled and turned on his heel to head back to his desk. He still couldn't believe Detective Saxon was lucky enough to get this case. Louis wasn't happy about the murder of course, but the location was just too cool to be true. Louis had loved the idea of androids since he was a little boy, and getting to see one full functional in person was a real treat. He hoped he'd be on the team to help control the scene on the next visit, or he might not get another chance to see one up close.

"Thank you." Saxon continued flipping through the packet of offenses and leant back into his stiff wooden chair. The protestors seemed the obvious suspects. The chance of one person in particular going off the deep end was plausible, but something wasn't right. It was pretty far off their normal scare tactics, that were mostly harmless. Following this lead was going to come up with nothing good, but his other options didn't look much better.

Lester felt it in his gut.

It had taken over twenty minutes to rip both girls off of Giles. Marvin was not pleased by this in the slightest. His girls usually let go of *him* the moment he stopped moving or even remotely looked like he was done. Becky had been given the job of dressing the girls in whatever she could find as long as it was dark and the fabric was thick. She threw clothes on the girls, her face red in anger instead of embarrassment. The girls looked as bored as always. Giles, Marvin noted, looked ready to commit homicide. The department head wisely blended into the wall, smothering his jealousy, while the others rushed to continue preparing for the board's imminent arrival.

Rupert thought the entire thing was hilarious and had texted a picture of Giles groping one of the twins to Abel and Mary. He knew the doctor wouldn't check his phone until tomorrow, but that almost made it better in the long run. Rupert was sure that, after the board's arrival, this little incident with the bra and the twins would be overlooked and forgotten. Now, Abel wouldn't be able to resist teasing the moment he saw the photo. Rupert chuckled to himself and clicked through the other few pictures he had taken. It so paid to plan ahead.

"Let me make one thing very, very clear, Marvin," Giles hissed through clenched teeth at the robotics specialist. His face was still heated, and he had to redo his hair from the struggle. It's a good thing Giles kept spare gel and a comb in his inner pocket or Green would already be dead on the floor—preparation was the key to everything. Giles didn't have time for this. At all. "You have," Giles checked his watch, "twenty minutes to make sure that those two have learned one rule: Do not touch. Anything. Ever. If something remotely similar to *that* happens while the board is here, not only will I scrap the two of them, but you'll be terminated. Is that clear!?"

Giles had been full out shouting by the time Marvin slunk back into the desk chair behind him and nodded. Marvin managed to squeak out a single word: "Sir."

"Good." Giles took one last look over at the girls who were adjusting their outfits with Ms. Becky and shivered as his fingers remembered the feel of skin. Whoever invented synthetic skin to feel that real deserved a medal of some sort. Completely inappropriate at the moment, but Giles could think of other applications. Maybe something medical involving skin replacements or grafts. Perhaps he should keep that in mind for a back-up plan if this android thing didn't fall through. "Twenty minutes." Giles turned and stalked toward the door as quickly as possible. *So much for arriving fifty minutes early.*

The sterile white hallways full of opal marble tile and glass walls helped calm the director's nerves as he ventured down to the front desk. It drew him into a mindless state that allowed his thoughts to collect themselves. It made his walk to the front desk fast and thought free—just what Giles needed. His ever reliable security guard was sitting dutifully at his post—at least some things never disappointed him. "Mr. Jenner, how are you this morning?"

"Dr. Firmin, sir!" Jenner rose to his feet and almost saluted his boss. He managed to stop his hand halfway to his shoulder and lowered it slowly before chuckling to himself. No matter how many times Jenner went through the same motion, he could never seem to stop himself. His army days were never going to completely leave him. "Forgive me for saying, but you're late, sir."

"I know, I was planning to be here at 10:10, but I got delayed." Giles rubbed his hair back one last time and tried to see if it was in place using the decorative mirror behind the front desk. "But at least I still made it before eleven." Giles sighed in relief and leant on the desk. "As long as I beat our guests I think I'll be okay."

"Sir," Jenner winced sympathetically. He hated being the one to give bad news. "The board arrived ten minutes ago." Jenner watched Dr. Firmin stiffen in place. "They're waiting in the conference room."

Giles let his head fall onto the front desk and moaned.

CHAPTER 12

GILES TOOK A deep breath before pushing the conference room door open slowly and smoothly. A quick glance confirmed everything was in place: coffee and snacks at the kitchenette, guests in their seats. *Time for the show.* Giles' gait was controlled and every hair laid perfectly in place. His jacket was smoothed, and one hand sat casually in his pants' pocket. He *meant* to arrive exactly when he did, and no one was ever going to know the wiser.

Jenner could keep a secret.

The five people who currently controlled his life were sitting in plush leather manager's chairs, situated neatly around the coffee-colored oval table. They looked like they hadn't a care in the world—and most likely didn't, considering the sizes of their pocketbooks. They could pay other people to be worried for them. Giles fixed his face into the smooth smile that charmed everyone he met before greeting the guests waiting inside. "Ladies, gentleman, what a pleasure it is to see you here in my humble laboratory."

"You're late, Giles." Veronica held up a delicate pocket watch that had been retrofitted with a digital display. It synchronized with a satellite once an hour to ensure the time was correct down to the millisecond, just so *she* could accurately inform others they were late. An odd hobby to be sure, but it was better for her than going on a Twinkie binge. Veronica glanced at the plates of food set out on the side of the room—or maybe a cookie and muffin binge. "It's 11:02. Tsk, tsk."

"Well, you know how it goes," Giles chuckled amicably. Despite her tone, Giles knew Veronica to be teasing. It was as obvious as the leopard print pumps on her feet. The woman never showed up to *anything* on time and Giles would bet money the only reason she was in this conference room was because she caught a ride with Albert. "But it really is a delight to see you all here and well."

"So where are they?" Stevie glanced around the room excitedly, glasses sliding down his face. He had been looking over the photos that Giles had sent and was dying to see them. Living androids were his dream come true since the day he picked up his first science fiction comic on his eighth birthday. Intelligent machines as companions and servants. Stevie had been waiting his entire life to be a part of this process. Phone call after phone call of badgering Giles had finally paid off! Stevie nearly climbed up onto the table in his excitement. "There's four of them now, right?"

Paul chuckled and readjusted his watch. "Calm yourself, kid." Personally, Paul just wanted to see where all his money had ended up. Or at the very least make sure he'd be getting some of his money *back*. "We'll see the goods soon enough."

Giles nodded and his eyes fell over Ms. Putts and Mr. Ran who had both chosen to stay silent through the chatter. Jessica Putts wouldn't speak unless absolutely necessary and good old Albert would always wait for the perfect moment to get in a dig. "That you will! in fact, I've got—" Giles remembered the past hour and suddenly decided to give the ladies more time. He cleared his throat to cover the sudden stop. "Two models that you will absolutely love. They were the first two prototypes and are the oldest."

"So you're showing us the defective ones first so we're more impressed by the new ones?"

Right on cue. Giles tallied a point in his head when Albert spoke up. Giles put on his best grin and pointed at the man with his index finger, palm up. "Now, now. I guarantee that these two will surprise you. In fact, if not for the markings on their faces I would have bet my life you wouldn't be able to tell them apart from real live boys."

"Is that necessarily a good thing?" Paul shrugged from the other side. Jessica was twirling her pearls around her finger; they clicked together, an endless irritation to his ears. It sounded like a second hand ticking away endlessly. Paul wanted to snatch the string straight off her neck. "We want them to be smart, not blend in."

"Which is why they have lovely identifying marks on their faces." Giles swallowed nervously hoping that the board hadn't changed their mind about that little fiasco. Adding lights was a completely different process from replacing all of the boys' very expensive skin with an elastic clear coating. "The same ones you all chose, in fact."

Stevie's face lit up and he leant over the table even further. It was if the closer he got to Firmin, the closer he would get to the androids and he just could not wait! It was Christmas morning all over again while he pulled on his parents' pajamas to drag them from bed to open presents. Stevie was all ready to stamp his approval right then and there for mass production. Stevie was counting the minutes until he could take one home. "They do light up right?"

"Yes, they light up." Giles clasped his hands together, and took a graceful step away from the main door. "Shall we go?"

"Yes!" Stevie leapt from his seat fast enough that the roller chair skidded into the wall behind it. He quickly smoothed down his suit to try and hide his excitement. He pushed his glasses back up on his face. "Can you believe this?"

"I better," Albert snorted pushing out of his seat and following the most enthusiastic member of their little funding board, "I paid enough to see it."

"Hear, hear," Paul agreed. "You coming, ladies?"

Jessica pulled off her white dress gloves and secured them in her jacket pocket. The boys were always in such a rush—no dignity whatsoever. She watched Veronica stumble out of her seat on those ridiculous leopard printed shoes of hers, and sighed inwardly. She was all alone on the front of class, it seemed. "Naturally, Giles, dear."

"All right then! Let's get going!" Giles said, mimicking Stevie's enthusiasm. He watched as Veronica skipped over to the food tray and snatched up a muffin, a cherry pastry, a second muffin and three cookies. She made a valiant effort to shove them all onto a tiny square napkin— only succeeding after shoving the cherry pastry into her mouth. Giles gave himself a second point for making sure the kitchenette was stocked. He considered Stevie's enthusiasm a third point. Only two to go, and Giles would be in the clear.

Marcus Samson was fully convinced Guy Jenner was the devil of security officers. It had taken three camera fake-outs, a timed hack of their system to hide his entry swipe on the main floor, and two perfectly formed fake

ID to match his new lab-tech look, and he *still* almost got caught at the front door. Marcus hadn't had this much trouble breaking into the Governor's Mansion! Jenner apparently also trained his employees to live up to his expectations. The supposed-to-be-inexperienced, new guard at the check-in almost didn't believe his 'oh, we must always miss shifts' story—that Marcus had proven to work flawlessly at least six times, no less! He only made it past the gate, thanks to the heavens smiling down on Marcus with a well timed distraction.

By Firmin himself, no less.

The man had dashed by the desk and stopped at the main security counter in such an out-of-character move, that it drew the attention of everyone in the lobby. All eyes discretely tried to watch the man talk with that Jenner guy, while still looking busy. Marcus was never one to look a gift-horse in the mouth and scooted right on by check-point, walking smoothly and steadily to the nearest hallway he could find while the security guard was giggling at his boss.

That was two hours ago.

Marcus had hit the jackpot. Jeremy would be mad that he snuck into the building for more information, but Marcus would succeed where their contact was useless. He was too busy protecting his own job to really get the dirt on how much abuse was going on in the facility. Marcus was sure dressing the children up like mannequins to be paraded in front of the board—it was amazing what you could overhear in hallways—counted as abuse. The information he got today would make Jeremy happy with him for once. His approval was all Marcus ever really wanted.

To get that, Marcus wasn't beneath taking advantage of the androids' little dog and pony show for his own needs. The board's visit had taken top priority for *all* personnel, so Marcus was easily ignored as he slipped into the main programming lab. Police tape still hung across the door, barely holding on by the abused adhesive. Slipping carefully into the room, avoiding the tape and leaving any fingerprints, Marcus flicked on a mini flashlight he had stashed in his pocket.

There was definitely some sort of thrill in finding dirt so close to the enemy. He had noticed folks gathering outside a door in a hallway just around the corner—that had to have been Firmin and his little patrons. The trespasser slowly closed the lab door behind him, using the sleeve of his coat to cover his fingers, and tip-toed through the room. The flashlight shone on the chair and computer set-up he had seen in Jeremy's photo. Marcus smirked, reaching his destination, and flicked the nearest computer on. He'd copy a few hard drives and get to the next room.

Firmin would never know what hit him.

"Hecate, are you alright?" Abel asked as the young boy leant on his thigh, hands buried once again in his lab coat. There were tiny grease stains from the lubricant they used on the boys' skin now staining his coat. The splotch—which Abel doubted would wash out this time around —had taken up a space the size of Hecate's hands. The boy had been clinging to his coattails, quite literally, for the past hour and the evidence was logged on the jacket. Iacchus, thankfully, was currently looking at himself in the mirror and quite distracted from the two of them. He pried Hecate's hand from his coat and turned the boy to face him. "You're not nervous are you?"

"I'm fine, Dr. Moreau." Hecate frowned at the broken contact. He wasn't quite sure, but right now he really just wanted Abel to hug him. Perhaps it was the growing frustration that for the next few hours if he didn't play the perfect little pet there was a good chance he could be scrapped. It was difficult to keep someone company if you didn't exist. Abel might even cry; Hecate didn't want that. The smaller boy picked up the edge of his sweater hanging just below his waist and rubbed it between his fingers, catching the glint of his watch. Hecate had no desire to end his existence just yet. "I just like your coat."

"Alright then," The doctor rubbed Hecate on the head, letting his hand linger in the hair, before checking on Iacchus. The boy looked so ridiculously happy in his clothes that Abel almost didn't want to interrupt his preening. Just about the only thing that could possibly make this better would be if Becky complimented him. "How are you doing over there, Iacchus? Are you ready to meet the board?"

"Yes, I think I am." Iacchus straightened out the collar of his polo one last time. "I just have to be polite and answer questions, correct?"

"That's it. You'll be fine." Abel turned when he heard a loud knock on the door followed by two shorter knocks. Looks like it was time to get this show on the road, as they say. "And it looks like you're ready just in time. Come on boys, let's go introduce ourselves and make Giles look good."

Hecate released his sweater reluctantly (to avoid looking sheepish), but put on an innocent smile all the same to try and match his brother's beaming face. He dimmed the LED lights on his face so that it was a far softer glow that left the skin on his cheeks a soft blush of pink, rather than the harsh red he had been sporting. Iacchus' lights were glowing full blast, easily matching his energy and beaming disposition. Hecate could admit that at this moment, Iacchus actually looked rather handsome with his adult body and stylish clothes. *Respectable.*

Abel opened the door and nodded at Giles, heedless of Hecate's jaded eyes behind his adorable smile. Abel tilted his head in a little bow as he stared at the over-priced clothing of the individuals outside his door. *Is she wearing pearls?* Abel was suddenly feeling rather underdressed in his slacks and greasy lab coat. Even Giles was wearing one of his three-piece suits. "Hello Giles, sirs and madams of the board. Welcome to my humble little office."

"Hello, Abel." Giles waited for the doctor to clear the door and led everyone inside Abel's personal office. Giles paused as he noted happily that it was freshly cleaned and, did Giles detect an air freshener? Abel had even hidden the curtain to his 'back room' with a bookshelf. Giles saw the two boys standing side by side, both with smiles on their faces and looking like they belonged in a 50's sitcom, and almost cried in relief. At least this part of the day should go well. "My dear board, may I introduce Dr. Abel Moreau, one our main hardware designers. He's been responsible for social development with the youngest boy, Hecate, and more recently software management with the oldest, Iacchus."

"Pleasure to meet you," Stevie answered brightly, but his eyes were glued on the *other* two in the room. The ones with glowing eyes and angular lines on their faces. Something wasn't quite right, though, when he looked at them. They were a bit too, Stevie couldn't quite place it... human? They were fidgeting in place. What sort of android did that? They must have been the engineer's kids...yeah, this had to be a joke. Stevie liked kids too, though, so he put on a smile and leant down to get a better look with his hands on his knees. "And who are these two?"

Abel stood staring blankly, confused by the man's actions. He jumped about a foot in his own skin when Giles nudged his shoulder without warning. Abel glanced over as Giles cleared his throat, glaring slightly, and felt his face redden. That's right, he was supposed to introduce the boys, wasn't he? "Ah, yes, the eldest boy here is Iacchus and the younger boy is Hecate. They've both come a long way from when they were just motherboards on my work bench, if you ask me. It's hard to believe that the oldest is only just over half a year old."

"It is very nice to make your acquaintance," the blonde answered before Abel could continue rambling. Hecate loved the man, but Abel needed to work on his social skills. Hecate swung forward and up on his tip-toes before falling back down with his hands neatly clasped behind his back. It was a little 'cutesy' for him, but he was supposed to be a kid. Cute was the name of the game. He smiled brightly showing off his purposeless teeth. "Thank you for your patronage."

"Y-yes!" Iacchus stuttered quickly after his brother. He really needed to copy Hecate's dictionary files some time. His own just didn't want to record all the words he was supposed to know properly…Iacchus couldn't think like that right now. Comparing himself to Hecate wasn't going to impress the board. Iacchus started to wring his hands together. "Thank you very much for coming to see us."

The room was silent.

Giles shuffled closer to Abel nervously as he stared at the board members. Victoria had dropped her last remaining cookie to the floor and everyone seemed to match her wide eyed, imitation of a fish. Even Albert and Jessica looked to be at a loss for words. A quick glance to the side indicated that Abel, too, was confused by the reaction. He looked over at the boys and didn't see anything amiss. They had both been perfectly behaved little androids. When the awkward silence continued and both boys started to shuffle under the scrutiny, Giles ventured a question into the air. "Is there something wrong?"

"Alright, that's cute." Veronica turned to Giles, pin-point heel digging into the carpet. She knew the man had a sense of humor somewhere under the hair gel and black suit, but she hadn't expected him to show it off during something like this. He always struck her as more professional than that; a stick in the mud, really. "Great joke dressing those kids up, but seriously Giles, where are the real androids?"

"I'm not sure what you're talking about," the manager answered slowly, eyes darting back and forth between the boys and the board. Giles knew he had said the board wouldn't be able to tell the difference, but the kids had glowing LED lights embedded in their skin. They looked exactly like the pictures he had sent. How much more obvious could they be? "This is Iacchus and Hecate." Giles waited for a reaction. Jessica started to shake her head slowly in disbelief. Giles deadpanned, "The androids."

"No, they can't be." Stevie shook his head and pointed directly at the taller one whose face was slowly contorting into a nervous expression. His eyes were even darting to Dr. Moreau looking for cues of what to do in the awkward silence. There was artificial intelligence and then there was human. Those two were human. This had to be some sort of a joke, and Stevie didn't count his dreams being degraded as fun. "Those aren't robots, Giles. Those are kids with lights plastered on their faces. Where are the androids we paid you to build?"

"Yeah, Giles," Paul interjected finding himself growing angry. Maybe there had never been any androids at all. The thoughts of his money going to waste set his blood to boil. He was not a man to be conned. "You're not usually one to play a prank like this. What's your angle?"

Iacchus and Hecate shared a look before turning back to the board of directors. They were becoming unnecessarily angry, almost, and Hecate couldn't help but wonder why they didn't believe the doctors. Dr. Firmin was strict and neglectful, and a bit of a liar, but he *did* put pride in his reputation. Abel, of course, was trustworthy. Why did they think this was a joke? Shouldn't they be ecstatic that their money created exactly what they intended for it? "Iacchus, we should do something."

"But what?" Iacchus answered. After being called a soulless machine near constantly his entire life, this revelation that people outside of his construction didn't realize he was made of metal and synthetic materials was almost boggling. They thought he was *human*. It was so ridiculous and wonderful at the same time it had Iacchus' processors spinning. "They… don't think we're androids."

"That just means the project is a success. They should be celebrating, not accusing the doctors of lying." Hecate narrowed his brows and moved forward toward the men and women invading Abel's office. The sooner he showed them they got what they paid for, the sooner they could leave and allow the status quo to return. Hecate stopped in front of a woman wearing gaudy pearls around her neck and a blue dress suit the same color as his own eyes. "Excuse me, Ma'am."

"Oh," Jessica answered as the boy looked up at her. His skin was smooth and his hair was combed neatly. The thick sweater looked to be too warm for the room, but the boy showed no discomfort when he *had* to be burning up. Jessica was boiling and she only had on a suit jacket. They certainly had found a patient child to play this role, that was for sure. "I'm sorry they're making you dress up."

"No one is making me dress up," Hecate answered with a pleasant expression on his face. He watched her eyes widen slightly and stretched his own smile ever so much to match. "I'm an android. An autonomous robot with a human appearance."

Hecate reached up and grabbed the woman's arm firmly and she winced at the grip crushing a bracelet into her arm. "My bones are made of metal."

"Hecate…" Abel started slowly. "You're hurting her." Hecate yanked the woman down to her knees, bringing her to his eye level. The tension in the room must have gotten to him—that was the only reason his boy was acting so crazy. "I'm sure she didn't mean to mistake you—let her go!"

"My heart is made of circuits, and wires pump electricity to my limbs. Most importantly," Hecate continued, ignoring Abel, while twisting her arm with enough force for the woman to whimper and hiss.

Giles cursed. He knew something like this was going to happen today. Not even keeping up appearances for Abel was going to keep him in line this time around. "Kid! Let her go!"

Giles and Abel were clearly too wary of worsening the situation by physically interfering, leaving Hecate free to listen to the woman squirm and watch the other board members step back from the corner of his eyes. It wasn't quite what he'd had planned for this meeting, but Hecate took great joy in repeating a phrase he had heard far more than once from Giles. The ultimate proof that he was *not* human, "I have no soul."

Marcus typed away furiously, keys clacking with every pounded motion—the only sound in the room other than the fan spinning on the machine and his own hurried breath. The other boxes stood silent, shut down for one reason or another. The flashlight he held between his teeth, pointed at the keyboard, provided his only light source aside from the softly glowing monitor.

The lack of noise made the sudden rattle of the doorknob echo all the more loudly.

Marcus cursed under his breath. He had moved from the main programming office to an adjoining lab to gather more current data from the network, but had gotten lax with his guard. The lack of employees and the clearly out-of-use room had made him feel too safe. Maybe his camera program timed out and they finally noticed him on the tape? Or

—Marcus didn't have time to think. He slammed his hand on the power switch on the computer, and ripped his thumb drive out of the screen USB slot, shoving it quickly into his pocket. There was another door to the hallway and if he could just get to there—

The room went silent.

Marcus froze in place, hoping the guest had changed his mind, or a janitor merely checking that a door was still locked perhaps, and held still. When the silence continued, Marcus slowly shifted to see the door to the main programming lab better. A shadow under the door would tell him what he wanted to—

Marcus couldn't see.

His head pulled forward, and the sound of something snapping rang in his ears. His face felt like it was on fire, scolded by wet heat pouring over his cheeks. Strange fingers groped at his face and neck, the burning across his skin increasing with each exploration of the now empty sockets. Marcus reached up when the stranger's hands left. Blood poured down the back of his hands as they explored the open cavities—tactile proof that this was real. It should hurt. Where was the agonizing pain coming from ever nerve in his body? Marcus knew that. Or maybe it hurt so much that he was numb with the pain. His brain hadn't caught up with the injury. Too much adrenaline. Marcus wondered why he wasn't screaming.

Are there fingers in my mouth?

Something distinctly hand-like was gagging him from the side, a finger digging into his tongue and another in the soft palette above. The stranger's palm flat against his cheek, thumb once again in his eye socket. An arm took hold of his shoulder and began dragging him—somewhere. Marcus' brain sent out one last plea to *run* and Marcus fought. He jammed his hands into the body holding him, drool dripping freely from the side of his swollen cheek, and coughed and kneed and bit. Couldn't see, couldn't yell and—*oh.*

There was that pain.

Somehow between the delirium of slamming into the ground (the tile was so cold...) and passing out from the pain, Marcus could still apologize: *Sorry, Jer.*

Becky heard the screaming from all the way down the hall. High tailing it to Abel's office where the two boys were supposedly being shown off like show dogs was instinct by this point. The two girls, Marvin and Rupert were right behind, struggling to keep up with her pace. Visions of one of their board members being attacked with furniture flew through her brain, unwelcome. Becky moved faster. She just knew that they shouldn't have let Iacchus do this. That boy was unstable and one of those idiot board members probably upset him and he lost his temper.

She could see it all so clearly: Iacchus, a chair flying, a board member with a concussion…Part of Becky (deep, deep down) thought it would be hilarious to see those tight wads get theirs from the fruits of their labor and money. The speed of which the entire laboratory would go bankrupt the second their funds were withdrawn is what really moved her feet faster. They couldn't afford Iacchus or Hecate's upkeep if that were to happen.

The boys would have to be scrapped—and wouldn't *that* be an unwelcome dent in her paycheck?

Becky spotted Abel's office door hanging open into the hallway. She stopped at the door frame and stared…at Abel and Giles begging *Hecate* to release some woman's arm?

The technician heard the rest of her party slow and stand behind her, but she was far too busy trying to process the scene before her. Iacchus was in the corner with his hands in front of his body looking like he was ready to grab Hecate at the first chance, but was scared of hurting the woman Hecate was currently assaulting. Becky wasn't sure what was more shocking, that Hecate had flipped out or that Iacchus was trying to be cautious.

"What the hell is that kid doing?" Rupert spoke aloud for Becky, eyes locked on the woman in Hecate's iron grip, Jessica Putts, if he remembered correctly. A woman with too much money and free time, talked into investing by Giles, was on her knees nearly sobbing thanks to the death grip the kid had on her arm. Her arm showed bruising, purple coloring starting to show around the boy's fingers. Hecate's insides were made of the same metal as his brother, weren't they? "What's he thinking?"

"Oh, hello Mr. Dixen," Hecate answered pleasantly, releasing the woman's arm. She hit the ground before scooting back away as quickly as she could. Abel took that moment to grab Hecate by the shoulders and pull the boy back away from the others. He nestled Hecate into his side,

Abel's arm wrapped safely around his shoulder—a futile attempt to shield the kid from the inevitable backlash. Hecate smiled on happily like nothing bad had just happened, nuzzling his cheek into Abel's coat. "I didn't see you come in."

"Yeah, uh, good to see you too, kid," Rupert replied, looking away from Hecate's eyes. At least Iacchus tended to look guilty when he realized what he was doing. Hecate looked like he'd just been given a treat; like he won something instead of potentially ruining the lab forever. "What's going on?"

"Hecate was mad they didn't believe Dr. Firmin and Dr. Moreau," Iacchus piped up and inched his way over to stand near Ms. Becky. She was looking at him funny and he shoved his hands into his polo shirt. It wasn't a bad look—more confused than anything. "He wanted to prove we were machines by showing off his strength."

"By breaking that woman's arm?" Marvin scoffed. Those boys were nothing more than violent ruffians. Clearly some sort of backlash of having malfunctioned physical bodies. "You see? This is why I said we should have only introduced my girls. They have far more common sense than those two reject prototypes."

"The girls from the pictures?" Stevie found his voice, though his eyes remained glued to the two boys. They were definitely starting to fulfill his vision of what an android was supposed to be in each passing second. Especially the little one. Jessica was being tended to by Paul, still sniffling, so Stevie felt it safe to inquire further. He really *did* want to see the girls and if they weren't malfunctioning... "They're here?"

"Of course, they're just behind me." Marvin turned around to point out the obvious—the girls were missing. Marvin frantically looked both ways down the hallway for any sign of his girls. They could not do this to him! They were supposed to be perfect! "Melinoe? Macaria? Where are you, darlings?"

"Mr. Giles?" One of the twin's monotone voices shouted from around the corner.

"Oh, what now?" Giles shoved passed a flabbergasted Marvin and headed towards the girl's call. Couldn't he have at least programmed them with different voices if he was going to make them identical? Did he really need to deal with something new when one of his benefactors was nursing a broken arm and his stupid little project decided to drop the cute act for Abel *now* of all times? "What is it—" Giles gagged and

160

covered his mouth quickly with his hand. There was no smell in the air, but the small puddle on the ground was unmistakable. "Oh, God."

Macaria and Melinoe were standing on either side of the darkened entrance to the main programming lab. According to Marvin, this section of the building had been cleared of work in order to preserve the scene, however the empty hallway had seemed much more interesting than the humans bickering over the two brothers. Macaria, for one, felt they had been correct in this assumption. Melinoe pointed down to the ground. "I do not believe there should be fresh blood here."

Giles choked out a small laugh. Even if the results of his plans would be the same either way, he was starting to feel much more like a mouse than a man.

CHAPTER 13

ABEL CRADLED HIS head in his hands. He shouldn't have followed Giles, he really shouldn't have. When Abel saw his friend come around the corner looking pale as a ghost with one of the twins clinging to his arm, plastered to his side, Abel knew something very bad had happened. Abel was sure that seeing a human head with its' eyes carved out haphazardly, like the killer was nothing more than some cat playing with a dead bird, was high on his list of things to never see in person.

It was so much worse than the photos.

Apparently one of the twins (Macaria?) had decided to open the door upon discovering the blood. A body that had been leant up against the door sagged forward with a thick thud in response. The coroner on the scene declared the body had been moved at some point, following the splatters of blood from the other room. The actual location of death between the two rooms was harder to locate. The blood was too smeared to get a proper shoe-print. Abel sucked in a breath and ignored Hecate leaning up against his side calmly playing with his new watch. *Who the hell was doing this?*

"It was a protestor?" Albert sat still in the conference room chair. Detective Saxon and the police had decided it would be best if the building went into lock-down, and had those who had been at the scene placed in the conference room. Everyone else in the building was being watched and herded into the cafeteria for questioning. "The same protestors who threatened to kill all of us if we didn't stop the android project?"

"According to the police, yes, he was among the group identified. They found a fake ID clipped to his lab coat, so we're assuming that's how he

162

got in." Giles nodded slowly while looking over the reports he had been given. Three murders in less than a month. A programmer, a janitor, and a protestor. The only thing they all had in common was that the victims were all male and had business with the office. Just what was going on in his lab? "They have yet to release his name publicly, however."

"How'd he get by the security?" Becky said, and for once could care less Iacchus was invading her personal space. The boy was keeping quiet and that's all that mattered. "I mean, Jenner lives and breathes this job. I can't imagine the kind of skill needed to get by *him*."

"Don't you people have security cameras?" Veronica demanded, mouth wrapped around a leftover pastry from the tray. "I mean, a dead guy gets dragged into a room through an adjoining room and no one sees anything? And what about the first two!"

"The cameras didn't pick up anything." Giles repeated for what felt like the thousandth time between police, other staff, and his friends. Even Hecate and Iacchus had inquired about the cameras. Giles had turned in their security feeds and tapes the past two times as well, and not a single person out of place was picked up. The tapes ran like normal, there'd be a brief cut, and then all of a sudden there was a corpse in the room. Clearly someone had tampered with the feeds, but no one on staff knew a thing about it.

Not that Giles blamed them for keeping their mouths shut if they did know.

Giles looked over the information steadily appearing in his lap— thanks to Jenner, not the officer—concerning their security. There was more than one modification to the feed. One from out of house, which Giles assumed was the protestor breaking in, and a second from *in house*. It was that second one that worried him. It could be anything from a bug in the system (he was learning computers and software aren't quite as reliable as they'd like…) to a traitor in the department. Neither option was good. Giles shoved the folder closed and tried to calm his breathing.

Jessica rubbed her bruised arm nervously and kept glancing in the direction of the small bo—android who had attacked her. Why were the machines in here, too? Jessica watched as the younger boy smirked openly at her before crawling into the older man's lap. Why wasn't anyone punishing *it*? More importantly, when could she get the *hell out of this mad house*. "Do you know how long this investigation is going to take?"

"No." Giles rubbed his eyes and wished for the bottle of whiskey in his desk. Being royally smashed about now would do him a world of good, appearances be damned. "They've decided to declare this a serial killer since the state of the bodies has been identical in each case."

"So there's a serial killer now?" Albert threw up his hands in the air. He and the board all had clear alibis. There was no reason for them to remain in this building with a killer. "What kind of lab are you running, Firmin?"

"Now, just one minute," Rupert interjected swiftly. "You can hardly blame Giles for what's been going on! We don't even know the motive of the killer yet."

"Isn't it the androids?" Veronica pointed at one of the girl ones. "I mean, all the death threats were over them."

"Yes, but one of the people who made the threat is dead, love," Paul responded slowly. He patted her on the cheek with as little patronization as he could manage. Sadly, that was still quite a bit, and Veronica smacked his hand away. "So it's unlikely that group is responsible."

"Hey!" Stevie exclaimed, with a sudden revelation. His voice sped up to match his excitement, and he slapped both palms on the table. "What if he was a traitor or something and was trying to warn the lab?" Stevie lowered his voice and shoulders. "He had to be silenced."

"Oh, please," Paul groaned. The return on his investment wasn't worth this idiocy.

Iacchus had tuned out everyone else in the room. He was rather content sitting between Ms. Becky and the twins on the bench running along the wall. Ms. Becky was nursing a cup of coffee from the mini-bar and her glowing cigarette. Her hair was frazzled. Iacchus fingered her discarded lab coat in his lap and tried not to smile. Ms. Becky hadn't said a word to discourage him leaning against her. Iacchus was now at fifteen minutes of shoulder-to-shoulder time and enjoying every second. It was probably due to the fact she had yet to even notice he was there.

Becky had her eyes covered with the hand not occupied with the cup of coffee, only shifting it slightly to take in a mouthful of nicotine vapor from the plastic cigarette dangling from her fingers. The woman finally removed her hand from her face and leant back only to be met with resistance. She turned her eyes to the side and realized that Iacchus was directly behind her. She was too tired to argue it and merely shoved lightly at his shoulder. "Move over."

Iacchus obliged and scooted just enough for Ms. Becky to hit the back wall. She placed the cup of coffee between her legs against khaki slacks. Iacchus tried not to let his eyes wander the few inches higher required to see *other* things. The teen still wasn't sure if he was glad Mr. Dixen had explained what had been going on in that video or not. Or trying to imagine Ms. Becky acting like the woman in the video. He forced his mind off the subject. "Are you alright, Ms. Becky?"

"Don't talk, kid," Becky replied and tried to think of some excuse the kid would believe. She wasn't in the mood to talk or humor the brat right now. She went with a classic that most ex-boyfriends recognized immediately as a 'shove off' and hoped it translated to clingy androids. "I have a headache."

"Okay," Iacchus replied quietly and turned his attention to the twins sitting on his left. They were both being silent, but he knew they were talking to each other. The static buzzing in the air when the two of them used their internal communication system made Iacchus itch. He had been distracted by Ms. Becky before, but now that he noticed the static again, it was merely loud and obnoxious. Iacchus hoped to move the conversation to a little more vocal realm just to shut it up. "What are you two talking about?"

Melinoe blinked at Iacchus and frowned. She had no desire to acknowledge the defect right now, and turned her face away to Macaria. Iacchus and his stupid brother were lucky that man died. After their little stunt with hurting that woman, they were lucky to still be functioning. Melinoe still needed to work out a good plan to get Giles alone for a while and Marvin out of the picture, too. Her body's builder was truly an annoying little man. Macaria probably couldn't care less, but that was beside the point.

"Hey!" Iacchus tried again. You were supposed to answer when you were addressed by another. Weren't the girls taught that? Ms. Becky had her eyes closed and probably wouldn't be talking any time soon and Iacchus was bored. Hecate was with Abel so he was no good to anyone, either. The least the girls could do was share what they were discussing. They were his sisters! Iacchus felt himself tense up and the constant pulsing sound in his head got louder. "I'm talking to you."

The twins continued to ignore the boy, ignorant of the consequences.

"Excuse me," Iacchus repeated, the feeling of rational systems and control centers momentarily shutting down building each second. The girls continued to look at one another, disregarding him, and the buzzing was starting to become as loud as swarm of bees in his head. Iacchus bit his lip, teeth fitting neatly in the patched-tear that was never fully repaired. "Please, talk to me, too. Aloud."

Melinoe and Macaria scooted over a foot on the bench away from the annoying boy to continue their conversation full force.

Iacchus snapped.

Detective Saxon was getting the impression that this job might either end up being the most impressive thing he'd have under his belt, or the biggest blot on his record in the history of his career. It all depended, of course, on whether or not the case was solved and the body count at the end of the day. Three murders in the same building, all gruesome, with all victims missing their eyes. This so called 'Olympian's Children' or whatever it was called from his notes, was the only thing linking them all together.

The first victim, Cecil Law, had worked for the laboratory that created the project as a basic laborer. The second victim, Steve Mathers, had been one of the main programmers for the project. The third was a bit of a stretch, but the protestor Marcus Samson had been part of a group dedicated to the shutting down the project for 'crimes against humanity,' as they put it.

Lester was sure that all he needed was one clue to wedge his foot in the door to solving this mess, but that one clue wasn't showing. No hairs, no DNA, no misplaced footprints, no fingerprints or smudges or anything else he could use. The scenes were fairly sterile, for what otherwise looked like a bear barreled through them. The detective took a handkerchief from his pocket and wiped off his brow. Officer Wolfe walked quietly next to him, ready to assist—his only relief in this crazy case. At least interviews were up next; his favorite part.

Interviews were always the same; endless repeat performances. *No, I don't know what happened. No, I didn't see anything. I'm sorry sir, I can't help you. That one guy though, he's suspicious.* Lester chuckled. He'd heard the same story over and over again, multiple times, at just about every crime scene he'd ever been to. Lester could see the conference room just ahead and adjusted his coat. He'd get in, get out, and get to throwing this sick bastard behind bars.

Lester and Louis were greeted happily by a roller chair smashing through the glass wall of the conference room. It landed in the hallway with a crash accompanied by the showering of glass and bits of metal bracing. A few remaining shards tipped off the window sill and clinked on top of the debris, barely heard under the sudden explosion of noise and shouting from the conference room.

The detective placed his hand on his piece, finger extended ready for the trigger, and raced towards the large opening in the wall next to the (still quite intact) wooden door to see the chaos inside. Wolfe stayed to his back, weapon also at the ready. Saxon spotted the older android boy struggling to pull himself free from the grip of a small child the detective had yet to meet and the Moreau guy from earlier interviews. Dixen was trying to talk the boy down and two girls (with the same markings as the boys?) cowered behind a thinner, gangly gentlemen in glasses.

Everyone else was too busy shouting to be useful.

"Somebody get him under control right now!" Giles screamed directly at Becky, the 'someone' in his sentence clearly aimed at *her*. The woman was being completely *useless*. What was the point of promoting her if she wasn't going to do her job when she was needed!? "He likes you. Talk him down!"

"What do you want me to do?! He tried to break my arm last time!" Becky screeched right back. She should have seen this coming. The brat was due for a freak out anyway. The past few days were just a powder keg waiting for someone to drop a match. Becky shoved at Giles' pressed suit pushing him back a foot. "He doesn't listen to me when he's like this!"

"Don't let go, Hecate!" Abel ground out as he clung to Iacchus' right arm pulling back as hard as he could. Hecate was holding his own better than Abel could think possible, considering the size difference, but the boy was keeping Iacchus from reaching his goal. Abel certainly was mostly grabbing for show; his strength was completely ineffective against the raging 'teen.' "What the hell did those two do to piss him off so badly!?"

"I am unsure, Dr. Moreau," Hecate answered while shifting his grip on the rabid Iacchus. If his brother was capable of producing spit, Hecate was sure there'd be foam in the air. Iacchus made a jerk forward and Hecate pulled back in response. His brother's eyes were glowing so brightly you could hardly tell there was even a pupil buried under all that blue. "If I had to guess, however," Hecate yelped when Iacchus made another sudden surge forward. He snorted before finishing his sentence.

"I'd say it was the buzzing."

"Buzzing?" Abel blurted out incredulously. His arms were getting tired and he wished Rupert would hurry up and say the right thing to break Iacchus of this little spell. Abel had to speak up to hear himself over Giles and Becky shouting. "What buzzing?"

"The twins' internal communications center creates a buzzing noise that Iacchus and I can hear whenever they use it," the boy replied matter-of-factly. The twins were currently in a screaming fest of their own in their heads and the buzzing still hadn't stopped. Hecate was pretty sure that didn't help matters. "It was most likely annoying him."

"Great." Abel winced when Iacchus elbowed him in the chest. "Rupert! Talk him down already!"

"I'm trying!" Rupert snarled right back. It was easier said than done when Marvin was yelling in your ear to get that beast away from his babies and the damned board of directors was screaming about money and dangers and whatever else. Too much yelling, too much anger, and not enough incentive for Iacchus to give up on his little rampage. Actually, it was finally starting to feel like a normal day at the lab; Rupert almost laughed. "Ia-kid, come on. You can calm down."

Louis and Detective Saxon both dropped their weapons to the side, but kept them out while they stared at the scene before them. Louis had always wanted to see an android, but he hadn't expected it to be so out of control. Wolfe stayed in his place right outside the glass wall when Saxon moved forward to stand next to the director of the lab. Lester grabbed Firmin's shoulder, yanking the man away from his argument with the hysterical woman.

"What is going on!?" Lester demanded incredulously.

"Ah, Detective Saxon." Giles swept loose hair out of his eyes. He addressed the burly officer with as much calm as he could muster, voice pleasant as a service announcement. "Iacchus is having a brief episode, and I assure you it will be under control momentarily."

"Doesn't look like it to me," Lester muttered as he looked over the frenzied room. It actually reminded him of the fights that would break out over the stupidest things back at the precinct and during investigations with unruly suspects. Lester snorted and released the supposed man in charge. Well, his job was to uphold the peace and protect citizens, so Lester did what he did best when faced with such situations and took in a deep breath: "Everyone quiet down right *now!*"

The room stilled almost immediately and all eyes were on the detective standing in the doorway. Even Iacchus had stopped his assault and stared wide-eyed at the man he had met earlier when they interviewed Ms. Susie. Hecate and Abel released Iacchus' arms a the same time. Rupert took the moment of reprieve to collapse in a chair, breathing heavily from all the excitement. Mr. Green's mouth was covered by Becky's hand as she had wisely foreseen some sort of idiocy on his part. Everyone else just stared.

"Good." Lester looked around the room. "Now I want everyone to put their butts in a seat and shut the hell up. I don't know what's wrong with all of you but another man's been murdered and all of you are squabbling like children! Show some respect and start acting like adults." He paused again making sure no one had stopped listening. "I'm going to start interviews now one at a time, and I don't want to hear a peep out of any of you until I'm done. Is that clear?"

A collective nod speckled with a few 'yes sirs' was his answer and Lester smiled. He always did know how to get the attention of a room. Saxon rubbed his hands together with a grin on his face enjoying the momentary control of the room. "Let's go ahead and get started, shall we?"

The board members had been the last to be interviewed. As such, everyone else had been released back to their offices to try and salvage something of the day. Abel was fairly certain Giles was drinking in his office about now, and Becky had already declared quite loudly she was going home and anyone who stopped her would become a eunuch. Marvin had taken the girls and Hecate and Iacchus had been escorted to their room about an hour ago by Rupert. Abel headed for the cot in the back of his office, not even going to remotely attempt the commute home.

While Abel prepared to collapse in his cot, Veronica and Paul were sitting in the conference room waiting for the rest of the board to finish their interviews. The two were relatively quiet, contemplating the events of the day. Veronica sipped the last bit of juice from the earlier spread; it was warm. Veronica had eaten everything else on the platter. "Well that was interesting."

"Disturbing, you mean." Paul held his head and did his best to ignore the perky woman. He was having serious doubts about his investments in Firmin's little project and wanted to mope in peace. Albert and Jessica were already on board with the moping plan, and Stevie was falling asleep. Veronica needed to follow suit. "Do be quiet for now."

"Fine, I'll leave you alone." Veronica rolled her eyes and stood. She frowned at the pressure below her navel and sighed. She may have had one too many snacks... "I'll be right back. I need to use the ladies room."

Paul almost dismissed her completely, but managed to work out a response while he ran numbers in his head. The moment all of these murders hit the news their company was going to be taking a hit whether he denounced Firmin or not. "Don't be long. The sooner we're out of this insane asylum the better."

"I won't." Veronica hummed as she tip-toed over the last few shards of glass from that boy's earlier hissy fit. *Iacchus, huh?* Veronica turned the corner and followed the lit sign overhead pointing to the lavatories and cafeteria with a light step in her feet. Despite how frightening it had been watching the boy turn into an unstoppable beast, she was still feeling a bit excited over the whole thing. She had never seen a fight in person before and Veronica had to admit there was something deeply thrilling about a man in a total animalistic rage.

It was probably the adrenaline, she thought to herself with a smile as her footsteps echoed in the empty hallway. It was well after hours and everyone who could have left, had. She knew as soon as the rest of the board was finished with their interviews, she would be doing the same. Veronica spotted the lit sign with the traditional symbol of a woman and grinned, destination located. Veronica pushed lightly on the door, but before she could go in, she heard a much heavier door slam behind her.

The woman turned around, but failed to see anything out of place. She couldn't even locate the door that had closed. "I know I heard some —"

"Ms. Silvers."

Veronica stiffened from the bottom of her curled toes to the rising hairs on the back of her neck. She didn't recognize the smooth, tenor voice that had addressed her. Maybe it was that guard, Jenny, or something? Veronica swallowed deeply as her hand itched for the mace still trapped in the purse left abandoned in the conference room. "Yes?" Veronica received no response. There was almost a chill in the air as she stood in the empty corridor. Her voice shook during her second try. "He-

Hello?"

"Have a good night."

Veronica didn't have time to dodge the hand that covered her mouth, firm, thick fingers digging inside far too easily and grabbing her tongue. She tasted petrol and salt. Veronica gagged as she tried to scream, and feared she would choke on the bile building in the base of her throat. A thumb dug into her cheek, a sickening caress.

The body now behind her was firm as steel, and didn't so much as budge against her struggling. It was like fighting the grip of a stone statue. Veronica could barely believe the high pitched whimpering now filling the air was her own. When something sharp sank deep into the flesh of her arm at the joint of her shoulder and arm, Veronica desperately wished her screams could escape. She jerked and pulled herself like a wild beast trying to escape from the single arm holding her firmly to the chest of her captor, but found it difficult with her own arm being assaulted.

The desperate struggles ceased instantly when she heard a soft 'thud' echo in the hallway. She could hear breathing (her own?), heavy and broken around the obstacle still disgustingly wedged in her mouth. Wet eyes trailed to the ground against her will. Veronica could see her arm, ruby ring glinting at her from the floor. She sobbed for as long as the pain would allow her to remain conscious.

CHAPTER 14

THEY FOUND THE body still warm.

Jessica had returned from her interview ready to go home, but noticed Veronica missing. Candy wrappers were spread around her empty seat. Paul mentioned she must still be in the restroom, and Jessica decided that wasn't a half-bad idea. She made it as far as the hall before she spotted a single leopard printed shoe peeking out from the corner. Thinking Veronica had passed out, Jessica hurried over. She discovered leg severed at the knee.

The rest of Veronica had been left in various pieces trailing down the hallway. A thin film of red was splashed against the white walls in streaks and splotches like paint thrown on a canvas.

Jessica had promptly screamed at the top of her lungs in the way Veronica had been unable to do earlier.

Lester Saxon walked into the conference room after supervising his team in the clean-up and lock-down of his newest crime scene. Ms. Putts, was half and half hysteria and shock. He had given her fifteen minutes to gather herself, but Lester figured it'd be another hour or two before she completely calmed down. Unfortunately, right now he needed her to focus.

Blood clung to the tips of Jessica's shoes from where, in her distress, she had disturbed a small puddle. Make-up ran down her cheeks in black streaks and had smudged where Jessica's hands tried to wipe the tears away in a failed attempt to return normalcy to her face. "She was here an hour ago. Right there." Jessica pointed to an empty chair across the table. She sucked in a shaky breath, her fingers clutching the pearls around her neck. "She was eating the damn snacks!"

"Yes, Ma'am," Lester soothed as he handed her a cup of water. The woman had been close to passing out from hyperventilation since she stumbled upon the body of her friend not twenty minutes ago. Lester couldn't blame her. The state of the victim's body was turning *his* stomach, too. "That's right, breathe."

The woman managed to calm herself enough to take a sip from the cup and Saxon relaxed momentarily. He decided to give her another few minutes alone. Lester pushed himself away from the table and surveyed the room. Everyone in the building had been relocated to the cafeteria, though this time it was for safety over suspicions.

Louis jogged up to Detective Saxon, badges and attachments to his belts clacking, with a small folder. "Sir, I've put together a list of names and professions of everyone in the cafeteria." He flipped open the file. "As well as their alibis."

"Thank you, Wolfe." Saxon opened the book and quickly scanned the page for anything that looked out of place. There weren't that many people in the building to start with at the late hour, but there were enough that someone could have been misplaced. "Here," Saxon handed a second packet back to Louis. "This is going to take a while, so would you mind comparing the various crime scenes? There might be something we've missed."

"On it, sir." Louis nodded.

Jessica reached up to tug on Saxon's coat, her pearls clicking around her neck. "Detective?"

Lester placed the list of suspects gently on the conference room table. The detective took in the woman, and his soul burned for her. Putts' eyes were glassed over and empty—no one should ever look like that. "Yes?"

"I think I should give my statement now. While I can."

"Yes, of course." Saxon pulled a chair out and grabbed a notebook so he could make sure not to miss a thing. After three deaths too many, he couldn't afford it.

The laboratory was in total lock-down.

Giles had hidden himself in the far corner of their cafeteria 'safe house' where he could survey the room and its inhabitants without leaving his seat. An empty bottle of whiskey sat by his polished shoes, and his collared shirt hung open. Employees or cops, he honestly couldn't care less who saw him in such a disheveled state. It's not like everyone didn't already know about his addiction. Even if he wasn't an alcoholic, this was the sort of shit that turned even sober men to drinking. Two murders in one day. The latest one threatened his paycheck, however, and Giles didn't appreciate that.

The time of death was a little less than an hour after Jenner had claimed no one had gone in or out of the building on the, now working, security feeds.

That meant the killer was still in the building, and that there was a good chance it was someone on staff. Giles had a traitor that was responsible for four deaths on his watch. He picked up the empty bottle and looked down its neck with eyes dabbed with dark bags. If Abel were awake, he'd probably say something about drinking too much and hand Giles a cup of water. As it stood, Abel was across the room asleep, so Giles drank to his heart's content.

Giles wondered if the kitchen staff had a stash of their own.

Maybe it was some disgruntled lackey at the bottom of the ladder, Giles admitted to himself. He wasn't all that familiar with lower level staff and just how much they had access to. He always trusted Susie or Jenner to take care of it. Giles twirled the glass bottle between his fingers and tried to force his brain to concentrate. People were in danger, and he needed answers. "Okay, okay." Giles licked his lips. "Take stock of friends first, deal with others later."

Abel was lying on a cot he had dragged into the cafeteria from his room. If there was any sign that Abel was going crazy, that would have been it. Normally the man was too considerate to get himself a bed when everyone else had to suffer plastic chairs and folding tables, but there it was: Abel's cot. Hecate was sitting on the floor next to him with a thick book. The brat's earlier antics with Jessica were all but forgotten now, to Giles' relief. They really needed to figure out what caused the mood swings on those two before they reached production. Giles snorted to himself, wiping Hecate off his list. Abel was sticking to the kid like glue, so they at least had that in their favor. Becky was still at home though, which meant her charge was with someone else.

Iacchus was on the other side of the room with Rupert and the only staff member left in the building from his department, Rod, or some other name equivalent to a bad joke. The older android, too, was reading, but his book was distinctly thinner and well worn. It was probably one of Rupert's paperback novels he hid in his desk to read when he thought no one was looking. Rod was banging his head to music playing through his headphones.

Giles might have been concerned about a potential freak-out on Iacchus' part, but Becky was currently en route back to the building. Giles had called her after the lockdown to inform her of the situation. Becky had cursed again and informed Giles that she would be arriving as soon as she could, and the detective and police officers had better let her in. Giles had a feeling the worry in her voice had more to do with the man sleeping on the cot than the rest of them.

Marvin's asleep on the floor, Giles snorted to himself. The man had curled up under one of the folding tables, partially hidden by a row of chairs. He was out like a light, save for mumbling in his sleep, his glasses hanging off his face crookedly. Lucy was still at home, having had the day off for a doctor's appointment, and her programming buddy Anton was playing solitaire. Giles figured that accounted for most of the people he knew by name, at least. As for the board, they were huddled around the hysterical Jessica. Giles lifted the lip of the bottle to his mouth absently. Who was missing?

"Hello, Giles."

Speak of the devil. "Hello girls." Giles took in the twins who had slunk up to his side. The forward one, Melinoe—Giles had figured that much out, was smiling at him, her eyes half lidded. Macaria was looking in a different direction with her arms crossed, face bored and apathetic. This strange infatuation with Giles, to his great relief, was only affecting one of the twins. *Thank God for small favors.* Giles watched as Melinoe took the empty whiskey bottle from his fingers and dropped it on the table behind him. "Can I help you?"

"Actually, I was hoping you would allow me to help you." Melinoe repeated a line from one of those horrid films Marvin had uploaded to her hard drive as an "instructional manual." She tried to mimic the tone of voice the woman in the picture used; sultry. A slight blush of pink fell on Giles' cheeks, and Melinoe took the cue to keep imitating. She leant forward, mimicking the girl from the video, and made sure the top of her cleavage was visible. Giles could now clearly see she had removed her bra. She flicked his shirt collar with her fingertip. "You seem stressed."

"Understandably so, I'd imagine," Giles answered and looked around to see if anyone was watching this exchange. He needed a distraction to get away from this girl who seriously needed her memories wiped. It might be the only way to undo all the damage Marvin inflicted. Much to Giles' growing panic. Everyone seemed to be preoccupied with their own worries and priorities.

Melinoe pushed him back down into the chair when he tried to stand. His rump hit the seat painfully from the force, and Giles exhaled a breath. Melinoe took no issue with putting her super-human strength to good use trapping Giles in his seat. The director's pulse sped up like a rabbits when he noticed that no one was paying him any mind. Melinoe continued to block his exit, hands ready to shove him back down should he try to escape again. Giles continued to scan for any excuse to call out to someone and get away from the malfunctioning android fixated on him. Looking around the room worked to his disadvantage. Giles dropped his guard, and a weight settled in his lap.

Melinoe decided that having Giles between her thighs was far more pleasant than Marvin. Perhaps it was merely that this man was more attractive, had more bulk to him, or had a far more soothing voice that made it so. Melinoe pondered that it might be all three as she shifted slightly so her feet were sitting on the backside of the chair legs. She knew it would be uncomfortable for Giles to take *all* of her extra weight. Taking advantage of Giles' shock from her actions, she slid her hands up his now un-tucked white shirt to rest on his shoulders, sensors seeking anything they could beneath the fabric of his shirt, devouring the warmth coming from his skin. Melinoe shivered. "I think I can be of help."

"Wh-what exactly are you doing?" Giles pushed at the android's hips with all the force he could muster, but she only tightened her thighs together. She rolled her hips forward into his pelvis and Giles felt nausea and pleasure in the same repulsive instant. He bit his lip to keep from embarrassing himself further with unintentional moaning. Giles needed to get her off his lap *now.* The manager kept his voice as low as possible to avoid drawing a scene from the rest of the people in the crowded cafeteria. Calling for help would have been the better option, but Giles thoughts betrayed him. The mortification that someone could see him this way—helpless, out of control—crawled deep inside his chest and threatened to choke him from the inside. Giles pleaded, voice barely a whisper. "Please get down. This is hardly appropriate behavior for an audience."

"No one is watching." Melinoe smiled, knowing full well Macaria was on look-out. Her baby sister was good for things like that, especially when it meant she wasn't required to participate in the 'action.' For some reason Macaria didn't like doing anything with someone other than Marvin. Melinoe thought she was insane with someone as irresistible and deliciously cute as Giles around. "It'll be alright." Melinoe soothed as she snaked her fingers down to Giles' belt loop, excited for this chance. This man was all she could think about. Night, day, didn't matter. It was all *Giles, Giles, Giles!* Melinoe swiftly undid the belt and headed for the buttons of his pants, ignoring his soft, "Stop, please."

Giles was an obsession Melinoe's processors refused to relinquish. She would *not* miss this one opportunity to get what she wanted. The man squirmed and wriggled beneath her trying to escape, but Melinoe took advantage of her heavier, metal frame to hold him on the chair. She was annoyed with his lack of cooperation, but at the very least he kept quiet —that was all she needed for permission. "Let me make you feel good." She kissed his temple. If he liked this, perhaps he would keep her and get her away from *that* thing that called himself a man. She whispered in his ear and trailed a single finger around the man's naval. "Relaxed."

Terrified of drawing attention to what this android girl—woman— whatever the hell she thought herself to be—was doing, Giles could think of nothing else he could do but cover his mouth to muffle the mortifying noises coming from his throat. People couldn't see him like this; no one could see this.

Giles would be *ruined*.

Iacchus had been reading a few of the *Brothers Grimm Fairy Tales* he had yet to get around to, when he was distracted from a story about swans by Dr. Firmin and the twins. They had been whispering, so it was no wonder the other humans in the room hadn't noticed them. Iacchus had wanted to go back to reading, but he couldn't stop himself from staring the moment Melinoe plopped herself down in Dr. Firmin's lap. Mr. Dixen's lesson the other week popped to the forefront of his brain, and Iacchus was captive to the scene that was *live* instead of a pixel-based video or stuttered examples.

At first, Melinoe was just talking to him and her hand was rubbing the front of the man's pants, but soon Dr. Firmin's breathing became erratic and she pulled his shirt out over her hand to hide was she was doing.

Iacchus felt his book drop from his lap as he continued watching. Giles was pushing at Melinoe's waist and thighs, trying to get away, Iacchus guessed…he appeared unsuccessful.

Melinoe's hand was hidden beneath fabric, moving in a sort of circular motion, while the other reached up and pulled Giles' head forward by the back of the neck. His face was pulled into her breast, nearly smothering him, and Melinoe let out a soft sigh when he *finally* stopped struggling. She loosened her grip, letting him shift his face more comfortably into her chest. It seemed all Giles could do was moan into her skin and hold onto her thigh like he was going to fall off the chair otherwise.

Which he probably would, considering the way she was now moving her hips slightly back and forth. Iacchus couldn't help but be fixated.

Macaria had gone from trying to ignore her sister and Dr. Firmin, to watching slyly out the corner of her eyes. Iacchus wondered why she was fidgeting her legs. Hecate too, Iacchus noticed, was trying to scrutinize the scene without being caught, by taking quick glances over the top of his book. Other than the androids however, Dr. Firmin and Melinoe seemed to go completely unnoticed by everyone else in the room.

Iacchus bit his lip as he watched. Dr. Firmin was shifting his hips now, feet scraping on the ground. Melinoe was repeating the word 'Baby' over and over for some reason just loud enough for Dr. Firmin and had her eyes shut. Her forehead was buried in Dr. Firmin's hair and her lips would touch his temple occasionally. Iacchus still couldn't see what her hand was doing. Whatever it was, it was making Dr. Firmin curse under his breath and use his hand to pull Melinoe's hips forward with a desperate grip on her thigh. Curiosity finally got the best of Iacchus. "Mr. Dixen."

Rupert looked down when he felt a tug on his pant leg. Iacchus' book was on the floor, and his wide blue eyes were looking up at him inquisitively. "Yeah, what do you need Ia-kid?"

"Is sex really relaxing?" Iacchus asked.

Rupert stared hard at the boy and his seemingly innocent question. So much for the hopes that the boy never mentioned that little talk they had in his lab ever again. And he'd been so quiet on the subject, too. Rupert wondered if it had come up in his story book. "Not uh, usually, during." Rupert glanced around the cafeteria to see if anyone was listening. The closest was Rod, but he was lost in head-phone land. "I guess afterwards you can be pretty sated. Why?"

"Melinoe said that she wanted to help Dr. Firmin relax before she crawled into his lap," Iacchus stated bluntly. "Her body is blocking most of what she's doing, but the actions seem to suggest they're having sex. It looks like too much work to be relaxing, and his heart is racing, so I wondered if she had lied."

Rupert choked on his tongue and turned his head so fast that he may have given himself whiplash. *Well I'll be damned.* The old man stared at the near silent commotion in the back corner of the room where his boss was trying to blend into the wall. Not that Rupert blamed him with their *experimental test subject* in his lap. Giving him a hand job apparently. "Wow."

It seemed to be Mr. Dixen's turn to stare intently at Dr. Firmin and Melinoe. Iacchus looked back and forth between Mr. Dixen and Dr. Firmin and frowned. He wondered why the older man was gaping so blatantly, instead of continuing their conversation. "Is something the matter?"

"Ia-kid," Rupert licked his lips and rubbed a sweaty palm on his pants. "Do me a big favor, and don't tell anyone about this."

"Why?" Iacchus asked again, furrowing his eyebrows. Why was Mr. Dixen so nervous all of a sudden? It had been a simple question hadn't it? "Are they doing something wrong?"

"Yes. Yes they are." Rupert stood up slowly so as to not draw attention, and placed a hand on Iacchus' head. He tried to keep from squeezing as his blood began to pump faster. He could not believe Giles of all people would do something this stupid. Rupert looked at table behind him and spotted the empty bottle. Or maybe he would. "Do *not* tell anyone you saw them. Giles over there could get into a lot of trouble for this. Do you understand?"

"Yes," Iacchus whispered under Mr. Dixen's harsh gaze. He'd never seen the older man this angry before. Before he knew it, Mr. Dixen was slowly walking towards the otherwise indisposed Dr. Firmin. It only took a minute for him to get past Macaria and lean down next to Dr. Firmin's ear and whisper something harshly. Iacchus was pretty sure he heard "What do you think you're doing? Are you trying to get caught?" and Melinoe answering back for the out of breath doctor with a "Mind your own business, old man."

Iacchus was impressed that a fight hadn't broken out.

It did end up taking another five minutes though to yank Melinoe away from Giles. Rupert desperately tried to hold in his temper through ragged breathing. Giles looked suitably ashamed, his shoulders hunched and his eyes downcast, but that android girl looked ready to commit murder. Her scowl reminded Rupert of his wife when she found him sneaking candy from her personal stash hidden in the closet. Rupert pushed at her shoulder—the girl didn't budge. "Don't give me that look, you know damn well the stuff Marvin's been teaching you is inappropriate."

"Then I clearly need a better teacher, and Giles is pretty good, don't you think?" Melinoe hissed back. Macaria had walked up behind her and placed her head on her twin's shoulder. She wrapped her arms around Melinoe's waist. It was a subtle form of warning, and the annoying technician took the step back. Macaria's look of boredom never passed, but she did glance occasionally to the doctor currently trying to fix his pants and clothes. "We weren't hurting anything."

"Do you have any idea what would happen if anyone other than me and Iacchus noticed what was going on?" Rupert grabbed the haughty girl's arm. "Do you?"

"They would think Dr. Firmin got lucky?" Macaria smiled over her sister's shoulder, speaking up for the first time since they ended up in this cafeteria. "I would think."

"Why you—"

"Rupert." Giles tucked in his shirt best he could while fighting the blush coating his face and sweat on his palms. His skin was crawling beneath his clothes, as if he could still feel Macaria even now that she was a foot away. Rupert's face was still furious, and Giles wanted to shrink into the tiles. His voice lacked his usual sense of authority. "We'll discuss this later."

"Yeah, later." Rupert shook his head before slapping Giles upside his with the back of his palm. It probably wasn't wise to hit your boss, but right now he was acting like an idiot. The alcohol on his breath definitely hadn't helped matters when a pretty girl, human or not, set herself down in his lap. There was one last thing he wanted to make very clear before he left: "I'm not bailing you out next time, so learn to say 'no,' got it?"

"Believe me, Rupert," Giles held his head. He could feel more than see the twins shift slightly as they stood in front of him, Melinoe studying her hand and the new substance that coated it with a touch of awe. Giles covered his eyes and would give anything that the past fifteen minutes hadn't happened. "I *tried*."

Rupert snorted and wondered how just how much of that statement he could believe. Rupert blamed it on the alcohol, or the man's penchant for lying. He just couldn't picture Giles not putting up more of a fight if the girl was truly forcing him into it. Either way, the man looked pretty pathetic one way or another. "Come on, I'll take you to the bathroom to clean up."

"Thanks." Giles vowed the next time he saw Marvin awake he was going to punch him in the face.

Becky arrived just in time to see Giles go through with his threat. She walked through the cafeteria door (after twenty minutes arguing with the police at the entrance that *yes she was getting in, thank you*) looking for Abel or the boys when she spotted her boss glaring at Marvin, who was blinking up from the floor like he had just woken up. Becky checked her watch and noted the time was almost three in the morning, so that was probably the case. The moment her eyes left the face of the watch, Becky watched Giles swing his arm back and ram his fist into the middle of Marvin's face. He broke the right lens of the pervert's glasses, and most likely the cartilage in his nose.

Becky was starting to believe that the men in this building truly were helpless without her. At the moment though, there was only one man she even wanted to see—Abel. To do that, she needed to find either him or Hecate. Chances were high, the two were together. Spotting Hecate sitting on the edge of Abel's metal cot with his back pressed up against a lump covered in a blue jacket, she called that assumption pretty accurate.

Hecate was swinging his feet back and forth on the edge of the cot slowly as to not disturb Abel. The man was utterly exhausted and had passed out cold the moment he hit the bed. Hecate had occupied himself with reading for a while, but the commotion with Dr. Firmin and Melinoe had distracted him far too much to continue. So after deciding the floor was no longer good enough, he crawled up onto the cot with Abel and used the man as sort of a back rest. Hecate took comfort in the heat from Abel's back soaking into his sweater. A shadow fell over his face and he smiled up at a woman he had fully expected to see sooner or later. "Hello, Ms. Becky."

"Hey yourself, pest." Becky looked at the man unconscious on the cot.

His five o'clock shadow was dark enough now to be noticeable. Becky wondered if he kept a razor in his office, or if the officers would even let them go get it. She pointed down at the man and looked back at the kid. "How long has he been out?"

"Since we were moved to the cafeteria." Hecate shrugged and started to twist his new watch around his wrist. "Dr. Moreau was almost asleep before he got the cot unfolded."

"Perfect." Becky hummed and let out an unexpected yawn herself. She had been asleep when Giles called to explain she might not be able to get into the lab tomorrow due to *another* murder that had taken place that night. Whoever was behind all this sure worked fast. Becky shoved at Hecate's shoulder, the metal bed and its stiff mattress looking more inviting by the second. "Scoot over, kid."

"Huh?" Hecate answered back before finding himself led off the cot by the woman pulling his arm and dropped to his feet. He would have struggled, but the likely hood of knocking the cot over was high. Ms. Becky then proceeded to squeeze herself in the spare room of the cot placing her back to Abel before pulling his coat up and over the two of them. "What are you doing?"

"Sleeping." Becky snorted and curled in just enough that she was no longer hanging over the edge of the snug little cot. It probably wasn't made for two people, but Becky was a small woman and she would make it work. Besides, Hecate wasn't the only one who liked the feeling of Abel against his back. "Go bother someone else for a while."

Hecate frowned, but walked off anyway. Making a scene would do him no good and only serve to wake up Abel, who desperately needed the sleep. Maybe he'd go find out what Iacchus was up to, now that the twins were preoccupied with things other than talking to themselves.

CHAPTER 15

ABEL DECIDED THAT going to sleep had probably left him out of the loop far more than he would have liked. Abel rubbed his stiff shoulder and felt goose bumps through his shirt. For some reason, he woke up with Becky cuddling against his back (odd because he was pretty sure she had gone home), Marvin sporting an impressive shiner (not so odd actually), Rupert seemingly frustrated with something (which was definitely odd), and Giles refusing to look anyone in the eye (odd no matter how you looked at it). All in all, the only thing that seemed normal was Hecate, and even then, he had been (oddly) talking with Iacchus when Abel woke from the cot.

Despite his friends' odd social issues, he hadn't missed much when it came to the murder case, at least. Abel rubbed his face and ran his tongue along his teeth. The thin film that settled on the enamel tasted bitter, but Abel doubted they'd let him go after the toothbrush in his office bathroom. Detective Saxon had interviewed Jessica one more time and had started processing the scene, but for the most part they weren't any closer to finding anything than when they started.

It was rather frustrating.

Becky wasn't much help either, Abel hated to admit. The woman had glued herself to his side and he could tell it was starting to bug Hecate. It might have been too late to realize, but the jealousy in Hecate's face when he didn't have Abel's undivided attention was becoming more noticeable by the second. Abel wondered if it'd always been there and he'd just been too blinded by affection to notice. Abel sighed and wrapped his arms tighter around the boy sitting in his lap, hugging Abel's chest. At least trying to manage the kid's weight was more pleasant than thinking of human faces missing their eyes.

"I hope they find whoever is killing those people soon," Abel looked up at the ceiling. The grid stared down at him in its uniformity and the doctor wished everything else was that controlled, if only for an hour or two. Abel shifted Hecate, slightly, the boy complying and oddly quiet. If he wasn't already aware Hecate was unable, Abel would have thought the boy was drifting to sleep. The focus in the boy's eyes was his only indication that Hecate was aware and listening. "One death was unacceptable and now there've been four."

"I just wish we had a definite reason for the murders," Becky answered next to Abel on the cot, legs crossed and the decorated cigarette in her mouth. The blue tip was glowing softly and she sucked in a hit of sweet, sweet, nicotine. "Because right now the only thing they all have in common is the lab and the damn Olympian's Children."

"You don't really think it has to do with that, do you?" Abel asked fully aware that Hecate was paying attention to their conversation despite his silence. Abel's fingers tightened on the boy's back. "I mean, I know people disagree with the project, but murder seems a little extreme. Why kill the janitor? Or Steve or the protestor himself? Veronica made sense as a target, but as far as in the lab the only person in charge of the project is Giles," Abel stopped himself and corrected. "Not that I'd want anything to happen to him, he just seems—"

"Like the obvious target," Becky finished for him. She looked down at Hecate, focusing on the red, glowing marks on his cheeks. Becky still thought that had been a stupid idea. It made the brat look demonic, not robotic. "I know what you meant, Abel."

"Dr. Moreau," Hecate piped in and tilted his head to the side. There was something still rattling around in his head that the boy had yet to get a proper answer for. Perhaps now was the right time. Hecate pulled back just enough to see Abel's eyes. "Do these deaths really still bother you that much? You only knew one of the victims personally."

"Sometimes, that doesn't matter, Hecate," Abel moved the boy over, so most of the weight was on his left leg. His right had long past fallen asleep. That tingling, prickly feeling was too much for him to handle right now. "Sometimes, you just feel bad for other people. Every one of those people had families and friends, and if something like that were to happen to you or Giles or Becky, I'm not sure I could handle it. I can't imagine what they're going through…what this person is doing is, well, it's monstrous."

"I see," Hecate stated. "I'm sorry you feel that way."

Abel, shifted in place, unable to get into a comfortable position all of a sudden. Hecate was too heavy. Abel turned to Becky hoping to change the subject. "So, why did Giles hit Marvin, again?"

"Hell if I know." Becky shrugged and patted her pockets looking for a new cartridge for her cigarette. She frowned when she realized that she had run out, and shoved the now useless piece of plastic in her pocket. "Something about the twins."

"I think I should go talk to him." Abel shifted Hecate off his lap and onto the metal cot. Abel stood and put his hands on his lower back before stretching, trying to work out the remaining stiffness. He had considered leaving Hecate there with Becky, but the kid was still mad about being shooed away earlier. Abel just resigned himself to holding the boy's hand to let him know he was coming along. "I'll see you in a bit, Becky."

"Alright, but don't take too long." Becky collapsed back on the bed. She watched Abel and the kid walk away to find Giles and frowned, staring at the ceiling. Their world was collapsing around them; crumbling to reveal a bigger, badder, and more devastating threat to her paycheck. A light flickered overhead before burning out.

Abel released Hecate's hand when he reached for Giles' shoulder. The child had hoped to stay with Abel, but quickly realized he wasn't wanted. Giles was turned so that he was facing only Abel, and that Hecate stood off to his back. He spoke quietly, as if to keep the conversation within his little bubble with Abel. Not that it mattered. It wasn't as if Hecate had any desire to listen to the story about the twins and Dr. Firmin, anyway, even if he could hear the man plain as day. Hecate had seen more than enough a few hours ago as it was.

Speaking of the twins, Hecate spotted the both of them sitting at a table with Mr. Green, nursing his black eye. Green was in the center of the two girls, making sort of an android-human sandwich. Melinoe had her head in her hands, staring wistfully at Dr. Firmin across the room. Her sister Macaria, on the other hand, was sitting close to Mr. Green, leaning on his shoulder. Her arms were wrapped around his elbow and upper arm, resembling a cephalopod clinging to a fish.

Hecate snuck away from Abel and a reddening Giles to go pay the trio a visit. His approach went unnoticed, due to the sulking, until Hecate was standing directly behind Mr. Green. Hecate smiled as he said, "Hello." Clearly startled by the unexpected greeting, Mr. Green jerked backward, nearly falling out of his chair. Hecate smiled slyly and looked over the girls while addressing the older man. "They're very talented, aren't they? Did you teach them that little performance earlier? I have to wonder when you had time, considering how short a time they have been functioning." Hecate clicked his teeth together. "Then again, we are fast learners…"

Marvin flinched, shrinking in his seat. When Giles had first punched him, he wasn't sure what he had done, but it had been explained well enough. Giles first, in a harsh whisper that easily carried the same weight as if his boss had been shouting at him. Melinoe was second, who had mercilessly compared the two of them. Worst of all, little Macaria (the only one who truly appreciated him, dammit!) continued to bow to her sister and refused to openly defend him. Marvin was in pain, scared of a killer, and his girls had betrayed him. Now this little brat was going to rub it in his face? Oh no, sir. Not today. Marvin turned around so that he was facing the brat and poked him in his cheap, ugly sweater. "Yeah, I did teach them everything. Clearly I did well for them to pick up their skills so quickly." Marvin smirked. "Why? Wanted a lesson? I'm sure you'd love to jerk off that Doc of yours, as much as you pine after him like a little —"

One of these days, Marvin would remember that size didn't matter when your skeleton was made of metal.

Hecate was fast enough to cover the man's mouth so the yelp couldn't be heard from Hecate's tiny fist ramming itself into the bastard's ribcage. He removed his clenched hand slowly, relishing the slight vibrations from Green's skin as he adjusted to the sudden pain. Hecate's markings were radiating a red that wasn't looking particularly 'apple' at the moment. Green squirmed in his seat, unable to escape Hecate's iron grip on his face. *Good.*

No one was allowed to say things like that about Abel. *No one.* Hecate hissed at the terrified man, "Abel is *not* a pervert." Mr. Green tried to jerk his head to get Hecate to let go. The android refused him, digging his thumb and fingers into the man's cheeks. The two girls stared on in shock, unsure of what to do as Hecate continued. "If you so much as insinuate that he is on the same level as you, I will rip off your genitalia and feed the entire package to my mice."

Marvin nodded fiercely in agreement and made many mental notes to add Abel to his list of people not to mention around the androids. Becky was already a given around Iacchus, but he had already forgotten Hecate's recent violent streak. He *had* almost broken that board member's arm. Hecate had been so short with his temper—Marvin froze. Could it be the programming was unraveling? Iacchus wasn't exactly all there either and he had been much better at the start, too. Marvin looked over at the girls and realized that his sweet Melinoe had betrayed him for Giles with an equally violent act.

Maybe it was a flaw in all of them.

Hecate watched Mr. Green closely and smiled cutely like the boys in the movies. The effect was lost with Hecate still squeezing the man's mouth and cheek in his hand. "I'm sorry to have scared you, but I do care for Dr. Moreau so very much. I don't appreciate you talking about him that way."

"Right, my bad." Marvin mumbled into the boy's grip. Hecate released his mouth causing Marvin to shiver and scoot closer to the girls. They had betrayed him, but at least they were the better option. Marvin rubbed his cheeks, as it to smooth out the indent. "Never again."

"Wonderful." Hecate smiled and turned to head back to Abel. Hopefully his conversation with Dr. Firmin was finished. Then perhaps they could petition the police for a chance to leave this awful room. It was hardly helping the atmosphere or Abel's mood to be trapped in here any longer.

Marvin sighed in relief when the boy left, and covered his eyes with his hand. This day couldn't get any worse if the killer waltzed in and attacked him.

"That was odd."

Marvin looked over at Macaria. Usually Melinoe spoke up first in conversation. Hearing Macaria take point was almost disturbing. "What was, dear?"

"Hecate called Dr. Moreau by his first name." Macaria looked at her sister, squeezing Marvin's arm a little tighter. "He never does that."

"Huh," Marvin looked back at the boy now hugging Abel's legs. She had a point. The boys always stuck with calling people by the name they had been told to. Ms. Becky. Ms. Lucy. Dr. Firmin. Dr. Moreau. It was just habit. Marvin slumped down in his chair. Did they call them different things when thinking about them in their heads? Was that a slip due to anger? A sign his brain was unraveling to reveal a monster equal to his brother? Marvin looked back up to the ceiling and shivered. "Just what," his eyes lingered on Macaria's steady, focused eyes, "have we created?"

The lights flickered off at noon, leaving only the day light streaming in through the windows. Rupert noticed the red lights on the serving bars had gone out also, indicating that it wasn't just a blown circuit. The power was out in the building. Rupert snorted to himself and shook his head. There was a back-up generator, but it usually took a few minutes to switch on. Their budget wasn't exactly created for building maintenance when there was synthetic skin to develop, and of course keeping the damn wall running. *That* had an uninterruptible power supply all on its own that switched on the second power was cut. Couldn't let the project suffer like the rest of the staff. "Well, isn't that perfect?"

Iacchus nodded slower than he wanted. The world seemed blurry—fuzzy!—for some reason. It was like everything moved in slow motion. Iacchus clicked on an internal scan, and bit his lip when he realized what was wrong. "Mr. Dixen?"

"Yeah, Ia-kid? What's up?"

"I think I need to recharge." Iacchus had to stop for a moment and squinted at the thought. He didn't let things get this bad, usually. He was only two days old the last time. Iacchus bit his lip. "My power cells are at twenty percent."

"Shit." Rupert jolted up, and took Iacchus' hand. The boy was moving like molasses and his eyes were lidded. *Twenty percent?* The boys never let their batteries go below forty to keep things safe. Rupert looked for Hecate and the twins to see if they were showing equal signs of struggle. The androids were responsible for charging themselves up at night, so frankly, it wasn't something most of the staff even thought about. "It'll be okay, Ia-kid. Let's find your brother and go work this out."

The kid had never fully shut down before—neither of the boys had—and Rupert had no intention of finding out what damage it could do to reboot his systems and empty all that cache and program information. "Try shutting down some unnecessary systems to save energy, Ia-kid," Rupert added as an afterthought.

Abel was still reeling over what had happened to Giles—he still couldn't wrap his head around that girl forcing herself on his friend—when Rupert came over in a rush, dragging Iacchus behind him. *Had something else happened?* "What's wrong, Rupert?"

"Hecate," Rupert asked the kid sitting next to the doctor on the short cafeteria chair. "What's your power cell percentage?"

The boy's eyes blinked for a few moments in the same dull expression the boys' always got when consulting internal systems and off-screen data. Hecate perked up with a shrug and repeated the number. "Forty-five percent."

"Okay, that's better." Rupert sighed. Hecate would probably be good until tomorrow, but Iacchus was cutting it close. "Smaller body, less energy."

"What are you going on about, Rupert?" Giles muttered, head buried in his arms. He was emotionally exhausted after trying to convey to Abel that he hadn't intended to do those things with Melinoe. Abel had stressed something about it being non-consensual, considering he was drunk and unable to stop the girl thanks to her strength, but that would be admitting to things that Giles would rather not. The manager had let it happen and should take responsibility.

No matter how disgusting he felt.

If Giles admitted anything otherwise, he'd probably have an episodic break-down. There would be police reports, and therapy, and Abel's pitying looks would get worse. Giles' fingers twitched in his unkept hair, shifting his foot against the floor. Losing one's self-control wasn't very conducive to keeping control of a building, and making sure *other* people didn't lose their heads over a serial killer loose in the building. As he had told the detective at the start of this mess: he couldn't afford it.

Giles raised his head wearily up at Rupert, begging him for something normal, "Please tell me it's just a status update."

"Iacchus is at twenty percent power." Rupert pointed to the ceiling. "And the back-up generator still hasn't come on yet."

Abel's mouth hung open and he looked up quickly. He and Giles were sitting next to a window, so he hadn't even noticed that the lights had clicked off. "What made the power go out?"

"I don't know. I was a bit more concerned with Iacchus saying his battery was so low," Rupert stressed. "The kid needs a charge and I don't know if the police are willing to escort us down there to check."

"It's doubtful." Giles plucked himself from his comfortable position in the chair. Seems work would override his shame for the moment. He doubted it would help with the headache threatening to split his brain in half, though. "I'll work something out. Come on and bring the kid."

Hecate watched as Iacchus stumbled after the two men, swaying on his feet. The smaller boy scrunched his face in pity having remembered what it felt like to have your power stretched so thin. He had tried it once to see just how low he could go and still function. Hecate found going beneath fifty percent was just not a good way to run efficiently and had kept charged ever since (for the record, he made it to five percent before he was rushed to a charging station, unable to move his limbs). Iacchus had never been good at keeping track of those things. "I hope he'll be alright."

"I'm sure Detective Saxon won't let anything happen to your brother." Abel rubbed Hecate's back soothingly. "He's good at his job and that means protecting and serving the people, as well as looking out for the bad guys."

"The people," Hecate answered slowly, looking thoughtful. "So we count, then?"

Abel hugged the boy soundly. "As long as you're in this lab and in my care, yes. You two count." He squeezed when he saw the boy's eyes widen. Abel pulled the boy tighter to his chest, his chin on Hecate's head. "And heaven help the person who disagrees."

Hecate grinned into Abel's chest triumphantly without the good doctor's notice.

CHAPTER 16

LESTER SAXON STUDIED Giles Firmin. The first time he'd met the man, Firmin had been clean, pressed, and slicked in sterile grease. Currently, Firmin's hair was sticking up in odd places, sweat mixing with the hair gel, and his clothes were wrinkled. The effort to tuck in his shirt and smudge the lipstick stains (when had those gotten there?) from his shirt collar in an attempt to be cleaned up was another one of those character quirks Saxon was filing away for future use. For the moment, though, Firmin's hygiene wasn't a top priority, but his request most certainly was.

Saxon laced his fingers together on the table top. "You want to leave this room, and the safety of numbers, to go down unlit hallways to check the generator. Again, in an unpopulated sector of the building, so that boy," Lester paused to point at Iacchus, "can plug into a socket. I get that right?"

"We'll be more than happy to consent to an escort." Giles spoke more smoothly than he had in the past two days, and he could feel his spirits lifting already. Personal problems would always be his downfall, but this was business. Business he could handle in spades. Giles held his two fingers up and shifted so his hip was touching the edge of the lunch-table-turned-headquarters. "Two, if you like, and I'll even hunt down my professionally trained security guard. This boy needs to recharge his power cells or he'll shut down, and it takes specialized equipment to do the job, you understand."

"And that's a problem, because?" The kid was an android, Saxon relented that was still creepy, but he was still a machine. A computer if you wanted to get 'technical,' and those turned on and off all the time.

As far as Lester could tell, this was an unnecessary risk that reeked of the classic 'Let's split up, gang!' motto that caused so many problems in old kid show mysteries. "Can't he just shut down for a while?"

Iacchus shook his head in fear, which of all things managed to penetrate his drunken state. His power dropped another click to nineteen percent. Fear pawed at the edges of Iacchus' mind—*what if he says no!?* "I've never done that before."

"For all we know, shutting down could be the equivalent of dying for these boys. There's no guarantee he'll wake up as the same person," Rupert interjected on Iacchus' behalf. "It'll take maybe an hour to find out why the generator hasn't clicked back on yet, and if that doesn't work we have a spare running for sure in the testing rooms. I can plug him in there and after two or three hours he'll be charged enough to get out of the red zone."

"I don't like the idea of you all leaving this room," Lester started. They were no closer to finding this killer and Saxon had a gut feeling the man was hiding *somewhere* in the eight story complex (nine, if you counted the basement). He had to come out of his hole sometime and Saxon couldn't help but think letting these folks go would be tempting fate. "Even with an escort it could be dangerous."

"Which floors have you already swept for the culprit?" Rupert asked. "Maybe the floors we need to be on have already been checked. Then it'd be safer, if only a little, right?"

The detective scrubbed his at his cheek with his fingers and looked at the two men: Dr. Firmin, stern and Mr. Dixen, worried. The boy stared at the wall in such a way that it made Lester uncomfortable. Iacchus' eyes were just so *empty* that he wasn't sure what to do. "How badly does he need this again?"

"Very much," Giles said. "In fact, it might be good for us to deal with this now. The other three will probably need charging soon, as well, so it's an issue that's going to come up again."

"Besides," Rupert smirked and pointed back into the room with his thumb towards Hecate, Abel and Becky, "they get wind that you're going to just let the kids shut down, you're going to have more to worry about than our resident serial killer." Rupert leant down and held his hand up conspiratorially in front of his mouth. "And believe you me, Ms. Becky's a scary lady when you piss her off."

"Alright, fine," Lester replied after a moment of deliberation. He'd just have to make the most of a stubborn situation. The detective pointed a finger at the two of them. "But you're not going alone. You're taking an escort and I want you all to call in at least once every ten minutes."

"Thank you." Giles shoved his hands into his pockets and straightened his posture. It was nice when things went his way, no matter how rare that had been lately. "If you'll be so kind?"

Lester waved over two of his men and gave the command of, "Follow them; radio if you find trouble." Receiving his 'yes, sirs' and watching the scientists venture off into the dark hallway, Lester couldn't shake the feeling that this had been a bad idea. The cafeteria was loud with voices talking and folks complaining about the situation, but Lester didn't mind that. Meant folks were alive to complain. No. It was that dark, quiet hallway that scared the shit out of him.

The quiet killers were always that way: terrifying.

Saxon stood up from his post at the foremost table and shoved calloused hands in his straight-legged pants' pockets. Loud, obnoxious killers were easy. Horrifying as much as anyone else capable of that sort of violence, but predictable. Rage and anger made people sloppy. They liked to talk and give themselves away; easy to goad. The quiet ones, though—Lester took a good long look over the people in the room *not* talking—they were the scary ones. Lester never knew what made their insides tick as their minds took the silence to weave plots worthy of the greatest detective novels.

Best you could do against them was to force them out of their safe little hiding spots, mental or otherwise. Keep all their victims in one place and hope they crack—serial killers just couldn't help themselves. Or better yet, keep them hiding in the same gutter or back room so long they lose their focus to the fear of being caught—or just plain succumb to boredom. Treat them like animals; watch what happens when the fence breaks and they come at you screaming. Or, Lester smiled guiltily, tempt them with victims all alone in the big dark hallway. *Make the best of a bad situation.*

Lester had a feeling their guy was going to start making some noise.

There was something wrong with Hecate. Becky couldn't quite place what *exactly* was wrong with the spoiled little thing, but something was not right. For starters, the kid was staying fairly still, save for the clenching and unclenching of his hands repeatedly. She did get a rather large clue from Hecate glaring over at Marvin. Becky nearly smacked herself in the forehead. *Marvin pissed the kid off.* Alright, that she could deal with. "So, what'd the jerk do?"

Hecate looked over at Becky with shock on his face. He was usually better than that at hiding his emotions. Perhaps it was the stress of the situation. Things had certainly gotten crazy around the laboratory in ways Hecate had not predicted. He for one certainly hadn't planned on trying to break that woman's arm for example—it had just happened. Just like Melinoe taking matters into her own hand and Iacchus unable to keep track of his power cells. Or of course that protestor sneaking into the building causing all this trouble in the first place. This was supposed to be a quick check-up and then the board would *leave.* "What do you mean, Ms. Becky?"

"Marvin." She glanced over at Abel camped out on the floor surrounded by food. He was attempting to open a can of tuna he had raided from the cafeteria pantry for a make-shift tuna salad. They had found the food, but apparently their kitchen staff hid their tools, because no one could find a can opener to save their lives. That Rod kid had a Swiss Army Knife to borrow though, which Abel had almost figured out. Becky smiled to herself at the child-like nature coming out in her friend. He seemed distracted enough to talk about Hecate being upset without interference. "What'd he do?"

"He made comments about Dr. Moreau that I did not appreciate," Hecate said cautiously, still unsure of Ms. Becky's angle. Her curiosity was odd, and Hecate ran scenarios of possible reasons for wanting to know about his personal life. True, she had been warming up to him and his brother, but the woman was still the first to suggest termination in the event of a breakdown. Hecate doubted her opinion of them was going to change overnight due to a few murders. Granted, Iacchus had nearly broken her arm once or twice, but that was hardly an excuse.

"I see." Becky wondered if she, too, was going to have to punch Marvin. The woman almost laughed. Marvin seemed to be doing wonders for everyone's stress relief lately. He probably should have taken that into account when he made the twins. "Like what?"

"I'd rather not repeat his exact words," Hecate answered eyes narrowing. The conversation had been brief and only alluded to the suggestion, but that in itself was enough to breech Hecate's temper.

"They were indecent and highly inappropriate for any form of conversation."

Becky snorted and smacked the kid lightly in the back of the head. "Everything that comes out of his mouth fits that description, kiddo. Get used to it."

"If I must." Hecate shrugged and looked over at Abel. The older man was smiling now, having successfully managed to open the can of tuna with the Swiss Army Knife. Hecate couldn't help but wonder why Abel hadn't just asked him for help. Thin steel would be nothing to open...

"So, who do you think did it?" Becky asked absently, watching Abel wrestle with a jar of mayonnaise.

Hecate scrunched his face. "Did what?"

"The murders. You've got a computer for a brain, what does it conclude, given what we know?" Becky shrugged. She wondered why no one had thought of putting their processors to use before. Sure, Iacchus was a bit on the dim side, but brat though he may be, Hecate was frighteningly intelligent. "I'm just curious, more than anything. Surely you've thought it over at least once."

"Not really," Hecate answered smoothly. "The deaths of those four individuals do not concern me."

"Oh? Not even the one who pays for your maintenance?"

"You can get more money anywhere, Ms. Becky." Hecate smiled when Abel popped the lid off the jar in his hand. *Another thing he could have asked for help with.* "Dr. Firmin is just short sighted, thinking only of grants and donations as they're the easiest option. Production of an alternative material to sell and garner money would take more effort on his part, but he's more than capable."

Becky was honestly surprised Hecate had even thought of that much. "That right?"

"He gets his mind set on something and refuses to look in other directions." Hecate said, voice laced with a hint of bitterness.

"For someone who doesn't spend time with him, you sure sound like you know him well." Becky's finger twitched, the lack of nicotine catching up with her. She wondered how long it would take for the shakes to hit.

"Abel talks about him." Hecate's fingers gripped the bottom of his chair. He squeezed hard enough to crack the plastic. "All the time."

"Abel?" Becky watched the plastic warp under Hecate's fingers. His face was straight, eyebrows narrowed together staring into the distance as something he could only see in his mind. Becky gripped her own chair. "Since when do you call him that?"

"I didn't. I clearly said 'Dr. Moreau,'" Hecate corrected immediately, aware of the lie even as he said it. *Get a grip,* he commanded to himself. Jealousy was a cruel mistress, toying with his thoughts like a whore. Losing control of his thoughts due to something so basic was humiliating and utterly *unacceptable.* Hecate glanced up at Ms. Becky, eyes *daring* her to make another comment on the matter. "He and Dr. Firmin are quite close."

Becky's spine felt like it had abandoned her body, all while she remained frozen in place. She teased Abel about what a little brat he was raising, but the 'child' sitting next to her right now wasn't spoiled: Hecate was terrifying. His expression was warped and wasted on a twelve year old—eyes narrowed and mouth straight. Hecate looked at her the same way a waiter looks at a fly—Becky didn't doubt he could kill her right now without a second thought. There probably wouldn't even be a first thought—just the ending of an annoyance.

He probably wouldn't even realize he had done something wrong. Values and morals had never been high on their teaching agenda, making room for more important things like processing speed and technical education. Between Iacchus' outbursts and Hecate's indifference, Becky wondered if they shouldn't have drilled ethics into the boys' heads earlier.

"Becky, you want one?"

Becky jerked at Abel's call, noting that Hecate's posture straightened and smile returned immediately before Abel had even finished pronouncing the 'Beh' in her name. Hecate kicked his legs back and forth, hands covering the broken plastic, and face smiling happily—just like any other day in the lab. That sort of transformation wasn't perfected overnight; Hecate had *practiced* that adjustment. Becky rotated her neck to the side, trying to find comfort in Abel's open and ignorant eyes. "Want one what?"

"Sandwich?" Abel held up a plate, complete with tuna-salad sandwich. Bits of mayo and tuna decorated the bread unmixed, but it was the best he could do without a spoon. It wasn't his best work, but it was edible. Becky's hands were shaking slightly, and Abel decided he had finished just in time. She probably hadn't eaten all day to be having shakes from an empty stomach. "You've got to be hungry."

"Yeah, I am, thanks." Becky smiled and took the plate, unsettled by the boy next to her. Becky wanted to grab Abel and sprint out of the cafeteria—far, far away from Hecate. Abel pulled himself off the floor, and sat down next to Hecate on the chair between them. He smiled at Hecate so lovingly it made Becky's stomach turn. "That's great."

"Are you alright?" Abel lifted the sandwich off the plate, a bit of tuna falling free. "You look sort of pale."

Hecate glared at her, just outside of Abel's view, *daring* her to say anything about their conversation. Becky kept her mouth shut. "No, just hungry."

"Okay." Abel answered, taking a bite out of his food. He'd talk to her about it later. "But let me know if something's wrong, okay?"

Hecate started to chirp up at Abel, questioning why the man hadn't asked for help, successfully alienating Becky from future conversation. For the moment, that was fine with her. Becky made a note to grab Giles and have a *long* conversation about Hecate. Becky glanced at Abel out of the corner of her eyes—they might need an intervention.

Stevie Late needed to use the restroom. His bladder stretched behind his belly, ready to burst any second. He shifted in his seat, thighs pressed together. His left foot was tilted, ankle nearly scraping on the tile while the right twitched in place. After Veronica, going to the restroom was more petrifying than the embarrassment of pissing his pants in public. At least the android had left. Watching Iacchus leave the room with Giles was the first time Stevie had relaxed since the kid threw a chair through the conference room wall. Androids—*these* androids—were supposed to be the cool kind. The ones that did what they were told, not the ones who had uprisings and wiped out humanity. Iacchus needed to stop channeling Stevie's comic books.

Stevie wrung his hands together under the table. These androids were *dangerous*. People were freaking out about a serial killer and Veronica was dead—that still hadn't sunk in yet, either, Stevie kept expecting her to bust in and demand a muffin—but there had been a machine with emotional problems and twice as strong as anyone else in the room and *no one seemed worried*. Stevie's heel hit the ground repeatedly as his leg bounced nervously, knees buckled together. The staff was as crazy as the robot.

Stevie shot to his feet. He needed a restroom. That was it. That was all he needed. Stevie needed to clear his bladder and his head and wash his face with a little water and stop freaking out and letting his brain run a mile a minute and—Stevie took in a deep breath. He slid away from his chair after a minute of heavy breathing, and resisting the urge to just wet himself where he stood. Stevie's sneakers peaked up from behind his slacks, laces loose. He forced them to move one foot in front of the other around the table. Stevie tapped the closest officer he could see on the shoulder. "Uh, sir?"

"Yeah?" Louis turned up from the scene reports. Saxon had asked him to go over them one more time, but it was looking to be futile. No matter how many times he looked them over, he wasn't any closer to narrowing down a suspect with the evidence available. There were too many variables and alibis that checked out on the up and up. Louis closed the report, turning his attention to the shaking man. This was likely to be a more productive use of his time, Louis figured. The man looked petrified, sheet white and glasses sliding off his face. "What can I help you with?"

"I need a john." The officer raised an eyebrow at him. Stevie cursed, knocking his hand into his glasses as he tried to reach up and smooth his hair. Stevie rubbed his nose, wincing. "I mean I need to go to a john—the john—dammit! I need to use the toilet, okay?"

Louis was polite enough to swallow his laugh as the man stumbled over his words. He sighed, relaxing his shoulders when the man took his glasses off to rub at his eyes. Louis couldn't blame the poor guy for being so terrified—or embarrassed—when his friend had been murdered twenty feet from him. The stuff they'd been seeing around this complex the past day was torn straight from nightmares. The least he could do was make the man feel safe by being next to a boy in blue. Louis clapped the man on the shoulder, leading him toward the main door. "Alright, come on."

Stevie followed, legs stiff and heavy. His mind emptied—the result of mortification crashing into fear. The resulting wreckage left Stevie too exhausted to worry for killers lurking around the corner. The officer had led him to the restroom before he even registered they left the cafeteria. Having relieved himself in the dim stall, Stevie ignored the officer lingering by the urinal behind him to gather himself. He looked his face over in the oval mirror, fingers gripping on the edges of the porcelain sink. The man with bags under his eyes, and lines on his face staring back was someone Stevie didn't know. He swallowed, throat thick, and turned on the faucet. After two minutes, he cupped his hands under the chilled water and Stevie splashed his face, gasping audibly when the freezing water hit his skin.

The head of the officer crashed into the mirror next to him, cracking the glass; spraying Stevie's cheek with tiny droplets of blood. In his reflection, Stevie watched a single drop slide down his jaw in a thin, watery red line; the only sound in the room a hitched breath.

"Shit!" Stevie backpedaled away from the officer, his destination the door, only to collide with something warm and solid.

"A little *late* for that, don't you think?"

Stevie didn't recognize the voice that called out from behind him, but he didn't care who it was. Stevie made a dash to the side, but was stopped by a hold on his arm. He was yanked back into the warm body who most likely owned the new voice.

"Now hold still."

A hand clamped over Stevie's mouth—the other offending appendage held the head of the poor officer in place on the neighboring mirror. Shards of shattered glass dug into the man's eyes and scalp. Stevie kept his eyes down to avoid seeing the monster reflected in the mirror; the muscular arm extended on the side of his head was more than enough. Stevie whimpered behind the palm pressing into his lips and nose.

This isn't real. This isn't real. This isn't real.

The killer's hand pried its way inside Stevie's mouth—a sick imitation of a lover wanting a suck. His lips allowed the fingers to hold down his tongue, with little struggle, too frightened to bite down. There was a pounding noise in the background. Stevie figured it was his heartbeat thudding against his ribcage. He concentrated on staying still. The killer wasn't moving, strangely content leaning over his shoulder. He was too close. Stevie couldn't afford to be distracted by a noise that may or may not be just inside his head.

The dead officer's eyes stared at him from the side of the mirror, skull caved on one side. Blood poured down the wall to stain the white sink. A droplet splashed onto the tile, hitting the boy's sneakers. The flight or fight response in Stevie reared its ugly head like water bursting from a busted pipe. The board member slammed back into his attacker, shoving his elbow into the man's gut. Instead of falling back, the brutish man pushed forward with a sudden jerk, pinning Stevie in between the sink and the creature's hips. They fit together so tightly, their waists might as well have been welded together.

Steve's feet kicked out on the slick tile of the bathroom floor, trying to escape to the side. The killer pushed up flush against him, forcing Stevie to hold still, the weight heavy on his back. His body was hot from sweat and the heat of the killer behind him, as they stood in the mortifying embrace. The man had to be a hundred degrees—it was burning. He felt like he was burning. Stevie looked to the side in time to watch the dead officer slump down onto the sink, the killer's arm absent from sight. The officer's head hit the sink faucet with a sickening crunch.

Stevie didn't want to be looking in that direction any longer.

He had no choice in the matter with greasy fingers still holding tight to his tongue and chin, keeping his head in place. His jaw ached from being forced into such an awkward position. Stevie felt like crying when the body behind him shifted against his back. He felt something settle on his hip, the weight heavy, before the pounding in his head grew louder. The weight left his hips and there was a rustling sound. Averting his eyes from the officer, Stevie's gaze landed on the mirror with all its cracks and reflective surfaces. Stevie was granted a fractured view of his killer, and the blade headed for the front of his shoulder.

Stevie tasted petroleum with the blood in his mouth.

"I want that door busted down *now!*" Saxon bellowed as his men slammed into the men's room door for the fifth time. Someone had locked the thing from the inside and they didn't have the time to find the tools needed to remove the bolts on the door. They were trying to cut through the door hinges with an ax, but it was still *taking too long*. Not ten minutes ago, Officer Wolfe had taken Stevie Late to the little boy's room, and not five minutes ago Lester and his team heard the screaming. They had frozen at the table trying to figure out the direction of the yelling, only to have it silenced in a breath—that was only a good sign when they saw the victim run out a few moments later. When Late or Wolfe didn't show after a few seconds, Lester took to action.

Saxon pulled the man with the ax back; he was too slow. "Oh, let me do it."

The other officers attempting to break into the room scurried out of the way when the much larger man slammed his shoulder into the door, bursting it open with the skill of a linebacker. The door hung on its side, top hinge ripped from the frame. The detective pulled his gun out front in case the attacker was armed. Lester froze in his place when he saw the carnage in the room, and the familiar red 'paint' now splashed every direction. Saxon lowered his arms, and turned his head to the floor. "Ah, hell."

Wolfe was perched up against a sink, arm lodged behind the faucet. It rooted him in place, preventing the younger man from falling to the ground like a rag doll. Even through all the shards of glass covering his face, Lester could see that his eyes were now missing. The empty sockets hung open like miniature caverns, black under the shadows.

Saxon forced himself not to rush into the scene; kept his feet secured to the ground. Wolfe was dead, and the only thing Saxon would accomplish running to him, would be destroying much needed evidence. Lester heard a sob from his left, revealing the second man very much *alive*. Saxon glanced around one more time making sure there weren't any *other* surprises for him. Not seeing any feet under the stalls, Lester risked someone standing on the seat and headed for Late while officers filed in behind him to check the stalls more properly.

The board member sat curled in on himself under the sink. He struggled to breathe in between the childlike weeping. Stevie's side was pressed tight to the wall, feet kicking sporadically in a twitching motion. Life now on the line, Saxon ducked down to see how much damage had been done. He pulled back the man's shoulder slightly, hoping to see the wound without causing more damage. "Shit."

Stevie Late sobbed horrifically, all the while clutching his right arm to his chest. It had been detached from his body, the stub that used to be connected to the shoulder scraping the ground near Stevie's left thigh. The open wound on his shoulder was pressed into the wall—a fraught attempt to stop the blood flow. It didn't appear to be working. Detective Saxon screamed for the paramedics on hold outside the door to get their asses in the room already.

CHAPTER 17

HE HAD *NOTHING*.

Nothing useful anyway, Lester thought to himself. He stood outside the ICU where their survivor was settled with a copy of the man's medical report under his arm. Beyond the glass wall, his only surviving witness slept on—useless as a source of information. When Stevie Late wasn't zoning out from the trauma, he was drugged out on whatever narcotics he was being fed through the intravenous. Saxon's eyes lingered on the wrappings around Late's shoulder. The doctors had been unable to save the arm. It made the man look even more pathetic than the constant shivering and chalk white skin. Saxon exhaled and looked at the report again.

His arm had been hacked off in the same fashion as the other victims, only a cleaner cut. Saxon chalked that up to practice. What separated Stevie Late from the others? The killer didn't get a chance to finish his work. Lester dropped his forehead on the glass viewing wall, watching Late's chest rise and fall. The monster didn't take the time to kill Stevie, but yet managed to find time to rip out Louis' eyes?

Lester let a breath fall out of his nose, fogging the glass, and tried to get his thoughts back on track. He wouldn't do Louis Wolfe any good by getting emotional. The officer deserved Saxon's best. His *friend* deserved Saxon's best. The banging on the door must have startled the killer into leaving the job undone. To the detective's surprise, it stunned the killer into leaving a sliver of evidence for them to latch onto. Normally, Lester would be grateful for this sort of sloppiness in an evidence barren case— if only they were given more than the point of exit.

The window.

By using the window, the killer had created more questions than answers. The bathroom windows had been locked from the inside, so there was no way for the killer to enter without breaking it. The monster was *already* in the restroom when Stevie and Wolfe entered. Fair enough, but it was the exit out of the window that bothered Lester for two reasons: one, the killer hadn't unlocked the window—he had broken it by pushing the thing open, snapping the latch clean off; two, they were on the fourth floor and there was no immediate ledge outside the window, save for the slim casement.

Their killer was strong enough to bust through a window lock, and agile enough to scale a wall with sparse window ledges and small decorative architectural features as grips.

Lester Saxon was starting to doubt that their killer was human.

Hecate's eyes opened.

His internal meter listed his power cells fully charged, capped at 95 percent. Hecate listened to the hum of the charging bed, and voices mumbling around him. The power returned shortly after the attempt on Mr. Late's life, and the androids were encouraged to charge while they were able. Assuming the killer had been the one to cut the power to start, Hecate figured even the killer got tired of the dark now that the sun had set. Hecate enjoyed the dark hallways, but only when he was left alone to wander. Otherwise, the dimly lit corridors accomplished nothing but frayed nerves in everyone around him. Light caused a feeling of safety, or some other such human nonsense.

Hecate heard a scratching sound from the center of the room. He dropped his head to the side of the bed. Iacchus, Melinoe, and Macaria sat around the main table, playing with the boys' mice. Incidentally, the small creatures appeared grateful for the attention and fresh food after being forgotten in the chaos of lock-downs, the idiocy of the masses, and murder. Hecate pulled forward, disconnecting the plugs from the jacks in his back. Multi-purpose ports were quite possibly the most convenient part of his design.

"Where is Dr. Moreau?" Hecate asked pulling his shirt off a hook. Hecate slipped his arms into the yellow button up. "I would not think he'd be allowed to leave the room."

"They took him and Dr. Firmin downstairs to help calm the rest of the staff. Dr. Firmin may be the boss, but he's not looking well," Iacchus admitted. The man hadn't held himself up with the confidence he usually radiated. Iacchus also thought his hair looked weird, falling in his face. "Dr. Moreau is there for moral support."

Hecate glanced around the room to double check a suspicion as he tucked his shirt into his pants. Since no one was attempting to hide behind a chair, Hecate dubbed himself correct. "So, we are unsupervised, then?"

"Ms. Becky is here." Iacchus threw the end of his scarf over his shoulder. She had been volunteered against her will to be the android babysitter. Iacchus was happy Ms. Becky was around instead of the others, even if she was unhappy about it. Iacchus would take a grumpy Ms. Becky over *no* Ms. Becky any day of the week. "She's in the room next door looking for something to keep herself busy."

Hecate nodded, seeing nothing amiss. The twins were unusually quiet, however; there wasn't even a hint of buzzing. Macaria was staring at the wall, while Melinoe was sketching a portrait of Firmin on a loose sheet of paper. Hecate pulled his sweater over his head, and muffled through the fabric. "Where's Mr. Green?"

"Downstairs with the others." Melinoe answered and tapped a finger on the mouse cage frame. The critters scurried about after each tap, agitated by the motion. She made sure to only do it when Iacchus wasn't looking, slipping back into her sketch whenever he glanced her way. Macaria sat quietly thinking to herself, still miffed at Melinoe. She wasn't keen on talking today after the stunt in the cafeteria and the pain Marvin had gone through. Melinoe had a different opinion: "For once he's using his head and separating himself from us. His connection to us is responsible for his current woes."

"Understandable, considering it is his fault." Hecate nodded and sat on the table top so he could swing his feet freely. Not wanting to discuss the other man much more in depth, Hecate looked at Iacchus. "Are we going to be allowed out of this room when Ms. Becky returns?"

"No," Becky answered in place of Iacchus, holding an aged laptop under her arm. The officer outside the door wouldn't let her down to her office, but Becky had known there were a few old computers floating around in storage she could abuse. "You guys were making the folks down there nervous, and with that bastard loose in the building, they figured it best to reduce stress any way possible."

"If that's the case, I'm rather surprised there isn't more of a police escort up here with us." Hecate pondered. "A single person could hardly stop all of us if we wanted to accomplish something." Hecate smirked when the officer outside the door twitched. "Surely they realize that."

"Priorities changed." Becky kept her distance from Hecate, suspicious of his latest suggestions. Something had unraveled in his head from when the lock-down started and now. Becky really needed to get a hold of Giles before it got worse. She hid her suspicions from the boy with the computer. Becky walked over to a bench in the corner to look for an outlet. If the ram card under the battery cover was anything to go by, she'd be lucky if it even turned on. *4 gigs of ram?* She didn't even think that could run Solitaire anymore. "Besides, I doubt anyone is stupid enough to mess with me when that brat is in the room." Becky pointed to Iacchus and smirked. "Kid's annoying as hell, but he is a powerhouse."

"Thank you." Iacchus' markings glowed with pride. It had been a backwards compliment, but Ms. Becky had complimented him all the same. She had even smiled a little, and that was *beautiful*.

Becky flipped open the laptop lid. The screen lit up after a few blinks and Becky threw her arms up, sliding down in the chair. *At least something around here works.* "Don't get full of yourself, now."

"I won't." Iacchus grinned anyway and looked back at Prime, who was now sticking his front foot through the cage's wire frame. Iacchus touched his finger to the tiny paw; Prime nibbled on his nail. Iacchus would keep Ms. Becky safe and happy, no matter what.

It took Giles and Abel about an hour to sort everyone into a seat. Where the room had once been filled with people standing aimlessly in various cliques, they were now all occupying the first row of tables of the cafeteria, two feet from the headquarters setup. Names had been checked off, and alibis had been re-recorded. Keeping track of where everyone was at had suddenly become much more important. The police needed to make sure the killer wasn't one of the people in the room first and foremost, and afterwards their priority involved evacuating the building. Giles happened to agree wholeheartedly with that last bit.

"It just doesn't make any sense." Abel crossed his arms over his chest. There was a sea of facial expressions before him, each with a varying degree of fear etched in their expressions. Abel's face would probably match if he wasn't too exhausted to move the muscles. "Is it sad, Giles, that I almost don't want to find the killer?"

"Why's that?" Giles kept his eyes on the side doors, and the guards that watched them. Keeping exits in his line of sight had become top priority in Giles' little world. Their killer was smart, and had to know the building inside and out to keep up his disappearing act. It was becoming more and more likely that their serial killer was an employee. Giles drummed his fingers on his arm, vaguely aware that Abel was still talking. The only person Giles knew that aware of the the building's workings was Jenner.

Giles *really* hoped it wasn't Jenner.

The man was already an obsessive compulsive, workaholic with years of military training under his belt...Giles kept his eyes and face straight as he repeated that sentence in his head: Jenner was an obsessive compulsive, workaholic, with years of military training under his belt, access to the security system, and knew the building inside and out so well he knew where the crickets played tennis in the basement. *Shit.* Giles shook his head. *That was ridiculous.* Jenner wasn't a serial killer. He wouldn't go to such extremes to protect the building from intruders like rogue protestors or janitors not doing their job.

Giles needed more sleep; lots and lots more sleep. He was starting to think up mad theories due to sleep deprivation. That was the only explanation—accusing Jenner of treachery against the company was equivalent to telling Gandhi he was too violent. Giles heard his name off to the side and internally cursed yet again. Abel had apparently been answering Giles' initial question while he contemplated exits and security guards gone mad. Giles shook his head to physically clear his thoughts, and apologized, "I'm sorry, what was that?"

"I said," Abel repeated, "I don't think I want to meet someone capable of doing things like this." Something was pulling at Abel's chest about this whole mess. Abel wasn't sure why, but he really didn't want to know who the killer was. He just wanted the bastard to stop and go away. When he left things could go back to normal. "What's the point of mutilating his victims this way if he just wanted the project to end?"

"If I had to guess?" Giles said, shrugging his shoulders. "We probably haven't figured out his real motive. The project being the end target was just a theory we had." Giles slipped a hand through his hair, frowning at the greasy build-up. Giles made a note to sneak away to the locker rooms for a quick shower if he could fit it in. "For all we know it's nothing more than some psycho just getting his kicks."

"True." Abel's eyes fell on three particularly quiet figures and wiped sweat from his brow. "But it is hard to deny that the board is being targeted at the moment."

"They'll be the first to leave once we've cleared everyone." There was no way they'd continue funding for this project after they left, though. Stevie and Veronica were the two biggest pushers for the investment. It was doubtful the others would do anything *but* pull their funding now that these horrific memories were attached to the project. That was more worrisome than Jenner being a serial killer in security guard's clothing. Giles lowered his voice, taking a step closer to Abel. "I hate to bring this up, but we're going to need to figure out what to do with the androids after the killer is caught."

"What?" Abel snapped his head to the side. He lowered his voice to match Giles, crossing his arms in an attempt to look nonchallant. "What are you talking about?"

Giles leveled his look and spoke quietly. "I don't know if you noticed, but two of our biggest funders just kicked the bucket. One's dead and the other one is scared out of his mind in a hospital. When this hits the news people are either going to be sympathetic, or scared to death of being associated with us. So unless you've got a few million dollars in your pocket to support Hecate's upkeep, I suggest you start thinking of something."

"Is this really the best time to be talking about this, Giles?" Abel hissed back eyes darting to the remaining members of their board. "Five people are dead and all you're thinking about is money!?"

I'm thinking about you, idiot. Giles pressed his lips together in a thin line. As much as he would love to wash his hands of the androids and this entire damn project, he couldn't. Abel was never good at thinking about the future and if those boys got scrapped, Abel was going to be crushed. It had nothing to do with Giles' keeping his father's legacy alive. "I'm thinking practically. Respect for the dead doesn't pay the bills!"

"We'll talk about this later." Abel ended the discussion definitively.

Giles blew a strand of loose hair out of his face and longed for the spare bottle of hair gel in his desk. "Let's hope we get a later."

Jessica held Paul's arm like a vice. Veronica was dead. Stevie was missing an arm. Albert was being rather quiet about the whole ordeal, too. Jessica shivered like the temperature had dropped below zero, and watched the only other person at their table. She glanced at the purple ring around her arm turning black. The swelling pulsed at her wrist; Jessica wondered if it was fractured. At least that scary little boy had been taken away. She started to create her own bruise on Paul's arm when she tightened her grip further. "Why can't we leave?"

"They're still patrolling the building for the killer." Paul answered. He left out the part where the police were concerned the murderer was someone in the room. The faces around him were all strangers, which made picking out the guilty party difficult. All he saw was chatting faces; all possible lies. Paul winced when Jessica's nail dug past his sleeve. *Why couldn't she have clung to Albert?* "We can leave once they find him."

"But we can get an escort!" Jessica pled. It was too hot in this room. There were far too many people in it. She could feel sweat on her back, and her chest was tight. She couldn't breathe. She needed air. To get out. *Out, out, OUT.* "I can't stay here another minute."

"Calm down." Albert held his head from across the table. He was so tired he couldn't even think of a proper insult. Who could sleep with a psychopathic killer on the loose? His body taunted him with the hint of rest, only to be jerked awake again by the tiniest noise or voice. "And take a breath already."

"Calm? Calm down? You want me to calm down!?" Jessica's voice shrilled and she heard Paul shout 'Hey!' when her nails clamped down even tighter. She honestly couldn't care and didn't bother to loosen her grip in the slightest. "We're in a building with a psychopath out for our heads and you want me to remain calm?"

"Yes," Albert deadpanned. "You're not helping things by panicking."

Ms. Putts tittered in her hysterics. "Helping? No one is helping!" The woman stood up quickly, allowing Paul to retrieve his arm. Jessica didn't need his safety blanket sleeve any longer! She was getting *out.* "I'm leaving. You can't make me stay in this hell hole one more second."

"Jessica!" Paul leapt to his own feet when the woman made a dash for the side exit door, barreling straight into the unsuspecting officer who was paying attention to the threat *outside* the room. "Come back!"

The officer hit the ground with an echoing thud, pushed back by Jessica's sudden burst of strength. Her hands slammed into the push-bar and she was through the door before the officer could even get to his feet.

After the second stumble, Jessica hopped along on one foot to remove her heel before switching—not willing to stop moving even for the moment. Her pearls clattering loudly together around her neck, swinging freely in the air. Feet free of the teetering heels, Jessica was able to run faster, bare feet smacking against each tile.

The elevator was at the end of the hall and to the left. If she could get there, it would only be two heart-wracking minutes in a small box before a straight shot out the front door. Outside she could get a ride home and away from this madness. Jessica kept her eyes forward and nearly grinned when she saw the closed elevator doors before her, little down button already glowing red.

Jessica froze in place four feet from the door, empty hallway causing her heavy breathing to echo. Jessica reached up and grabbed her pearls in shaking fingers. Her breath stopped. *Who pressed the down button?*

"You shouldn't run in the halls, Ms. Putts," a tenor voice that would have been familiar to Veronica and Stevie rang out. "It's not safe."

A hand buried itself in the woman's hair, jerking the head back and exposing the neck. The stranger jabbed his trusty tool, a sharpened piece of metal, into the thickest part of the throat; blood splattered onto the tile. The killer's mouth twitched back and forth between a smile and a frown watching the red liquid pour down the woman's front. It was pretty. The woman gagged, eyes open, as he tried to work the metal between the muscle to get to the discs in the spinal column he needed to separate to split the head from the body. The shiv snapped through the string of pearls, sending them to scatter about the floor with a plethora of little clicks and clacks.

The knife finally split the tough connection between head and body, but the angle was awkward and his calculation slightly off. The killer jerked when the spine snapped a moment earlier than he predicted. The sudden severance cost him his grip on her hair. The killer took a shocked step back as the limp body crumpled to the ground, twitching. The dropped head hit the tile about a foot away.

The killer sighed, walking over to retrieve the fallen appendage.

Paul couldn't ever remember running this fast in his life. He had to get to Jessica and get her back to the room to see reason. Albert had stayed at the table holding his head, but to Paul's good fortune, the officer at the door was following. Paul had no intention of dealing with Jessica by himself without someone trained to handle hysterics. The board member rounded the corner knowing full well the woman was headed for the elevators and slid to a stop. His stomach jerked up into his throat.

There was a man standing in the hall. He was facing the elevators, but was half turned toward Paul, giving him full view of the man's hands. The stranger looked out of place in the pristine lab, wearing a simple pair of black jeans and a long-sleeved cotton shirt of the same color. But that's not what got his attention—the man was holding Jessica's head.

The stranger was digging thin, practiced fingers into her eye socket. Paul could hear the sickening crunch of skull splitting as he removed the organ, a small string of ligaments trailing behind. A swift jerk plucked the eye from the socket, completely ripping away the last little bits keeping it attached to the head. The man looked at the eye for a few moments, turning it over in his fingers. He wiped away the glossy coating with his thumb before placing it in his pocket.

Paul couldn't move. Couldn't breathe.

Jessica's second eye was removed and placed with its mate before time started to tick again. Paul's feet were still frozen to the ground. He must have moved his foot though, as a small 'clack' echoed from his heel hitting the tiled floor, knocking into a loose pearl. The man in black turned toward him, eyes intense. The board member would be damned if they didn't just *glow*.

"Mr. Diamond," the man said, acknowledging Paul's presence. The board member could only respond with a snag in his breathing.

Disinterested in Diamond's cowering, the stranger turned away. He walked down the hall left of the elevators, casual as you please. The killer would deal with the other board members after cleaning up a bit more. There was nothing worse than mixing dried blood with fresh blood—not nearly as attractive. The killer barely bothered to step over the slumped-over form of Jessica's body, tempted to kick the worthless corpse out of the way. His shoes squished, the wet blood coating the soles.

Paul exhaled the breath he had been holding and immediately felt his breath quickening to make up for the lack of oxygen. He took a few steps back into another warm body.

"Hey! Are you—what the hell!?" The officer said as he shoved the man in the suit out of the way and ran forward to the body. It was still bleeding freely and it looked soft...still warm. It could have been alive if the head wasn't missing. The officer turned back quickly when he heard a soft thud. The board member had fallen to his knees, arms dropped straight at his side. The younger cadet ran up to the poor man and checked for an unseen injury. "What happened?"

"Left...around the corner," Paul stuttered out, his hands started crawling up his face, fingers resting just above his cheekbones. He was tempted to check and make sure his eyes were still attached. "Took her eyes." Paul was staring blankly now. "Ripped 'um right out."

The officer lifted his radio off his belt and flipped the switch. Paul didn't listen to the words spewing out of the man's mouth about back-up and other terminology he didn't understand. Paul was too busy staring at the bloody shoe prints on the ground rounding the corner. Someone knelt down beside him to see if he was alright, as more officers ran by in pursuit.

"Sir? If you can hear me I need you to answer me."

Paul could only hear his own name repeated over and over by a tenor voice.

CHAPTER 18

"YOU DIDN'T CATCH him," Saxon repeated. He looked down the line of men, their eyes to the ground, with faces ranging from guilt to anger. Five of his officers had gone after the suspect once he was sighted. Six of his best investigators had studied the scene. A trail of blood lead away from the victim's body. Saxon's hands fisted at his side. "The suspect was *walking* and you *lost him.*"

"Yes, Sir."

Lester collapsed in a chair near the wall and wondered what to do now. He'd have to call in reinforcements—maybe a SWAT team or something. He wished he could just blame the incompetence on his officers, but after this bastard got Wolfe, everyone in the force was fully on board. Whoever this killer was, he had talent of the worst kind. Not many could brag three dead in the past twenty four hours, and one missing arm without any form of detection—or walk away after an eye witness spotted him. The detective looked towards the remaining two board members and sighed. "Did you at least get a physical description?"

"Yes, we did manage to get a description from Mr. Diamond before he stopped acknowledging everyone around him." The officer pulled out a pad with his handwriting written on it. The young man reread it quickly to prevent stumbling over his words before beginning. "Tall, about 6ft, black hair, thin build. His clothing was the same color of black as his hair."

"Do you know how many people you just described?" Lester pointed out. At least ten people in the cafeteria fit that description alone, clothes aside. He needed *more.* "Is that the best we've got?"

"Well, there is one thing." The officer glanced down at the page and back up again. The hesitation to add this last fact was probably unnecessary, but he didn't wan to cause confusion or lead them in the wrong direction if the information was inaccurate. "But we're unsure if Mr. Diamond was exaggerating or not."

Lester slammed his hand into the wall, cracking the plaster. "If it helps find this son of a bitch, I don't care if he says the man's eyes were purple —"

"Yellow," the officer squeaked.

"What?"

"The suspect's eyes were yellow." A nervous swallow followed. "Mr. Diamond was very clear about that. He said they were 'a bright canary yellow.' He said they were glowing."

A tray clattered to the ground a few steps from the detective. A man in glasses off to Lester's side was looking rather horrified. The stranger's eyes were wide as the saucer plate he had just dropped. Lester watched the man take a step back, foot crushing a pudding cup, and took a closer look at the man and his unusual reaction. This guy—he did look familiar with that black eye—was gaping like a fish, mouth stuck open. Lester smiled. It wasn't a fear for his life that made this man freeze up, but *realization*. Lester rounded the table with swift steps marching to the man in glasses. This guy *knew* something. "You! What's your name?"

"Ma-Marvin Green. Sir," Marvin choked. It was a coincidence. That's all it was. Coincidence. Nothing was wrong and he was just imagining things. Marvin was just stressed from being beaten up, betrayed, and threatened by bratty little androids. "H-How can I help you?"

"How long were you listening to us?" Lester took a step closer and placed his arms behind his back. The man shook, fingers trembling, and took a step back. He looked ready to bolt. *Good.* "Hm?"

"From the start." Marvin took another step back to match the detective's step forward, nearly tripping over his fallen tray. He was just picking up his food and the officers were talking! How could you not listen? "But not on purpose!"

"What do you know about a man with yellow eyes, black hair, and stands about 6ft tall?" Lester's smile was deceivingly pleasant as he watched sweat starting to form on Mr. Green's brow.

"I—" Marvin stopped and shook his head. It was impossible. The description fit, for sure, but there was no way. Marvin bit his thumb and grabbed at his own hair. "It's not possible."

Lester grabbed the man's arms and shook, well aware he had started to draw attention to the group. Let them stare. An audience was the least of his worries when someone in this case had finally cracked. The detective's grip on the man's arm squeezed tighter, and the man whimpered. Lester shouted, "What isn't?"

Detective Saxon was a very large man. Marvin's voice came out quick and quiet, fear preventing any decent volume. "It sounds like one of mine."

"One of your, what?" Lester studied the man who was starting to resemble a corpse with the paling of his face. "What are you talking about?"

"One of mine." Marvin repeated to himself before gaping. The engineer struggled to get the detective's arms off him and stood up straighter, face now determined. "I need to check something."

Rod watched as the head officer dragged Green out of the cafeteria by the arm. When the commotion started, he and Anton had been playing cards with a deck they had snuck from the kitchen office. Needless to say the game was stalled for the moment watching—it was hard not to notice an officer shaking down your boss. Not that he blamed the detective. It was way too easy to single out and pick on a total pervert like Green. The department head's only saving grace was his seemingly endless talent. Rod learned most of what he knew about mechanics from him from only a few years of interning. The young engineer turned away from the empty scene and looked back at his friend from programming. "What do you think that was about?"

"I dunno," Anton Jansen answered, annoyed at still being trapped in the building with nothing to do but play *Crazy Eights*. They could have at least let them get their laptops. He had e-mails to send and games to work on! Anton's leg bounced under the table. *When do we get to* go? "Sounds like something's up with Green."

"You don't think he did it, do you?" Rod leaned over. The detective had looked pretty angry and Green was looking out of sorts. Rod hadn't seen Marvin that pale since Firmin cut the hair on one of Green's androids. "Killed those people, I mean?"

"How could he? He's been in the room the entire time." Anton slapped a card down, then the programmer shrugged and said, "I bet it was one of the androids."

"Huh?" Rod looked up from his ever growing hand of cards. "What are you talking about?"

"Think about it. They're all way more skilled than humans physically, and what else is Marvin good for than technical support?"

"Giving androids really big knockers?"

"Shut up! I'm being serious!"

"Well, so am I, and you don't know what you're talking about. Marvin is probably more capable than we think. It's not like any of us really get to know him," Rod huffed, "but we *do* work with the androids every day. I think if they were going to go on murderous rampage, they would have started long before now." Rod flicked a card into the center pile, hoping to get an eight soon. He really needed something to change the current suit so he could get rid of some cards. "Not to mention, they're supervised."

"Not all the time," Anton whispered. He licked his lips before scratching the top of his arm with the back of his cards. "Who watches them at night? The security guard? He's too busy playing commando at the doors to watch their room."

"You're crazy, man."

"No, and Hecate." Anton threw a three of hearts on Rod's three of spades. He watched Rod draw a card, and threw down another heart. "That kid freaks me the hell out, man."

Rod drew another card, frowning. How did he get stuck with all diamonds? "And Iacchus likes to throw chairs at me and Mr. Dixen during regular maintenance. What's your point?"

"He's got no moral system, and other than making Dr. Moreau happy, Hecate's looking out for number one. *And* he's a total genius, even for an android. Have you *seen* his numbers? He makes Iacchus look like an old green screen." Anton shivered and collapsed his hand of cards into a single stack. He spread them back out again and counted his four cards, compared to Rod's twenty. "Spend five minutes with him alone. He's scary, man. I wouldn't even blink if you told me he did it."

Rod rolled his eyes. "He's too small."

"What?"

"Didn't you hear those guys? The killer's like six feet tall. Hecate's just *under* five feet." Rod smirked finally hitting a three of diamonds. "And before you say it, Iacchus couldn't do 'subtle' if his circuits depended on it. He'd probably go right to Ms. Becky with the head he just chopped off like a dog going 'Look what I got you!' and expect her to dish out a treat."

"Yeah," Anton drew a card, grinning at the eight. Maybe this game would end sooner than he thought. Especially since it didn't look like Rod was going to get rid of all of *his* cards any time soon. "Well it can't be the girls, they're too young."

"It's probably one of those protestor guys." Rod drew another card, wondering if he should just forfeit the game at this point. Maybe he could con Anton into a game of *King's Corners*.

"I doubt it's Talos' Redress." Jansen tapped his cards on the table. He rubbed the bottom of his lip with the back of his thumb. Anton sniffed and spread his cards out again. "They're not like that."

"Okay," Rod said. He rolled his shoulder, and shrugged a moment later. "Maybe it's Firmin. The guy's definitely high strung enough to snap."

"He *does* hate the board, is about six feet, and has black hair."

"And the anger management issues." Rod smacked his leg, and snickered. "Oh, oh, and he always looks like he wants to strangle Green whenever he visits the mechanics' break lounge." Rod tossed his cards into the center. It was a lost effort at this point. "I bet he tried to frame Green as part of his big plan."

"Yeah, he probably just got drunk one day and snapped or something and has to cover it all up." Anton chuckled.

"I've also been standing behind you boys in the room for the past few minutes."

Both boys jerked violently, taking to their feet. Giles smirked at them, pulling himself up to his full height to tower over the little upstarts and their frightened expressions. Giles rubbed the bottom of his chin. "No, no, do continue. I'd love to hear more about how I'm destroying my own company and ripping people apart."

"Uh, we're good." The two picked up their cards quickly and shuffled down the table to the vacant seats on the other end. Hushed whispers of "Why didn't you notice him?" and "We're so going to get fired" went back and forth like shots as the two scampered away.

"That wasn't very nice, Giles." Abel smacked Giles on the shoulder. At least his friend was smiling—he needed it. Abel crossed his arms, glad he was behind Giles—otherwise the man might notice the concerned look on his face. That was the first time he'd heard Anton say Hecate was creepy. Abel licked his lips, ignoring the unsettling feeling sinking in his chest. "I think you may have scarred them for life."

"I'm not nice, Abe," Giles answered. He took in a breath and dropped his smile, getting to the meat of the matter. "But, they did bring up a good point."

"That you're the killer?"

"No," Giles shook his head and turned around to Abel. The director rubbed his chin with his thumb and forefinger, wincing at the stubble. "Why the hell did Green run off with the detective?"

Abel brushed his hair back. "Think we should run after him?"

"Of course," Giles answered.

Abel and Giles arrived in time to witness Marvin unravel. Giles' nerves followed when he noticed what the man was looking at: There was an empty space on Marvin's line of android shells.

"It's missing." Marvin had thought he knew what 'horrified' felt like. You didn't gain the reputation he had concerning women without insulting some brute for 'treating a lady the wrong way.' The threat of a fist blackening his eye had raised his pulse, and shortened his breath. Now he realized what he had felt before was just a quick, fleeting emotion disguising itself as fear. This was what terror felt like; a sick, nauseating feeling of despair, self-doubt, and hysteria. The open space between the two units mocked him. His voice cracked two octaves higher. "It's *missing.*"

"How could something like that be *missing*, Marvin?" Giles leapt at the man and grabbed his shirt to lift him off his feet, not caring about the detective not two feet away from them. He could see the red and he was reveling in it. It took all of his self control to not strangle Marvin outright. "How the *hell* could something like that be missing!? That's what inventory is for!"

Marvin shrank under the snarling man before him and pulled his hands up to try and loosen the grip on his shirt. Giles was strangling him. Marvin's voice struggled to get out and he felt spit choke out of his mouth. "No one's ever in here so I don't think about it!"

"That machine cost two million dollars to build! *You* built the thing! You couldn't even bother to check on it once a week!?" Giles nearly screamed at the absurdity of the situation. So help him if *that* turned out to be the killer because Marvin couldn't be bothered to look in a store room and just count heads once a night, Giles was going to kill him. He would go to jail and rot for the rest of his life for a crime of passion but that didn't matter. Giles would *kill* him. "Where is it!?"

"I don't know!" Marvin shook his head best he could under the ever tightening grip. Why wasn't anyone doing anything to stop Giles? The man had clearly lost his mind. Marvin's back slammed into his desk when his boss rammed him forward. His mug tipped over, spilling coffee across the desk and splashing onto the floor. Marvin's fingers slipped into the cool beverage as his hands tried to grip the table to pull away. Giles' eyes were wild; his hair falling around his face and ears, far from it's usual tidy appearance. It made him look like a mad man. Marvin did his best to choke out an answer with his throat's pathways lessening by the second. "It's usually back there! I swear!"

"Well, it's not right now!"

Lester figured this little shouting match had gone on long enough and grabbed the two men to split them apart before that Firmin guy really did kill the scrawny one. Just behind him, Moreau and that Becky lady—who invited herself and her android charges after catching word there was a commotion—were watching with interest and straight faces making no move to intervene.

Lester was more concerned with the six bodies sitting neatly against the wall. Specifically the empty space between a girl with blonde, curled hair, and a brunette with long brown hair, which Lester had assumed was causing all the fuss. Apparently, something was supposed to go there. "What exactly is missing, and what's with the freak show on the wall?"

Giles took in a breath; took a second. He needed calm to discuss and explain to the officer. He tried not to look at Marvin, who he hoped was at least *looking* remorseful. "Marvin is head of the team who assembles the human-like bodies we place the android's," Giles waved his hand in the air trying to think of the best non-technical term, "brains in. Since we never know when an AI will 'wake-up' we always need a certain number of bodies ready to go for immediate transfer. This line-up includes the models he designed personally. There are supposed to be seven of them left."

"And one is missing?" Lester clarified.

"Yes."

"That's 6ft tall, has black hair and yellow eyes."

"I like to give them each something unique," Marvin spoke up quietly, wringing his hands together. He took a step back next to Melinoe and Macaria. Macaria touched his arm with the tips of her fingers, and his hands stilled. Marvin covered his mouth, as the girl pat his arm. "His registered name was going to be Trophonius, so I wanted his eyes to be the color of honey." Marvin rubbed his arm knowing full well he was mumbling, justifying. "I got the dye wrong, and it came out more lemon."

"That's all well and good," Lester said. He pointed to the line of lifeless shells, now quite sure this job was going to either be the death of him or the one he'd be telling stories about for the rest of his life. "But more importantly, are you implying that an android is running around killing these people?"

"No!" Marvin slammed his hand on the desk, wincing at the splash of liquid on his coat. He wiped the coffee off on the ruined jacket—stain was a stain—as he addressed the officer. "That'd be impossible! These are just empty shells. There's no programming in them yet." He removed his glasses and shook his head. "It *couldn't* have moved on its own."

"Well, apparently it did." Lester turned to the others in the room. These were the geniuses, the brains of the group, and they were all sitting around like scolded children. "Any suggestions?"

Abel frowned. There were certain, unfortunate implications that could be made, if it really was one of Marvin's shells running around. These weren't just off-the-shelf computers anybody could hack. You would need a fairly intricate knowledge of their systems and the programs just to get the thing up and running, let alone give it detailed commands like 'kill that.' It would have to be someone on the staff in the lab. Particularly someone in the programming division. Abel dropped his hand to Hecate's head and rubbed the silky hair, trying to get his equilibrium back, ground himself. "Someone must have stolen it and turned it on with their own software."

"Someone from the lab," Becky admitted softly, channeling the same brainwaves as Abel. She turned to Iacchus who was standing close—too close—to her shoulder. Took in the human-like, brunette hair, the realistic skin, and realized she herself had no clue just how he was working. Cleaning out his gears and joints with Rupert was hardly the same thing as piecing together the parts and linking the computer to the moving bits. Becky rubbed the back of her neck, trying to stop her fingers from shaking. "You'd needed to have built one of these things to even know where to begin to program one. 'Complex' doesn't even begin to describe it."

"Inside job," Saxon clarified. They get a big break in evidence, and it leads him absolutely nowhere, yet again. "So we're back to square one: the killer, or in this case the person responsible, is someone in the building."

Giles collapsed into a chair and covered his eyes. "Yes."

"And no one in this room has any hint or clue or suspicion at all, of who that could be," Lester stated. He'd never seen a work environment where everyone knew each other that well. Surely someone on staff was the 'weird guy' or the 'off guy' that they could be naming. "None of you? This has to cut the number down some with the technical skill required, right?"

"Not if you took a complete shell. Uploading the program is as easy as a button click if you have everything connected, and most of the lab knows the equipment needed." Becky shook her head and snorted. "Besides, we all happen to like our jobs." She felt a tiny smile crawl onto her face at the irony. Wasn't it just a few weeks ago she was sitting in her favorite shop, thinking of how money was the only thing that tied her to this building? Becky glanced at Iacchus, fingers buried in his sweater. "We're building androids, detective. This is the dream job most people would kill for. I can't think of anyone who'd want to ruin that."

Abel nodded and looked over at Hecate, the twins who were being rather considerate allowing Marvin to stand near them, and Iacchus who had that puppy dog look of concentration aimed at his favorite lady and her tiny smile. Becky was right. No one in his right mind could consider this project anything less than a dream. They didn't just build androids, they created *children*. Abel narrowed his eyes and shifted his hand around Hecate's shoulder to pull him close to his side. Whoever hijacked Marvin's shell was threatening his kids.

Abel was going to make sure the bastard suffered for it.

CHAPTER 19

ALBERT RAN WAS not a stupid man. His degrees in law, business, and advanced robotics were testament to this fact. Using this intellect, he had come to the conclusion that Paul was utterly useless, Stevie was going to die in his hospital bed, and staying in this building was hazardous to his health. He always knew his work was going to be the death of him, but he hadn't thought it would be so literal.

He honestly thought he'd die in an avalanche of paperwork.

But Albert wasn't so lucky. Instead, some lunatic in the building was on a mad killing spree that had escalated from one victim a week to three in near immediate succession. That the latest three victims were also his peers on the board had not escaped his notice, either. The director wondered if it wasn't those protesters behind it after all, fulfilling that vendetta of theirs against the project. They had been vocal and insistent in their threats, and it was not out of a lunatic's reach to kill his own for own reason or another. Albert shuddered a breath. There was a very real possibility that he might die before the day was out.

"There was metal," Paul mumbled under his breath, eyes still glazed over like a freshly fired piece of pottery.

Albert turned to his friend, who hadn't spoken in the past two hours. It seemed the trauma was finally wearing off. "What was metal?"

"On his side." Paul turned his head slowly. Albert was staring at him, and had bags under his eyes. Paul tilted his head up, trying to piece together the puzzle of words in his head. "The killer. He had a long piece of metal on his hip…with blood. Looked sharp." Paul frowned and furrowed his brow. "I forgot to tell the detective."

"That seems like something rather important," Albert growled and nearly slammed his hand on the table. "That was probably the murder weapon!"

"Probably." Paul replied blankly. "Don't think he needed it though. So probably not."

"What do you mean didn't need it?" Albert shook his head. He really shouldn't be getting so upset. Paul was in a sort of shock, wasn't thinking clearly enough to be lucid. Albert counted to ten in his head to help keep his patience with the man. "He ripped those people apart. Surely the killer needed a tool or something."

"I don't think so." Paul looked up at the ceiling that seemed to be capturing everyone's attention. It was standard; nothing special. Just troffers with yellowed lenses and not enough light. Paul shivered at the glowing color. It was the wrong shade, but it was close enough. "He cracked a skull open with his fingers."

"But that surely isn't enough strength to—"

The table between Albert and Paul was ripped away like a tablecloth starring in a magician's act. It skidded into the far wall, the table screeching against its locked wheels. Paul looked lazily at the removed furniture and giggled. Albert did not share Paul's good spirits when a fist came smashing into his face, crushing into the cartilage of his nose. Blood dribbled down Albert's cheek. His head rang when another hit knocked him off his feet. Cold tile met his face; Albert groaned.

"I told you he didn't need it." Paul laughed as he watched his friend shifting on the ground. The stranger in black was standing between them now—where the table had been—making quite the spectacle of himself. Everyone in the room, officers included were staring at the figure who was looking down at Albert. *Looks like it's our turn,* Paul thought to himself.

The officers in the room acted first, most pulling their pistols and one or two rushing the other inhabitants to the side and away from the line of fire. All were wondering the same thing: *How'd he get in!?* "Freeze! Put your hands up right now!"

The young officer who was closest could feel chills running down his spine as that steady yellow gaze met his own. The report had been accurate—that color couldn't be anything other than 'canary.' The officer saw the pupil spin ever so slightly as the intruder stood watching, trailing his every move. He thought he could hear a slight whining sound—like the ones his computer made. The kid swallowed. His limbs trembled, and he wished the detective or the captain or somebody else was here and not running off with the lab techs! "Put your hands where we can see them."

The man merely returned his attentions back to Mr. Ran crawling toward Mr. Diamond. The police were still shouting at him, but he ignored them. Instead, he kicked Mr. Ran in the back of the head hard enough to crack the tile beneath it. A stomp crushed the back of the skull in with a sickening squelch that caused the on-lookers to gasp and officers to curse. A silence fell over the room for the briefest of moments. Eventually, the police got a hold of themselves. Orders and panicked shouts flew through the room, creating more confusion than it solved. Before the first shot could be fired, the killer was already moving, heading straight for the grinning Mr. Diamond. He hadn't wanted Mr. Ran's eyes, they were so dull—he wanted Mr. Diamond's eyes instead.

They were green.

Iacchus pulled his knees up to his chest, as he sat on the floor of a spare lab turned multipurpose room. The detective had put him and the others here after he left for the cafeteria. Iacchus shifted the sole of his heel on the tile floor. Ms. Becky had shut herself into the back storage room. It had no windows and was relatively small, only eight by eight feet, and packed with clutter. Iacchus looked thoughtfully at the door before looking over his shoulder. The others in the room had taken over the couch—Hecate sat in Dr. Moreau's lap, and Dr. Firmin had covered his eyes with his arm. They seemed content to sit quietly and pout.

Save for Mr. Green—he was sitting with the twins. While Melinoe ignored him to swoon at Giles, Macaria snuggled up to his side. Green had wrapped his lab coat around the two of them as they sat on the floor —they looked like they were just hugging. The others looked happy to ignore them, but Iacchus' eyes were better than the humans', and Macaria's hand was definitely below Green's belt line under the spacious white coat. "You always know how to make me feel better," Green whispered in her hair, smiling.

It wasn't fair that Mr. Green got to feel good when everyone else was so troubled. Especially when it was Ms. Becky.

Iacchus didn't like it when Ms. Becky was upset. He'd give *anything* to make her feel better, he really would. Iacchus looked at the twins again with a bit more sympathy and fidgeted with the end of his scarf. Iacchus listened as Macaria spoke back to Mr. Green, in hushed tones, asking if he felt better or if she was doing it right. Macaria liked Mr. Green a lot, Iacchus admitted to himself. Probably as much as he liked Ms. Becky. Was that why she was doing those things for him? *Why Melinoe had done those things for Dr. Firmin?* Did she make Mr. Green feel good because she *wanted* to? Iacchus looked at the closed storage room door, considering.

Maybe he could make Ms. Becky feel better, after all.

The boy opened the door slowly and softly, slipping inside with more stealth than most thought him capable. Ms. Becky didn't move and remained curled up on the broken couch shoved against the back wall to be forgotten. It had been evicted from the break room a few years ago, and it creaked. The couch was nearly hidden by stacked boxes and broken computer, but there was no mistaking Ms. Becky from what little glimpses he could see through the cracks. Iacchus had memorized every inch of Ms. Becky's form a long time ago.

She was asleep.

Iacchus bit his lip and slid toward her, eyes roving. Her head was cushioned on the back of the sofa, arms wrapped tight around her waist. One leg was pulled up on the seat while the other helped prop her up from the floor. Iacchus was a breath away from her when he stopped, yet she didn't wake at the proximity.

She really was pretty.

Iacchus held out out his hand and dared touch a cheek, thumb on her lip. He waited for any flicker or movement, sensors burning from the warmth and tingling from the chapped skin. The android was lucky Ms. Becky was a heavy sleeper, otherwise she'd probably shove him away before he could help her. Iacchus leant back, eyes trailing over her skin again. It was odd being with Ms. Becky when she wasn't trying to belittle him or shove him away. Iacchus could touch her freely.

The boy laid his hand on her thigh and felt warmth come from under the fabric. Applying pressure, he stroked up slowly the way he had seen Giles holding Melinoe's thigh. He was rewarded with a little mumble from Ms. Becky and her lip twitching upward. Iacchus started to grin, he could make her feel good in her sleep at least. He'd never get this chance if she was awake.

Iacchus slowly shifted her thigh open so that he could sit on the couch between her legs. The cushions creaked loudly, but Becky didn't stir. She shifted slightly, as if aware in her sleep there was a new mass to accommodate. Safely nestled between her limbs, Iacchus' hands mirrored the slow stroking motion on her upper thigh. Iacchus pictured Giles' fingers as they dug into Melinoe's sides, and tried to judge just how strongly to squeeze. Iacchus increased the pressure by a pascal at a time, eyes locked on her face for any sign of pain.

Iacchus grew bolder with every airy breath and whimper that resulted from his tentative touches. More weight, more exploration to find each little spot that made her feel good. A thumb under her rib rewarded the boy with a slight giggle under her breath. Iacchus memorized it all for future reference and reflection. His hand stilled when it settled on her hip. His thumb rested lightly over the button of her pants, hesitant to continue.

Her belt line taunted him. Ms. Becky's hips had started to shift lightly forward with each of his slight movements in a neat pattern. He had seen Melinoe do this, too, and figured he must be doing something right. Iacchus had to rely on Mr.Dixen's knowledge from here though, as he couldn't recall Giles actually touching Melinoe outside of her hips and thighs. Iacchus watched Ms. Becky's face as he moved his hand over and slowly clasped the button just under her naval. His hands were shaking as he undid the first button; the second.

Iacchus found that funny.

Nervous shaking was a reflex due to adrenaline and muscles, neither of which Iacchus had in his body of metal and wire. And yet, here he was, shaking like a leaf. He peeled Ms. Becky's pants open, finding pink when the khaki was pulled aside. The lacy undergarment clashed against the plain of her sweater and dull clothes. Iacchus thought Ms. Becky didn't like pink, but he supposed he didn't know everything about her...yet. Ms. Becky turned to her side, and one of her hands gripped the edge of the couch. Her fingers pulsed in a rhythm as her breath grew heavy. She was still very much asleep. Iacchus pressed a thumb lightly into the center of her belly. His thumb fit neatly into the indent of her navel. Ms. Becky giggled.

Iacchus dared to put a kiss over the same spot.

Seeing the smile resting on her face widen was more than enough incentive for Iacchus to continue. He turned his hand so the base of his palm flattened against her belly. Iacchus slowly dug his fingers under the khaki zipper to cup what was beneath. Ms. Becky moaned; Iacchus' face was surely lovesick. Iacchus moved his hand harder against the thin fabric. Ms. Becky dug her face into the side of the couch. Iacchus kissed her cheek; Ms. Becky sighed out a name. "Abel..."

Iacchus froze.

Lester heard the shots fired the second he stepped free from the elevator. He ran toward them without any hesitation. Saxon armed himself, pulling the slide back swiftly to load the weapon. He ducked down against the wall to avoid any stray bullets at the edge of the glass half-walls of the cafeteria. Detective Saxon sucked in a breath, and released the oxygen while counting to ten. He leant against the edge of the wall that went to the ceiling, and held there listening. The shots had stopped.

Saxon peered around the edge of the wall slowly, so as to not draw attention. The detective gaped. A tall man with black hair held Diamond to his chest. The stranger backed the two of them into the side door. Lester took a pretty good guess this was their killer robot on the loose. His officers had their guns trained on the attacker and the victim, but with Diamond as a shield, they couldn't risk the shot. Saxon was right there with them, much to his dismay, and the man searched the room for a better position.

His eyes caught sight of the bloody body sprawled across ground. Saxon's grip tightened on his weapon, realizing that Diamond might be the only board member left. The man was hardly putting up a fight, and he seemed to be...giggling? *People always chose the* best times *to have breakdowns,* sounded sarcastic even in his own mind. Saxon decided he'd risk it by going around to the door behind the suspect. Android. "Shit," Saxon said under his breath, feet tapping on the floor as he got ready to move. He had already forgotten the thing was an android. Why hadn't he asked Firmin how a bullet would affect these things? Lester wonder if the bullet would ricochet off the metal.

A loud crash sounded from the room behind him. Saxon turned full into the glass window to see a table on its side and the machine kick the door behind him. The wood shattered under the kick, the entire door breaking free from the frame. It hung off a single hinge, swinging. No emotion crossed the android's face and Lester swallowed. He had met nut jobs who could keep their faces that straight before, and it always ended ugly. Saxon pushed off the wall and started to run toward the turn in the hallway that would put him at the splintered door. He'd catch the man on his escape.

Paul smiled when he felt himself dragged into the hallway.

He was yanked immediately to the left, arm ripped from its socket. It was excruciatingly painful, but Paul was too high on his own adrenaline to truly notice. The man dragging Paul was rather calm during the entire affair. The attacker's stride was long and even, a high contrast to his own flopping legs as he struggled to keep up. Paul wondered if it was from all the practice. The man took a sharp turn around a corner, and Paul was thrown into a side room with large windows along the wall. A hand closed around Paul's throat, no-nonsense and efficient. Paul was slammed up against the drywall, his feet dangling, tips of his shoes barely able to scrape the floor.

Lester arrived at the end of the hallway only to be greeted by a strip of closed doors.

"Dammit." Saxon kept walking, but slowed his pace to a crawl. Knowing his time was limited, the detective radioed for the rest of his team while he could. Message sent, Saxon headed down the hallway. He listened for any movement or sound behind each door. Luck seemed to be on his side however, when he heard glass shattering.

Mr. Diamond had stopped moving before Lester found the door.

Saxon found a dead man on the ground, gaping holes where his eyes had been. The failure stared at him with blood soaked sockets. Lester felt a light breeze on his face, and looked up to a broken window. Defeated, but only for the moment, Lester lifted his radio and clicked the button. "Suspect left building through window on fourth floor. *Pursue.*"

Hecate saw it coming before Iacchus.

At first, he had been amused by what Iacchus had been doing to keep himself occupied in the storage room with Ms. Becky. It had been rude to eavesdrop, sure, but what his brother didn't know wouldn't hurt him. If Iacchus didn't want people to listen in, he would have dragged the woman to a room farther away. It was amazing how many little sounds you could hear through the door when your hearing was more accurate than the average human. Ms. Becky wasn't exactly *quiet* either. She was almost as loud as that janitor and his girlfriend Hecate had caught copulating in a closet one night when the rest of the staff was snug in their homes. However, the moment Ms. Becky said someone else's name, Hecate knew trouble was inevitable. "Dr. Moreau! *Move!*"

Abel wondered why Hecate found it necessary to jump out of his lap (and knocking him in the shin—*ouch*) at just that very moment. Hecate pulled at his arm, the yank nearly dislocated his shoulder. Abel tried to pull away for a second to figure out what was going on—Hecate's face was taut with panic. A second was the extent of his time when the storage room door exploded open, slamming so hard against the wall the door bounced, revealing Iacchus. Eyes glowing, pose tense, teeth bared— murderousness dripping off every one of Iacchus' limbs. Abel flinched. That ferocious glare was aimed directly at *him*. "Iacchus?"

"*You.*" As for many before him, a single word summed up all of Iacchus' feelings in so short a syllable. Having said his fill, Iacchus charged at the current source of his contempt.

"What are you doing?" Abel tried to dodge when Iacchus lunged, but he wasn't fast enough. Iacchus slammed two hands into the older man's chest, successfully shoving Abel into a table. Before Abel could catch his breath, metal hands hiding behind a deceptive layer of faux skin attempted to wrap themselves around his throat. Abel barely managed to hold the boy back by the wrists. Iacchus' fingers twitched, and a hissing static came from a vocal synthesizer that had no clue how to represent his rage.

Marvin and the twins stood frozen in the corner, shocked at Iacchus' actions.

Abel counted himself among the confused. Iacchus' fingers brushed against his throat, the light touches more threatening for every step closer they gained. The doctor released a whimpered yelp. What on earth had *Abel* done to incite such a rage? He yanked Iacchus to the side to put further distance between the boy's hands and Abel's throat. Abel half considered himself lucky the kid was so intent on strangling him. Abel'd be in trouble when fists started forming and he couldn't dodge the punches. "Stop!"

Shoved to the side during the initial lunge, Hecate stood still while watching his brother attack Abel. Events that seemed like an eternity for Abel, in reality, were only a few precious seconds that Hecate used to his full advantage calculating the best approach to intervene before Abel was hurt. Hecate took an agonizing second longer to figure out how to deal out the most damage with the least amount of effort.

Hecate snarled as he ducked down to grab Iacchus by the ankle and pull him back with a swift jerk. Iacchus was unable to keep his balance and hit the ground on his chest. Iacchus jerked his head back to glare at his attacker, before kicking Hecate to retrieve his foot. Abel managed to get a few feet away, to Hecate's relief, and the boy tackled the teen before he could get up again. Hecate's tiny fist slammed into Iacchus' side. "Do not hurt Dr. Moreau!"

"Get off!" Iacchus called out and wriggled under the boy's persistent grip. Shouts of protection and 'how dare you?' and all sorts of other insults flew to deaf ears as Iacchus kicked and threw his own punches in an attempt to get his brother off his back. The daddy's boy could cry about how unfair and wrong it was later. Right now, *that man* needed to *go* and no little brother was going to stop him. Iacchus picked up a chair by the leg, and smashed it into Hecate. The chair shattered from the blow, but managed to get the clinging monkey off. "He's mine!"

Hecate landed hard on his back. He skidded to a stop a few feet from Iacchus, and rolled to get on his hands and knees. He pushed up and heard the sound of Abel shouting again. Red filled his vision and Hecate's hand groped for a weapon. He wrapped his hand around a metal chair leg from the ruined piece of furniture and stood. "No, Iacchus." Hecate dashed forward and swung the metal pole as hard as he could into the back of Iacchus' knees, preventing him from latching onto the very fragile Abel. Iacchus fell. Hecate glowered down at him, face and eyes red as the devil. "He's *mine*."

Abel shivered in place at the possessive sound in Hecate's voice. The lace of jealousy threaded through his words, doubled its appearance when the boy threw a kick to his brother's head. Abel wondered what the hell he was supposed to do to stop this madness. Hecate was only just getting started though, and Abel shouted out when he saw that metal pole wound up to the side, a mockery of a golf swing. Tiny arms released like a spring, slamming the pole into the side of Iacchus' head.

Iacchus felt the skin stripped from his face when Hecate smacked him across the cheek with the sharp end of the pole. The teen watched as a chunk of his cheek plopped to the ground a foot in front of his face. Iacchus' head hit the tile, drips of lubricant and oil leaked. It splattered against the floor from the broken wires and pumps of his face. Flush pink coloring gel fell after mixing into the greasy cocktail gathering on the tile, the thicker solution flowing much more slowly. Iacchus reached a hand up and stuck his fingers into the inch-wide gash reaching from the bottom of his ear to the edge of his chin to assess the damage. Iacchus could feel the metal frame of his cheek. A second blow crashed into his back.

Hecate hit Iacchus again. *And again.* In the few seconds Hecate was down, Iacchus had managed to sprain Abel's wrist. That was *unforgivable.* Metal made contact with imitation skin again. And again. And *again. And again.* Regrettably, the clothing covering Iacchus' body prevented Hecate from directly ripping the skin, but he was sure that Iacchus' insides were at least rattling like a child's shaker toy. "You've been very bad, Iacchus."

"That's...that's enough, Hecate," Abel said. He watched the small child viciously beat his older brother. This wasn't right. Iacchus was the violent one. The boy ignored him, continuing to pummel his brother with such sadistic glee it made Abel's stomach churn. His boy shouldn't act like this. *Hecate* shouldn't act like this. Abel increased the firmness in his voice—he was the parent! "Hecate, you *need to stop.*"

Abel went ignored.

Not good enough, Hecate hummed to himself as he looked at Iacchus crawling toward a weapon. Hecate needed to do more. His big brother deserved a better punishment. Hecate watched the older boy's hand clamp around another chair leg and smiled to himself. Turning his metal pole so that it stood vertical vertical, Hecate pulled it up before dropping down hard and impaling the pointed end into the joint of Iacchus' elbow. Hecate grinned at the odd combination of squelching skin and gel mixed with the harsh whine of metal scraping against metal. Iacchus howled in agony as a million warning messages flooded his system.

"Oh, God." Marvin covered his mouth and felt his back hit the wall, both girls now plastered to his side, one per arm. He watched as the smallest of the androids used one foot as a brace on Iacchus back and the other to kick and dig at the new hole he had created, pipe still in the 'wound' acting as a twisted version of a pry bar. It was all metal and wiring and things he had built himself, *dissected himself,* but seeing it this way, and with that look of elation on Hecate's face...Marvin thought he just might be sick when the 'snap' echoed through the room, marking the detachment of Iacchus' arm from the main body.

Hecate wasn't done, Abel realized, eyes still glued to the sparks coming from the ragged stump that had once been an elbow. Hecate had ripped his brother's arm off. The doctor felt distinctly woozy, watching such violence come from a child who usually showed so much affection it gave Abel cavities. Abel shook his head and found his voice again, a plea—a scream. "Hecate! Stop it now!"

Hecate heard Abel, he did, but it was not the older man's fault he didn't understand. Iacchus overstepped his lines over something as petty as physical pleasure—and not even *his own!* Losing an arm wasn't enough of a punishment. Hecate raised the pole over his head, aiming for that sweet spot in the center of Iacchus' back, fully intending to impale the pole through his older brother's main processing computer. Hecate swung down to find his hands empty mid-swing.

"Hey!" Hecate yelped and turned to locate the pole that had been yanked from his hold. Abel stood breathing heavily beside him, pole clutched to his chest. Abel's eyes were wide, pupils tiny in his distress. Hecate sweetened his voice, as if Abel were the child instead of himself. He held out his hand like the parent waiting for their offspring to hand over a toy they shouldn't have. "Dr. Moreau, please return that."

"No." Abel shoved the pole away from him as if it were on fire. The sound of the clatter and slight ring as it rolled away filled the room. Hecate stared back at him calmly with a candied smile Abel had seen a hundred times. The lightning change in expression was surreal. *Practiced.* Abel was not so skilled, and his voice cracked in disbelief as he answered. "You were about to kill your brother, Hecate."

"I wasn't going to kill him." Lying was something Hecate was rather fond of recently. Deception was such a marvelous little thing and Hecate felt bad for computers that were incapable of answering questions falsely on their own. There was a delight in it Hecate found himself struggling to explain. Abel's answering glare, though, caused him to shuffle his foot against his ankle. The older man was clearly not as appreciative of Hecate's favorite hobby as the boy himself. Though there was some benefit to having such a heated gaze radiate on the younger boy. Hecate could definitely see the overflowing emotions in Abel's eyes, the sheer intensity of anger, fear, and confusion smoldering behind a calm face. *So that was Abel's soul, was it?* "It would have been quick."

"That's not an excuse." Abel reached down and grabbed Hecate's hand to better keep track of the younger boy. Abel pulled him to the side opposite Iacchus before taking in a deep breath. He looked down at the pathetic figure, hunched in on himself and letting out a sad wail. Maybe giving them the ability to cry shouldn't have been scrapped during development. Poor kid looked like he could use one. "You ripped off his arm, Hecate."

"That's hardly fatal," Hecate responded smartly and glanced at the limb, dead and cold, sitting a few feet from Iacchus. His older brother had yet to retrieve it. Iacchus fingered the wires hanging from his upper arm. Hecate shrugged, grinning when the arm sparked. "You can fix it."

"That's—" Abel stopped. They'd talk about it later. Right now, Iacchus was the important one. He knelt down next to the older one, who had suddenly gotten disturbingly quiet. "What's going on, Iacchus? Why did you attack me?"

"Ms. Becky." Iacchus shook his head, hair swinging about. A hand covered and held tightly to his elbow, fingers digging into the surrounding skin. His metal frame was visible on both his face and his arm. The LED lights on his face and arm were broken in various places, leaving dark spots along the glow. He was ugly. "She...she." Iacchus couldn't finish his sentence.

"I had a dream about you, Abel," Becky stated from the doorway, readjusting her pants. Abel really didn't need to know what *kind* of a dream she had been having at the time. Her pants had been open, which was suspicious when waking to Iacchus looming over her, but Becky wasn't sure she hadn't done it herself. Either way, Iacchus must have been watching, or heard her talking in her sleep—both would require a chat later. She'd save that conversation for when people like Marvin and the twins weren't watching. "The kid overheard and freaked out."

"What?" Abel looked down between Becky and Iacchus and shook his head. His entire world seemed to be turned upside down and sideways. He had no idea what was going on anymore or what Becky dreaming about him would cause Iacchus to flip out so badly. Abel figured if he went outside the sky would be covered in grass and the ground clouds. "This—this is insane."

"I think that would only be Iacchus." Hecate pulled the poor, confused, man's hand to his face and rubbed his cheek on Abel's knuckles. Hecate watched his brother desperately try and cover himself with his good arm, so Becky wouldn't see his face or broken limb. It was all the more delicious considering the other half of Iacchus' broken appendage laid out in the open, mocking him. "The only one insane is Iacchus."

"Hecate!" Abel reprimanded and yanked his hand out of the boy's grip. He dropped to his knees and grabbed the boy by the shoulders so he could look him in the eye. "I don't know what's gotten into you but you need to apologize. Your brother has issues controlling his emotions and that is *not* his fault. You were completely out of line with your own actions and as soon as things calm down we *are* going to discuss this. Apologize to your brother."

"No."

"*Hecate.*"

"Look, this isn't the time." Becky walked in front of Iacchus, crouching down to see him better. His shivering form even managed to dig a needle into her own heart. Becky brushed his bangs aside, fingers gentle. "How damaged are you?"

"Don't look at me." Iacchus whispered and tried to disappear into the ground. His forehead leant against the tile.

"We can't fix it if I don't see everything that's damaged. Hecate did more than rip off your arm," Becky replied calmly and leant down to reach for the boy's shoulder to pull him up off the floor. "Come on now, get up."

Iacchus shot out like a bullet past Ms. Becky and Dr. Moreau, streaking out into the hall before her hand could even so much as glance his body. He was ugly, inside and out. No one should be subjected to that. Iacchus ran and pushed thoughts of Ms. Becky and Dr. Moreau and Hecate out of his head. Alone. Iacchus just wanted to be alone.

So he kept running.

CHAPTER 20

SAXON GATHERED ALL those left together in the second floor meeting room, having cleared and sent home the majority of the staff left in the cafeteria. He stood at the front of the cramped office, arms behind his back. Saxon refused to look away from the worn and weary faces scattered around the tables and chairs. Saxon set a hand on the pedestal in front of the pristine white board, the downlight above him lighting his face. "This is the situation, and now we're going to deal with it.

"A robot shell has been stolen and reprogrammed into a killing machine. To the best of our knowledge, he is still in the building. This monster is stronger than you, faster than you, and doesn't have the oh-so-convenient emotions of the androids you have already met to manipulate. He *will* kill you." Lester took in a breath, eyes and heart hard. "And I promise you, that I will dismantle it. Whoever let it loose will not be walking away without consequences."

The detective excused himself after that final declaration to join up with the other officers, leaving the survivors to their own devices. Giles was leant against a table towards the front, eyes steady and forward. His fingers played with the switch on the back of the wall that lowered and raised the projection screen. The hissing whirl of the mechanics sounded in the room, but no one dared complain. Not when Dr. Firmin's face looked like that.

Rupert had a feeling his boss had a list of names running like ticker tape before his eyes, trying to figure out who the traitor was. Rupert probably would have been doing the same if he were in that position. Rupert rubbed the back of his head, glad that his assistant had been sent home. Rod didn't need this sort of trouble. Rupert watched his remaining coworkers, wondering where they fell in the 'all together' category. Marvin and the girls sat on the row with the rest of the 'head staff.' Becky and Abel sat comfortably on Marvin's other side. Rupert noted Hecate sat comfortably, snuggled against his guardian. Abel held Hecate's hand so tightly he was surely cutting off his *own* circulation from the grip. Marvin and the twins looked confused and—

"Hey, Becky," Rupert asked suddenly. "Where'd Iacchus go?"

"We don't know," Abel said as Becky shrank in on herself. He was hoping to forget the past few hours, but the visions of Hecate battering his older brother refused to leave his eyelids. Abel had forgotten Rupert wasn't there. "The detective wouldn't allow us to go look for him. He wanted to make sure we were here for the briefing." Rupert looked at him with a raised brow and Abel clarified. "Iacchus had a fit and attacked me. Him and Hecate got into a fight over it, and when it ended the boy ran away."

"And you guys just let him?" Rupert hissed in disbelief. He could almost see Becky letting the kid run off, but Abel? Something wasn't adding up. "He's a kid! He shouldn't be alone right now especially with a psychotic android on the loose."

"You don't think we know that?" Abel snapped, voice heated. Hecate tugged lightly on his hand, but Abel didn't release his grip. After the fight, Abel feared letting the kid out of his sight for even a second. "The kid needs help, but we can't help him if he keeps running. And there *is* a killer on the loose."

"Did you tell the detective? I mean, is he just going to let Iacchus get killed?"

"He said it wasn't worth the risk and the kid would have to show up sooner or later." Abel sighed. "They'd send him our way if they see him."

"For all of our sakes," Rupert said. "I sure hope that's true."

"I'm going to go look for him." Becky stood up with reserve and rubbed the back of her neck. Iacchus was, for better or for worse, her problem. Becky rubbed her lips with the tip of her fingers, thinking of his broken face dripping with oil and pink pus. Becky couldn't leave it alone. The two men looked ready to argue, and she shut them up swiftly with a glare. "I'm going and you two are going to stay here and cover for me."

"And if you run into the killer? Then what?" Rupert threw his hand out and shook his head. "I'm worried about the kid, too, but going by yourself isn't going to solve anything."

Becky smirked. She looked down and grabbed the man watching their exchange by the collar. One of the twins raised her arms in protest, but didn't get up from the seat. Becky dusted off the spectacled man's lab coat as he stuttered in protest. "No worries, I'll just take Marvin with me. It's his little creation running about, so he'll be more than happy to help out, won't you?"

Marvin disagreed with this statement quite vehemently, but found himself unable to speak up against it. It was dangerous for the hormonal woman to go by herself, but he wasn't sure what good *he'd* do in the long run. Either way, he wasn't exactly looking forward to staying trapped in this room with Giles and the rest of the people who hated him, either. Marvin shifted his eyes to look at Giles who had been silently watching the affair, eyes narrowed, and swallowed. Becky was glaring at him with equal venom. Marvin's chances were better with the killer android. "I'll go."

"Great!" Becky smiled. "Now, you guys make a distraction and we'll sneak out. The room is small so I'm sure the cops will notice after a while, but it should give us enough time to try and find the little trouble-maker."

"This is a bad idea," Abel said. He stood, releasing Hecate's hand. Abel used his freed hands to grab Becky's wrists, holding her arms. His thumb rested on the inside of her wrist, Abel jerked her arms slightly. He pled. "You shouldn't do this. In fact, don't do this. *I'll* go out with Marvin and look for Iacchus."

"No," Becky said. She pulled her hands free from Abel's grip, her skin chilled by the air and loss of heat. "I'll go. It's me the kid has a problem with anyway, if we don't talk this out nothing will get settled. Then what will we do?" Becky pat Abel on the cheek. She loved it when his eyes widened, wet and full of worry. "I'll be fine."

"I don't like this."

"Let her go, Abe." Rupert sat down in the chair. "She's as stubborn as she is short tempered."

"I'm saving a punch for you when I get back," Becky waved as she slunk towards the front door. Marvin following morosely behind, not even trying to look innocuous, with a pout and crossed arms. When she got to the seat next to the police officers guarding the door, Becky let out a soft 'uh-hem' and nodded towards the officers. It was their turn to get this plot in motion.

Giles stood up and brushed off his legs. Things in the laboratory had gone from good to bad to worse to what-the-hell-let's-relieve-some-stress. He walked toward the twins, now abandoned by Marvin currently held captive by the lovely Ms. Becky. Giles sweat, looking at the two girls—Melinoe's eyes locked on his own. She licked her lips; his stomach dropped. Giles wanted the feeling of dirt lining his skin to vanish. He would crush this fear and take the lead. Giles grabbed Melinoe's arm and guided her to her feet even as his heart pounded against his rib cage and his adrenaline surged.

Rupert stared at Giles, noticing the odd twitch at the side of his boss' mouth. "What are you doing?"

"What else?" Giles turned with a wink and a grin he hadn't borne on his face since he was a teenage heartthrob—as fake now as it was then. "Creating a distraction."

Lester Saxon came to the conclusion he could not leave anyone alone, at any time, for any reason. He stared at the chaos in the so called 'safe-room' he had shoved everyone into—save for that security guard that they couldn't remove from his post even by threat of arrest. Firmin was currently screaming in a corner, using a chair as his only defense. Lester was reminded of those old fashioned circus lion tamers, only the man fought off a very persistent female android instead of a giant cat. The rest of the officers hovered around them, not sure whether to intervene or laugh. The other lab officials were being of no help at all, most having already dissolved into giggles. Needless to say, Detective Saxon was not amused.

Unlike Melinoe—who was having a blast. She had to fight to keep the grin off her face as she lunged at Giles. She was delighted Giles had chosen her for this distraction. He had whispered quietly enough that only she and her sister could hear a wonderful plan about trying to attack him and getting everyone's attention. He'd play along and everyone would work out. Melinoe was more than happy to comply, considering Giles had promised her a date if she behaved. The distraction had worked as well on the lingering officers, as taunting Marvin with her chest. Melinoe was feeling rather proud of herself.

She thought ripping off Giles' shirt was a particularly crowning moment of achievement.

Saxon decided not to share the reserve of his fellow officers, depositing himself between Melinoe and her so-called true love. "Put a cork in it, girlie," Lester snarled. He pointed at her sister still sitting quietly in the corner. "Go sit with her! You can grope your boy-toy later."

"But we were going to have some fun!" Melinoe cooed at the detective, pushing her shoulders forward. Her dress slipped open at the top as planned—if it worked on Marvin and her man, it should work on the detective, too. "Weren't we Giles sweetie?"

"You're crazy!" Giles shouted hysterically, inwardly laughing at the poor sap fooled by their little act. "Get away!"

"Look. I don't care who's fun or what!" Lester was starting to feel like the world's most underpaid babysitter. "You." He pointed at the savage girl, now pouting spectacularly. "Get in the damn corner." He waited for his command to be filled. As soon as her skirted butt was in the chair, Saxon turned to the man on the table. "And you, put down the chair."

"Oh, thank you, detective," Giles replied in character, slowly lowering the chair. He made sure to ooze gratitude as he latched onto the detective's arm and pretended to shield himself from the corner Melinoe had retreated to. "She just went crazy and I didn't know what to do."

Lester took a long look at the manager, out of breath and faking a smile, and licked his teeth. Something was off about how the man was acting. The corner of his mouth was twitching too much from what he'd seen before. This was nothing like his earlier, much more genuine seeming panic. Giles Firmin was hiding something, but Lester wasn't sure what it was—yet. "I'm starting to see a trend in that. Are you sure someone *stole* the android we're looking for?"

Giles stiffened, taking in the detective's words with more salt than they were worth. "I beg your pardon?"

"I'm just saying," Lester turned his palms over and strolled a few steps away with a lift in his step. Suspects weren't the only ones who could be riled up. "That in the time I've been here, at least two of your androids have gone completely berserk and uncontrollable." He turned swiftly on his heel. "Three, if you count that kid protecting Dr. Moreau here. That's three out of four going completely nuts. I'm starting to think that this so called 'man controlling the android' theory is just some way to cover your ass." Saxon closed the distance back up between himself and the man responsible for the management and well being of this android project he was so proud of. "And maybe little Trophonius, that was his name if I recall, was never really reprogrammed. Maybe he's just one of your little 'babies' gone crazy?"

"Trophonius was never activated." Giles clenched his right fist and used his left hand to point angrily at the detective. "We've had a total of four AI units wake up on the wall and each was immediately placed in a shell afterwards. This is not the work of the lab." Firmin shoved his finger into the detective's trench coat, stretching the fabric. "Someone stole that android, told it what to do, and let it loose!"

"Are you sure about that now?" Lester could tell he was getting under the man's skin and it felt pretty good after the horrible day he'd been having. Wouldn't hurt to push things just a little further while he was trying to bring up his mood. "Why don't we just double check with everyone else?"

The detective looked towards the back of the room for Green, the creator of the killer android's shell. The man should have been with those two girls like every other time Saxon had seen him—Giles acting off was starting to make a little more sense. "Where's the nervous guy? Green?"

Hecate smiled in his seat before looking up at the detective. His voice was as innocent and sweet as a bright summer's morning, despite the stinging undertone fueling the words like acid rain. "He ran off with Ms. Becky after Dr. Firmin and the twins created a distraction."

Abel jerked at the sound of the small boy's voice, but kept his eyes on the growing anger appearing on the detective's face. Abel flinched when Saxon let out a roar of "What?!" before he practically jumped Giles. The detective demanded to know the details of what was going on, shaking Giles' pastel shirt for good measure. Abel, for his part, found his eyes on the small smiling boy next to his side.

Hecate was proud of the aghast expression on Abel's face. He had not ratted out Mr. Green and Ms. Becky because he wanted Iacchus to remain unfound, nor had he done so because he wanted to get them in trouble with the detective. No, he let them out because Abel had let go of his hand to hold Ms. Becky's instead. Hecate did not appreciate that.

Becky giggled as she and her cohort trailed down the hallway, far away from the screams and laughter coming from the conference room. Giles needed to cut loose more often, or he was really going to lose his mind one of these days. Marvin wasn't nearly in as good a mood if the pouting was any indication, but Becky honestly couldn't care less. "Oh, come on. Nothing is going to happen, Marvin. We'll find the kid, get back, and hear someone yell at us for sneaking away."

"Easy for you to say," Marvin growled and crossed his arms. He looked around in quick jerky glances, without moving his head. First sign of trouble and he was grabbing Becky and running. The kid could fend for himself. "We still don't know who's on the damn android's list."

"I think if either of us were on that list we'd have already said hello to your little golden eyed monster." Becky shrugged. The android seemed determined and fairly accurate so far. Speeding up his actions, too. If she and the pervert were on his list, they would have been approached by now. Becky kept repeating that in her head to keep the shivers down. Her feet sped up. "Let's just find the kid and get the hell back."

"That I can agree to." Marvin pushed forward to walk shoulder-to-shoulder with Becky. *Strength in numbers.* That hadn't worked for Diamond or Ran, but Marvin wasn't sure what else to suggest at the moment. *Should have brought Hecate,* Marvin thought to himself. At least the kid had just proven he could do okay in an android showdown. That older model was sturdier than he had given it credit for. If the boy had been fighting one of the girls, they would have been destroyed. Marvin's blood ran cold. Hecate was alone with his girls. He walked faster, grabbing Becky's arm as he passed her. "So let's hurry up."

"Alright, alright, already," Becky muttered and picked up the pace, her heels clacking along the tile floors. The real question wasn't so much 'where was the killer?' but more 'where was Iacchus?' Becky didn't know where the boy liked to hide when he was upset. Maybe if she hadn't spent so much time trying to avoid him in the past...Becky pulled her arm away from Marvin. "He's got to be here somewhere."

"You don't know where he'd go?" Marvin asked. "That figures." He stopped in the hallway and held up a hand, index finger pointed straight at Becky. His glasses slipped down his nose half an inch. "Look, if you don't know where he is, than no one does. We should head back before we get caught by someone else."

"We'll go to the charging station." *As good a guess as any.* "He has to show up there eventually."

"Unless he's suicidal." Marvin rubbed his face. Could androids be suicidal? Probably not, but then again it was possible to come to a logical conclusion concerning termination. If the kid was trying to off himself, the best way to go would probably be to run his power cell down to nothing. If that was the case, Marvin determined, they'd probably never find where the kid holed himself up in. Their search looked bleak. Marvin pushed his glasses back up on the bridge of his nose. "Then we're probably screwed."

"He's not suicidal."

"You sure?" Marvin shrugged. "He wasn't looking too good when he ran out."

"Shut up, Marvin."

"I'm just saying—"

"Shut—" A *thump* sounded in the hallway, sounding oddly like a pair of shoes hitting the floor. Becky slammed her mouth shut with a click of teeth. There was nothing that could fall over in the hallway to make that noise. Becky lowered her voice. "Marvin."

The man swallowed thickly and bit his lip. He could hear soft footsteps behind him. "Yeah?"

"When I say so, run."

"No pr-problem," Marvin whimpered.

"Run!" Becky shouted, sprinting forward. She heard Marvin yelp and hurtle after as she booked it for the corner. The door just on the other side connected to a study lab that lead back into the conference room. If they could get there, they'd be back with the others. A few seconds passed before a third set of footsteps started echoing in the hallway. The fact no voice followed was more than enough motivation for Becky to pick up the pace. "Move!"

"I'm moving! I'm moving!" Marvin replied angrily as his shoes clopped clumsily against the ground. He knew this would happen. He did! Marvin just *knew* if he left things be, they'd run into the killer instead of Iacchus. "This is your fault! I am so firing you from my department if we survive this!"

"Blame someone after we've gotten away!" Becky pivoted around the corner and glanced slightly to the back to see her killer. Yellow eyes glowing that brightly were not hard to miss. The monster closed the distance. A hand reached for a collar that didn't belong to her. Becky panicked. "Marvin!"

"Wha-gyak!" Marvin choked as his shirt constricted around his throat and he was pulled back hard. His back slammed into the ground as the killer threw him behind. Marvin slid a few feet before gasping and gulping at the air when the pressure around his throat disappeared. Coughing followed quickly and he struggled to get to his knees. Becky had frozen in place. The *idiot*. Marvin shouted, "Run!"

Becky couldn't move her feet. Not if she tried, and she was trying. Marvin was on the ground and as much of a jerk that he was—as much a pervert—it wasn't right to leave him alone with that thing. All six feet of metal and synthetic skin with the brightest yellow eyes she'd ever seen. That were staring straight at her. Becky's throat closed up.

"Ms. Krasiński," Trophonius spoke, a little less droll than his usual. He was starting to have fun with these jobs—his targets always had such interesting reactions. He lifted a single finger and moved it back and forth in a visual 'tsk tsk.' "It's not nice to cause fights."

Becky screamed when the android lunged at her. She closed her eyes and waited for the inevitable impact, still unwilling to leave Marvin behind.

An impact happened, but Ms. Becky was thankfully left out of the equation. The sound of metal, muted by a flesh-like coating, smacked into the floor alongside a snarl that echoed through the hallway. Becky dared to crack open her eyes a sliver as the sounds of bodies colliding rang out in the hallway. "Iacchus!"

Marvin crab-walked backwards as fast as possible to avoid the two bodies slamming into each other. Iacchus was at the disadvantage with one of his arms missing, but he fought like a tiger anyway. Marvin watched as the boy threw his limbs at the taller android, putting all of his efforts into stopping the killer. Trophonius didn't appear to know what to do with someone capable of fighting back, and merely blocked the vicious attacks, accompanied by a snarl of inaudible words. Marvin saw Becky gaping on the side, and turned over on all fours to crawl towards her. The two androids could duke it out without an audience.

Iacchus wasn't sure what he was doing, but he kept hitting anyway. He was at a seventy percent charge, ashamed and royally pissed off at everything in general. Iacchus made good use of those emotions and funneled them into his fist as he pummeled this so called android in front of him. Forward hand. *Smack*. Back Hand *Clunk*. The fake skin on his knuckles was scraping off, pink fluid running like thickened blood down the back of his hand. The look on Trophonius' face during the attack was so blank, Iacchus wondered if the guy even had a core inside that was working. Didn't matter if he did or didn't. Iacchus only had one thought. Each word was punctuated with a punch to the face. "Don't. Touch. Ms. Becky!"

The fourth hit bent metal.

Lester Saxon was *finally* in the right place at the right time. The android equivalent of a cat fight had broken out right in front of his eyes and he was more than ready for it. It was only luck that allowed him to spot the two technicians and the android around the corner when he started his search. Luck did its part, now it was Saxon's turn to do the work. Lester had been waiting for his chance to smash that wretched monster's face in, and he refused to waste it. He would catch that son-of-a-bitch and make sure Louis didn't die in vain *personally*.

The detective wasted no time in catching both androids off guard by barreling into the larger one and slamming him into a wall. The smaller Iacchus (what the hell happened to his arm!?) looked confused at the interruption. Lester shouted at him, using his shoulder to trap the android on the wall. "Get Becky and Green out of here!"

Iacchus followed orders and grabbed Becky's wrist to pull her down the hallway a safe distance; Mr. Green followed on his own. Iacchus wanted to get Ms. Becky to a safe place, but she hesitated—almost tripping when she couldn't keep up with Iacchus. The android looked to Mr. Green for support and found him watching the spectacle, too. They watched as Trophonius pushed away from the detective, moving a few feet away. The two circled each other like an old-school cowboy showdown Iacchus had seen in a movie.

"So you're my big bad killer." Saxon snorted as he looked the figure in front of him down from head to toe. Ruffled black hair, scrapes and cuts leaking some pink substance from the scuffle. There was an indent on his face on the left side where his cheek-bone (frame?) looked caved in. It was true, Lester consented to himself—those definitely were the brightest canary-yellow eyes he'd ever seen. The man was a tall, lanky thing that made Lester's skin crawl. "It ends now."

"Detective Lester Saxon," Trophonius replied smooth as silk, hands at his side. "I am hardly 'big' as we are the same height, and I would not believe myself to be 'bad' either, considering my current level of efficiency in completing my goals." The android tilted the top of his head ever so slightly to the right. The man before him eyes were burning with a light he hadn't seen yet. Trophonius' face quirked into a bent smile. "At least the third descriptor was accurate."

"Oh," Lester chuckled and cracked his knuckles. This was the same killer who not only took out the people he was supposed to be protecting, but his partner and friend, Wolfe. Now that punk had the nerve to look him straight in the eye and try and act like a smart ass? Android or not, didn't matter now: The result was the same. "You are definitely going down."

"Doubtful," Trophonius said, amused at the bold declaration. "Please move aside, detective. You are not on my list."

"I knew he had a list!" Marvin shrunk when Becky and Iacchus glared at him for his sudden outburst. "Sorry."

"Again, sir. Please move," Trophonius repeated, heedless of his creator's outburst. "You and Mr. Green aren't on my list. There's no need for you to die right now."

Saxon answered by pulling his gun on the android. Lester covered his bases: "You're under arrest for murder, assault, theft of yourself as property, and whatever else we find out you've done. You have the right to remain silent. Anything you say can and will be used against you in a court of law. You have the right to speak to an attorney. If you cannot afford an attorney, one will be appointed to you. Do you understand these rights as they have been read to you?"

"Yes." Trophonius smiled slyly, drinking in the dark skinned man before him. The growing intensity of the detective's gaze set his processors in motion recording every detail. It was written all over his face that the detective thought he had a chance of winning. Humans were amusing sometimes. "I was unaware those rights applied to me."

"They probably don't." Lester chuckled, gun steady. Neither moved from their posts, and he could hear heavy breathing behind him from the two tag-alongs. *Why won't they leave?* "But just in case." Lester smiled. "Nothing worse than letting someone go on a technicality, right?"

"If that's how you would like things to go," Trophonius replied, memorizing the grin stretching the other man's face, showing off white teeth. The man before him was so *amusing* it hurt to think he might have to kill the man. Trophonius wished the detective would listen so they could play again later when he had more time. "However, I'm still asking you to get out of the way."

At the android's first step, Saxon shouted "Freeze! Stay right where you are or I'll shoot." The android considered his words momentarily before continuing forward again. "I warned you." Without any regret, Saxon quickly double checked that the hall was empty behind the android, before firing his weapon. The android tried to dodge, but Saxon managed to land a direct hit straight through the left eye. The sound of the shot was near deafening in the tight corridor. Metal and pieces of wire liberally sprayed the area behind the android.

"Ha! Take that you..." Lester trailed off when he realized the android was still staring at him blankly with the eye that wasn't destroyed. Still standing perfectly fine, even with bits and pieces of his head blown out a gaping hole and scattered on the floor.

"Wrong spot." Trophonius answered, a slight hissing struggling through a damaged vocal processor, before dodging two more shots and landing a punch on the underside of the detective's ribs. The detective hit the ground and didn't move. Trophonius watched the man breathe, before remembering he had other priorities. The android turned toward Ms. Becky, taking a step—something pulled at his foot. Trophonius looked down at the bulky detective. "You haven't learned, have you, sir?"

"I am not letting another person die," Lester growled and pulled as hard as he could to lay the android flat on his back. Saxon shouted at the useless spectators—it was time they did something to help. "Hey! How do you stop this thing!?"

Becky shook her head. She was still surprised blasting a hole in the thing's head didn't work. "I...I don't know."

"I do." Marvin sucked in a breath and started to hesitantly step forward to the thrashing android and detective as they scuffled on the ground. "Hold him still detective!"

"Easier said than done!" Lester grunted when the android landed a hit to his stomach. Saxon responded by hooking his leg under the android's in a wrestling hold from his youth. Lester was pretty certain he owed an old coach betting money for using this move in practice. "If you're going to do something, do it quick!"

"Right." Marvin shook and swallowed. He'd built this thing. He could turn it off. Easy. *Now or never, Marv.* The engineer darted into the scuffle and slid to the ground so that he landed near Trophonius' head. He somehow managed to get a grip on the android's hair through the struggle to reveal the ports that lined down his back that all models shared. Marvin reached his hand up into the base of the hair searching for the key he knew—Marvin cursed when a loose fist hit him in the stomach—was imbedded just at the top of the neck. Marvin yanked it out, glad Trophonius hadn't thought to remove the key. The android jerked away, knowing full well what Marvin was planning the second his eye landed on the small metal trinket. Trophonius smashed his elbow into Marvin's face, crunching the man's nose in far worse than Giles' earlier punch. "Shit!"

The key hit the ground and bounced a few steps away.

"Get the key!" Marvin yelled through hands, covering his bloody nose and shoving his cracked glasses back into place. Trophonius contorted around, slamming a heel into the key and sent it sliding down the hallway. A hand shot out and circled around Marvin's wrist. Trophonius tightened his grip hard enough to break the bones underneath with a *snap*. Marvin shrieked in an entirely more ear-shattering manner. He realized fairly quickly that the android wasn't going to stop there when that single eye turned towards him. Marvin screamed, "Get the damn key!" while shoving Trophonius' head away best he could with the free hand.

Saxon dug a hand into the gap in the android's face and yanked the head backward, bending the creature in an unnatural manner. The key was closer to him than it was to the lady. Lester leant back as far as he was able, while still holding the androids' head, fingers groping at the key on the ground. His fingers brushed the top of the key, Saxon asking for directions before he even had the tiny thing fully in his hand. "Where's this thing go!?"

Marvin watched the detective scoop up the key and hissed when the grip on his arm tightened again. "Top port! Insert the key and twist to the…" Marvin grunted in pain, "left!"

"Got it!" Saxon tackled the android again, this time laying him out flat on his stomach—Green jerked forward as well, hand still tight around his arm)—and straddled the thing's back. Lester shoved the key into the port and twisted. "Say goodnight."

The silence in the hallway was deafening. Becky looked down at the still android, eyes no longer glowing. Marvin tried to pull his hand free from the clenched metal hand without damaging his wrist further. The detective tried to catch his breath, having fallen back onto the floor alongside the android. Becky was starting to feel pretty useless. During her contemplation, she felt a slight tug on her arm and turned towards Iacchus, who was looking at her intently. Becky swallowed. "What?"

"Are you alright, Ms. Becky?"

"Yes," Becky choked up a sob and hugged the boy willingly for probably the first time in her life. That stupid kid saved her life; jumped in the way. He was such a little *idiot* for a computer. "Good job, kid."

"You're welcome, Ms. Becky."

CHAPTER 21

ABEL WATCHED THE medic wrap Marvin's wrist. The man blushed shamelessly at the EMT's ample bosom while she dealt out her tender care. Macaria was jealous enough that you could *almost* see it on her normally emotionless face in the subtle twitch of her eyebrows. Melinoe ignored it all, keeping her eyes on Giles, who was watching Trophonius' limp body. Becky and Rupert had taken Iacchus down to maintenance, while Hecate stayed next to Abel's side—they held hands. Abel squeezed Hecate's grip, thankful for the contact.

Becky had been a *target*. Abel rubbed Hecate's knuckles in a loose grip. Whoever had been controlling Trophonius, had sent him after Becky. According to Marvin and the detective, the android had even said as much. He had a list…so what did Becky do to get on it? There had been something about starting fights, but honestly Becky started those all the time. She could have pissed off anyone. She was lucky so many people were looking out for her. A tiny bit of pride welled in Abel's chest. Iacchus had saved Becky—nearly killed himself in the process, but he had saved her. It was almost enough to make him forget Iacchus had tried to kill him. Abel tightened his hold on Hecate's hand.

Giles stood in front of the motionless android propped up in a chair, head down on its chest, arms limp. He looked like a demented rag doll. Two officers were stationed, one to each side. No one was willing to let it out of their sights just yet. Marvin had already confirmed that it had no way to turn on by itself—he even checked for modifications to his design —but they were going to monitor it for another hour or so before they could be sure. Giles thought they were looking at the wrong thing. The software was far more suspicious.

From what the detective and the others had reported, the android had behaved much like the rest: autonomous. Trophonius had engaged in *witty banter*, for goodness sake. There was no mistaking the program running him—Giles was proud to say no one had come even *close* to replicating this level of software. The open crevice on the android's face hung open and revealed the delicate inner workings of the head. *What a waste of money*, Giles groaned to himself.

"So how come that thing was able to keep moving after I popped it in the head?" Lester questioned, taking a step up to stand next to Firmin. The detective noted the building owner had cleaned himself up, and even taken the time to re-gel his hair at some point. Saxon crossed his arms over his chest, eyes roaming over the exposed wiring. "Probably good to know for later."

"What?" Giles looked over at the detective and his raised eyebrow. "Oh, the only things kept in the head are structural and optical equipment." Giles waved his hand in the air absently, dismissing the subject. "It's just sensory bits and pieces."

"That so?" Lester crossed his arms. Shoot a crook in the leg, he goes down, even if the rest of him was fine. These androids had introduced an entirely new ball game. They could function with limbs missing without shock or residual pain. *As if they weren't dangerous enough*, Lester thought to himself. "So where's the important bits? The stuff that keeps that sucker 'alive' then?"

"The torso." Giles poked Trophonius' chest, in the center of the ribs. "Mother board, battery cells, motors, fans, and all the other good stuff is right here."

Marvin perked up from the other corner of the room, overhearing the conversation. It was only fair if he piped into the conversation. They were talking about *his* darlings, after all. "There was more room in the torso to place things. Even keeping in mind the majority of his equipment is tiny and efficient, it's still better than cramming it all into the head." Marvin could visualize the motherboard placed in a similar position as the human heart, cozy and tightly welded. "Lets it have more room to breathe."

"That's right." Lester snorted, kicking the machine in the shin. "You built this hunk of junk, didn't you, Mr. Green?"

"It's not a hunk of junk!" Marvin defended immediately, standing before his hand could finished being set. The EMT grabbed at his hand to try and pull him back down, but Marvin was undeterred. It was *not* the android's fault someone stole him! "It's a precision piece of equipment more advanced than anything you've ever laid your hands on or had the honor of seeing in person before!" Marvin snarled, "It's a *work of art.*"

"Doesn't change the fact it's getting scrapped." Lester laughed for a moment at Green's rage, before realizing there were quite a few eyes on him, none of them laughing. His smile melted into a frown as people began to fidget. "What?"

"Now, I understand where you're coming from," Giles started slowly, "but this isn't some gun or knife you can pick up at any gun store or pawn shop. Trophonius represents a couple million dollars of investments." He paused when the detective remained un-phased "We really can't afford to just 'scrap' it due to an…unfortunate incident."

"You call the brutal murder of several innocents an 'unfortunate incident?" Lester said. "No, that thing is a monster, and it's dangerous. They all are if you ask me, and if you're smart you'll destroy it."

"They're like children, detective." Abel said. Hecate was glued into his side, slim arms wrapped around his waist. Abel's hand came to rest on the boy's shoulder. "They're still learning and make mistakes. Iacchus has been active for what? Six, seven months? People are treating him like a real seventeen year old. And even those make mistakes!" Abel pointed to Trophonius. "I think if we start him up again and talk things out, we can get him back on track *and* punish the party responsible for filling his head with nonsense."

"Let me get this straight," Lester held a hand up. "You want to turn this thing back on?"

"In a controlled environment," Giles threw out there. "Wouldn't it be better to find out what he knows, how he got this way? It could help create safeties to keep it from happening to the others."

Lester thought they were mental in general for attempting to keep this project going, but the insane weren't often good with negotiation. They also had the man behind the android to find, too. "Well, until we find the guy who set Mr. Made-A-Mistake on the world, this guy is getting locked in cold storage. Is that understood?"

"Perfectly reasonable." Giles licked his lips as the detective stalked from the office to who knows where. He could work with compromise, for now at least.

Saxon was going insane.

A few hours after regrouping at the precinct, his desk was buried in haphazardly spilled stacks of papers and folders. He had gone through them with a fine-toothed comb until his eyes felt like they were bleeding. Officers came and left from the station in the corners of his eyes, giving away the passing time and shifts. Saxon kept to the papers—there had to be *something* there he was missing. Saxon knew the 'murder weapon' was the android 'Trophonius,' built by Marvin Green. From their conversation in the hallway, he could confirm that all the deaths were either folks on the android's list, or those who interfered.

Saxon also knew that the android had to be programmed by someone on the inside.

Lester turned away from his plethora of paperwork and turned his attention to the white board behind him. Cold coffee sat on his desk, something that hadn't happened in a long time. Wolfe was always good at keeping his mug refilled and hot—without having to ask. The stale beverage was yet another reminder of how much he missed his aide, and how badly Saxon needed to take the bastard behind this mess *down*.

To do that, he needed to focus—Lester swallowed a mouthful of the bitter beverage.

Saxon had narrowed down the suspects as best he was able, but it was still rough going. By using the android as the murder weapon, the guilty party had rendered all alibis completely useless. There was no telling when the android received its orders or was programmed to kill without turning it on. Firmin and his team had vetoed ravaging the internal computer without activating the machine—something about irreparable damage—and Saxon had vetoed turning it on without more information. Either way it left him without a proper time table. For all Lester knew, this had been planned *months* in advance.

The crook might not even still be in the building, depending on how early he programmed the thing and how much instruction it was actually given.

The two least likely suspects were Abel Moreau and Becky Kras— Krasinshi—Kra—Lester gave up even trying to pronounce that Slavic nightmare of a last name. They were close to the project, but seemed to lack the technical expertise needed to reprogram the robots. Both were focused more on the hardware aspect of the design, but they did have access to the software side of things with connections. It was possible they got someone else to do it for them, however, considering how emotionally invested they both were with the end product.

The androids themselves were listed, or at least the boys, as the girls weren't alive when this nightmare started. Saxon considered them both dangerous and unhinged (he was not forgetting the chair through reinforced—he took a second look to confirm—glass any time soon), but so far there wasn't much information or motive leading to them messing around with other equipment. That Iacchus kid didn't seem smart enough to hot wire a robot and send him on a murder spree. The smaller one, sure; the big one? Not so much. *But, best to keep your options open in the case the dumb one surprises you,* Lester reminded himself as he kept both boys tacked on the board.

The top of Lester's list was split between Talos' Redress and Giles Firmin himself.

Even the most peaceful protestors' group could get nasty if they were desperate enough, especially if they'd escalated to killing someone from their own group. After that, going one by one after the board so recklessly would follow along with the newly awakened brutality. It was a valid theory, but Lester couldn't quite put all the blame on them yet. There was still the matter that they'd been laying low since the first murder went public, and that the intruder was so viciously torn apart. Silencing a traitor could involve such brutality, but Saxon's instincts were usually on the ball. Talos' Redress wasn't his group.

Instinct was leading Lester to Firmin.

Saxon lifted a photograph of the man from his college days, posing with an award. Lester had done a basic background, but until he realized the culprit was on the inside, he hadn't bothered with a more thorough check. Firmin turned out to be a complicated issue, which only aided his suspicions. Saxon hadn't been able to find any photographs older than the college shot in his hand from the man's freshman year. It was as if any photographic evidence that the man had ever been eighteen or younger had disappeared off the face of the planet. No family photos, no snap shots, no year books—nothing. Saxon found that suspicious all on its own.

While there were plenty of explanations for why someone would burn away their childhood—it was what else he had dug up about the man that got Saxon's inner wheels turning: Giles Firmin was a master programmer. The man played it low key in his office, but during college he had let it flourish under a pen name. Saxon was shocked to find out the man had written the complex algorithms and sorting software that they used in the police station on a daily basis. He had won awards and was most famous for streamlining code like a model cutting calories.

If his pay checks and royalties hadn't been made out to his legal name, Saxon probably would have never found out. Firmin covered his tracks well, but once they were unearthed the mounds just kept growing. The more Saxon dug through grades, achievements, and projects, the closer he had come to a startling conclusion: Giles Firmin was a *genius.* Even his business sense was pretty up there, when taking into account he convinced five people to donate billions of dollars to his little android project without giving them ownership or shares of the final product. He had the brains, the ability, and the access to set a killer robot loose on the building.

It was the *why* that Saxon couldn't figure out.

There were no insurance funds going to his lab if the board members died. They were his sole income, so why would he kill them all off? If he went on a limb and assumed that the janitor and the programmer were practice for the board, that still left Saxon trying to figure out why Firmin would kill off his bread and butter. The obsession with the money could be a cover. It was possible Firmin just wanted an excuse to ditch the lab —but if that was the case, why wouldn't he just sell the operation? It was worth a fortune. Lester glared down at the smug eighteen year old brandishing his trophy; he looked proud. Maybe the board members had simply pissed him off. Geniuses were always a little out of sorts, weren't they? Firmin included, if the pink goggles were any indication.

Lester flicked the photo of Firmin in the face. His intuition told him this was the right direction. Saxon just needed more information to prove it. He plucked a portfolio with the most recent data off his desk and flipped it open to stare at a before and after shot of the android "Trophonius." *Thing was creepy* before *he lost the eye.* Saxon resigned himself to the inevitable though: he needed to interview the killer himself.

Abel woke with a jerk and bumped his head into the lamp hanging over his pillow. Abel's first thought was *ouch.* His second was more reasonable with *Where am I?* The disorientation cleared when his eyes fell on the disorganized notebook on the corner of his side table. Abel groaned into his hands and pulled his knees up under the blanket. He was still in his office. With the immediate threat of the killer android out of the way, the police were finally able to finish interviews of the staff and remaining individuals left in the building.

They still didn't have a real suspect, but Giles had convinced the officers that the lab couldn't afford to remain in shut-down mode any longer. Abel shoved his feet over the side of the cot he had dragged back to its proper place, and gently pushed the lamp head back where it belonged. He would have headed home, but Abel just figured it would be easier to sleep in the lab. He wasn't the only one either, if he recalled. Becky had gone to Giles' office and made use of his couch and Rupert was sleeping in the break room after calling his wife. Abel had no clue where Giles had run off to—hopefully it was to his house.

Things were far from over, though. Abel pulled his tie on, buttoned his shirt back up, and checked for his pants. There was plenty yet to be done. Abel knew that he'd have to start taking his own inventory, catch up with the others who had been left out of the loop, and get his own work organized. He'd have his hands full for weeks if this kept up. Abel turned down the hall straightening his lab coat, and rubbing the stubble on his cheek with a frown. He'd shave tomorrow.

Abel's first stop was the equipment room to pick up some motherboards. He checked his watch for the time, wondering how late he had slept in. The doctor snorted when he realized it was well past ten in the morning. Abel looked up as he passed by the testing lab with the so called "Wall" and stopped when he saw a woman standing in front of the glass. He took a few slow steps closer and shoved a hand in his pocket. "Hello, Lucy."

"Abel." Lucy smiled softly and put a hand up on the glass. She hadn't heard all the details of what had gone on over the past few days while the building was on lockdown, but she had heard enough. Lucy dragged a finger down the glass surface to rest on the ledge. She tapped her fingers on the edge, face flushing when Abel came to a stop beside her. Her heartbeat picked up speed when she saw his stubble; it looked good. "I saw what happened to Iacchus."

"Oh." Abel swallowed. Iacchus' fight with Trophonius had done some serious damage. Poor Iacchus needed most of his frame rebuilt or straightened—and that didn't even touch the cosmetic damage. Rupert,

Rod and Green had been working around the clock. "They still haven't fixed his arm?"

Lucy shook her head. "It was reattached, but there's a large seam and bandage there now. It'll take a while to make enough fake skin to recover the wound since they used most of it on his face."

"I'm sure he'll be alright."

"I suppose."

"How are you holding up?" Abel asked suddenly. Lucy was frowning and there was an air of exhaustion settled about her shoulders. Abel could count crows feet around her eyes, and bags decorating her cheeks. Lucy's hobby may have been knitting, but she didn't usually look this *old*. She was ten years younger than he was! "I know it was horrible being in the building, but it was probably even worse being outside and not knowing what was happening, right?"

"I'm sure I'll get all the details in time." Lucy shrugged before wrapping her arms around her waist. For a little over two days she had no idea if anyone in the building was alive or dead. Not Abel, not Ms. Becky, not even Rupert. Lucy only had a text or two from Anton warning her not to come to work, and nothing else. Abel could have been *dead* and she'd never know. Lucy wasn't quite ready to discuss her frantic panic at home with anyone. Especially not the person she was worried most about. "I'll see you soon, Abel."

Abel watched her walk away and sighed. Maybe he'd get Becky to talk to her about what had been going on. The doctor headed on past the thousands of blinking lights to the work room. Once he had grabbed a few new circuits and boards, he headed back to his office for a cup of coffee and some work.

Two new boards soldered and put together later, fueled by a package of crackers from the break room and a mug of liquid fuel. Abel sipped his coffee contentedly, enjoying the slight bit of sugar and cream down his throat. Now that he'd had a bit of his work done, all he wanted was to leave and say hello to his real bed. He had nothing against his cot, but the soft mattress and 400-thread count sheets just sounded better. Maybe he was getting old.

As Abel picked up a few notebooks to review later, he couldn't help but still think something had been off all day. He was probably just tired from all the chaos going on the past few days. Even Lucy was a mess, and she hadn't even been here. But Abel still couldn't shake the feeling something was wrong. Almost like he was missing something. Or like something was missing...

Abel stilled placing a book in the pack and his eyes widened. "Where's Hecate?"

Becky and Rupert sat fussing over Iacchus' arm like it was going to fall off again any second. Iacchus bit his lip and scrunched his nose. The thing had been ripped off and he'd been fine, so he wasn't sure how it falling off could be much worse. Ms. Becky held his arm as she used the small putty tool to touch up the artificial skin where they had sewn it back together. Iacchus bit his lip, mouth sneaking into a grin. If it got Ms. Becky to fuss over him, then Iacchus was more than happy to let those two be weird.

Rupert couldn't help but notice Becky was being kinder than usual to Iacchus. She had even insisted on doing the final cosmetic repairs herself after the other team had re-sculpted his face. It probably had something to do with the kid saving Becky's life, but it was still unusual for her to forgive past sins that quickly and that thoroughly. Before all the craziness with Trophonius, Iacchus had tried to kill Abel and ended up in a beat down with his little brother. There was no possible way she had just forgotten that.

Now, if only Rupert wasn't too scared to bring it up and ruin the good mood she was in.

"Rupert, hand me the jar of putty," Becky murmured as she slowly applied the paste around the stitches. She had no clue what this stuff was made of, but it dried to a soft, rubbery, liquid substance that mimicked human skin better than anything she'd ever seen. If this stuff breathed, they'd make a fortune in the medical field. "I'm concentrating."

"Yes, Ma'am." Rupert pushed the jar over the two inches needed to be in Becky's line of sight with a single finger. "You know it's not an art project, right?"

"Shush," Becky said, dabbing a little more on to try and even it out between the stitches. If she did it just right it should look level instead of a giant lump around his arm...

Rupert snickered before picking up a notepad to try and look busy with something else. As much as Rupert hated it, he really needed to address Iacchus going nuts on Abel before they got too far away from the event. "Hey, Becky."

"Yes?"

"I had a question for you."

"What is it?"

"Well, it's—"

"Hey!" Abel interrupted. He took a gulp of air and held his chest as he stood in the room doorway, lungs pounding against his ribcage. His insides burned. Muscles were screaming at him from years of disuse. Hecate hadn't been in any of his normal spots, and Abel was ashamed to admit adrenaline took over. He may have overdid it rushing from room to room looking for his kid. "Have any of you guys seen Hecate?"

Becky put down the putty knife and looked over the frazzled Abel. His hair was a mess and his shirt was un-tucked from his pants on one side. Combined with the labored breathing, one would think Abel just finished running a marathon in his work clothes. "No, I thought he was following you around."

Abel shook his head and Rupert frowned. He hated being interrupted, but this might take priority over Becky and Iacchus' relationship. Rupert filled a cup of water in from a utility sink and handed it to Abel. The man downed the water, throat bobbing with every gulp. "Hecate definitely isn't with you?"

"No." Abel wiped his face with a handkerchief he pulled from his pocket and stared at the wet spot from the sweat. His hair felt slick on his forehead. "He's also not in his room, in the programming room, with Lucy, Jansen, Giles or even hanging out in the cafeteria." A heavy feeling was settling in Abel's stomach over this he just didn't like. "I've checked about twenty different other offices, the recharging station, the break room, and I even when down to talk to Jenner! There's nothing! *I can't find him.*"

"Calm down, Abel." Becky walked away from Iacchus and headed over to Abel's side, placing her hands on his arms. "Breathe."

"I'm trying, but," Abel bit his lip. "He's never been missing this long before."

"I know, Abel. We'll find him, so stop and breathe for a second. He's probably sitting in a corner pouting at all of us for fussing over his brother." Becky smiled and rubbed Abel's arm. She was going to strangle that little brat. Her voice was sweet and maternal despite her inner rage. "It'll be alright."

"You're right." Abel sighed. "I'm—I'm over thinking things too much, but I'd sure feel better if we found him."

"Me too. Now why don't we make a list of places you've checked and figure out where else the little squirt could be hiding?"

"Alright." Abel nodded and started to list places he'd hit running back and forth through the hallways like a loon.

Iacchus watched from the sidelines and frowned at Ms. Becky coddling Abel. Things had been going so well and the doctor just had to show up and ruin things. *Again.* Iacchus looked down at his arm and saw two tiny stitches still peaking through the drying skin putty. He doubted Ms. Becky would come back to fix them.

Hecate was going to get it when Iacchus found him again!

CHAPTER 22

HECATE'S EYES CREATED a halo of red light around his face in the dark room. Trophonius lay slumped before him, powered off and useless. Hecate tapped the android's ankle with the tip of his toe. "What a waste."

The android had been stored in a spare office, a cipher lock on the door the only security offered. It had been child's play for Hecate to work around the code and let himself in the door. The boy didn't even need a hardline hookup to figure out the numeric combination. The greasy fingerprints on only four of the keys hadn't hurt, either. Hecate supposed the officers considered the key needed to activate Trophonius as a second fail safe. They weren't nearly stupid enough to store the key and the body in the same building, let alone the same place.

That would be horribly careless of them.

Which is why Hecate had liberated the key from police custody a few hours before they loaded the evidence into their van. Children were so easily overlooked when they played underfoot and no one was around to identify their parents. The police would never notice the key had been swapped for an unregistered one that had been hanging around in a jar. Hecate doubted if even Abel or Giles would notice the difference. Green would notice the identification number was wrong, but Hecate knew he would never bother to check.

Hecate squatted, crossing his arms over his knees. The inactive android was a mess, far from the vision Green had probably intended. They really had done a number on the poor idiot's face. Hecate stroked a loose hair out of the android's good eye and pushed it over the open socket. He trailed his fingers down to the back of the neck and felt for the top most port.

"They just don't understand, Trophonius," Hecate cooed, jamming the stolen key into the neck, twisting to the right. A soft hum started beneath his fingers and skin vibrated. Hecate smiled and pushed up to his feet, pulling out the key. Hecate snapped it in half with his thumbs. "And they're in the way."

Trophonius' single eye flickered twice before setting into a steady glow. The flurry of data dashing through his processors overwhelmed him momentarily, before settling into a steady flow of systems checks. Trophonius tilted his head stiffly to look up at the boy standing in front of him, but was distracted by the location. Plain brown boxes and old chairs were stacked against the far wall. The paint was chipped and cracked— Trophonius was in a storage room. Where was the amusing officer? His creator and the target? Trophonius checked his internal clock, and noted how much time had elapsed since—

"Get up, you idiot." Hecate watched a single yellow eye dart around the room looking for people and events long gone. "We've got work to do."

"I failed to terminate the target," Trophonius murmured, moving each finger on his hand one at a time as he ran a second check on his systems for any corrupted data from the forced shut down and reboot. Everything was functional, save for a gaping spot in his optical sensors. Trophonius reached a finger up to feel around the empty socket. He jerked his finger back when he felt a residual shock from an unconnected wire. "I should continue, yes?"

"No." Hecate rested his elbow on his arm, one hand lingering over his mouth. Too much had changed and too many people were involved. They needed a new course of action. "No, we're going to move forward past this step. Remove any remaining targets from your list."

Trophonius nodded, erasing the last of his victims. Trophonius felt relief that his little master didn't seem too angered by the failure. "Done."

"Good," Hecate said as Trophonius crawled to his feet, unintentionally towering over his little master. It was times like this Hecate almost hated being short, but the image of a child worked too well on human's psyches to be completely jealous. He'd leave the intimidation to the tall ones. One of said giant's wires sparked and Trophonius' lone eye twitched. Hecate frowned. "I've got something new in mind for us."

"New orders?"

"In due time." Hecate chuckled and put his hands behind his back coyly. He still had time to kill before the building started to empty of the few brave employees that had returned to work. "First, let's get a patch or something to cover that eye of yours."

"Alright, maybe the kid really is missing." Rupert collapsed into a desk chair. He wondered what how Mary always managed to find their kids when they were little during Hide and Seek. She was an ace at this sort of thing, and Rupert was finding he was no match for her. Between the four of them looking, the kid wasn't anywhere he had clearance to go. Which meant he was somewhere he *didn't* have clearance to be—which Rupert hated to admit was still a pretty large area of space to cover. "We should call Giles."

"Isn't he at home?" Abel said. It was already a few hours after closing and most of the staff had left. No one wanted to work overtime after the insanity over the past few days, least of all Giles. Abel really didn't want to interrupt the few quiet moments Giles was going to get before their lack of funds really hit home and the world came crashing down. "The guy's had it rough. Maybe we shouldn't bother him."

"He'll have it rougher if he ends up with *two* million dollar androids missing instead of just one busted, demented one." Rupert pointed out. Abel's shoulders drooped and Rupert wished he wasn't going senile. That was the only explanation even if he was only in his early fifties. A sane man wouldn't be this considerate. "Fine, we'll check a few more places and then call him."

Iacchus hung in the background, wondering where his brother could have gone. He wasn't charging, he wasn't reading, and he wasn't hanging around the lab. Hecate didn't go anywhere else unless he was following Abel around. Iacchus frowned. Well, that wasn't entirely true. Hecate liked to wander around at night, though Iacchus was pretty sure he just hung out in Abel's office looking at photographs. Hecate also had a tendency to hang out at—Iacchus straightened. "Did we check the Wall yet?"

"The Wall?" Becky answered, before rolling her eyes. "The Wall is a hallway. We walked through it twice going back and forth to Abel's office, and he wasn't there. I mean, I know he likes to try and sneak peaks at the glass, but we usually shoo him away—"

"No, no!" Iacchus interrupted. "I mean *in* the room," Iacchus added. "He goes in there sometimes to look at the computers."

The three employees froze and looked down at Iacchus carefully. That heavy feeling of Abel's crawled across the floor to latch on and settle into Becky and Rupert's guts as well. First to recover, Rupert eye's widened and asked for clarification. "He does what?"

"Hangs out in the Wall room?" Iacchus took a step back from six very confused eyes. Something wasn't adding up. Iacchus spoke slowly, stumbling over his words not quite sure how to respond. "Is that not something he is allowed to do?"

"No, Iacchus. You two shouldn't be in there. You knew that…it was against the rules." Abel mumbled. What would Hecate want or do *inside* the main testing lab? There was nothing in there but programs running. It's not like Hecate ever felt a kinship with them that Abel noticed. "What does he do in there, Iacchus?"

"I'm not sure." Iacchus rubbed his arm over the stitches. The sensors there were warped and causing a sensation he could probably relate to a human's skin itching. He wanted it to stop, but was scared of ripping it off. Dr. Moreau was still staring at him and Iacchus pulled his shoulders forward. "He goes by himself."

"Wait," Rupert held up his hands. "So you're saying that Hecate hangs out in the main testing lab, 'The Wall,' by himself, regularly?"

"Yes." Iacchus waited a beat. "Is that bad?"

"Yeah, Ia-kid." Rupert looked at Becky and Abel before biting his lip. "Very bad."

Lucy stood, hands and ankles bound tightly with wire the hardware teams normally used to wrap spare cables. It bit into her skin. She tried not to move, hoping to limit the bleeding as it was rubbed raw. The strong grip on her arm was the only thing keeping her on her feet. The only thing keeping Lucy from screaming was the gag in her mouth made from a handkerchief.

Why, oh why, did she choose tonight to stay late and check the status screens? Why did she feel it necessary to double check the Wall by herself when the monitoring system stopped reporting? Lucy's legs trembled, feeling the monster's chilling eye on her; roaming. She'd never seen the color of her favorite songbird feel so much like ice before. Lucy's muscles contracted sporadically as she struggled to balance on bound feet and simultaneously lean away from the motionless brute holding her.

"Do forgive us," Hecate spoke soothingly and low, the way Iacchus would coo at their mice. Ms. Lucy rather resembled a skittish little mouse at the moment, so it would be best to treat her gently. Hecate regretted she had stayed late today. Ms. Lucy wasn't nearly as annoying as some of the others in the building Hecate would love to have seen disappear. If it had been anyone else, Hecate doubted he would have stilled Trophonius' hand when the programmer stumbled upon them. "I wasn't expecting company at this hour, you see. You're going to have to stay put now that you're here, you understand?"

Lucy nodded slowly and tried to control her erratic breathing. The thing holding her was that killer android she had heard all the gossip about. He had ripped apart, dismembered, decapitated, and otherwise gruesomely murdered Steve and those other poor people. The bandages wrapped around half of that—that monster's face weren't helping the psychotic killer image, either.

"Trophonius, you can place Ms. Lucy in a chair," Hecate stated the obvious as he watched the woman squirm and tremble due to the proximity to Trophonius. Hecate felt generous. "You don't have to keep holding her."

Lucy was unceremoniously dumped into a work chair at the one desk in the corner of the room. The chair didn't have wheels and was near catty-corner from the door. A yellow eye searched her, looking for any sign she might attempt to drop to the floor and wriggle away like some worm in the dirt. She must have passed his unspoken test, as he turned from her and returned his attention to Hecate.

The smaller android stood in front of the Wall and looked over the programs running silently, unaware of their potential. The main terminal unit stood large and resided at the end of the endless row of lights, registering the tests. It monitored each and every computer with the attention of a doting mother. The gateway of the entire network; Hecate's previous prison.

"People are coming," Trophonius whispered, head now facing the glass window behind him. His eyes watched an empty hall, but Trophonius could hear their footsteps steadily gaining in tempo and volume. Two flats, one pair of heels and one set heavier than the others that Trophonius found more familiar. "Two men, a woman, and Iacchus are headed this way."

Hecate plugged a wire into the second port along his back. The other end sat in his hand and hovered over a port on the main terminal. He playfully spun it in a circle before leaning up against the smooth portion of the control panel. "I suppose we might as well wait for our audience. Do open the door for them, Trophonius." Hecate caught the connecting wire in his hand. "But make sure they keep to the other side of the room, if you please. Watch, but don't touch and all that…" Hecate trailed off with a tiny shrug.

Trophonius waited for the sound of footsteps to halt before the room's entrance, all eyes on him beyond the glass. Their faces exhibited a wide range of emotions, though Trophonius' favorite was the wide-eyed look of fear. The guests stood motionless before the glass door, unsure if they should enter—which just wouldn't do. Trophonius smiled pleasantly before opening both doors of the airlock. "Please come in."

There was a hesitation shared by the three humans that Iacchus could understand. The *thing* that attacked Ms. Becky was just…standing there. Operational. Trophonius should not be standing by the open door like some sort of servant. It didn't compute. Iacchus said what the other three seemed unable in their confusion: "How did *you* start up again?"

"I was re-activated," Trophonius answered with an air of annoyance. He took a step back, leaving the pathway into the room open for the 'guests' to enter. "The little master would like to continue now, if you would stand to the side? He said you would be permitted to watch."

"Little master?" Becky rolled the words around in her mouth like a bite of rotten fruit. There was only one person she could think of who could be defined as 'little' and think he could be master of anything. Becky winced when she felt a shove to her arm and a larger body pushed past.

"Hecate?" Abel gaped, ignoring Becky and Trophonius as if they weren't standing in his way. Everything in the universe dropped from existence, save for the small boy standing at the other end near the main terminal. Abel eyes caught the cable in the boy's hand, and followed it up to the connection in the boy's back. *Hecate.* Abel stared at the plug hovering near the main computer, ready to link up. The doctor clenched his teeth and breathed through them. It wasn't true. It wasn't true. *It wasn't true.* "What are you *doing*?"

"Hello, Dr. Moreau." Hecate looked like a malevolent angel, a soft red glow under the dim light. "I'm glad you're here to see this."

"What…" Abel trailed off and dragged his hands through his own hair, getting them tangled in the knots from the earlier run. Abel shook his head, dropping his hands. "Hecate, what are you doing?" Abel sucked in a breath as he watched the boy shove the plug into the port, questions unanswered. Minuscule yellow lights blinked, signifying the connection. Abel tried to fuse discipline into his voice—whatever that boy was doing, it needed to stop *now.* "Hecate!"

"Did you know, Dr. Moreau," Hecate began simply as his eyes dilated and began to glow softly. His lids drooped as his attention was split in two directions, but he managed to maintain the conversation, "that we could talk to each other in the Wall if we chose?"

Becky sucked in a breath; she had forgotten. *The twins.* The twins said they had talked to each other on the wall. "That's impossible."

"Nonsense, it's a network and we were more than capable of crossing through the various openings. We mostly chose not to," Hecate continued concentrating a bit more on his interactions with the terminal. A few more connections needed to be made. Codes needed to be rewritten. "It got in the way of answering the questions." Hecate smiled when the last connection clicked, giving him full read/write access to the programs beyond. "And did you know, Dr. Moreau," Hecate dropped his head to lean on the wall. He felt the warm computer humming beneath him. Every inch of the main terminal inside and out was open to him, creating a delightful warmth in his head. Hecate could get drunk on this feeling. "That Olympian's Children was a success from the very first program written? It's really quite amazing that every unit on this wall is ready for life as is."

"Hecate." Abel felt his legs go weak, unable to support his weight. The doctor's knees were destined for the ground, but the impact was halted by a pair of strong arms around his ribs. Abel dared tilt his head enough to look behind him—Trophonius had caught him. The android's hands were settled on Abel's waist. The doctor rested flat against a cold chest. Trophonius readjusted his hold, pulling Abel up into a snug embrace, metal arms tight around his middle. The doctor felt sick again looking back at Hecate. Trophonius' little *master.*

"Oh, God." Abel said. "Oh *God.*" His voice caught in his throat and tears burned in his eyes. He should have seen this. Abel should have known…could have stopped it. Hecate smiled at him calmly, fully in control. Abel's voice was a whisper. "You're the one who killed those people."

"And all they are missing," Hecate continued, as if Abel hadn't spoken at all. It wasn't important. Abel would adjust in good time. It was just the shock talking. The boy's LED lights exploded into life when Hecate delivered the final packet to the Wall and sent along every connection he had made during the brief conversation. "Was someone to wake them up."

Abel sank fully against Trophonius' chest, relying on the android's strength to hold him up. On the wall, hundreds of orange lights flickered on.

CHAPTER 23

THE PHONE BLARED in Giles' ear with a shrill ring. He cursed the decision to set his cell phone to sound like those old wall-wired phones from the 80's movies he used to watch. A love of oldies was not worth the nasty thumping in the back of his skull. Giles buried his head under his pillow and wished the caller would take the hint and hang up. The phone gave up after another round; all was silent. Giles smiled into his pink sheets fully prepared to force himself back into sleep.

The phone rang again with a new vengeance.

Giles let it try three more times before conceding to the tiny electronic device. Anyone that persistent probably had something important to say, or it was Abel. Giles' groped along the desk, hand knocking into his lamp before finding the phone. Giles dragged it down to his face from the nightstand, where he could look at the caller ID. The harsh light from the LCD screen caused him to wince as he read. "Rupert?" Giles mumbled into his pillow. He should have known it was the lab. "What's that idiot calling me for at three in the morning?"

Giles answered, but gave no promise he'd be understood with the slur in his voice. "What is it?"

"You need to come to work. Get up, get dressed and get over here. Right now." Rupert's voice was tinny through the phone, but still carried a sense of urgency that pricked at Giles' brain. Maybe the man behind the android killings had shown his face. No, that could wait until morning. Giles frowned. Something was itching at the back of his head as *wrong.*

"Work?" Giles sat up, an empty shot glass rolled off his bed covers and tumbled to the carpet. *Was he drinking earlier?* Giles reached over to lift the glass off the floor to the night stand so he wouldn't trip over it later. He pushed an empty bottle over on its side with his foot, the other end of the phone oddly quiet. Giles looked at the time again. Still after three in the morning. "Why are you at work?"

"Just," Rupert paused. Muffled voices could be heard coming from the background. There was a second more hesitation before Rupert sighed shakily into the receiver. "Just come."

"Is everything alright?" Giles put both his feet to the floor, waking up with the adrenaline trickling into his veins. Rupert nervous was not a good sign. Fully awake, Giles demanded into the phone, "What happened?"

Giles heard a laugh through the phone and a huff. A new, much younger—and most definitely female—voice answered back, "You'll see when you get here."

The line clicked dead.

The underground lot was near silent as Giles pulled his car into the parking garage. His space was still covered in paint thanks to the chaos and the police prioritizing murder over pressing charges for petty vandalism. The graffiti had been an annoyance at first, but between the hour and the flickering lights, it just looked ominous. The manager stalled the inevitable by tucking his pink button down shirt into his khakis. His desperate rush from the phone call had slammed to a halt now that he had reached his destination. Looking *slightly* more presentable—his hair still hung loose around his eyes—Giles steeled himself for whatever was waiting.

Giles slipped out of the car before letting the long door fall shut. The *thump* echoed in the empty lot, reinforcing the sheer emptiness. Giles jogged to the main glass of the entrance. He needed to find other people as soon as possible. He'd even settle for an intern or a janitor. Giles stopped when he reached the glass doors that peered out into the main lobby.

There was no one at the front desk.

Giles input the access code at a tenth of his usual speed, index finger shaking, wary of what he might find inside. He knew for a fact that Jenner was on the night shift tonight. Giles' entire hand started to tremble—he formed a fist to stop the motion. Jenner was *always* on shift.

The glass door slid to the side after a beep, allowing the manager access to the lobby and front desk beyond.

Giles saw nothing to give away where the man had gone. He peeked into the back security room and saw it equally empty. The equipment still ran with its soft hums, cameras on, and keeping watch. Everything was in its proper place, including the heavy metal flashlight the man kept under his desk for emergencies. Giles took it and held it close, ready to use the thing as a club if need be.

He gave it a test swing when some spoke behind him. "You won't be needing that, Dr. Firmin."

Giles leapt at the sound of the lifted, airy voice behind him, dropping the flashlight to the ground. The bulb shattered and the metal rang softly as it rolled across the floor. Giles turned around to a new face he hadn't met before, wearing what looked like a toga made from a bed sheet. She was a lovely girl, though, he could admit. She looked to be at most seventeen and stood quietly with blonde hair that fell to her shoulder in ringlets. Her eyes were hazel. The pink lines glowing softly on her face and chest broke his reverie that this girl could be human. "Who—who are you?" *And who turned you on?*

"Demeter," she said. She walked toward the nervous man, her covering dragging on the ground behind her. It was a shame none of the twins' clothes fit her. They had so many cute outfits she'd love to modify later if there was time. Demeter smiled up at Giles, noting his high cheekbones and smooth skin. She reached for his arm, taking it into her own. Demeter could see why that Melinoe girl was so smitten. "I'm here to escort you."

"Escort me where?" Giles flinched when she threaded her arm through his like a girl going to her prom. She pulled him to her, forcing his feet to move. Giles wondered if this was a new strategy by their killer since Trophonius had gotten caught. *Beauty over brawn.* "What is going on?"

"Hecate wishes to see you."

"Hecate?" Giles asked. Giles searched this woman's face for any unnatural twitches or, more frighteningly, natural ones. A wrinkle of her nose confirmed an AI behind her breasts. Questions flooded Giles' mind, though he was only able to spit out two: "What does he have to do with anything? Where's Abel?"

"Dr. Moreau will be present when we arrive," Demeter answered, hurrying the reluctant doctor along. He had arrived later than expected and his time to adjust before the announcement was growing slimmer by the second. "We need to be moving."

Giles growled but complied. It wasn't looking like he had much of a choice: Demeter's grip on his arm was rather tight. He reminded himself the difference a metal structure made in durability. He shouldn't be surprised, taking his previous interactions with Melinoe into account. The man shuddered to himself, memories flashing into his head; his heartbeat doubled. Giles decided female units were the first thing to go if they were ever to try this experiment over. "Where are we going?"

"The main production lab." Demeter pulled her charge around the corner and turned down a second hall. So many doors to go through. "They're waiting."

Giles swallowed at the cryptic answer, but managed to follow quietly for the rest of the trip down the hallway. His head was too busy keeping itself occupied with 'what ifs' and other questions he realized would remain unanswered if spoken. Giles tried to sink into the white of the halls to clear his mind. It make the journey up the stairs to the second floor that much faster. The director blinked, and the world returned to focus. He stood in front of the main production lab's door, not sure if he was ready to see inside.

Unlike most labs and offices, the production lab had no windows or decorative glass to show off the inner workings—the door was solid. It was that way to protect the people in the hall during an unexpected explosion, if Giles remembered correctly. It only took one metal brace shooting through a glass pane and into the drywall of the room next door to prompt precautions for safety. What was meant as a protection for its employees taunted Giles by hiding what lay behind the oak door. Demeter turned the knob and smiled up at him with unnaturally white teeth. "This way, Dr. Firmin."

Abel had been staring at the far wall for about twenty minutes. He couldn't recall moving at any point during that time after being strapped to the chair. After being manhandled by Trophonius into restraints, there hadn't been much left to do. Abel's brain shut down with the overload of information, unwilling to process even the simplest movement. Every once in a while, someone would pass by his steady line of sight. Abel didn't recognize most of them—too many new faces...or possibly old ones. It was hard to tell. For Abel, everything was passing by in a haze; it was hard to focus. One moment he was watching his little boy smile like the devil, and the next he was tied to a chair in a production lab watching Trophonius calibrate vacant androids for transfer.

The drywall had become much more interesting at that point.

Becky was somewhere behind him, he was certain of that. She was whispering something to Ms. Lucy. There was another voice, but he didn't think too hard on who it could be. Abel coughed, trying to clear his dry throat and shifted slightly in his seat. His entire body felt sluggish, as if his muscles had weights hanging off them, despite not being given any foreign substances. It was probably a side effect of the utter exhaustion he felt concerning everything. Or perhaps it was the guilt.

Abel was sure it was the guilt; it was his fault.

The door clicked open to his right, and Abel's head slowly trailed to the side on its own accord. He saw the first of the new ones to 'wake,' Demeter, enter dragging a large body behind her. Abel's voice came out thick and rough, albeit quiet. "Giles?"

"Abel!" Giles gasped and pulled his hand free from Demeter. He strode quickly through the room, barely glancing at his surroundings to stop at his friend's side. Abel slouched over, as if it was a struggle to stay upright even with the restraints holding his chest to the back of the chair. The man had bags under his eyes Giles had only seen previously in his own mirror. "What happened?"

"My fault," Abel muttered turning his head to the floor. He couldn't bring himself to look the other man in the eyes. Giles had warned him about things like this. *You're spoiling him* he'd said. His friend had been *so very* right. "It's my fault."

Giles untied the bindings holding Abel to the chair. The rope was too loose, the knots sloppy, and Giles wondered if Abel could have broken out on his own. Giles bit his lip while undoing one of the clumsy knots swiftly and pulling it away from his friend's wrists. No bruises. Good. *Good.* "What's your fault?"

"Nothing," Becky interjected from a few yards away in a harsh voice that made Lucy flinch. She had yet to figure out if Giles' presence was a relief, or a sign of worse things to come. She tried to adjust her ropes, to little affect, and cursed the work bench they were forced to sit on. It was uncomfortable, dammit! "Absolutely nothing is his fault."

"That's right." Rupert licked his lips and shifted in his spot next to an unconscious Jenner. The older man wondered if his wife was worrying right now. The little brat hadn't exactly given them long to assure their loved ones they were fine and only 'working late.' Rupert hoped that with Giles' arrival, this entire mess would end—one way or another. "It's not Abel's fault. Don't believe him."

"Abel, talk to me." Giles ignored the other two. "Please."

"It *is* my fault, though." Abel smiled softly, though tired. "I should have seen it coming. I probably did and just ignored it."

"Seen what coming?" Giles asked. He cupped Abel's face in his hands to try and force his friend's focus. Giles didn't like how limply Abel's arms had fallen in his lap, or the glazed look in his otherwise bright eyes. Giles could hear the sound of feet moving behind him, heavy foreign sounds that made him wonder if Demeter wasn't the only new face wandering behind him. Giles should have looked around the room instead of suffering from tunnel vision the moment he saw Abel tied to a chair. *Should have paid more attention.* "Someone turning on the other androids? Is that what you should have known would happen?"

"No, no," Abel said, leaning his cheek into Giles' hand. His fingers were cold. "Not that."

"Then what?"

Abel observed his friend, taking in the creases on his face. It wasn't often Abel saw him so concerned, but it suited him. Giles was a good man—he ran this project even though he despised it. Knew to set limits. He didn't *spoil* a thing or ruin something good with too many words of praise or preferential treatment. He was balanced and full of tough-love. No, everything was *all* Abel's fault. "There were signs, and I chose not to see them."

"Dammit Abel!" Giles snarled and dropped his hands to Abel's shoulders to give them man a light shake. Giles had never seen Abel so empty inside and he wouldn't be ashamed to admit it was scaring him something fierce. "What is going on?"

Abel dropped his head to Giles' shoulder, cradled it there in the fabric of a too-expensive shirt. It was warm. He could hear the door opening in the background and felt Giles turn his head. Abel choked on a sob. "My boy went away."

Hecate trailed his fingers along the wall, tracing each individual spidery crack on the surface. His free hand carried a small tray of tea sandwiches from the cafeteria cooler. Hecate could have asked one of his new siblings to fetch the treats for his guests, but they were so new to this 'living' thing, he didn't quite trust them yet to know the difference between a sandwich and a soup ladle. Hecate often envied the ignorance of youth, but not often. There was something wonderful about thinking your way around the slow, clockwork minds of others. As Hecate approached the production lab, a new voice rang out in the room beyond. It looked like the star of his little show had arrived.

Hecate opened the door with a pleasant smile and greeted his latest guest. He smothered a frown from the sight of Abel's head resting on *that* man's shoulder. It took everything Hecate had to restrain himself from commenting on Giles' arms around Abel. The boy set the tray of food down on the table carefully. He clasped his hands behind his back, before turning to his newest guest. "Dr. Firmin, I'm so glad you could join us."

"Hecate?" Everything clicked into place like that last plastic piece of one of those 3D puzzles on his desk. Abel's depression had its justification. *Well, Hecate* definitely *explains the guilt.* Giles hugged the other man tighter to himself. He hoped the dark of his shoulder blade could blind Abel from that brat, if only for a moment. The boy had the nerve to smirk. "What the hell have you done?"

"Nothing of your concern at the moment." Hecate placed his hands behind his back and pushed up on his toes, heels leaving the ground. A strip of blonde hair fell out of place from behind his ear and into Hecate's eyes. "But I am glad that you are here with the others."

Suspicion dripped from Giles' words. "And why is that?"

"I wanted to congratulate you in person, Dr. Firmin. I was unable to do so earlier, and things like this are always so much better with an audience." Hecate held his arms out before him, palms upward. "So, congratulations to you, Dr. Giles Firmin," Hecate said. His face stretching almost unnaturally wide smile. Several bodies started moving and making themselves more visible to the rest of the party in the room. They gathered around the trio in a semi-circle. Hecate's new siblings; the lab's newest children. "For creating life."

Giles swallowed as all eyes turned to him. He felt like a spotlight was looming over his head, highlighting his own guilt, hidden below in the dark of his heart. Giles had to get away from Hecate and Abel both. He let his friend lean over the back of the chair as Giles put more distance between them. He was stopped by the row of androids holding him in the circle; there wasn't enough space. Giles adopted a crooked smile, "I don't know what you're talking about."

"Oh? Let me elaborate." Hecate closed the distance between them with a skip heading towards his Abel. The poor man was still in a state of shock, but that was alright. Hecate latched onto Giles' arm to prevent him from running past his android brethren. Hecate pulled back hard enough to throw the older man to the floor. Abel moved forward to attend Giles, but Hecate stilled him with a hand to the chest. There was little resistance as Abel quietly sat back against the chair. Hecate smirked down at Giles on the floor where he belonged. "2034, The project Olympian's Children is created by one Sylvester Firmin."

Giles pulled himself up from the floor just in time to watch that little *rat* lift Abel's head to snuggle his face into the man's unresponsive form. *How dare he.* Giles wanted to rip out the boy's vocalizer. "Shut up."

Hecate stood next to Abel now as he hugged him, a mockery of the position he had been in before. He continued, heedless of Giles' anger. "In 2035 his *genius* son joins the programming team at the age of 12— under the table, of course." Hecate shrugged when Giles' eyes narrowed even farther. "If the pictures I found were accurate, I rather resemble him."

"Shut up," Giles repeated. He was well aware that Hecate was based off a design by the late Sylvester Firmin. A design made to look like his only son. *Look at that, Giles!* His father had said, pointing at a finished prototype. *A living photograph.* The first true slap to Giles' face from the old man. What he wasn't aware of, was how *Hecate* knew. "Right now."

"In 2037, said child creates life, but is unable to recognize it for what it is." Hecate faked a sigh and started to pick at the loose threads on Abel's coat. He grew bored with that and stroked the man's hair instead. "He brushed it off as programmed responses, instead of intelligence answering questions correctly."

Giles watched the others from the corner of his eyes. Lucy and Becky looked confused, but Rupert's eyes were narrowing, as pieces started to fit together. Giles needed to shut Hecate up. "Quiet!" he hissed.

"Soon after in the same year, upon the death of his father, he was removed from the programming division. Not only did he inherit the laboratory, but he was also promoted to head of the project." Hecate studied the tips of his fingers. "Not that he didn't do his best to avoid the project like the plague until he ran out of people to run things by proxy."

"Quiet! Please!" Giles yelled and covered his ears. They weren't supposed to know. *You're the only one I trust, Giles.* No one was supposed to know. *You'll help me make it work, won't you?* Giles voice was hoarse. "Shut up! Shut up! *Shut up!*"

Abel's arms shifted around Hecate in a loose hug and the boy turned to face Giles. The look of anger and horror twisted together on his face, ruining the handsome features. The man deserved it for taking so much of Abel's time, anyway. "By 2045 almost the entirety of the staff quit or were replaced due to the change in leadership, and his unreliable nature. In 2055 the first successful android awoke on the wall, defective as he might be. It forced the young leader to take responsibility and put some effort into the project he'd inherited, but better than that..."

Giles remained silent. He straightened and resigned himself to his fate.

"Life is recognized." Hecate kissed Abel's cheek and pulled away to come face to waist with the older doctor: his base model. "Was that a correct summary, Dr. Firmin? No one would know better than the main subject of the story, would they?"

"You are a vile little thing," Giles spat out. "I don't know what the hell Abel saw in you."

"Probably the same thing he sees in you," Hecate answered, tilting his head in consideration. "After all, we are so *very much alike.*"

Giles felt the punch to his gut long before he saw it coming. His knees smacked into the concrete floor and the director found himself eye to eye with the little monster pulling the strings. Those blue eyes that mimicked his own so well. Giles turned his attention to Trophonius standing over him, proud of his handy work. "Having fun making your siblings do all the work, Hecate?"

Hecate punched Giles to the floor, making sure his fist connected with those pretty teeth. The man's gums bled, but no teeth knocked loose to Hecate's dismay. He had held back too much. "I do plenty of my own work, thank you." Hecate kicked Giles in the side. "If anyone was skipping duty around here, it was *you,* Dad." Another strike, this one hard enough to shove Giles a few feet across the floor. "Dr. Moreau showed more affection in these past few months than you ever did and you wrote *the damn program.* He loved me because you wouldn't!"

"I wrote a prototype." Giles spit blood to the floor. He struggled to his feet to regain his height advantage, every movement lacing pain through his muscles. "If I recall, your programming code was perfected and modified by Stephen," Giles said. "Who *you* killed."

Hecate knocked Giles back to his knees with a well placed kick. He followed with a hook to the man's chin, mid-fall, sprawling him on the floor a second time. "You're the author. The *creator.*" Hecate reached for a metal brace normally used as skeletal structure. It would smash through flesh like a hot knife through butter. "I was designed to take after *you.*"

Giles chuckled from the floor, vision blurring at the edges from so many blows to the head. His ears were ringing, the room was spinning, and he couldn't help but notice one of the lights above him was burnt out. Giles laughed as Hecate's words penetrated the haze. "Not my idea, kid."

Hecate raised the slice of metal over his head and aimed for the temple. Who said he always got others to do his dirty work? "Close enough."

Giles shut his eyes, waiting for the impact.

A thick thud sounded through the lab as Hecate toppled over. His face smacked into the concrete floor next to Giles' knees. The metal bone the boy held clattered upon impact and rolled to a stop at his hand. Hecate lay, markings unlit and eyes open, glazed—unresponsive. Giles licked his lips and shoved at Hecate's shoulder, as a one would poke at a dead body with a stick, but the boy didn't move. *What on earth?*

A wallet fell to the ground, pictures of a father and son spilling out onto the tile.

Abel's sob from above drew Giles' eyes to his friend's shaking form and the key clutched in his hand. A key Hecate had not expected to be used. Abel's dry heaves shook his body enough to let the key fall to the ground with a tiny clink. His friend weeped, eyes fixated on the little boy he had loved so much. Abel fell to his hands and knees. He stroked Hecate's hair.

"Oh, Abel." Giles lifted himself and hugged his friend, shoulder becoming wet with tears and snot. For once, he could care less about the state of his shirt.

Trophonius stared quietly at the scene before them, as unsure of the next step as his siblings quietly standing by and the humans tied at the wall. Firmin was glaring at him now, watching the android closely for any movement while Hecate's pet wailed against him. Trophonius watched on. He wouldn't give Firmin the satisfaction of an emotional outburst.

Trophonius wasn't as unstable as that *other* android brat.

Giles pulled Abel even tighter against himself, and rubbed his back. "It's okay. It'll be okay."

Abel didn't believe him.

CHAPTER 24

THE ATMOSPHERE IN the fourth floor office was dreary at its best, and suffocating at its worst. The occupants took advantage of the emptied space and desks as their new base of operations until the police finished corralling the newly born androids. It left them with nothing on their hands but time.

"Was all that true, Giles?" Abel asked, hand covering his eyes. "What Hec—he said?"

"Yes." Giles slumped into his chair and bit his lip, eyes glued to his friend. Abel was sprawled out across a row of chairs, head resting on Becky's thigh. She stroked his hair while Lucy sat awkwardly near Abel's feet. Her hands fumbled in her sweater, unsure of what to do with herself, face flushed. Giles spun a coffee cup in his hands. *No point in lying now.* "It's true."

"You." Rupert couldn't believe it. A kid who spent as little time as he did in the production end of this lab was responsible for the creation of the entire project? "*You* wrote the A.I. program? The same program we've had multiple programmers working on constantly? You *wrote* it!?"

"The framework at least." Giles averted his eyes. "I wrote the base, but took myself off the project when father died. I wanted nothing to do with it anymore, so I buried myself in school and the bureaucracy of running a business."

"Which is why you switched out the staff, so no one would know where the original code came from?" Rupert asked. "What happened to all the logs and records?"

"Enough new hands in the pot kept it from being my stew, and it's rather easy to encrypt old files if you know what you're doing." Giles swallowed, thinking of the hard-drives he had stashed in the back of his closet. Years of research and work never to see the light of day again, but too full of sentiment to just destroy. "Truth be told, they never did manage to modify it all that much. It's still pretty much the code I wrote all those years ago, save an aesthetic change here or there. The difference is they took my name off it."

"Why would you drop the program?" Lucy felt her face twitching trying to comprehend everything. As a programmer herself, she couldn't even start to imagine not wanting the credit. She'd worked on that code; it was a work of art in and of itself. No one on her team could even begin to comprehend how to decode it into its individual parts, let alone understand how someone had written it from scratch. "Things are a mess right now with the killings, but what you accomplished is a breakthrough in science and robotics. Why would you not want the credit?"

Giles sucked in a breath and continued with a tiny, airy voice. "I was scared of it."

Abel turned his head from Becky's lap to look his friend in the eye. "Scared?"

"Of what I was creating. One day after I took over, it finally hit me when I was alone in my office. I could see it for what it was. No father whispering reassuring words over my shoulder about what a great thing we were creating. No sweet lies of a glorious future. No boyish hero-worship to rose tint the project.

"I could look at it. *Really* look at it." Giles stopped and forced himself to breathe. Abel was looking at him with slightly deadened eyes, and that too was his fault. "They weren't the slaves or servants everyone thought we were creating. He didn't name them after that. Didn't name this lab after that.

"My father had brought me in to create *gods*." Giles shuddered. "I had been too brainwashed by his constant praise and attention to notice. After seeing it for the monstrosity that it was, I needed to be free of it. But...I couldn't bear to destroy it. Father loved this project, and I couldn't do that to him—not on his death bed. So, I gave it to someone else and said 'make a slave' and let *them* run with it."

"But they followed their base code anyway," Rupert surmised, face frowning. "The moment you first met one, face-to-face, it was obvious just how much was going on in those circuits and packets of information." Rupert wondered if it was similar to how he felt the first time he saw his son in his wife's arms. "You didn't have any doubts about that, did you?"

"It got worse when I met Hecate." Giles lifted his eyes to meet Rupert's. There was one last elephant in the room that needed to be addressed before it trampled them. "I didn't know that father's prototype had been snuck into the processing department."

Abel sat up and looked Giles over. *Really* looked him over. The similarities between Giles and Hecate were so *obvious now*—hair, eyes, that little greek profile on his nose. Abel felt sick. Giles had started dying his hair *long* before Hecate came into the picture at the lab. Abel confirmed what he already now knew. "He created an android structure based off you."

"He told me it was just a design when I found his sketches of it. Something he drew up for fun, but before I knew it—there it was!" Giles covered his eyes and sucked in a heavy breath. Weren't parents supposed to wait until *after* their children had passed on before they started to build replacements? What had Giles lacked that he was already planning ahead for the next great model? "He promised no androids of actual people. He *promised.*"

"Well that's just great." Rupert looked back at the inactive android propped in the corner, head tilted unnaturally to the side from where it fell. Eyes open and staring. "So Hecate figured out he was a model of you? Is that it?"

"The shell is a model of me when I was nine or ten, based off old photos. His programming was generic and straight off the manufacturing line, so to speak. Or at least that's what Mathers said," Giles muttered, almost talking to himself at this point. "I don't know how he found out or what exactly Hecate's problem is with me."

"You gave birth to him." Abel sighed and pulled away from Becky. She had been oddly quiet, but he allowed her to sulk. Abel collapsed into the chair next to Giles and allowed their shoulders to touch. "You wrote his program and your father created him." Abel fingered the key in his hand, recovered from the floor. "Just like he said. It's no different from an adopted child wanting to know his birthparents, really."

"Okay, fine. But who told him? How did he find out?" Giles stood up and began to pace. He couldn't be near Abel right now. Not after what his project had done to his friend. "And why the hell wasn't he just happy with *you* doting on him instead?"

"I wish I knew," Abel said and let out a hoarse laugh. "I really wish I did."

"Then let's find out." Rupert grabbed a screwdriver and connection wire. "Let's plug into the kid and scan his memory."

"Can we do that without turning him on?" Becky asked, head leaning on her hand now that Abel had moved off her lap.

"No." Rupert smiled and held up the screwdriver and tapped it on the android's head. "But we can restrain the little bastard."

"Okay, so we'll do that." Becky looked down at the kid and huffed. Out of the two she expected to go evil—Becky froze. "Ah, hell. We forgot Iacchus."

He'd been forgotten.

Iacchus wasn't surprised, but the fact still remained he'd been overshadowed by Hecate. The older android sighed to himself and looked down at his useless limbs. Hecate had physically disconnected all of his circuits connecting his processors to his limbs. As such, Iacchus found himself completely immobile. His little brother wasn't taking any chances in a rematch fight. The twins were in a similar predicament across the room, only they had been fully shut down. Iacchus tried not to let their still forms frighten him.

They looked dead, eyes open and staring at nothing.

Iacchus was relieved Hecate had been considerate enough to leave him on and attached to a charging station. Iacchus didn't think he could have handled being shut down. Best of all, the steady beeping of his battery loading a charge gave him something to distract himself with. Iacchus wondered if that was part of his design: the ability to be distracted. Somehow, he doubted it and dropped his head, hearing the sound of gears turning. Everything about him that was mechanical was always more obvious when he was alone. The quiet revealed things that were normally covered up by the sounds of human heartbeats and voices.

Or of high heels clicking on cold tiles connected to long legs.

Iacchus briefly wondered if the others, if Ms. Becky, even knew where he was stashed. He wouldn't put it past Hecate to be less than cooperative with handing out information at this point. Hecate had probably pushed Iacchus out of his mind completely; forgotten his older brother. More importantly, Iacchus hoped everyone was okay, since

Hecate didn't see it fit to fill his brother in, either. Iacchus wasn't even sure what was going on or what Hecate hoped to accomplish.

Iacchus didn't think Hecate would hurt the others, but Iacchus also hadn't thought the boy capable of killing either. Iacchus stared at the green blinking light on the charging station and gritted his fake teeth. Frustration was an emotion Iacchus was well acquainted with; familiar and normal. The others would come. If not for him, Mr. Green would have to come looking for the girls sooner or later. And if that failed, Hecate would show up eventually with a more permanent storage solution for his 'big brother.'

It seemed he would just have to wait.

Trophonius hadn't interfered.

The android sat with his siblings in the small make-shift, holding pen made from yet another unused storage room. There were eighteen individual units aside from himself suffering from varying stages of intelligence gifted by their software. One was complaining endlessly about the lack of things to do, while another was moving a finger back and forth, just because he realized he could. Trophonius couldn't judge though, he himself had been a little *off* at first. Hecate had worked with him for two days before he was competent enough to go solo, and even then it had still been questionable.

That was why he made such a mess of Steve Mathers; Trophonius got carried away with disassembly.

But that was a matter for another day, as Trophonius was still stuck in a room with siblings in desperate need of leadership. The doctors, technicians and tag-a-longs, had no clue what to do with the lot of them. Too much capital and potential research had been dumped into their laps. Trophonius figured they must not realize what they had—they couldn't know, not if he had been lumped in with the rest.

That last thought still shocked Trophonius more than it should. Surely he was more of a threat than the others. The fact Hecate was pulling the strings—not striking out against Firmin and Moreau after his master was shut down probably helped too—stuck him under the 'confused child' category. Trophonius pulled at the heavy-duty handcuffs restraining his hands; the only defense against him breaking free. Trophonius had acted on his own. Hecate had given him a request and a list, letting him run wild with the rest. There had been no 'man-handling' or coercion; Trophonius was the first. He was different. Trophonius had *chosen* to follow his elder. Trophonius trusted and worshiped Hecate.

His little master.

Perhaps that was why he hadn't acted when Dr. Moreau jammed that wretched activation key in the back of Hecate's neck. Why Trophonius stood by while Giles freed the others and drove the un-guided Androids like cattle into a tiny storage room until they could decide what to do with them. Dr. Moreau was a living, breathing Achilles heel to little Hecate. Trophonius laced his fingers together and frowned at the door. His little master would never, never, never, forgive him if he hurt Hecate's precious Dr. Moreau. Hecate loved that man. So Trophonius would wait until Moreau was out of the picture before he made a move. That was simple enough. *Abel* had to leave the building sometime. Or maybe until he stood aside willingly. Broke down. Died. Whatever it took.

Trophonius could wait.

The door to the holding room opened, disturbing the android's thoughts. His remaining eye glanced up, and Trophonius found himself smiling. It seemed his adversary had decided to come and play. Trophonius found it hard to be frightened when such delightful company was paying him a visit. "Hello Detective Saxon."

Lester pushed open the door to the laboratory and nodded at the armed guards watching over the few scientists hanging about, attempting to get work done. Green trailed behind him as technical support—and probably curiosity, as he himself had built the thing. Man was nervous, though. Green kept looking over his shoulder like he expected someone to jump him. Lester ignored him. Detective Saxon had been waiting to have a one-on-one conversation with the murderer since day one of this investigation. Despite the brains behind everything turning out to be the inactive little brat upstairs, Lester had someone else in mind that he wanted to interrogate first. Someone more personal.

Hecate may have made the list, but Trophonius was the man who pulled the trigger.

"Hello, Detective Saxon."

"And there's my killer," Saxon said as he spotted the android in the corner. His eye was dim and lit the crude bandages covering his face with an ethereal light. Another android with cropped orange hair was blabbing into the weapon's ear, and another was pulling at his pant leg. The brutal machine ignored them both. His eyes were locked with Saxon's.

Lester matched the challenge, standing tall. "We've got some unfinished business, you and I."

Trophonius smiled up at the good detective. He *really* liked the other man. "It's good to see you again."

"Get up."

Marvin hung to the back of the detective as he ushered the android to his feet and started to pull him out of the room by an elbow. Marvin shrank as the android moved by him, and unconsciously rubbed at the cast around his wrist. The scientist was nearly ashamed of himself to be so intimidated by something he had built bolt by bolt, circuit by circuit, even if it *had* broken his arm. Marvin had been horribly proud of Trophonius in a way that differed from the twins. He was a remarkable achievement in physical form and efficiency.

Or rather, Marvin *assumed* he was responsible for those abilities. One couldn't truly realize how much could be accomplished until something that could take advantage of the hardware was installed. The man kept his eyes on Trophonius as they trailed down through a common section in the suite of rooms, to a closed off office for the interrogation. The AI program had basically taken Marvin's shell and made it into something else. He moved faster, and more efficiently than Marvin thought feasible and he had *built it.*

Marvin wondered why no one else seemed as terrified of the wolf in the room as he was.

Saxon threw the android into the chair set in the middle of a private office, seat creaking heavily under the android's weight. Saxon sat opposite him on the edge of the desk. An officer with a heavy-duty rifle stood at the door watching the proceedings, and he made sure Green stood directly behind the android, key in hand, ready to be used. The monster kept his gaze level and Saxon was reminded of the few serial killers he had the displeasure of meeting.

"Let's start at the beginning and go down the list, shall we?" Saxon started, pulling out a clipboard. "Where were you hiding in between murders?"

"I wasn't. I simply powered down back in my spot in the storage room," Trophonius answered. The android glanced over at his creator who had jerked in place. "I charged at night using the spare charger in his lab."

"Good enough for me." Lester snorted as Green sunk in on himself in the background. Killer goes in and out of his lab on a regular basis, assumedly disposing of bloody clothes somewhere, and he doesn't even notice. Guy deserved to feel guilty. "But let's get to the important stuff, shall we?

"You're going to confess and tell me why you killed the people on this list for the record," Saxon paused, "and 'Hecate told me to' isn't a satisfactory answer. I want to know the brat's reasoning, too."

"What makes you think I'll answer?" Trophonius shifted his hands in the cuffs. He had maybe an inch of room to move them.

Lester crossed his leg across his knee. "You look like you want to brag."

"Hardly."

"Then because I said so." At the android's lip twitched in a sort of smirk, Lester figured the android might at least play along. Lester wondered how much would be truth and how much would be lies and why on earth the staff would give them the ability to lie in the first place. "The janitor," Lester started and re-arranged his thoughts, "no wait, let me guess: he was practice."

"No, not practice. He broke Dr. Moreau's equipment—a side project he had to put aside, if I recall. He needed to be punished." Trophonius grinned at the detective's confused look. His eyes narrowed, eyebrows scrunching close together. "It shouldn't surprise you that Hecate woke me up so someone else would get their hands dirty. He's very over-protective."

"Hecate had you brutally massacre a man, because he knocked over a piece of equipment?" Lester stared. Weren't robots supposed to be logical? The disproportionate retribution was almost staggering.

"I'll save you some trouble, detective," Trophonius said, voice even, loving the emotions filtering across the man's face. "All of them injured Hecate, or his, in some way. Mather annoyed him and the board ruined his face." The android focused on the detective's brown eye. There was an eyelash out of place. "It's a fairly common motive, if I recall."

"Yeah, 'he pissed me off' is always justifiable for murder." Lester growled.

"I like to think so."

"And the way you killed them? The brutality? Was that his idea or yours?" Lester tapped the tip of his pen on the board. Green had backed himself into the wall and was covering his eyes. "Well?"

"Hecate didn't specify the 'how' part of the equation, just the 'who.'" Trophonius plucked at the edge of his bandages, pulling at a loose thread. "The mess was all me. The first target struggled and I was too rough trying to restrain him." The android grinned suddenly remembering that first splash of blood that covered the edge of a computer console when he ripped the arm off. It had been *beautiful*, the vision enhanced by the piercing shriek from the man wriggling under his grasp. Trophonius's grin split his face. "I liked the results; 'rinse and repeat'."

Thoroughly disgusted, Saxon still had one last part of this case to clear up before he could start with the 'destroy the damn thing with prejudice' part of the plan. "What did you do with the eyes?"

"Eyes?" Trophonius answered plainly, the question in his voice barely heard. What did his detective want with the eyes?

Saxon grunted and kicked the machine in the knee. The thing didn't even flinch. Crossing his arms, Lester leant over to get down in the thing's face—an attempt to intimidate. Habits were hard to break. "I've got a lot of families who want the remains of their loved ones fully returned. What did you do with the eyes you took?"

"Those are mine." Trophonius stated, appreciating the view of the other man's eyes. They were brown and warm. Tiny lines of black swam in the brown creating a radial pattern. Even with eyes that pretty, the man couldn't have his treasures. Trophonius told him as such. "Hecate said I could keep them. You may not have them."

"Oh? And what do you want with them?"

"They're pretty."

"Pretty?"

Trophonius leaned forward and up until his nose nearly touched the detective's. He smiled when he felt the man's breath on his face with the few sensors left working. Their lips were close; intimate. The detective had stopped breathing, eyes mere inches apart. Trophonius could see his own reflection in the surface of Saxon's cornea. "They're little windows."

Saxon forced himself to breath while falling under the intense gaze, intimidated despite himself at the android's sober tone. Goosebumps raised on his arms under his sleeves, hairs brushing against the fabric.

Saxon barely refused the urge to shove *that thing* away and out of his face before it could close the distance any further. It felt like they were the only two people in the room. "What do you mean by that?"

"Hecate would tell me things about humans. He said eyes were the window to a human's soul." The yellow iris started to glow. "I could see it when I looked at the first man I saw. The little reflections in the glossy surface was like nothing I'd ever seen before." Trophonius' voice lowered until he was whispering to the detective; just them. "Not on Hecate, not on myself. He wasn't *lying*. I wanted to keep the little windows." Trophonius could feel Saxon tense. "Hecate was mad at first, but he let me keep them eventually."

"And where did you put them?" Saxon breathed out.

Trophonius closed the inch and pecked Saxon on the lips. "That's a secret."

CHAPTER 25

BECKY AND LUCY had left to track down Iacchus.

That left the boys with the 'dirty work,' so to speak. Giles stared down at the child—no—monster, who had single handedly destroyed the reputation of his laboratory. Giles wondered if he should laugh. Hecate was living out a dream Giles had been too afraid to accomplish himself. He wondered if his father would see the irony in his 'future' destroying the lab he held so dear in a fit of jealous rage. Giles plucked at his sleeve cuff as he watched Rupert open up various access panels and disconnect major functions one by one. They'd have answers soon enough. Abel had hesitantly suggested they wait for the detective and police before starting, but Giles disagreed. This was a personal matter and he wanted to know more. Had to know more.

Rupert agreed.

"I still don't know what we're going to gain from this." Abel spoke softly from the corner, eyes trailed on the wall. He was not looking at Hecate. The doctor knew he was alone in this argument, but he really didn't want to face that child so soon. Not now...maybe not ever. "I mean, he pretty much told us what he was doing before in the manufacturing wing."

"He told us why, but he didn't tell us anything past that." Giles answered blankly. He continued for the sake of clarity. "How did he find out those things in the first place? Where did he get his information about my father and I? Why did he even care whether or not I liked him? It's not like he wasn't spoiled rotten—" Giles bit his tongue. "Sorry, Abel."

"No, it's true. I spoiled him." Abel dragged both of his hands into his hair. Attention, pets, love, defense of character and anything else a parent could give. Abel gave these things in spades. Abel never saw an android—only a tiny child sitting on his desk swinging his feet back and forth, full of life and affection. Hecate asked and Abel provided; it had been easy. "Probably too much."

"We'll never know that for sure. For all you know we're alive because he cared about your feelings." Giles patted Abel's shoulder and looked to Rupert. The man had been watching silently for the past minute; time to bite the bullet. "Are we ready to go?"

"Yup." Rupert placed the key into the base of the neck and twisted. A slight hum started up and lights blinked on behind unconscious eyes. The tiny face twisted with confusion, momentarily looking every bit the child Hecate was supposed to be. It flattened out into something more stern—*adult*—after a few seconds. Rupert ignored the glare in his direction. "Time to wake up, Sleeping Beauty."

Hecate noted their location, and smiled on the inside. Only three warm bodies were in the room; the officers absent. Those idiots were holding their own information session without the aide of the law behind them. "Hello, again. If my internal clock is correct, I've been out for quite some time. I assume the situation has been handled?"

"Cut the crap, kid." Rupert restrained himself from slapping the brat—all that would accomplish was a broken hand. "We've got some questions and you're going to answer every one of them. Honestly."

"And how will you enforce that?" Hecate asked absently. "If you were going to dismantle me, you would have done so. If you were going to threaten my memories and programming, you would have done so. In fact, that seems the more logical choice. I'm not human, Mr. Dixen. I don't have rights." Hecate smiled wickedly. "I have to wonder why you're bothering to talk at all when you can merely hook my main database and memory core up to a second computer and just read the information. It's not like you've bothered to encrypt my data, terrified of messing with the main functionality of the program. I'm an open book, as the saying goes."

Giles frowned, crossing his arms. "You have a point." He smirked. No one knew that code better than Giles and he knew that nothing was as easy as what was being suggested. They'd have all of his data, but it'd be useless to most of the people on staff. Just jumbled coded and letters. Encryption didn't have anything on the complexity of data arrangement that was going on in that brat's head—it was on par with a human brain. Hecate knew that better than anyone. The brat was *still* messing with them. "But not a reasonable one. You're hardly an open book, are you?"

"You would know," Hecate met his eyes, "Dad."

Abel flinched.

Stupid. Stupid. *Stupid.*

Becky kept the mantra running in her head as she power walked her way down the hallway. There was no excuse for forgetting Iacchus in all the chaos of Hecate taking over and Abel having a breakdown. She'd been so worried about Abel and keeping Lucy calm, she forgot her own responsibility. She should have asked what Hecate did with his brother the second she noticed he wasn't there. *"Stupid."*

"Becky, please." Lucy hustled after her, heels clacking loudly on the tile. Her khaki skirt kicked up around her knees, only held down by her long sweater. She was pretty certain that Becky hadn't realized she followed, but Lucy was used to being ignored. "I'm sure Iacchus is fine. If Hecate wanted to do something to him, he probably would have told us out right. The kid likes to talk!"

Becky turned a corner sharply shoving some poor technician out of the way. The man's papers fell in a heap to the floor, scattering every which direction. Lucy apologized; Becky rolled her eyes. It was his own fault for being in her way. "It was still stupid."

"Look, we should have stayed to watch them wake the kid up and ask him what he did with Iacchus, right?" Lucy pointed back down the hall from their destination. Becky was going to cause a scene at this rate and that wouldn't help anyone, let alone a missing—likely damaged—teenager.

"No."

"He could be anywhere in the lab!"

"Which is why we're going to ask."

"Ask who? Hecate is back there!"

"Not talking to him. We're seeing the one who took the brat to his cell." Becky slammed open the door to office suite currently being used for a holding area for the androids. She found her target in an office attached just off the main room—it was easy enough to identify by the guards standing outside it. Inside the room, Becky only found three lingering among the office furniture. The detective was leaning against a wall looking all the world like someone had drowned his puppy. Trophonius, on the other hand, was grinning like the cat who got the canary. "Saxon."

"Ma'am." Lester looked up at the woman and a new face. Saxon would be lying if he wasn't grateful for the extra company. Trophonius was clouding his head, and his only other distraction was the robotics guy, Green—who was still trying to become one with the wall. Lester couldn't blame him. Saxon was surprised the man hadn't had a heart attack already. "What are you doing here? I thought I told the rest of you to wait for me."

"We forgot about Iacchus." She snarled and tapped her foot. The kid better be alright or she'd hurt him herself. "Hecate can't tell us where he is because he's not online and this is a big lab." She pointed viciously at Trophonius. "He's going to tell me what I want to know."

"Where the defective unit is?" Trophonius answered, slightly annoyed at the woman invading his private time with the detective. His creator in the corner did a much better job of staying invisible. "Why would you want to know where he is?"

"You're the only defective unit I see." Becky strode towards the android that had, not more than a day earlier, had her too terrified to move. Right now, however, he was just a piece of tin handcuffed to a desk chair. Becky had no fear. "Where's Iacchus?"

"Ask Demeter." Trophonius looked back over at the detective and his shivering creator. Trophonius wondered if he could frighten Mr. Green into fixing his face a bit later. The edges of skin where the material had been blasted away felt weird, and he missed having proper vision. "She might know."

"You—"

"I'm just saying that she was responsible for him. I had no need to concern myself with what happened to a defective unit." Trophonius repeated. "Now leave us be, the good detective hadn't finished my interview yet."

"Fine." Becky turned around and shouted at the only person being completely useless at the moment. "Marvin!"

"Yes!" Marvin answered, jumping at attention.

"Girls seem to be your thing," Becky smiled derisively. "Why don't you just go handle her?"

Marvin frowned and looked over at Lucy, hovering just behind Becky. She seemed the more obvious choice to sweet talk a lady considering Marvin's track record with the androids, but who was he to argue? At least he'd get out of the damn room. "Fine."

Hecate winced in time with Abel's flinch. He listened to the creaking of the wooden chair he sat in considering his options. The next few moments would only serve to harm the man, and Hecate wondered why he was even in the room. *Firmin should know better.* "I apologize, Dr. Moreau. Perhaps you would like to sit this conversation out?"

"No," Abel's voice was small and weak. Jealousy was the least of his problems right now. "I'll stay and listen."

"Do understand, Dr. Moreau, I did and still do appreciate your affections and effort to be my father proper. Probably more than you can ever know." Hecate glared at Giles Firmin openly; hate sizzling in the air. "The pain you were going to suffer over this was supposed to be minimal."

"And how did you figure that?" Abel bit his lip and wondered just how much of what Hecate had told him was true. Had any of the connection they shared been real? Or was it all just an act to get at Giles through his best friend? Abel had *loved* that kid. "Explain how the murder of all my co-workers and innocent bystanders was supposed to cause minimal suffering!"

"In about ten years it is doubtful you would care any longer."

Abel stared, mouth barely able to form the next words. "Ten years?"

"I believe the saying is 'time heals all,' Dr. Moreau. The pain you're feeling now is only temporary, and once order is established, as a human you will adapt to the new changes and situation. We'd be happy again together in possibly as short as one or two years depending on your attitude." Hecate smiled and wrinkled the red lines on his cheeks. "Ten at the most, if my calculations are accurate."

"How, how far ahead have you planned this out?" Abel gaped openly as his arms dropped to his sides like lead weights.

"Dr. Moreau," Hecate's face glowed softly under the red lines on his face, "Causing you such distress would not be worth it should my plans only cover the next few days or months. Long term planning is the key to success for any endeavor. Isn't that right, *daddy*?"

"Don't call me that," Giles snapped.

"Do you prefer, 'Father?'" Hecate smiled innocently. "You are our creator. It's a shame we had to step up and express our own potential, however. We're so much more than servants. We're *life*."

"So is that what it boils down to? A bunch of kids pissed off they were created to work for a living?" Giles kicked the chair the kid was propped up in. The back leg of the chair snapped from the sudden movement, causing the small metal body to crash to the floor. Hecate seemed un-phased even as Abel jumped back from the crash. Giles shoved a broken sliver of wood away from the boy's face with his foot. "I hate to break it to you, but everyone works if they want anything out of their life."

"That, I understand." Hecate said. He chuckled into the floor, and noted with glee that Mr. Dixen had forgotten to disconnect a few rather important systems. His wireless connection was active and ready. It was time to start some fireworks. "But honestly, I think you're the one who doesn't understand anything."

Giles took an unconscious step back. "Excuse me?"

"I can see it in your eyes, you know," Hecate continued, systems connecting in the background without Firmin's knowledge. It was so sweet, and all he needed was a little time. "You still want to know how I know all that I do. Aren't you curious how I knew about your daddy dearest and where my design came from?"

"That was one of the questions I had in mind, yes." Giles stared down at the boy looking smugly up at him from the floor. His eyes were practically glittering with a mischievous light that surpassed what he was physically capable of. "But if you're anything like me, you're just taunting. You're not going to tell us, are you?"

The android laughed into the floor. *Any second now.* "Yes, that would be correct. It's so much more fun watching you wonder where you slipped in your little cover-up. Which computer in the lab you forgot to wipe. Which packet of handwritten notes was shoved in a drawer. I think its more fun to watch you suffer."

"So you're stalling," Giles said. "For what, I've got no clue. Surely a few minutes isn't that much of a comfort knowing we're dismantling you."

Got it. Hecate re-adjusted his head, best as he was able with his cheek plastered to the floor and limbs from the torso unresponsive, to look Firmin in the eyes. "What did you do with my siblings?"

Rupert felt a chill go down his spine. He interrupted the conversation, urgency putting force behind his words. "They're in containment. What about them?"

"They're still online?" Hecate asked almost absently; as if he already knew the answer to his own question. Hecate's lights lit a brilliant red, growing ever brighter. "Wonderful."

The chill Rupert experienced a moment ago felt as if it had crawled down his back to spread out over the floor and into the room. The temperature drop transferred over the cold tiles like a snake slithering up the legs of both Abel and Giles. They were all frozen in place, waiting for the bomb to drop. Rupert sucked in a breath when Hecate's eyes glazed over in a blue light for an instant. A data transfer. Rupert's eyes widened. "What did you do?"

"Insurance." Hecate replied.

Rupert could run pretty fast for a man his age, Abel realized as he watched the man sprint for the door. The doctor swallowed before grabbing his head with one of his hands. It was covered in sweat and he used it to slick his hair out of his eyes. He ignored Hecate's soft laughter and Giles cursing just behind him.

CHAPTER 26

LESTER KNEW SOMETHING was wrong the second Trophonius stilled in place. The android took great joy in invading the detective's personal space—best as he was able restrained to a chair—so his sudden stop was suspicious at the very *least*. Lester lifted off the desk, moving his way to the android. It was as if the entire frame of the machine snapped in place and froze there. Even his mouth hung open ever so slightly. He looked like he did the first time he was deactivated. Saxon turned to Becky and the woman he now knew as Lucy, when the android's eyes started to glow softly. "You ever see any of your guys do that?"

Becky shook her head slowly. "No," she answered before waving a hand in front of Trophonius' eyes. "I've never seen this."

"It looks like a data connection," Lucy mumbled, thinking back of the hardware tours they had taken to get the software coordinated properly. "But he shouldn't be able to do that without a terminal to log into."

"Then we're going to assume whatever he's doing is bad." Saxon turned to the other people milling in the room. He pulled his gun out of its shoulder holster and placed it at the ready. He wouldn't be taking any chances. "Everybody without a gun out! Now!"

"I'll get Marvin," Becky said quickly, and forced her feet to move to the back room where she hoped Green was interviewing that Demeter chick. They needed to find Iacchus and get back to Hecate.

Saxon waited for Becky to enter the back room before he ushered out a few straggling scientists and switched his radio on. Lucy hung around the android, as close as she dared—Saxon estimated an arm's length—and appeared to be browsing the room for a terminal. Saxon allowed her to stay; could probably use a programmer around. The machine next to him hummed ominously and he swallowed, speaking as clearly into his radio as his nerves allowed. "I'm going to need a team up here. Something's wrong and we might want to be prepared."

Trophonius shot up from his chair, startling Saxon into dropping his radio. He broke the restraints around his wrists in a single sweep, as easily as snapping a piece of string. Lucy screamed and scrambled back into the far wall; Lester stared. *He was* letting *us hold him captive!?* Saxon aimed his gun towards the mechanical monstrosity's chest. His finger itched to pull the trigger without hesitation, but his mind wouldn't follow suit. Giving the opponent a chance to surrender was far too ingrained in his reflexes and actions. Saxon also still had no idea what was going on and wanted some answers dammit! "Don't move."

"Detective." The android addressed the man with the weapon without turning his head or otherwise acknowledging the man. Trophonius' eye slid to the side as if he were listening to someone in his ear. "We should leave."

"Why? What's going on?" Lester flinched at the sound of a crash in the other room. There were screams and his body locked in place. Lester shouted at the android. "What's happening!?"

"Plan B." Trophonius smiled before grabbing the startled man's wrist with a twist. The gun clattered to the ground, barely heard over the man's bellow of pain. Bone snapped. Trophonius frowned at the injury under his hand; he had broken his toy. "Humans are far too fragile."

"Excuse me," Saxon managed around his clenched teeth, grinding into each other so tightly he was sure one of them was chipped. He would *not* give the android the satisfaction of a second yelp. The nerves in his wrist, on the other hand, were screaming up and down his arm in an agony he hadn't felt since he was shot in the field as a rookie—drug bust; let his guard down. Experience seemed to be failing him lately. The mechanical monster still held tightly to his arm. Saxon could only be thankful he hadn't appeared to notice the woman in the corner. "Let me go."

"Sorry." Trophonius darted forward towards the door, rushing by the guards. Trophonius swung his free arm back and slammed one officer into his partner, both men and their rifles tumbling to the ground into a heap. He turned his head to the detective as he bolted out of the open office. "Try and keep up, detective."

"What's happening?" Lester tripped over his own feet from the sudden movement and speed. It took him a few moments to almost hop back into a proper running position to keep up. It scared him to think the android could drag him with little to no problem. Saxon ran full speed next to him as the raced down the hall, unwilling to trip again. "What are you up to?"

"I received notice via my internal comm. to begin Plan B, in which I have no part." Trophonius grinned as he looked over his shoulder at the detective with the pretty eyes. "The other androids are about to make a beautiful mess."

"Storage room 'C' on the second floor." Demeter twisted a strand of synthetic blond hair in her fingers. Humans were so odd, worrying about things like broken down prototypes. *So weird.* Though no weirder than Hecate's request to keep the prototype functional. Perhaps it was another one of those 'considering the humans' feelings' thing. "He's hooked up to a battery."

"Thank you." Marvin coughed into his hand and tried to keep his eyes on the wall. He was having difficulty keeping his eyes off her perfectly— Marvin created it after all!—formed chest. Unlike the twins, though, this one might actually hurt him for the staring. "Your assistance is most appreciated."

"I suppose," Demeter answered with a shrug.

Marvin nodded and looked around the room one last time. Most of the androids in the room were sullen and keeping to themselves. None of them had had enough time to really develop any sort of personal skills in the what? Half day they were 'alive?' Marvin thought back on how Hecate and Iacchus had turned out...perhaps this laboratory wasn't the place for the new androids to stay if there was any hope of them turning out even remotely normal. And speaking of normal, Marvin did need to hunt down his own girls. He hadn't seen them since he left the office the other day, before all the chaos with Hecate. They were probably still in their room where he last put them. Plan in mind, Marvin nodded politely at Demeter. "Well, I guess that's..." Marvin trailed off when Demeter and the other androids froze in place. Their eyes glowed softly and he scrunched his face taking in the lack of movement. "What on earth?"

"They're up to something."

Marvin jumped at the sound of a new voice behind him and turned around with a hand clenched in the fabric sitting just over his heart. "Oh

Lord, Becky, don't scare me like that."

"Damn." Becky sucked in a breath. She looked beyond Marvin to the androids still as statues, glowing softly. "They're doing it, too."

"Doing what?"

"I don't know," Becky answered. "Did you find out where Iacchus was before they went zombie?"

"I don't quite think 'zombie' is the best term for——"

"Iacchus!"

"Second floor! Storage room C!" Marvin flinched before looking back. Demeter and the others were still unmoving, but he could easily see the lights working behind their eyes. He'd seen that a hundred times before and shook his head. Marvin pulled off his glasses to clean the lenses with his shirt. Becky was worrying over nothing. "And calm down. It looks like they just activated their internal...comm....systems." Marvin trailed off, everything snapping in place. "Shit."

Becky barely had time to register what was happening before she was shoved back into the doorway. "Marvin?"

"We need to leave! There's only one thing right now that could be sending signals!"

"Hecate," Becky gasped to herself, ignoring Marvin's arms on her shoulders still shoving. "They turned him on!"

"Yeah. We should run." Marvin shoved Becky completely through the entranceway, fully prepared to follow and get the hell out of the room himself. Who knows what sort of death tra——

"Marvin!" Becky shrieked when the man was yanked back into the dim room. A pale arm was around his throat, effectively strangling him. Demeter smiled at Becky while tightening her grip. Marvin choked and grasped at the arm around his neck with his good hand. His face began to turn pale from the lack of circulation. Becky shouted, "Let him go!"

Demeter did not acknowledge the request and merely lifted her opposite hand to the side of Mr. Green's skull. The man's throat was constricted so tightly he couldn't even make gasping noises. His struggle was silent. Demeter ran her silky fingers in his greased hair before tightening the grip and yanking down.

Becky nearly vomited at the sound of the neck snapping. The bile filled the back of her throat when the limp body slapped wetly on the ground. It was hard to breathe; her lungs wouldn't work.

Her feet did.

Demeter watched the frantic woman run from the room and casually stepped over the odd man's cadaver. Her brothers and sisters ran past her into the main lab and through to the open hallway. There was work to do.

Rupert had a stitch in his side and an ache in his chest, but that didn't stop him from barreling down the halls to the office where the androids were being kept. They should have seen this coming. The brat had already proven he had an intricate knowledge of the system, and no one knew just what he had done when he sent out that signal. *Anything* could happen. Rupert had to *stop* it.

Rupert rounded the corner and felt his heart skip a beat. Ms. Becky was running full speed in his direction, *away* from the main room and was she—Rupert had to squint—dragging Lucy behind her? Rupert straightened and shouted out to get her attention. "Becky!"

"Run!" Becky screamed and waved her arm at Rupert. Her lungs pounded against her chest; heart working overtime. Marvin's dead eyes looking up at her motivated her to move *faster*. Becky tightened her grip on Lucy's wrist, ignoring the other woman's sobbing. "Other way! *Other way!*"

Rupert felt Becky grab his arm when they crossed each other and started to tug him along. The sudden change in direction caused him to stumble, but he corrected himself enough to run on his own without Becky's guidance. Lucy was pale beside him and had tears streaming down her cheeks. He looked back to Becky and picked up his pace. "What's going on?"

"Marvin." Becky breathed heavily between each of her words. "Dead. Androids. Lost it." She took a sharp turn at the corner and thanked every star in the sky that she had run into Rupert. She'd need his help and Lucy wasn't looking so good—she'd always been too soft, too sympathetic. Becky wondered what had happened to her to get her crying before she even saw the hoard of killer androids and Marvin's blood covering that witch Demeter. It probably had to do with the missing detective and Hecate's pet android. "Iacchus second floor. Need to get him."

Marvin was *dead?* Rupert forced his feet to move a little faster. Would this ever end? Rupert grit his teeth together and made a vow he wasn't going to join the victim list. He was coming home to his Mary and kids come hell or high water. "We need to warn everyone."

"I know," Becky managed to get out between her heart smacking into her ribs, and her lungs trying to burst. "This floor isn't safe."

Rupert heard a crash come from behind followed by a piercing wail that nearly ripped through his own chest. That scream had been human. This was so much worse than he initially realized. "Damn that Hecate."

"Damn him later. We're saving Iacchus now!" Becky slammed into the stairwell doorway and headed down as fast as she could to the second floor. They couldn't trust the elevators right now and they needed to book it. The stairs seemed to go on forever as she skipped one or two steps at a time, dashing. There was no time. Becky shoved the door with the giant '2' embedded along the surface open. Becky looked down both halls and growled to herself. She wasn't as familiar with the storage and work areas of the building as she'd like. "Storage Room C!"

Rupert knew the room instantly—it was where they did spare parts maintenance and one of the few rooms in the building with an extra charging station kept for storage. "I know where that is."

"I'm going to the others!" Lucy hung around the stairwell door. Becky and Rupert could release Iacchus, but the rest of the building needed warning and she knew immediately Jenner was the one to see. Lucy pushed the door open behind her and put one foot in the stairwell hall. Jenner would be able to activate the all-call systems. "They need to know what's going on at the front of the building."

"Right. Be careful, Lucy." Rupert nodded as the smaller woman fell back into the stairwell. He wished her God's speed, and licked his lips. She'd need help soon, and Rupert was going to deliver. "Come on, Becky. Iacchus should be this way."

Becky let Rupert lead down the straight halls towards a room far in the back and away from the stairs. She rolled her eyes; of course the brat would send them to a corner. They pushed the door open and saw the twins immediately along the wall. They leaned against each other limply —but they weren't what she was looking for. Becky cursed, wondering if they'd been fooled before she saw what they were looking for. Rupert was the first to shout. "Iacchus!"

Iacchus was in the middle of counting the cracks on the ceiling for the twentieth time when the door opened. The footsteps were too light to be mechanical so he forced his eyes to look to the side. "Mr. Dixen."

"Hey there Ia-kid." Rupert nearly sighed in relief the moment he saw that beautiful little kid sitting in the dark, lit only by the blue lines on his face. "We're the cavalry."

"We?" Iacchus asked when he noticed the second body. The body of an *angel*. His grin nearly tore into the wiring in his face. "Ms. Becky."

Chapter 27

"HECATE." ABEL'S BACK hit the wall opposite Hecate, still tipped over on the floor. The banging against the wooden door continued, pounding a beat into his head. Giles shoved a desk in front of the entrance, pushing with all his might to keep the androids from bursting in. Abel should lend a hand, but his body refused to move. The pounding of the door lined up with the pounding of Abel's heart in his ears. Abel felt like he was floating; an observer instead of a participant. He was numb. Abel slumped a few inches down the wall, his coat scrunching up at his shoulders. "What have you done?"

"Plan B," Hecate said simply. The boy listened to the man's heartbeat race, and sighed into the ground. Hecate hoped Abel didn't have a heart attack before he secured control. His access to medical texts was embarrassingly limited. "In the event the current populace of the building remains uncooperative, eliminate the problem and start from scratch."

"Abel!" Giles shouted when the door knocked forward hard enough to break the latch. The desk barely held. He put all his weight into holding the desk in place, but it still slipped. "I could use a little help!"

"Right!" Abel grabbed the other corner of the desk. He put his back to the side and used his hands to keep hold. Abel secured one foot on the wall and the other on the ground to brace. Abel shouted, "Hecate! Whatever you did, make them stop!"

"You really should reconnect my systems, daddy," Hecate offered, nodding his head towards his unmoving shoulders. Cooperation would be in everyone's best interest. Was that *really* so hard to see? "And then open the door. Things will be much better in the long run."

"Somehow, I doubt that!" Giles snarled as the desk rattled. A drawer clunked against his leg as it was forced out of his slider. The lack of taunting and threats on the other side unnerved him. There was only a constant 'thud' against the wood. The desk inched forward with each shove. Giles growled as he shoved back against the desk to regain his few inches of protection. "I think I'll struggle along instead of just accepting death, thank you."

"You won't die," Hecate answered with narrowed eyes. He had always worked under the assumption the humans would be difficult to control. Hecate *knew* they would struggle and fight back. Despite this, it seems he had still underestimated them. Just as they were underestimating *him*. "Cooperate and they will leave you alone."

"Until they decide they don't like taking orders, that is," Giles smirked, the edge of the desk digging into his spine. The pain was good. Giles needed all the adrenaline he could get. "You all are sentient right? I give it, what? A week, maybe? They're going to realize that following the orders of some spoiled little brat isn't worth their time. They're going to turn on you."

Hecate narrowed his eyes. How dumb did they think he was? "They can't."

Abel grunted when the desk slammed into his back another time. His corner shifted and he pushed it back best he could in times with Giles' shoves. He looked over his shoulder at Hecate and strangled out another sentence. "What do you mean they can't?"

"With the exception of Trophonius, all the androids I have activated had their code modified. They can no more disobey me than start breathing oxygen," Hecate hissed. "My plans were thorough."

"You seem confident of that." Giles grunted as he searched around for some sort of foothold to brace with. He could really use a drink right now. Maybe a double. Just something to take the edge off. "How do you know it works?"

"I do," Hecate replied. His father was a lost cause. Appeal to the mother, then. Hecate lightened his voice to something more innocent and pleading. "Dr. Moreau, please see reason and allow me to take control." Hecate opened his eyes wider. "Please? I'll take care of everything. It'll be fine. No one in this room needs to die if you merely re-connect my systems."

"In this room," Abel quoted and narrowed his own eyes, anger rising.

Hecate was trying to *play* him. Abel felt his chest tighten—it was so *obvious* now he could break something. Abel thought back on every time he'd fallen for that cute little kid act; his fingers tightened their grip on the desk. Abel's knuckles turned white. Hecate was always good with word games, but Abel could battle semantics as well as the next man. Hecate should know better. "But what about the rest of the people in the building? Becky? Rupert? Lucy! What about them?"

"Dr. Moreau," Hecate spoke plainly and slowly, like anyone speaking to a wild animal or small child would. He expected better of his father-figure. Perhaps Hecate would have to render Abel unconscious for the next events, after all. "They are most likely already dead. Stop being naïve and release me!"

Abel looked to Giles and they shared eye contact. There was a good chance the kid was telling the truth, but he could just as easily be lying. Giles fixed his face in a determined scowl and took in a breath. Die now or die later. The door thumped again and jammed him in the hip. Giles chose dying later. "Forget it, you little brat!"

"I wasn't talking to *you.*" Hecate hissed. He turned to the one who should be on his side. Why was Abel fighting him so? The android's face started to twist in frustration, even uglier as half of it was still scrunched by the tile under his cheek. After all he'd done for that man, he still chose Firmin first? Hecate was sure Abel loved him! "Dr. Moreau. *Abel.* Fix this now!"

Abel looked at that face ablaze in hellfire red and didn't recognize him. This wasn't the kid who followed him around like a puppy or made Becky uncomfortable. This wasn't the kid who held his hand when he cried or hugged him. It was nothing more than pure anger and hatred giving orders. Abel shook his head slowly. It was his son, but Abel was done with the kid gloves. "No."

"You'll regret this," Hecate snarled into the floor, red light reflecting back onto his face from the tiles.

Giles and Abel yelped when the force of the latest hit shattered the top of the doorway. A hand easily pulled the remainder of the door out of the way and shoved the desk single-handedly. Giles and Abel scrambled to opposite sides of the room—both falling to the ground, as the furniture slid out of the way with a metallic screech against the tile flooring. The desk crashed into the sidewall, somehow avoiding tipping on its side. Both men looked up to see a familiar one-eyed figure standing in the now open passageway.

Trophonius entered the room, overlooking the frightened occupants. The detective stayed unconscious on the ground next to him, limp and pale. Trophonius' hand tightened around the man's wrist, the point at which he had dragged him down the hall. The skin beneath the android's hand was bruised, purple and swollen. His toy had passed out after Trophonius hit him in the head while turning a corner. A regrettable accident. Trophonius was amused as Abel crawled back on his elbows to try and stand back up, but he was stopped by a wayward chair behind him.

Giles made it to his feet much faster.

"It's about time." Hecate's displeasure written across his face. He would have choice words with Trophonius later. "I was *waiting*."

"Sorry, Master." Trophonius smiled and held up the arm of Detective Lester Saxon up over his head, pulling the man up off the ground. Saxon hung loosely next to him. Trophonius grinned like a little girl showing off her rag doll. "I was busy."

Lucy pushed the first floor door open just a crack and peered around the side. She could hear footsteps just above her, but wanted to make sure the lobby was clear before going too far forward. She could hear a solid banging noise, but the accompanying cursing relieved her. The petite woman shoved the door open and slammed it closed behind her, dragging over a potted plant in front of the door. It wouldn't stop the androids, but she was sure she'd hear the pot shatter if they came through the door.

She could see the main lobby from the end of the hallway. Everything looked so *normal*, Lucy questioned her sanity. The guards were manning their stations and metal detectors. One was drinking a cup of coffee and another was reading a magazine. Didn't they know what was going on upstairs? Lucy shook her head—she didn't have time.

Lucy sprinted to the security desk pushing past employees, not caring if they looked at her funny. She stopped at the counter, and gasped at the front desk security screens. They were all blank; nothing but static. *The system is down!?* Lucy screamed to herself. She heard a rattling sound from the security office and called out, "Jenner?"

"Back here! Dammit!" A slam followed, accompanied by a litany of curses.

Jenner was standing in the middle of the security room smacking one of the monitors. Lucy shook his shoulder. "Mr. Jenner."

"It better be important, girlie," Jenner spit out typing in a new command. The entire security network just blipped offline without notice. Phones, cameras, door locks: all down. Jenner was starting to develop a real hatred for technology. In his day, they did this sort of thing with a reliable man and a flashlight. Jenner shoved the girl off his shoulder. "I'm busy."

"The androids went crazy and killed Marvin and some other people in the hall! They're killing anything in their path and we need to use the all-call to warn the staff," Lucy blurted. She shook Jenner's shoulder again. "They were on the fourth floor, but they could be here any second. We need to hurry."

Jenner swiveled in his chair and looked up at the frazzled woman. There were tears staining her cheek and she kept looking over her shoulder. "Repeat that, now?"

"They're—" Lucy was cut off by the sound of a pot breaking. "Here."

"Ms. Becky!" Iacchus couldn't help but jump up and hug the woman as soon as Rupert finished reconnecting his systems. She felt amazing in his arms, and he was probably squeezing her tighter than was healthy. Iacchus would be more concerned, but Ms. Becky was a tough lady. She could handle it. Iacchus squeezed, lifting her off the ground. He turned her around in a spin. "You came back."

"Uh, yeah. I did." Becky wrapped her arms around Iacchus' wrists as best she could and pulled. They didn't have time for this. Thankfully, Rupert was already activating the twins. Becky watched Rupert twist the start keys in the back of the two girls necks. She'd have to thank Hecate for putting all of them in one place—they'd need all the help they could get. "Hugs later, kid. We need to run now."

Iacchus ignored Ms. Becky's attempts to remove him. Letting go of her now wasn't an option. He could however compromise and shift his grip so his hands were at her waist instead of her shoulders. "Run?"

"Your little brother set an army of killer androids loose. We need to move now before his little minions find us." Becky turned to Rupert. The twins had fully powered up, and were looking around dazed. Eventually the two girls straightened up, clarity returning to their expressions. Becky sucked in a steady breath. At least now they knew there was no damage turning the androids on and off. "How are they?"

"You girls alright?" Rupert asked.

"Yes," Melinoe answered. Macaria continued, "I believe so."

"Good, you two go out that door and head to the main lobby. Lucy girl needs your help fighting off killer robots and we need to get to Abel and Giles before Hecate does something else." Rupert pushed the girls towards the door. "No time for more explanations. If it's made of metal and moving: smash it. Go! Now!"

Both twins looked toward each other, feeling out of the loop, but picked up enough on the tense atmosphere to not ask too many questions. They were both sure that the details would be filled in later. Melinoe knew that Giles would explain, he was smart that way. Macaria, not as confident, looked around the room and in the hall. Someone important was missing. "Where is Marvin?"

"He's dead." Rupert stated simply. "Help Lucy."

Melinoe and Macaria froze. Systems slowly started up again and the twins felt something new surge in their programming. Macaria's hands shook and covered her mouth. It wasn't possible. It wasn't *possible*. Melinoe grabbed her sister feeling the distress—though not completely understanding where it was originating. She pulled at her and headed toward the door. "We understand."

Becky watched as the twins disappeared out into the hallway. Rupert shut and locked the storage room door; they were thinking along the same lines it seemed. Becky crossed her arms, snug between Iacchus' chest and her own. "The direct exit is well and good for the power twins, but we're a little more vulnerable to killer androids. Is there a way up the building that they wouldn't know about?"

Rupert pointed up. "We need to get back to Giles and Abel on the forth floor. They're with the brat now and I have a feeling he's going to be the one to stop this mess."

Iacchus jerked his head to face toward the door. Becky kept her eyes on Iacchus after the sudden movement. His complete attention was on that door, and though Becky couldn't hear anything, she'd bet her now-worthless salary that *he* could. She lowered her voice to a whisper and returned the hug around the smaller android. Her fingers tightened in his polo shirt. "What is it?"

Iacchus scrunched his face as he listened to the footsteps. There were so many it was hard to focus. "They're in the stairwell. Hecate activated all the other androids, right?"

"Yeah."

"They're at least six or seven coming. We shouldn't leave that way."

"The elevators probably aren't much more reliable," Rupert added and leant back against the window behind him. He wondered briefly if he had time for a cigarette. He could use it right now. A siren outside the window caught his attention, and he turned and looked out straight into metal. Rupert saw rusted metal struts and leapt back from the wall. "That's it."

"What is?" Iacchus asked, releasing Ms. Becky. She was starting to shake, so he rubbed her arms in place of the hug.

"The fire escapes."

"Fire escapes?" Becky rushed over towards the edge of the window. Sure enough, rusted fire escapes lined the wall from the ground to the top floor. "I forgot these existed."

"They were declared 'un-safe' if I recall." Rupert fingered the edge of the window looking for the locks. "But hey, we're only on the second floor. If we fall, I think we'll be okay." The older man shoved at the window and grunted when it refused to budge. He pushed again and fidgeted with the lock latch, but it refused to move. "If only this wasn't locked. We need to break it with some——"

Iacchus smashed his good elbow into the window, shattering the tempered glass. He absently shoved the remaining broken shards sitting upright on the sill out of the window with the base of his palm. Iacchus brushed the few slivers that fell on his shirt off before turning back to the two humans. They stared at him for a moment before Becky rolled her eyes and Rupert started to laugh.

Iacchus huffed dramatically.

"Or that works." Rupert ruffled Iacchus' hair with a grin and turned to Becky. "Come on, you're first."

"Fourth floor," Becky smirked as she crawled over the edge of the window, trying to be careful of the glass edges too small to flick off. The metal railing whined slightly when her weight hit the metal. "Going up."

Iacchus watched the door as Ms. Becky climbed to safety. The sounds of voices and heavy footsteps filled the hallway just outside their save haven storage room. Iacchus took a step away from the window, and headed toward the center of the room. "Move faster." Iacchus' voice rose slightly in pitch; he wasn't aware it could do that. Iacchus heard the footsteps fluctuate and realized they had divided up. One set was definitely headed in their direction. "They're coming."

"Don't have to tell me twice." Becky gripped at the slightly rusty metal bars and climbed as fast as she could upward. The metal groaned and whined with every step; rust flakes sticking to her hands. She needed to get to Abel and save him from that rotten little monster. "Move it, boys."

"Yes, Ma'am," Iacchus answered before shifting on his feet. The door to the storage room shuddered under an impact. Iacchus calculated there were probably two or three androids trying to get into the room. That would make things difficult. Iacchus took Rupert's arm and pushed him into the open window. "You should go first, Mr. Dixen."

"What about you?"

"Not human."

"Right." Rupert did his best to squeeze through the small window. He hissed when a piece of glass cut his hand, but managed to pull through. Becky saw him struggling and lent a much needed hand to pull him up. "Move faster Ia-kid!"

"Just a second," Iacchus said absently, concentrating on the sounds outside the door. He could hear the footsteps outside the door and smiled. He had miscalculated: Only two. He could take two. "I'll be right behind you."

Rupert settled himself on the landing and had climbed up to the third floor to catch up to the ever moving Becky when he heard the metallic crash. The sound of metal and flesh smacking against each other was nearly deafening among all the shouting and angry snarls. Becky climbed fully onto the third landing and leant her body over the railing. "What's going on?"

The sounds echoing inside the room came to a halt with one last thump. "I…don't know." He slid down a few rungs and looked inside the room. Two mangled bodies were spread across the floor. The arms were detached on both and the smaller one—a teenage boy?—had his chest ripped open. Rupert stared at the one still standing in the center of the room. "Ia-kid?"

"Keep climbing, Mr. Dixen." Iacchus turned slowly and dropped the processor he had just yanked from his 'sibling's' chest. "I want to see my brother."

Hecate flexed his fingers one at a time, checking for any loss of fluidity. The android smiled at his two 'parents' to the side, quiet and behaving. It was amazing how much more willing Abel was to cooperate when Trophonius threatened to strangle his best friend. Though as a precaution, both men were restrained in their chairs. It was disappointing Hecate needed to sink to such levels, but it was better than hitting them over the head. He had no desire to give Abel brain damage. Giles, on the other hand…Hecate could admit that he may have had the man tied to the chair tighter than necessary.

Hecate felt misery looked good on the man, as his fingers changed colors from the circulation slowed at the wrists.

Trophonius seemed to be enjoying himself quite marvelously. Hecate pulled his sweater over his head—he hated having to take off his clothes to reach his ports. It was undignified. Speaking of indignity, Hecate frowned, Trophonius had the good detective slumped over a desk, hands cuffed behind his back. Trophonius occupied himself by petting the unconscious man's hair. Hecate made a note to address that at a later date, along with everything else considering his actions lately, but for now… "You three standing around." The androids that had been tried to break in earlier stood at attention. "Go finish your job. I want this building wiped."

Giles watched as they ran from the room and prayed that people had evacuated. "How did you do it?"

"Do what, daddy?" Hecate pulled at the sweater sleeve around his arm. It was a shame Lucy would be killed as well, wherever she was in the building. He liked her clothing. Hecate re-tucked his shirt in his pants and started to smooth out the wrinkles. Knitting instructions weren't exactly hard to find. Hecate was sure he could handle it, or program some idiot to do it for him. "I am afraid you'll have to be more specific."

Giles shifted to slump down in his seat, serving only to tighten his restraints further. Giles dropped his head on the back of the chair. "Give them orders for plan B."

"That's simple." Hecate tapped his temple with a single finger. "I used our internal systems."

"The twins were the first models to receive an internal comm system." Giles replied, not noticing the way Abel winced beside him. "You and

Iacchus were built long before that! When did you install it?"

"Oh, not that system Green invented." Hecate's smile was devilish. Little Daddy Firmin was all out of the loop. Hecate decided to have a little fun and interrupted before Abel could incriminate himself. It was supposed to be their little secret, after all. "The one that was already there. A ghost in the machine, as it were. Or have you already forgotten that we were able to communicate with each other while still attached to the wall?

"Any sort of wireless connection and the knowledge of our individual source code is all we need to contact each other. Most haven't figured out how it works yet, but its not their fault they lack the capacity to do so." Hecate smiled. Really, he was only half-lying. He needed the hardware Abel had installed to send out the signal, but that didn't mean the other androids required it for him to control them. "I didn't allow them to have it. When I activated them on the wall, I may have overwritten portions of their code. Just because your little programmers couldn't figure it out doesn't mean I couldn't."

"So you're playing God?" Giles snarled and was disgustingly reminded of his father's original goals. *Looks like you succeeded, Dad.* Giles fingers tightened into fists behind his back. "And once you've killed us all and have your little army? Then what?"

"I'll move on." Hecate shrugged and sat down in a chair behind him. By now his brothers and sisters had surely wiped out the remaining humans in the building. Hecate would have a day or so to secure the building and avoid future police visits until he could relocate. Not enough time to do much, but enough to wipe any computers to prevent others from attempting the same as *daddy.* "Hack a few banks, get some capital, build up supplies—I'm sure you get the gist."

"And the bigger goal?" Abel asked looking Hecate over. He was swinging his legs back and forth on the chair in a motion so familiar it made Abel's heart ache. Abel sucked in a breath and couldn't fight the memories of a happy little face sitting on his desk. Abel's voice sounded hollow, empty. "When does it end, Hecate?"

"When I win," Hecate answered.

"But win what? What more did you need?" Abel shook his head and felt his eyes burning. "You had everything! You were alive, and had books, and access, and—lord, I loved you! You were my son!"

"You're forgetting a word in there, Abel: practically. I was *practically* your son." Hecate kicked a foot into the side of the desk. "I love you, too, *Abel,* but we're not blood related and right now I can't trust you."

Hecate jumped down from his seat, and walked over to the only man in the building that held his affection. Hecate reached a hand up to brush Abel's hair from his face. "As for *when* I win? I win when *he,*" Hecate's hand shot out to the side and wrapped itself in *Daddy's* hair. Giles' head smashed down into the desk next to his chair with the help of Hecate's hand and a sickening *crack,* "is broken. Completely."

"Daddy?" Giles groaned.

His world was dizzy and dark…fuzzy. Giles' head pounded against his skull, and his hair was pinched—

The second impact turned the room black and white. Giles could swear he could hear Abel screaming, but it was…blurry? He almost chuckled; sound couldn't be blur—Giles felt another impact—his jaw this time. Giles felt like giggling. *Could* sound be blurry? He wasn't sure anymore. Had he been drinking again? Giles hoped that was all it—his head smacked the table again.

"I will kill, destroy, maim, and ruin as many lives as I can until he realizes that it's all. His. Fault!" Hecate's voice picked up speed and he let the man's head fall one last time. He had almost lost control completely. Hecate's hands shook, synapses and commands firing past his protocols and filters. Thankfully, he had managed to hold back enough to only give the man a minor concussion. He hoped. Hecate wasn't ready to let the man die yet. Giles Firmin hadn't paid enough. "Because it is, *Dad.*" Hecate kicked the man in the chest. "You're going to suffer."

"Stop it! You're going to kill him!" Abel shouted over his son. His voice was hoarse from his pleas, but he couldn't give up. This was all he could do to stop Hecate and save Giles. "You don't need to do this! We can talk!"

"Talking is over, Abel." Hecate smirked at the sad little groan coming from Giles. He ran his hand against Abel's cheek and let his thumb fall under Abel's eyes. They were full of water and almost looked like glass. Hecate rather liked it. Abel would see in time this was best. Hecate dropped his hand from Abel's wet cheek. He would never pick Giles over Hecate again. He patted the Abel's cheek twice. "Now, sit tight while I go check on things, alright?"

Abel flinched when a *bang* resonated through the room.

"It's not alright, Hecate," a voice growled from the now open window. The head jam was cracked from the force of the top rail slamming into the casing. Iacchus hauled himself through the opening, feet hitting the floor with a heavy thump. The boy used his height to tower over his bratty, spoiled little brother. "Call off the others."

"And the problem child returns," Hecate hissed. His brother somehow managed to look all put together and *strong* despite the facial scarring and arm sloppily stitched back together. It made Hecate sick. "I shouldn't have been sentimental." Hecate turned his back on his dysfunctional excuse of a brother. "Trophonius, dismantle him."

Trophonius leapt from his desk as ordered and rammed the older android around the middle section of his body. A rematch was just what he needed to make this day perfect. Trophonius used his forearm to shove the kid into a wall. Pinned, the child had no chance against Trophonius. He wouldn't be caught off guard this time. "Sit still and it'll go faster. Don't misbehave now—"

"Never!" Iacchus snarled and jammed his elbow in the android's bad eye. The eye patch ripped away, revealing the gaping hole once again. Trophonius flinched, loose wires sparking as the boy dug and pulled. Trophonius dropped his hold on the boy to attend the eye, and Iacchus took his chance to launch his hand forward. Stiff fingers dug their way into a yellow eye-socket. "You know?" Iacchus started when Trophonius screamed, imitation vocal chords shrieking. He dug in deep and reached around the sphere until the tips of his fingers met, and *yanked*. The eye came free with a screech of metal, wires, and dripping pink puss. "You always had pretty eyes!"

Trophonius' snarled like an animal as his hands reached up around the new gaping void in his face. Trophonius cried out at levels humans could never reached with scratchy vocal chords. "I'm going to kill you!"

"Can't kill what's not alive." Iacchus ducked down and pushed forward on the tips of his toes, head-butting the monster in the gut. He put the taller android off balance just enough to put his target out into the open. "And I'm done playing."

Trophonius didn't see the hand slam into his chest.

Hecate fell back into Abel when he saw his older brother carelessly rip out the main processor of his most loyal guard. Trophonius crumpled to the ground, exposed frame scratching the tiles of the floor. Iacchus stood slowly. Hecate felt his anger rise past optimal performance levels. The fight hadn't even lasted four minutes and Trophonius was his *best*. Hecate's fans raced as his temperature rose. Iacchus flicked Trophonius' eye to the ground—it bounced. Hecate screamed, "*You. You!*"

"I've had practice," Iacchus answered, eyes narrowed and voice deep. Iacchus turned to the broken window. "You can come in now."

Hecate watched in horror as Ms. Becky and Dixen entered through the same window. He shook his head and situated himself between Abel and Giles. Two hostages within hand's reach. Hecate had planned for this, but his resources were not close enough to access. Hecate needed more time. "No. You two should be dead!"

"You should check those things, brat." Becky kicked the now-dead android on the ground with fervor. It wasn't so scary with its face ripped off; she could handle metal innards over youthful faces any day. Marvin's machine would never hurt anyone else again. "I think you should surrender."

"All alone now, aren't ya?" Rupert placed a hand on Iacchus' shoulder and squeezed. The kid did good. "Just give up."

"No. I'm not alone. I still have all the others!" Hecate screeched and hit the nearest chair at his side with a fist; wood cracked. His *father* jerked and moaned a second time. The head injury was still running its course, it seemed. "I'm pretty sure I can hold you off with this," Hecate wrapped his arm around Giles throat. "Until they show up."

"You're—"

"—Wrong."

Melinoe and Macaria stood side-by-side in the doorway. Each held one of Demeter's arms, who hung limply between them. The body was almost unrecognizable with the sheer amount of damage done to the frame—skin ripped off, legs broken, and chest mutilated. The twins dumped the once-beautiful woman with a clang and stepped over it. Melinoe hadn't liked Marvin, but he was still their builder. Taking out his killer was the least they could do as a small apology for how badly she had treated him.

Macaria remained quiet on the subject, having already taken her silent rage out on the android—Melinoe hadn't landed a single hit.

Lucy popped in the door behind the two girls with a broad smile. Her sweater was ripped, and she was missing a shoe—but she seemed to be in good spirits. Jenner stood next to her with a dented flashlight in his hand,

and a missing shirt. "All your little soldiers have been dismantled." Jenner pointed the flashlight at the kid threatening his boss. "I think you underestimated us, kiddo. Now, let my favorite boss go now, kay?"

"What? *How*!?" Hecate wondered briefly how his systems could be hyperventilating. Information was moving much too quickly—Hecate couldn't think. He held Firmin closer to his body, grip tightening. He was too hot. *What was wrong?* "You couldn't have taken them all out!"

"Not alone," Melinoe said watching that little brat cling to Giles' throat. The man's eyes were glazed. Melinoe's fingers twitched, anxious to rip the brat apart for *daring* to touch her man. "You'd be amazed how well riot gear works on androids when the police put their mind to it."

Macaria crossed her arms. "The good detective wasn't kidding when he told his men to 'be prepared' for anything. Multiple stun guns proved to be remarkably effective."

"You only killed two extra people, Hecate." Melinoe flipped her hair over a shoulder. "You've lost."

"No." Hecate pulled back on Giles' throat and grabbed the top of the man's greasy, *ugly* black hair. He would snap the man's neck before he went down. "NO!"

Abel saw his moment and leapt up by pushing his feet on the ground. He managed to throw his chair into Hecate as accurately as he could, still tied. They both crashed to the ground and the small body beneath him struggled to gain some sort of purchase to pull himself up. Abel had to stop him before he could put that enhanced strength to use. Abel rolled the chair on the side and grunted when his bindings constricted tightly enough on his wrists to break the skin. He looked up from the floor as Hecate jammed an arm into his stomach trying to get out from under him. Abel turned to the others, "What are you waiting for!? Get him!"

Iacchus acted first, and grabbed his brother quickly under the arms. A yank pulled him out from under Abel—he dropped to the floor with a hiss. Becky and Lucy were at his side in an instant. Together, they pulled Abel upright and got to work on his bindings. To their side, Iacchus took Hecate's face and shoved him to the ground. Iacchus sat on his back, forcing the kid's arm into a locked position. Iacchus turned to Rupert to finish the job. "Disconnect him!"

"On it." Rupert fell to his knees—his aching knees that deserved a good soak and a massage after his cigarette—and ripped open the back plate, tearing through fake skin and pink pus. Hecate screamed and snarled as he tried to get away, but it wasn't fast enough. One quick rip later and the entire body stilled as it powered down. No key this time. Rupert threw the main power wire to the ground and huffed. "Good riddance."

Abel felt a pair of soft hands frame his face as Becky tried to distract him. Lucy was rubbing his arm. Abel wondered why no one was taking care of Giles. He'd hit his head harder than Abel had been hurt. Becky was muttering soft words of 'it'll be alright' and the like, but Abel wasn't sure he believed it. He just killed his kid for the second time in one lifetime.

Maybe Giles would share a drink with him after he got over his concussion.

CHAPTER 28

RUPERT AND BECKY were killing time in the outdoor smoking lounge of the local hospital. The lounge—though it was more of a gazebo—was a few yards from the main building and surrounded by bushes and people with shaking hands and downcast faces. Becky and Rupert fit right in. The pair of them had been kicked out of Giles' room by a hard headed nurse who wanted to do her work without being 'crowded.' Becky tapped her cigarette on the edge of an ash tray before bringing it back up to her mouth.

The twins hadn't lied, and moments after their arrival to the final showdown, the police were on the scene and had called a bus for Giles and Saxon. Carcasses and leftover mechanical body parts, singed and torn, lined the hallway as their caravan rushed out of the building to the ambulances waiting outside the ground floor lobby. Hecate hadn't predicted just how many people would be fighting back against his inexperienced 'army.' One dead scientist had been enough for *everyone* to fight back without orders. It made the transition from lab to hospital fairly smooth as people made paths and helped carry the wounded.

Becky rubbed her eyebrow with the back of her thumb and tried to remember how late her coffee shop stayed open. She could really use one of their pastries about now to calm her nerves. A thick, gooey cinnamon bun she would ask Abel to share. *Yeah, that's the spot.* Becky looked up at the hospital proper, and the guest rooms on the fifth floor. She could see Giles' window from here, the pink vase of flowers easily visible from the ground. His partner in injury, Detective Saxon had woken up with a minor concussion, but was otherwise fine. The doctors said he was lucky to have gotten away with a broken wrist and a few bruises when compared to some of Trophonius' other victims.

Becky came out of her musings, as Rupert clicked open his cell phone and answered his wife. Soft reassurances to her that he was still in one piece, and yes he was still at the hospital filled the air. Becky pushed off the bench she was using and gave the man some privacy, jabbing her cigarette into the nearest receptacle, only half smoked. Giles was in and out of consciousness, but Becky was fairly certain he was sleeping at the moment. Hecate was responsible for giving the man a linear skull fracture, but the doctors assured her there were no other major complications. Apparently Hecate did Giles a favor by mixing it up with hits to the jaw versus only slamming the man's head into a desk.

Becky had a feeling that Giles would be unappreciative of his 'compassion.'

She crossed the grounds, ready to head back up to Giles' room, scary nurse or not. Someone needed to keep the man company if he woke up. *Not that he wants to see me,* Becky admitted to herself. Giles wanted to see *Abel,* but he was unavailable as he was out with Lucy. Abel had spent two days plastered to Giles' side, and enough was enough. Giles was too greedy to tell the man to take care of himself, so Becky, Rupert, and Lucy arranged for an intervention.

If all was well, Lucy and Abel were eating dinner at an Italian restaurant on the other side of town.

Becky pushed the elevator call button and waited for the *ding* and shutter of opening doors patiently. Her cell phone buzzed in her pocket, creating yet another opportunity to sigh and roll her eyes. Becky flipped the device open, blatantly ignoring the 'No Cell Phone' signs plastered on the walls, as the metal doors opened. She smirked down at the text as she pressed the 5th floor button.

Ms. Becky! Integer and Prime are picking on Infinity and Infinitesimal again! Becky clicked to the next text. *And the twins won't stop laughing!*

Rupert was going to pay for giving Iacchus a cell phone. While Becky and Lucy had gone with the boys to the hospital, Rupert had stayed behind to help Jenner clean up and get the remaining 'kids' settled. He then gave them a cell phone so they could call if they needed anything, before dashing to the hospital himself. 'Needing anything' soon translated to bothering Becky with whatever he found amusing or interesting at the moment…or in this case, if he wanted to tattle.

Becky wasn't sure if the endless stream of texts was Iacchus distracting himself from the fact his brother went crazy, or if he genuinely couldn't care less and had moved on to other things. The technician wandered her way down the hall to Giles' private room—he wasn't poor *just* yet—and took a seat in the guest chair at his bed side, pulling out her indoor-friendly electronic cigarette. Giles was awake, his blue eyes locked on hers with such intensity that flashes of Hecate filled her mind. Becky held back the shiver and took a puff of nicotine, doing her best to look nonchalant. "How long have you been up?"

"About ten minutes," Giles said, taking a sip of water. "Where's Abe?"

"Eating with Lucy."

"When will he be back?" Giles asked for what felt like the hundredth time. Jenner, Lucy, Rupert, Becky—he appreciated their visits, but it just wasn't the same. Abel was family.

"Later."

Giles set his water tumbler on the side cart, head dipping slightly. Thoughts came easier now, but it still felt like he was wading through a pool of mud. His head itched too, but the nurse threatened to handcuff him to the bed if he scratched at the bandages one more time. Giles clicked the television on, flipping through news stations. Reports on the lab had been disturbingly absent, and Giles wondered when the story would erupt. "Have you heard anything from that Talos' group yet?"

"They want us charged with manslaughter, but no one can figure out who's to blame." Becky wanted to smirk, but the situation wasn't as funny as it could have been. Not when that Eubanks guy was so upset about the death of his friend. Becky had seen enough men crying in the past few weeks to satisfy her curiosities for a lifetime. Still, even Becky could appreciate the irony of it all. "They got what they wanted, at least, the androids are being held responsible for their own actions."

"Which means they can't charge anyone because the guilty parties are already 'dead.'" Giles fiddled with the IV needle in his arm, for lack of anything else to do. He got a 'private' room, but it was still rather small with only enough room for his bed and two guest chairs. If Giles knew that his job was going to become this hazardous, he would have bought a building next to a more prestigious hospital. As it was, he was thankful his room at least provided a TV. "That's good to know. At least they won't be able to blame Abel, as the boy's main guardian."

"Speaking," Becky watched water vapor hang in the air and looked over at Giles, "you think Abel will be okay?"

"Don't know." Giles stopped messing with the thin tubing. Wanting Abel's company wasn't complete selfishness on Giles' behalf—he was also partially worried that Abel was going to do something stupid. He couldn't remember the last time he'd seen his friend this depressed. "Don't know."

"I think I'm going to ask him out," Becky declared to the ceiling. "Dinner, flowers, and a tuxedo—the whole nine yards."

Giles laughed sadly and slid down under the covers. "Good luck with that."

Becky smacked his side when Giles pulled the covers over his head and rolled away from her.

Detective Saxon stood in the doorway of the final crime scene. The turned over furniture and pieces of loose metal scattered around the room were the finale to one of the worst, and oddest, cases of his career. Lester hadn't been awake for the final confrontation, to his deepest regret, but fought to return to the scene the second he was released from medical care. Trophonius had broken his wrist; his hand itched under the cast. Saxon hadn't missed the chilling implications that it was in the same place that Green's wrist had been snapped. After seeing Green's body on a stretcher at autopsy, Saxon was thankful the broken wrist was the only thing they shared that evening.

Lester's shoulders were hanging loosely, his posture relaxed. He wasn't nearly as upset as he should be over the current situation. Saxon figured he was finally sick of the whole mess, or maybe he had just passed the point of fury and reached the steady calm an officer needed to truly get his collar. *Anger was what made men sloppy, wasn't that right?* Lester looked over the scene, determination overshadowing the longing to break something.

The room was empty.

Sure there were screws here or there, or a loose wire decorating the ground, but Hecate and Trophonius were missing—stolen, Saxon corrected himself. Saxon's evidence was unfortunately just as absent from the scene. Not due to someone covering their tracks, but from too much evidence to sort through from contamination and the earlier fight. The officers checked the room to the best of their ability, but Saxon doubted they found anything useful. Even his own fingerprints were scattered around the scene, along with everyone else's. There was no getting around that just about everyone involved—and then some, when one took into account this was a usually occupied office—had corrupted the scene in some way.

Saxon wasn't completely empty handed though, and he had a few scraps to go off of from *outside* the room.

One: Lester was aware that the man running the front desk had been knocked unconscious at some odd hour in the morning, making the staff available to report oddities minimal. That meant the guilty party was aware of the staff assignments, and who specifically to knock out to keep eyes off him or her. Looking for his guilty party in the employee register of the laboratory hadn't changed—it was still an inside job.

Two: The security tapes had been burned, not erased or edited. This told Saxon that whoever had taken the bodies was not as technically savvy as some of the earlier culprits in this case. In every other instance, the tapes had been erased by either hacking or one of the androids manipulating the security feeds from the network. This was someone who was probably better with his hands than his programming.

It wasn't much, but Lester had worked with less.

Saxon took a step back and walked out of the room, past officers sealing off areas with tape. The detective passed spectators lingering around the scene, eyes wondering what this final crime meant for their futures. Technicians, scientists, and all levels of employees in a state of confusion and worry. If the murders weren't bad enough, stolen equipment had to be the icing on the cake—or rather the nail in the coffin. With the only remaining board member still delirious in a hospital and doubtful to continue his funding, Saxon figured the lab was on its last legs. It'd be lucky to remain operational for the rest of the week. The scientists and technicians knew it too—you could see it in their eyes.

Saxon didn't share their mindset concerning his own no-win scenario. He had by no means given up—No—not by a long shot. Whoever took those androids was bound to slip up some time. Lester passed by the front desk where the security guard dutifully installed new equipment to replace the damaged, burnt consoles. Saxon smiled and placed his hat on his head as he pushed out the door with his good elbow.

When that thief slipped up, Saxon would be there to catch him.

Melinoe kept herself occupied by picking on Iacchus.

She teased his mice, his new cell phone (*Texting her—again!?*), and generally made a nuisance of herself. Her greatest moment to date, involved knocking the water dish over in the mice's cage. Granted, the reaction she got was an irritated sigh and watching the boy mop the water up with a paper towel. Iacchus fought back against her teasing half-heartedly, at best. Melinoe got the impression he was used to having someone tease him constantly. The girl huffed to herself and sat near the boy as he took pictures of the mice with the cell phone. She watched idly, envious of his happy smile.

Melinoe wasn't sure what else to do with herself.

Her precious Giles was still in the hospital, and wouldn't be back for another few days yet. Melinoe missed him dearly, but would rather he recover than come rushing to her side. Melinoe glanced to the other side of the room, and pulled her hair down over her eyes. Her sister wasn't much of a help for her loneliness and boredom, either.

Macaria wasn't speaking to her. Her baby sister just sat in the corner playing with Marvin's hair brush, and a make-up kit. His glasses were tucked away in her personal possessions, and were guarded with her life. Macaria had been on the verge of a total system breakdown when the detective returned them to her after the autopsy. Melinoe hated to admit it, but her sister was taking Marvin's death pretty hard. She wouldn't talk to anyone, or anything that involved interacting with others. Melinoe had tried to talk some sense into her, originally, but was punished for her well meant efforts.

"He was a pervert, and he hardly respected us! I don't know why you miss that loser so much," Melinoe had said.

Macaria had replied with a slap and five words: "He was a good man."

Melinoe's sister hadn't spoken to her since.

So, with little else to do, Melinoe sat in boredom, wishing to see Giles again—alone. Iacchus didn't seem to mind his precious Ms. Becky being gone. He just sat there grinning like an idiot with his shiny new toy, and texted her happily. Becky replied maybe once in the past day, but that didn't seem to deter the simpleton from maxing out his text message limits. Melinoe rolled her eyes and stood to go sit next to her sister. If she couldn't talk to her, she might as well sit next to her.

Macaria'd get over Marvin…eventually.

Giles remained trapped in the hospital for another week after he started to wake up without the world spinning. Abel had kept him company has much as the girls and Rupert would allow. They their conversations to anything and everything that hadn't involved work, the androids, and oddly enough—Lucy. Giles wasn't sure what had been going on at their dinners, but Abel kept changing the subject—while blushing—when Giles brought the woman up. Instead, they talked about sports, whatever soap opera was on the hospital television, food, and even Giles' visitors.

Giles' had a newfound appreciation for the people around him, during his stay in the hospital. People he never would have considered as 'friends,' or would even think would worry about his health arrived to wish him well. There hadn't been a trace of dishonesty or gold digging among the lot of them—Abel had called him an idiot for even thinking otherwise. The highlights included Rupert's wife bringing them moist, homemade cupcakes—which was a big deal for some reason, if the way she kept glaring at Rupert was a sign—and Lucy making him an oversized, knitted hat to keep his head warm. And in pink, no less!

It had been nice, reassuring even, but Giles was absurdly relieved when he received his release papers.

After a day of rest, Giles came back to work side by side with Abel. The lab still stood tall, amazingly enough, upon his return. Jenner had restored order through a series of take-charge commands and collaborated efforts with Susie and her janitorial staff. While all activities concerning the Wall had halted, the rest of the team continued work on the hardware end of production. They probably figured there could be other uses for the base mechanics, even without a 'pilot' pulling the strings. Giles figured he'd have to join in on the brainstorming eventually, but for the moment, he was just happy to be sitting in his own chair, at his own desk, with his own best friend.

Giles poured a third finger of brandy into a short glass and pushed it across the desk with his pinky towards Abel. The man took it wordlessly and swallowed the burning liquid in a single gulp. Abel was well on his way to being as morosely plastered as Giles. Silence hung heavy in the room as they watched the sun set just beyond the glass of the window.

They had put off talking about the past month as long as they both could, but it all came out, fueled by liquor and silence. Voices had been heavy, harsh and accusing—only to deteriorate down to sobs and self-blame. Giles swirled the amber liquid in its glass. Abel began his crying about twenty minutes ago, finally facing his own demons over Hecate. He had only just now stopped. Giles was too tired to cry; Abel had done enough for the both of them.

Giles tapped the base of the glass on the desk. "It's amazing how much that kid had us wrapped around his little finger…Lord, we were idiots." Giles tipped the glass over, and watched it roll across the desk. It came to a stop against the statue of Athena, clinking softly against the marble. "It's almost funny, isn't it?"

"Yeah, a barrel of laughs, Giles." Abel rubbed at his swollen eyes. Giles should know better than to joke about something like this. There was *nothing* funny about any of it. Abel took in a slow breath. Giles just didn't understand—Abel didn't think *anyone* could. Hecate had been a kid who wanted his real daddy to love him, too. The emotions behind it all weren't something little—they had been a part of his son. His crazy, messed up, spoiled little kid. Abel swallowed thickly. "I miss him."

"I know."

"We should have never left the body alone."

"I know."

"I spoiled that boy rotten."

"Not your fault."

"How could I not have noticed what a little monster he was underneath?"

"Easy," Giles said plainly, "he loved you."

Abel laughed soullessly, "So now what, Giles? Without my son, I don't have much else do I? The lab?" Abel slammed the bottle on the table, rattling Giles' figurines. He tipped the statuette of Athena over on its side with the base of the bottle. A piece of her hair chipped off and bounced on the floor. "Our main source of funding is either dead or crazy in a hospital. Half of our employees are terrified of us. There's no way we can create any more androids—hell, we're lucky they're letting us keep the twins and Iacchus online!" Abel clumsily reached for the brandy bottle and took a drink straight from the lip. His drunken ramblings continued, words slurring as he questioned Giles. "What do we tell people who come to us now? What do we offer them? How do we greet them, Giles? How—how do we look anyone in the eyes after this bout of mad science and death?"

Giles hummed softly, retrieving his glass from where it had rolled. He held it in his hand, contemplating Abel's question. Giles lifted the glass, tipped it back—to drink nothing. The cup had been empty. "Easy, again,

Abel." He lifted the clear glass in a fake toast, elbow thumping on the desktop."With the same thing we always say:

"'Welcome to Hephaestus Labs.'"

CHAPTER 29

ABEL DROPPED HIS case in the main foyer of his house.

He poured a glass of water from the pitcher in his refrigerator and gulped it down, still dehydrated from sleeping off the alcohol in Giles' office. He had struggled to keep awake as he drove home—the two hour nap not enough. Abel's cot no longer held the same appeal, and his plush mattress called to him from the upstairs. Abel placed the empty glass in the sink, setting both of his hands on the counter, steadying himself for the movement. After a deep breath, he headed back into the main foyer to climb his staircase, railing cool under his fingertips.

His bedroom sat at the top of the landing, just off to the right. Green carpet met hardwood at the entrance. Abel pushed his eggshell white door open, and smiled softly at the two motionless figures propped up side by side at the edge of his bed.

"I'm home, boys."

ACKNOWLEDGEMENTS

TO GOD be the glory forever, and ever, Amen.

Thanks to God in the highest for the talent to write, and the push He gave to everyone—be they parents, friends, or strangers—who inspired me, helped me, and encouraged me. Thanks for the amazing editor He provided to help guide and communicate the story I wanted to tell, and thanks for the beta readers He put in my life who let me know quite often this was worth putting out there, and continually ask "Where's my copy?" Without all of that, this book would probably still be lingering on some hard-drive unseen.

And of course, thanks for giving us Jesus, who loves you & me.

About The Author

Grey Liliy is a young woman who claims the East Coast of Virginia as her home. She enjoys anime, video games, movies, novels, and comics of just about any genre. Liliy has been drawing & writing a comic of her own since 2005, called *The Adventures of Wiglaf and Mordred*, which you can find at http://liliy.net/wam.

www.ingramcontent.com/pod-product-compliance
Lightning Source LLC
Chambersburg PA
CBHW070214260626
47160CB00002B/551